Leaving Hope

Golden Terrace Colony Book 1

R.L.S. Hoff

The Pencil Princess Workshop

ISBN-13: 978-1-7350742-1-4

Cover design by: UniqueDesignsREM
Printed in the United States of America

For Craig
My love and inspiration

Chapter One

Anastasia Cartier loved late afternoon in the greenhouses. She loved the way the light, set by some ancient, planet-inspired formula, slanted, highlighting sharp lines and sharper shadows. She loved the loose, well-worked feeling in her muscles. She loved the smell of mulch, flowers, and clean air. And she loved the freedom to find a quiet corner, sit cross-legged in some wide spot between plants she'd nurtured, and make beautiful things.

Today, Anya held her breath as she tickled the center of the flower she was light sculpting. She wiggled her pinkie to nudge up the illumination. Then she stroked the surrounding thorns, darkening them. She held nothing but light beneath her fingers, but she'd created an image so real she could almost feel the velvety petals and sharp points.

She steadied her left hand against her knee. This projection strained her armband's capacity past its normal limits, and she didn't want to break anything. But she was achingly close to capturing the inner radiance she'd seen in the trumpet flower images beamed back by the Shindashir explorers.

Some day she was going to get down there and see if the real-world plants were as glorious as the pictures. She smiled to herself and increased the illumination on the center a hair more.

"What kind of flower is that, anyway?" A voice at her shoulder broke her concentration. Her left arm wobbled. An alarm buzzed, and the flower dissolved into plain white light.

She stared at where it had been. Now it was a wide space where two greenhouse paths met. Dark thorny silverfruit bushes stretched in straight rows all around the metal mesh on which she sat. Below her, pipes gurgled as *Hope* creaked and hummed its way toward Shindashir. She could never hear it when she was creating, but now the ever-present ship noise sang in her ears.

She'd had her sculpture nearly perfect, and she wasn't sure she could do it again.

"Seriously, that was gorgeous. I've never seen anything like it before, and you know I'm stuck in here at least once a week. What was it?"

Anya turned, so she could see the speaker. Borsk King. Today his long black dreadlocks were pulled tightly away from his smooth tan skin. She wasn't sure she'd ever seen his eyes before. The bright greenhouse light brought out green flecks in the deep brown. He didn't appear to be laughing at her. He might mean what he said.

"It was a trumpet flower like the ones growing up the sign for the Golden Terrace Colony on their recruitment materials."

"Why were you looking at recruitment materials? You want to go down there?"

"I do."

"But doesn't your dad hate the Golden Terrace Colony?"

"My father doesn't have to know my plans."

"Plans? To what? Try out for the colony crew?"

Maybe not plans. What Anya had was more like faint hopes—she barely made the younger age limit for trying out, she had no special skills, and she had no partner willing to go. Colony leadership was looking for genetically compatible couples to bear the first land-born generation in centuries. Besides, as Borsk said, her father would oppose her.

But the more she remembered the glimpses of Shindashir she'd seen in the colony materials, the more she knew she wanted to—needed to—get close enough to touch and smell and see the planet, not just experience it through a screen or a simulation suit.

Her father might not like it, but she would find a way. She smiled at Borsk, faking a confidence she didn't feel. "Yeah, I want to try out. And for now, my father doesn't need to know."

"Won't your dad figure it out when he sees that?" Borsk pointed toward the place where her sculpture had been.

"I wasn't going to show it to my father, even if it hadn't vanished into the ether." She never showed her father her sculptures. He'd made it clear that art projects were a waste of her time, even more useless than her devotion to the greenhouses.

"What do you mean—vanished?" Borsk asked.

"Disappeared. Evaporated. Gone. I had to turn off my autosave when I started tinkering with my light output, and I'm pretty sure my last version is . . ." She tapped in the coordinates on the input panel on her inner arm, and her light sculpture appeared. The thorny cage she'd finished yesterday stretched threatening points toward a roughly-shaped-in pinkish flower.

"Crap," Borsk said.

"I was going to say a load of ferto, but, yeah," Anya agreed.

"You really don't have the final version?"

"I really don't."

"I, um, copied it. You want me to send it back to you?"

Borsk copied it? He had no business touching her personal software!

But if he'd copied it, he could give it back. She took a couple of deep breaths to reign in her anger. Once she'd cleared her head enough to think, she wondered why Borsk would copy her sculpture. Her art wasn't valuable.

Of course, he could have been hacking into her system.

No. If Anya could tell anything by the kind of detentions that landed Borsk in the greenhouses, this wasn't his kind of hack. It wasn't showy or challenging enough. He wouldn't even have needed to get by her armband's firewall. The code was projecting right out there with the light.

"I could send it to a safe file if you're worried about security," Borsk said. "I won't even keep a copy if you don't want me to."

Anya didn't mind him having the file now that he was asking instead of just taking it. In fact, she kind of liked having a backup that was immune to her armband's technical failures and her father's destructive searches. "You can keep a copy of this—or any of my art—if you want it. And a regular file will be fine." Anya figured he could hack into her systems through a safe file as easily as her personal message system, so why bother with the headache of unpacking a message with extra security? She shot him her address. "What made you save a copy in the first place?"

Borsk shrugged. "Second nature. I save everything I might want later."

"You thought you'd want it later?"

"Well, sure. It's good."

Once again, she couldn't see any sign that he was making fun of her. "Thanks," she said.

"It's nothing." Then he blushed.

An odd reaction. Was he hiding something? Still, he seemed to like her art. Amazing.

Her message tone pinged, and there it was. She opened the attachment, and her sculpture rematerialized in front of her, with even her last changes intact. Tears sprang to her eyes. She blinked them back. "I don't think you have any idea how much this means to me. Thank you." She closed the projection and tapped the keys on the inner side of her left wrist to save it to more permanent storage. *Trumpet flower trapped in silverfruit thorns—Wednesday—J1022—16:47.* "Ferto. Is that the time?"

"A quarter-to-five, more or less?" Borsk said. "Sure."

"I'll be late for dinner, and Father's going to kill me." The alarm that broke up her sculpture must have been her stop-work bell, not a system failure or a warning that Borsk was breaking in. Now she was seven minutes late and hadn't even started recycling. She scooped up the pile of silverfruit branches she'd trimmed earlier in the day, ignoring the inevitable scratches. "Thanks again, Borsk. Gotta go."

"Let me get them," he said. Her pile lifted as he pulled it into his own arms. "It's what I'm assigned to do anyway."

"What?"

"Old Greeley and I finished the tube-potatoes around four, but I'm stuck here until five. He told me to clean up and then help you trim bushes. I may have dawdled a bit."

"I would too, if Mr. Greeley had me doing a job *after* tube-potatoes." She took half the pile back. "Come on. We'll get it done fast." She rushed toward the recycling wall at the far end, keeping to the center of the turquoise-painted grate paths. The paths were narrow enough she scratched her arms, but at least this way she didn't get ferto crusted to her shoes. Long practice helped her keep her pile of branches from tangling with the living bushes on either side of her. Behind her, she could hear Borsk struggling to keep up.

As they got close, DeShawn Phillips, another of the detention-duty crew, was closing today's recycling drawer. "Hey, DeShawn, wait up!" Anya shouted. The drawer slammed. Had he pushed it deliberately?

"You shouldn't have done that, man," Borsk said, gasping for breath.

"Ooh—I'm scared. What are you going to do? Whine to Old Greeley?"

"I never whine," Anya said, dropping her branches and attacking the drawer. It was number four, in the muddy green row, the hardest to open of the bunch. Its lever-handle required the right touch of force and finesse, and if you managed to do it just right . . .

The door jerked open with a sharp hiss and a glop of compost. A shiny white grub slopped over the edge onto Anya's apron. She squealed.

"Now you know how the rest of us feel when we see your ugly white face," DeShawn said.

Anya looked down at the glistening creature inching its way up her front. The grub was bright white, like a screen that had blanked out. Even as a member of one of the few remaining pure-European-descended families on *Hope*, she had more color than that. Peaches and cream, Mother called their skin tone. She insisted it was beautiful and that those who disagreed were just jealous. Anya wasn't so sure. But she knew she looked better than a recycling grub. She straightened up, wishing she could think of something to say that would let DeShawn know his jibe didn't bother her.

"Shut up, DeShawn," Borsk said. He shuddered before dropping his branches into the drawer. "Do you want me to, you know," he said softly to Anya, pointing to the worm on her chest. His hand shook.

Afraid of recycling worms? Some people were. Nice of him to offer to deal with it if he didn't like them. He'd put himself between her and De-Shawn, too. She gave him a little smile. "No, I've got it." She scooped the little guy and his mulch back into the drawer. "They don't bother me, really. I was just startled at first." But now she would have to scrub up before leaving the greenhouse. She glanced at her armband. Five minutes until the shuttle. "Do you mind finishing with these?"

"I'll get them," said a gravelly voice. Anya turned in time to see Mr. Gree-ley hobbling around the corner from his office. His bald patch glinted when he stooped to pick up the branches she'd dropped.

"Mr. Greeley, you shouldn't have to clean up after us," Anya said.

"If you kids don't get out of here, you'll miss the shuttle. Parents will complain."

Borsk and DeShawn took off, but Anya bent to help the old man with the branches.

"Go on, child. You don't want to be late."

True enough. The last time she'd missed the shuttle she'd had to run all the way across the black zone to the inhabited side of *Hope*. She'd developed a cramp in her side that hadn't unclenched until morning, and she'd still been so late her father had grounded her from the greenhouses for a week. It had been almost enough to start her on an exercise plan. Almost.

"OK, Mr. Greeley," she said.

She ran to the clean-up station and quick-scrubbed with wiry brushes that nearly took her skin off. After a last splash in clean water, she dashed back through the maze of plants to the greenhouse door. If she only took two minutes to cross the suspension bridge to the greenhouse station, she could still make it. She crossed her fingers for luck and ran.

She was going so fast she didn't even see the engineer scrounging scrap in the black zone around the bridge until he shone his headlamp full in her face. "Who's effing *running* up there?"

Anya stopped cold. She'd forgotten this bridge crossed an unsound zone. "Sorry. I didn't think. It's just, I'm late."

"You're late? And this justifies shaking the ship apart?"

"Give her a break, David," said Borsk from behind her. "Anya's not big enough to do serious damage. And you'd run too if you were late for dinner with Thomas Cartier."

Anya ducked her head. She hated it when people made exceptions for her because of her family. "It's OK, Borsk. I should have waited until I hit a safe tunnel to run." She sighed.

"Yes, you should have," the voice from the darkness said. "You never know what idiot twice your size might be running along behind you. Perhaps a few more days of greenhouse work will teach you both some sense. Oh, and Borsk? Work on your plausibility, man. Late for dinner with Thomas Cartier? She wishes."

"B-b-but . . ." Borsk's armband pinged, and the sputtering changed to cursing. Anya tuned it out. Her armband had also pinged, and the details of her first-ever detention scrolled across her forearm. Five days in the greenhouses. Where she wanted to be. Anya laughed out loud. "Thank you. That's beautiful. Now, if you don't mind, I really am late for dinner with my father." She walked as fast as she dared. It would be too late for the shuttle, and Father would be spitting mad, but he couldn't take away her greenhouse hours. She had a genuine detention—if this David had guts enough to leave it once he learned who she was.

Behind her, Borsk stopped cursing. "What? David, tell me you didn't just give Anastasia Cartier a greenhouse detention. Are you utterly mad?" He chuckled.

He was still chuckling when he caught up with her at the greenhouse station where, unbelievably, the shuttle stood idling. Had it broken down?

No. The clock over the driver's seat showed a minute to five. She glanced down at her armband. Two after. Both supposedly ran off *Hope's* central clock. She opened her mouth to say something. Borsk stepped on her foot.

"Ouch!" She glanced up at his face.

His eyes twinkled.

He'd hacked the shuttle clock? Impossible! She stared at him, wondering.

He broke into a goofy grin. "Sorry about your foot. I'll make it up to you. You can have the last seat."

She glanced around. There was only one seat empty—next to DeShawn. "That's OK. I'd just as soon stand, and I know you had to wrestle with tube-potatoes today."

"Meaning she's too proud to set her fat white ass next to the likes of me." DeShawn shifted so he straddled both seats.

"DeShawn, no one wants to set their ass next to yours—why do you think I offered Anya the seat in the first place?"

DeShawn's answer was drowned out by an automatic warning about the doors closing. Anya gripped the central pole, smiled up at Borsk, and mouthed "Thank you."

Borsk shook his head, ever so slightly, and blushed again. Did gratefulness embarrass him?

She considered asking about it, but the shuttle started with a jerk. Borsk lost his footing and crashed into her. Anya caught him and helped him right himself.

"So, you two are dating now?" DeShawn said. "That's disgusting. Is she even red?"

At first Anya had no idea what DeShawn was talking about. Then she realized Borsk must be in the red dating pool. Anya hadn't bothered to check, but she did now, looking for the light on his armband, just under his wrist. Sure enough, red. So, who did that mean he was allowed to date? Anya hadn't kept track of who in her class was which color, though she knew it was all some of the kids talked about. After all, no one wanted to fall in love with somebody they couldn't get involved with, and nobody wanted to get involved with someone who wasn't their color. That was the way to wind up with in-bred genetic monsters for babies.

Borsk laughed. "I wish we were dating. I'd love to be going out with a great artist." He steadied himself against the support pole and flashed a light sculpture into the air.

Anya's heart stopped. Then she realized it wasn't the trumpet flower, but one of her others—silverfruit through superwheat supports. How long had he been copying her art?

Everybody on the shuttle leaned in, and someone behind Anya said, "Wow. No way does it look that good when I'm mending those lousy supports."

Anya turned but wasn't sure which of the four hulking guys on the shuttle's side bench had spoken. None of them seemed to be laughing at her. Her face got hot, and she looked down at the silvery, textured floor. "Thanks," she said, just loud enough to be heard over the shuttle's rumble.

"So, if you're not red, what color are you?" one of the giant guys asked.

Anya glanced at him. He was dark-skinned and had a skull tattooed on his right bicep, under a strategically placed tear in his uniform. Anya couldn't quite remember his name. Was he asking her out? No one had ever asked her out.

"Green," she said softly, not that it mattered.

According to *Hope* law, she could have kids with anybody, so long as he was green.

According to her parents, her choices were much more limited.

Tattoo boy was yellow, his friends on either side purple. The guys on the jump seat were orange. Then everybody was calling out colors.

In a car packed with twenty guys, not a one was green, not even the driver. What were the odds? The guys couldn't stop talking about it, all except Borsk, who tapped on his armband, raised his eyebrows, and said nothing, but looked thoughtful. Anya wondered what he was thinking but didn't feel she knew him well enough to ask. Maybe he'd worked out the probabilities of not a single green guy in a group with twenty-odd young men. She wasn't good at math, but her gut told her it was far from likely if you left nature to itself.

Not that she imagined this had happened naturally. She knew perfectly well that her parents had chosen who she'd marry before she was even born. Despite the fines and penalties that came if such a betrothal were exposed, they'd had her on purpose—to marry a particular guy from a particular family, so that pure-Euros would last another generation. They'd arranged the marriage even though it could cost them six months in the brig, ninety percent of their liquid capital, and half their physical property if the betrothal were uncovered.

Of course, they weren't going to chance her falling in love with some random guy on her preferred work detail.

Chapter Two

Borsk watched Anya scoot away from the shuttle stop, her legs moving as fast as the blades on his family's restaurant's salad chopper. She was surprisingly speedy for a short girl.

And surprisingly nice for a rich one. He wished he hadn't seen how respectful she was with Old Greeley, or how anxious she was to avoid special treatment, in both the greenhouse and out on the suspension bridge. He wished he hadn't seen the way her whole face lit up when anyone praised her art. He especially wished he hadn't seen her manage to seem disappointed, not relieved, when her dating pool color didn't match up with VJ Brown's.

He wished he could keep thinking of her as a stuck-up rich kid.

Then maybe he wouldn't feel so bad about totally ripping her off.

It had to be done, though. As Gramps was always saying, "Money doesn't fall from the ceiling supports."

"Hey, Borsk! Why so glum?" DeShawn sneered from where he was blocking the shuttle door. "I'm sure you'll find another flabby, pasty girlfriend-candidate in time."

"Shut up, dumb-ass." VJ bumped DeShawn from behind with a shoulder, hard enough to dislodge him from the entrance, but not quite hard enough to earn a violence citation.

The rest of the crowd behind them poured out of the shuttle in a roiling mass. Borsk lost sight of DeShawn, but VJ popped up next to him. "Quite a view, eh?"

"Excuse me?"

The big guy pointed at Anya's quickly receding backside.

"Um . . ."

"So, you were just kidding when you said you'd be interested in her if she were red."

Borsk hadn't been kidding exactly. He'd needed something to stop De-Shawn's put-downs. So, what if he felt no chemistry with Anya? Lots of people dated without that. "I really do like her art."

VJ grunted.

"Give me a break. She isn't red. It would feel like dating my sister." Borsk shuddered.

"Mmm. Sarka. Another fine piece of—"

"Watch it."

VJ laughed. "Relax. I'm yellow, remember? I'm never going to do anything but look."

Borsk wasn't sure he was comfortable with VJ even looking at his sister, but what was he going to do about it? "Talk to you later, VJ."

"Wait up. I have something to give you." VJ pressed a cold round disk into Borsk's hand. "It's for keeping Skreetches' soundstage open. Gran said it was valuable."

Borsk turned the thing over in his hand. Pure reddish-brown metal, with a raised bump on one side. "Is this a coin?"

VJ nodded.

"An Earth relic?"

VJ nodded again. "So, it's valuable?"

"Too valuable," Borsk said, handing the coin back to VJ. "You couldn't sell it until the antiquities people down at *Hope* Museum had a squint at it, and those guys take more than a month on stuff half this old, even when Thomas Cartier isn't sending them memos to go slow. Skreetches hasn't got that kind of time."

In fact, they had less than a week to find the money to buy out Thomas Cartier's share in the business.

VJ's face fell.

"Thanks, though. Really. Tell your gran it means a lot to us." Borsk steered VJ away from the shuttle toward the main hallway.

"We could contribute credits," VJ said. "I can only spare a couple, but if lots of people give—"

Borsk cut him off. "It's all traceable, VJ. And anybody who puts money toward the soundstage project lands on General Mercantile's blacklist."

"So what?"

Borsk rolled his eyes. He liked VJ, but the guy was dense sometimes. "Maybe you don't care about limited job opportunities and higher borrowing rates, but most people do."

"How much are we talking about for the soundstage anyway?"

"Fifty-thousand."

"So, it's gone."

"My mom will shut down the whole operation before shutting down the soundstage."

"She'd close Skreetches? It's been going half the life of *Hope*!"

"She's considering it."

"That's whacked."

Borsk didn't disagree.

℠ ℞

Anya broke into a full run as soon as she got into the semi-private corridors of her family's neighborhood. Even with Borsk's shuttle trick, she was running late.

At her door, she mistyped the curtain code. Swearing softly, she cleared her armband and started over. This time, the mag-field clicked off, and she dashed through the black beads that guarded their entrance.

On the other side, the table was already set up for dinner, filling most of the space between the kitchenette and the right-hand wall that held her bunk. Her father sat in the seat across from her, staring at a large reading tablet. He glanced up. "Where have you been? Ryan will be here in twenty-five minutes."

Ryan Lancet. The guy her parents intended her to marry. He was all right, Anya supposed, even if he was ten years older than she was. Certainly, he was better than Kenneth Llourdes, the bullying hulk they'd married her sister Kristi off to five years ago. But Ryan was only slightly more tolerant of her greenhouse fascination than her parents were, and so far, he'd dodged all her attempts to talk about the colony and possibly trying out. Anya had to make the discussion happen tonight. She was running out of time. She took a deep breath. "Sorry. I came as quick as I could."

Her father scowled. "Get cleaned up. I don't see how you can stand to be so filthy."

As if she liked having a thin layer of dust caught in the creases of her elbows and neck.

"Move!" her father barked.

She gulped. At least he wasn't getting up. She scooted around the table. "I'm going, I'm going," she said. "I really am sorry."

"Sorry's what you'll be if it ever happens again."

"Yes, sir," she said, thinking that right now, even if she knew for sure that Borsk had released viruses into all her father's systems, she wouldn't tell. She ducked under her parent's loft into the den and slipped through the silvery beads on the left that hid the bathroom. A few quick taps of her armband, and the beads softly clicked into firm alignment. She couldn't relax until she had that solid—well, as solid as bits of magnetized wire and plastic got—barrier between her and her father.

The shower was five minutes of heaven: pulsing sprays of hot water; slick, silverfruit-scented soap; sweetly aromatic steam. Anya basked in it, refusing to worry about her father or Ryan or anything. When she emerged, puffy and red, but clean and sweet-smelling, she couldn't help smiling at herself in the mirrored bathroom walls.

Her mother had hung a dress from the ceiling bar—an actual dress. It had once been Kristi's, which made it tight and long on Anya. Between that and her haircut—the exact same bob that Kristi's three-year-old daughter, Tiny, sported—Anya felt like she was playing dress up.

Her mom was coming in with tins of take-out when she got out of the bathroom. "Stacey! That dress looks great on you."

Anya grimaced. Her mom knew she thought "Anya" was a better way to shorten Anastasia than "Stacey." But Father liked "Stacey" better, so Mom almost always used it. Anya was surprised Mom had dared say anything about the dress before Father pronounced his opinion of it. Not that he ever noticed what she wore.

Except now. Father was looking her way. "Don't scowl at your mother," he said.

Anya smoothed out her face.

Father grunted.

It was as close as he ever got to approval. So, did he like the dress?

"Maybe we'd better put you back on that diet. No dessert tonight anyway."

Anya sighed. Dessert was the only part of take-out dinners worth eating. But after coming in late, she didn't have much leeway for arguing.

"Would you like help with your hair, sweetie?" Anya's mother asked.

"I guess." Anya stifled another sigh. She didn't see the point. No matter how much time her mom spent on it, her hair would still look exactly like Tiny's.

Her mom had barely finished fluffing and combing when Ryan arrived. He hung his hat on the pegboard next to the door, shook her father's hand, nodded at her mom, and said, "Hey, Stace. Anything new happening?"

Anya forced a smile. "Not really. Just pruning silverfruit today."

"I thought you were doing some kind of research—finding a low-light, low-water, complete protein, right?"

Anya shrugged. "Sure, I measured the B9s."

"Well that's something."

It wasn't, really. The B9s were fleshy, brownish plants with a foul odor. She wouldn't bother with them at all, but she knew her work on experimentals kept Ryan and Father from pushing her even more about quitting work in the greenhouses.

"Don't you like the B9s?" Ryan asked, tipping his head to one side. His white-blond hair glinted in the soft light off the kitchen. Anya wondered if she could draw that. She reached for her stylus, saying, "Sure, sure."

Ryan didn't accept that. "What's wrong with them?"

"They're ugly," Anya said.

Her father guffawed and maneuvered Ryan away from her into the den. Just as well. She knew he'd rather hang out with her father than her. And she was still focused on those glints.

She ducked into her bunk, glad she had a space of her own. If she'd had to share with a sister or cousins, she'd have an even harder time keeping Father from interrupting her art.

She set up her blank back wall to accept a projection of her drawing. She was half through a sketch of Ryan's face before she thought to consider how she'd feel with him looking down at her in the bunk. Not like he'd never been here before, but when he was helping with her homework, he didn't usually have this icy fire in his eyes. Her stylus faltered and she let it fall to her knees. It would take a few days to get this right, she knew. Could she live with him in her bunk for that long, staring down at her, gorgeous and godlike, burning but cold?

She was lost enough in her musings that she missed the thrum of the door chime and didn't realize it was Ryan's parents until Mr. Lancet gasped just behind her. Anya whipped her head around. Mr. Lancet was gaping at the image of Ryan on her bunk wall.

She moved to shut down the projection, but Mr. Lancet said, "Don't turn it off; it's gorgeous. Janet, have you seen this?"

Mrs. Lancet and Anya's mom both turned toward the bunk.

"It's beautiful," Mrs. Lancet said, but her forehead puckered a bit.

"You've made the eyes too . . ." Anya's mom started.

"Unsettling," Mrs. Lancet finished. "Though he does look like that sometimes."

"When he thinks no one is looking." Mr. Lancet laughed. "Who knew you saw straight through him, kid?"

"What's going on?" Anya's father growled from the den.

Not good, not good. Anya stabbed at her armband and the projection vanished, leaving her bunk wall blank again.

"It's just a picture, Thomas," Mr. Lancet said.

"Stacey's been drawing again? She's got homework to do!"

"Dinner's ready, everyone!" Anya's mom said, much too brightly.

They crowded round the table, talking lightly of the food and ship gossip, but from the thoughtful looks Mr. Lancet was giving her, Anya knew he was still thinking about her picture. She ducked her head and concentrated on eating. Maybe if she stayed quiet, everyone would forget about her and her artwork.

Certainly, no one mentioned the drawing during dinner. And maybe Mr. Lancet looked thoughtful for another reason. Near the end of the meal, he pushed his stool away from the table and leaned back, fingering his beard. "You know I enjoy our dinners, Thomas, but I wonder if these kids wouldn't like something a bit livelier. Isn't Steve Jackson giving a concert next week?"

"No. We've canceled that mess of propaganda for the Colonialists."

"And I hear you're pressuring Skreetches to keep him off their minuscule sound-stage. Do you really think that's wise, Thomas? Half the people on this ship wouldn't pay any attention to a new Steve Jackson piece if you weren't making all this fuss. And he's the best composer *Hope* has seen in a couple hundred years. If people listen to him, it might change minds."

"If you believe that load of ferto, George—"

"Stace, did you need any homework help?" Ryan cut in.

"Oh, Ryan, you don't need to—" Anya's mom said.

"But I want to," he said, sounding more sincere than usual. "In fact, I was hoping to get a little time alone with Stace."

Seriously? Was that good or bad? At least it might help her talk about the colony. Try-outs were close enough, she ought to be packing, not still looking for a partner. Anya smiled tentatively at Ryan.

He smiled back. "Actually, do you think we could have the bunk screen down this once?"

Anya dropped one of her chopsticks.

"Of course, of course," her father said as she dove for it. "You two enjoy yourselves."

Enjoy themselves. Yeah right. With a mess of Chemistry and a few quadratic equations. Unless Ryan wanted her alone for something other than homework. Anya's heart hammered against her chest. She wondered if they could all hear it, up around the table.

Ryan had never shown any signs of wanting anything physical before, but she supposed he had a right. They were going to get married one of these days, after all.

Still, she wasn't at all sure she was ready to be in a bunk with him with the screens down.

&   ⅋

Borsk walked VJ halfway to the Brown family quarters on the near, almost respectable, side of Sigmore Landing. The big guy seemed to need the company, and it gave Borsk an excuse to sneak into Skreetches the back way. If he was lucky, nobody would be making any deliveries or stocking the storeroom, and he could slip right to his bunk and get programming before anyone realized he was home and started him on restaurant chores.

At first it looked like luck was with him. The narrow back hallway for deliveries held nothing but their old hand truck, resting idle in the corner, like an ordinary black pallet. It wasn't floating, and its handle wasn't even raised. Borsk smiled to himself and dipped under the half-lowered shade of the storeroom door.

His smile disappeared when, before he could straighten up, he almost ran into a step stool. Someone stood on the top step, with their head and torso deep in the spare condiment shelf. All he could see was skinny legs in white restaurant pants above orange restaurant shoes.

"Hey, watch where you're going!" Sarka said. He must have actually run into her.

So much for getting quietly to his bunk. "If you put your stool smack dab in the doorway, you really shouldn't complain if people bump into you."

"Borsk!" Sarka backed out of the shelf and down the stool clutching a tub of mustard. Her dark eyes flashed. "Where have you been? Cousin Ketzia called in sick, and we've been shorthanded all afternoon."

"What, you're in charge of manning shifts now?"

"No, but when you disappear, I have to pick up the slack, and I'm sick of it." She shoved the mustard at him, snapped the stool shut, and slid it back into its slot between two cabinets.

"I had a detention. In the greenhouses."

"You went and got a detention this week? I thought we agreed to stay out of trouble, seeing how Mama already has so much to deal with."

"Agreed? What are you talking about? I heard your stupid lecture after church. Did you hear me say anything? Anything at all?"

Sarka stood there, glaring at him.

Borsk shoved the mustard back at her so hard that she crashed into the condiment shelf. Half a dozen things rattled, but she looked more angry than hurt. That was good. He hadn't meant to hurt her.

"Jerk."

"You know it." He walked between the rows of shelves. The archway to the kitchen was straight ahead of him, but instead of going through it, he turned left at the end of the row, toward the rest of the storeroom and the restaurant's private rooms that doubled as family quarters.

"Where do you think you're going?" Sarka shouted after him. "You've got work to do!"

"I'm cleaning up. Greenhouses, remember?"

"If I don't see your lazy ass in the kitchen scrubbing potatoes within ten minutes, I'm telling Mama what you really do in Sunday school."

Borsk turned. Sarka stood, panting, by the archway to the kitchen. She balanced the mustard tub on one hip. He smiled at her. "You don't think she knows I play computer games?"

"Run an online casino, you mean."

OK, maybe Mama didn't know that part. Borsk put on his best poker face and shrugged. "If you say so. Seems like you also say that you and Gabriel are studying Chemistry Friday nights at his house."

"We do study Chemistry!"

Borsk raised an eyebrow. "In his bunk, with the screen down?"

"How do you know . . ." Sarka started, but then seemed to think better of it.

Borsk widened his smile. "I'll get down to the kitchen as soon as I can." It was even true. If cousin Ketzia had called off sick, Mama would need him down there. But he didn't want Sarka thinking she could control him. He sauntered out of the storeroom as if he didn't have a care in the world.

Chapter Three

Anya's hands shook as she lowered the bunk screens and set the privacy code. If Ryan asked about it, she'd say she was excited, but she knew that nothing more than fear, plain and simple, made her tremble. She'd never been with a man, but she'd heard plenty back when Kenneth was terrorizing Kristi before they got married. Their bunk screens blocked noise from the main part of the quarters, but nothing stopped sound from traveling down from the upper bunk to the lower one where Anya cowered, curled up with her ears covered in a vain attempt to block Kristi's pleading and cries. Just the memory had Anya scrunching back into the corner again.

"Are you OK?" Ryan asked.

Anya put one hand on top of the other to hold it still. "Sure."

"You look pale. You never told me you get claustrophobic."

"I don't. I'm just a little cold." She rummaged through one of her cubicles and pulled out a ratty blue sweater. It didn't match the dress and tended to round her figure rather than slim it, but she didn't care. Grandma Anderson had given it to her, and right now she needed a touch of Grandma Anderson. If this went badly, she'd run up to the Sunnydale assisted care center and see Grandma in person—just as soon as the facility opened for visitors in the morning.

"We can have the screens up if it's going to bother you," Ryan said. "Really. I only asked to have them down so I wouldn't have to hear the wrangle our parents are about to get into."

Anya shrugged into the sweater. "Why? Usually you like joining the discussions."

"There's no winning this one. The way your father is handling the situation is wrong-headed, but I can't blame him for wanting to suppress the concert. The last thing *Hope* needs right now is a gifted musician convincing half the ship that the Golden Terrace colony is a romantic new beginning for all of us. Anybody with any sense knows that the colony will never be anything more than a supply station. But if Steve Jackson and his friends get everybody worked up, the colony will drain talent and resources we can't afford to lose."

"What if Golden Terrace is actually a new beginning?"

Ryan snorted. "Please. You're sometimes dense, Stace, but not usually about stuff like this."

That hurt. She knew she wasn't great at the engineering core, but she was reasonably smart otherwise. Plus, she wasn't the only one who thought going to the colony was the best opportunity in generations. And not just because of the generous compensation package, though that was tempting—A-level salaries, room and board (though the colonists would have to grow and make their housing and food), unlimited kid benefits on Shindashir, and letting someone in your close family on *Hope* have more than the usual two kids. It was a good deal for the colonists. But not the main reason she wanted to go. She wanted to see the planet. And she thought it was a great opportunity to start a fresh civilization.

She didn't like to argue, but if she was going to convince Ryan to try out with her, she had to help him see it her way. "I don't know. It seems like the colony will have a lot of advantages—more space, the choice for more kids . . ."

"But we have a millennium of culture and knowledge, not to mention a ton of technology and talent up here. *Hope* is going to continue to be the center of our civilization for quite a while to come."

"But not necessarily forever. In fifty years, or a hundred . . ."

"It might make sense for our kids or grandkids to move down there, once something's established and going. Not now."

Anya couldn't wait that long. "The people who go now will shape what that new world looks like and how it works."

"Not as much as *Hope*'s council and captain."

"Ryan, you're a lieutenant, not even old enough to run for the council."

"But you don't get to be captain by running down to the surface and spending the best years of your career mucking about in the dirt. Look, Stace, I came in here to avoid this conversation. I get enough of it at home.

So, his parents also thought going to the colony was a great opportunity. Or at least his dad did, and George Lancet wasn't stupid at all. Anya sucked in a deep breath, hoping some courage would come with it.

"Look, Stace, don't you have some homework we can work on?" Ryan reached across her toward her school tablet.

Now was the moment to say something, but her mind blanked. Then, as his arm turned, she noticed a small red light next to the green one on his armband. "You're recording us?"

"Of course. You're fifteen, Stace. Do you have any idea how much trouble I'd be in if I couldn't prove exactly how we spent our time in here together?" He glanced at her with his burning ice look. She shrank a little further back into her corner, and he glanced away, flicking on her tablet. "Ah. Algebra. How are you coming with those quadratic equations?"

So, he wasn't interested in being with her the way she feared. She felt strangely disappointed. It was almost like some part of her had hoped for physical touch—even though she was afraid. And maybe, if he'd wanted to touch her, and she'd let him, he'd have been easier to persuade. That was the way it worked in some stories. Though not for her mom or Kristi, so maybe this was for the best.

"Stace? Quadratic equations?" Ryan turned his icy fire look full on her.

She huddled into her sweater, letting one finger slip toward her tablet to open her latest homework attempt.

How she hated math.

℞ ☙

Borsk couldn't get away from potatoes. The tube potatoes in the greenhouse that afternoon had started it—nasty, messy things with worm-like growths all over them. Old Greeley had set him to digging the nasty bits out and planting them in stinky black ferto-eight. He'd have preferred the old man's job—screwing on the next section of tubing and squirting it full of more of the mushy growing medium, but nothing to do with planting tube-potatoes was fun. The process was dirty and time-consuming. He'd been afraid they wouldn't be done in time for him to spy on Anya. Then he'd have needed to figure out some new imperfect (but not too suspiciously imperfect) hack he could get caught doing to land him in the greenhouses again. Though, as it turned out, landing another greenhouse detention had been no problem. Who knew David Ryerson would be such a stickler for rules?

But he hadn't known that when he was working on tube potatoes and had been thoroughly relieved to finish long enough before the shuttle for him to capture some really good, high definition vids of Anya's eyes. Modeling electronic ones that could fool the identity scanners wouldn't be too much trouble if he ever got enough peace and quiet to do it.

Unfortunately, peace and quiet were about as plentiful as the money they needed to buy out Thomas Cartier's share of the restaurant. Before he'd even half finished his shower, Sarka banged on the water closet door, yelling at him to stop wasting water and get his ass down to the kitchen, which he did, only to be confronted with his second pile of potatoes for the day. These, at least, had no worm-like sprouts, but remnants of ferto-eight clung tenaciously to them, especially in the wrinkles and crevices formed by irregularities. Sarka handed him a scrub brush. "Be sure you're thorough. Last time we had complaints about the fries tasting dirty."

Borsk stuck his tongue out at her.

"I don't want to bring Mama into this, but I will if I have to."

Borsk rolled up his sleeves and grabbed the brush. "I'm scrubbing already. Don't you have some place more important to be?"

Sarka scowled at him until he started working. Then she flounced to the other side of the room to lend a hand with the fryers. Before he'd finished his first chopper-load, she'd finished with the fryers, run a set of dirty dishes through the washer, and set a new batch of salad going. Uncle Hirsch, their head cook, said one day she'd be an even better restaurant manager than their mother. Borsk, on the other hand, could barely be trusted with a pile of potatoes. He scrubbed the one he was holding so hard that bits of the skin came clean away.

"Careful," Sarka said from behind him. "Lose too much skin, and our nutrition numbers on the fries literally go down the drain."

"Like anybody's eating fries for their health," Borsk muttered.

"What's that?"

"I don't want to have to go to Mama either, but if you don't get off my case . . ."

"You're such a baby, Borsk. If you had any sense of responsibility at all—"

"That does it." Borsk lifted his hands out of the washbasin so fast, the dirty water snapped from his fingers into Sarka's face. "Where's Mama?"

"Are you two fighting?" Mama's low clear voice carried through the kitchen clatter even better than Sarka's shrill one did.

"No, Mama," Sarka said, wiping the damp off her face and heading for the hand sanitizer. "Borsk just didn't take kindly to one of my suggestions."

Mama paced toward them, elegant, even in the restaurant white and orange. "You two have to learn to work together," she said softly.

Borsk could see bags under her eyes and worry wrinkles in her forehead, so he choked back his speech about not intending to ever work with Sarka again once he got his degree and a job away from this place. There'd be time enough for that conversation another day.

"Sorry," he said instead. "It was a long day in the greenhouses, and I guess I'm a bit short tempered. By the way, I saw VJ Brown. His gran wanted to help out with the soundstage by contributing an old Earth coin to the cause."

"VJ's gran? Why didn't you tell me?" Sarka said.

Borsk glared at her. "I figured it would take too long to assess or authenticate or whatever. We couldn't use it, but we appreciate the thought."

"Surely we could get a waiver—" Sarka started.

"Borsk handled it exactly right," Mama said. "Now, Borsk, if you've had one work detail already today, what are you doing down here?"

"This isn't work, Mama, just a chore. There are no inspectors coming."

Mama's eyes got fiery.

"I'll run back to my bunk and do my homework as soon as these potatoes are scrubbed. Promise."

"You can't," Sarka said. "We didn't have a clean space for the new greenhouse shipment, and since your bunk was easier to scrub than the storeroom rack you failed to clean yesterday, we dumped the goods there. You can bunk in with Uncle Hirsch's boys tonight."

The hell he could. Even if he weren't trying to pull one of his trickiest hacking jobs, there was no way he was sharing a bunk with his nine and eleven-year-old cousins. Sarka would pay for this. Too bad he couldn't tell her so, but with Mama standing right there, it was too risky. He turned back to his tub of potatoes in dirty water, keeping his eyes lowered and his voice tightly under control. "I'll take care of it when I'm done here."

"Sarka," his Mama said in the deceptively gentle voice she always used when she was particularly upset with them, "Come with me to the storeroom for a moment."

Maybe he wouldn't have to think up anything creatively nasty for Sarka. Nothing he could do would feel half as bad as the quiet little "I'm-disappointed-in-you" talk she was probably getting from Mama right now. He smiled to himself as he scrubbed potatoes.

He even managed to be cheerful while cleaning out and sterilizing the storeroom shelf he'd neglected yesterday.

All remnants of cheer left, though, when he threw up his bunk screen and saw the ten-kilo bags of potatoes.

If he had to sign a contract with the devil himself to get it done, he'd make Sarka pay for this. Just as soon as he finished dealing with Thomas Cartier.

Long before he could get to that problem, though, Borsk's arms, neck and back ached. He was thoroughly sick of the family business. Maybe he should let the restaurant go the way of all things. Sarka would have to come down a peg or two and start paying attention in school instead of scraping by with bare passes.

Losing the restaurant would about kill Mama, though. She'd given her whole life to it. So had Uncle Hirsch. Every time he passed the kitchen, he could hear them talking softly to each other in worried voices as they served late orders and started nightly clean up. He could hear Sarka's whine now and then too, not well enough to make out words, but well enough to hear tension and worry in her voice. It was almost enough to make him feel sorry for her. She was a pain in the ass, but she didn't deserve this. He nodded to himself. Of course, they couldn't lose the restaurant. Even if he didn't care that much, the rest of them did. Besides, Thomas Cartier needed to know he couldn't bully everybody. Time to get to it.

He slung the last of the potatoes onto the storage shelf and eased his aching limbs back to his bunk. He had to wipe a layer of grime off everything before he could start, but at last he was alone, chest propped on a couple of pillows, with electronics spread in front of him, and his privacy screen down. This was his kingdom. It might not be big enough to sit up in, but he knew he was lucky to have a bunk of his own. He had shared with Uncle Hirsch's boys when he was younger. But when Gran and Gramps had retired and moved away from the restaurant, and Mama hadn't wanted to stay in the bunk she'd shared with Dad after he died, Borsk got his own space. He'd spent every credit he earned in the last three years at the restaurant making sure that in this bunk, everything was under his control. Not a sound, not a light, not an electron, could get in or out without him knowing and manipulating it.

This was the way he liked it. He'd work this way all the time if it didn't get so damn hot. He'd stripped down to his skivvies, but figured he'd still be miserable before he finished tonight—if he didn't get so caught up in his project that he no longer noticed physical discomfort. He smiled to himself as he connected his armband to his school tablet and a tangle of chips and wires that normally lived in a jumble with his other paraphernalia and his clean underthings. The resulting contraption looked bizarre, but with a little configuration, it sent out a signal indistinguishable from Anya Cartier's armband.

So far so good. The next part was simple, but time-consuming—rendering a digital mask for his eyes that could fool *Hope*'s financial service center into thinking he was Anya.

A good hour later, he stretched his sweat-slicked arms and took a swig from his water bottle. Now came the trickiest part of the operation—finding a data stream that could place him inside paranoid Thomas Cartier's quarters. He smiled in anticipation of the challenge, cracked his fingers, and started a careful approach.

Which proved unnecessary. Some fool was running a logged surveillance video from inside the quarters—from inside Anya's bunk in fact. Borsk raised his eyebrows. He didn't think she had a boyfriend, let alone someone close enough to make blackmail recordings worthwhile. Maybe Miss Cartier wasn't as sweet as she seemed. He copied the whole log, then used the data stream as a conduit to access first the house entertainment system, then Anya's bunk optics, and finally her armband.

Then he had to wait. He couldn't very well make the transfer while Anya was demonstrably busy with somebody else. While he was waiting, he might as well take a look at the surveillance log. He downloaded the feed to an old screen and played it back, from the beginning, triple time.

It wasn't at all what he expected. There was a guy, all right, but he and Anya weren't up to anything kinky, or even romantic, if he read the signs right. They just talked for a moment before bending their heads over what looked like Anya's school tablet. Borsk slowed down the playback enough to see details.

Math. The guy was tutoring Anya in math. Well, that was useless. Borsk would go over the feed in more detail later, just to make sure, but he didn't think this particular bit of data was likely to lead to anything valuable. He sped it back up, but even at triple-time, it was about like watching beans grow in the greenhouse. Even Anya didn't sit around voluntarily doing that. Borsk yawned and wished the two of them would hurry up. How bad could Anya be at math anyway?

Pretty bad, he realized, when the feed caught up with the current moment, and he heard the two of them in real time. Maybe this was a blackmail recording after all, just not the kind he'd first expected. He felt a bit sorry for Anya.

At last the guy left, and Anya's armband went into full-on art mode. Borsk smiled and captured the piece before slipping into the girl's financials.

Two minutes and a very tricky forgery of Anya's security swipe later, Borsk had full control of the girl's hundred-thousand-odd untraceable credits. Trust a Cartier to have more money at fifteen than most people on the ship would see in their entire lifetime. She didn't need it. And he wasn't really stealing it, just tying a hefty chunk of it up for a decade or so in an acquisition she'd certainly never make herself. One that could get her in a lot of trouble at home if anyone ever found out.

That made him queasy. So, he didn't believe his own justifications. No matter. He'd deal with his conscience later. He'd been hanging out leaving an electronic trail for far too long already. He made the deal, then backed out, erasing all trace of his presence as he went. Thomas Cartier's own hackers would be looking for signs of who made the purchase, and he didn't want to leave anything for them to find.

Chapter Four

Anya woke with a start before her alarm went off. She had the uncanny feeling that someone was watching her. She rolled over slowly and caught a glint of fiery eyes from the foot of her bunk. She jerked upright, tense, until she realized it was her portrait of Ryan. Thank goodness, the screens were down, and her parents couldn't hear her. She snapped off the projection and took deep breaths until her heart slowed. If just his picture gave her this kind of conniption, what would waking up with his actual person be like?

Not that he showed any signs of wanting to stay in her bed. Or of considering trying out for the Golden Terrace team. Somehow, she'd failed, again, to explain that it was important to her. Why couldn't she ever speak up for herself? She had barely ten days until try-outs started, and she was no closer to having a partner than before Ryan had showed up last night. She had to do something. Maybe Grandma would have some ideas. She wanted to talk to her about last night anyway.

Anya threw on a fresh, navy-blue school uniform and eased open her bunk screen.

"Caroline!" her father shouted from a few feet away. Anya shrank back into her bunk, letting the screen fall back to nearly closed.

"Yes, Thomas?" her mom said. Her voice came from up in the loft above the den but got closer. "Is something wrong?"

A few moments after her mom stopped talking, Anya heard a thump. Was Mom OK? Anya lay flat on her bunk and peered through the crack under the screen. Her father stood in Anya's line of sight, pressing her mom against the refrigeration unit.

"Is something wrong? Your mother buys out my portion of Skreetches, and you ask me if there's something wrong?"

Someone had bought Father's share of Skreetches?

Anya's mom sounded as shocked as Anya felt. "My mother? Surely, Thomas—"

"Your mother. Arnold Bates. William Newton. Oliver Forrest. Diane Rutherford. Those are the only people on *Hope* with enough untraceable liquid funds to buy out my share of Skreetches. It had to be one of them. Are you telling me that Arnie, Bill or Ollie did it? Or Di?"

"There must be another explanation, Thomas. There must be," Mom whimpered.

She was right—there had to be another explanation. Anya couldn't imagine the captain or any of Father's poker buddies crossing Father that way. Grandma would but couldn't have done it. She and Grandpa had made over their special untraceable fund to Anya before Grandpa died. Obviously, Father didn't know that. But it didn't make any difference. Anya hadn't ever touched that money. She never borrowed trouble.

"I want her declared incompetent to handle her own affairs. Now. And you and the girls are to stay strictly away from her."

"No, Thomas," Mom moaned.

Father picked her up and slammed her back into the fridge unit. Her head hit with a nasty cracking noise. "NOW!"

Anya held her breath. Part of her felt she should get out there and stop all this. A much larger part kept her frozen, hoping neither of her parents noticed her.

Relief washed over her when she heard her mom's voice. "I'm sorry, Thomas."

What was Mom apologizing for?

"I'll get started on the paperwork," Mom added.

No, no, no, Anya thought. But she didn't do anything as Father moved just far enough from the fridge for Mom to slip towards the den. He followed, probably to make sure Mom did exactly what he wanted.

Anya couldn't believe her mom would give in so easily. But then, Mom didn't usually stand up for herself, let alone anyone else. Anya herself was no better. Here she was, hiding in her bunk, when her mom was hurt and her grandma in trouble even though she had proof positive that Grandma hadn't done what Father thought she had. She could just tell him. And have all that anger directed at her instead of Grandma. She pressed down even further into her bunk, so that she could feel the weave of the mattress cover under her right cheek and her splayed fingers.

She was such a coward.

Well, if she didn't have the guts to face Father, at least she could warn Grandma. As quietly as she could, she grabbed her school backpack, and lifted the screen just enough to creep out of her bunk.

She'd nearly reached the door when her father's voice boomed out, "Where do you think you're going, young lady?"

"Library," she lied. "I've got a paper." Due in a month, and she'd already started on it, but it was a real assignment. He could look it up.

"Fine, but I'm watching you. No side trips anywhere else."

Ferto. That ruled out going to Grandma's, at least until she could figure out a way to mask her movements from Father's surveillance. She had no idea how to do that, and by the time she figured it out, any warning she could give her Grandma would be too late.

She shuffled along the half-lit corridors, close enough to the right wall that if she wanted to, she could run her fingers along the once-gold hexagons that ran in a waist-high stripe along all the halls in her neighborhood. She wanted to wash her hands after just thinking about touching the generation-and-a-half of grime that had built up since these walls had last been painted.

That reminded her that she'd skipped using the bathroom that morning. Surely Father couldn't complain if she stopped in one of the pay toilets on the way to the library, as long as the stop wasn't overly long. If she picked her restroom wisely, she might run into someone who could carry Grandma a message. Not on this level. The only public restrooms on Level One were over by the government buildings, and those would be crawling with her father's cronies.

Down a level or two, though, she might find someone Grandma trusted. Maybe on Three, just past the commercial district, in the law office area before the education sector.

Now that she had a purpose, she was tempted to speed up, but she reminded herself that it was still early. The longer it took her to get down there, the more likely others would be starting up their workday. She could find someone to help her. The library unit wouldn't open until seven anyway. She tapped her right earring a couple of times to start up a favorite ballad and slowed her steps to its leisurely beat.

The song reminded her of Ryan, who had introduced her to it. Music didn't speak to her, the way it did to him, but she enjoyed it. Since her father thought music was about as valuable as art, she'd have grown up in a silent world without Ryan. He really was a decent guy. Why was that easier to remember when he wasn't around?

She smiled to herself, and the music changed to an old lullaby that was almost her only memory from her father's mom. The woman had died when Anya was very young, which might be just as well. Everyone said she'd been a bitter old woman.

A bitter old woman who'd left her an art collection and a lullaby. Anya figured she couldn't have been all bad. Maybe not as wonderful as Grandma Anderson, but someone worth knowing, nonetheless. Anya couldn't afford to lose any more grandmas. She would find a way to warn Grandma Anderson before Father's lawyers locked her away.

She relaxed into the music, letting it calm her. Music was amazing that way. It touched her heart, even when her mind couldn't be reached.

A mind that couldn't be reached—like Ryan when she wanted to talk about Golden Terrace. Why couldn't he see the potential of the new world?

Could music help? If Skreetches was free of Father, they could hold Steve Jackson's concert—a concert Ryan thought would draw people toward the Colony. Hope rose in her. Maybe she could convince Ryan to go. The music would persuade him of what she'd been unable to explain.

As she moved toward the library, Anya hummed.

No one was in any of the pay toilets when Anya got down to the restroom in the lawyer's area on Three. As she stood at the row of sinks, tapping in her codes to pay for water, though, a tall, dark woman came in. She had bright lips and purple-painted fingernails half as long as her fingers.

The woman smiled at her. "Good morning, honey. Are you lost?"

"No—no. I'm on my way to the library." She tapped off her music so she could hear better.

"And they don't open for another fifteen minutes, do they? Well this is as good a place as any to wash up of a morning. Lord knows, it's better than the restroom in my hall. Do you mind if I use the mirror here? I've got to finish putting on my face."

Anya stepped a bit to her left, and the woman pulled a brightly flowered roll of fabric out of her briefcase, unrolling it on the metallic shelf beneath the mirror to reveal an intimidating variety of cosmetics.

Anya had never before thought about what mornings might be like in the parts of the ship where whole halls shared restroom facilities, but she could imagine how a restroom in one of the commercial districts might be preferable. It looked like this woman would be here awhile, though, longer than Anya could stay, and Anya had no idea who she was and whether it would be safe to trust her. She couldn't even think of how to discover the woman's name. She scrubbed her hands under the water she'd called up for longer than strictly necessary.

The woman leaned close to the mirror to draw dark lines around her left eye with a dangerous-looking stick. "I'm Laura Wilcox, associate at Brunner and Dyne. I've been coming here mornings since I was an intern."

Anya smiled at her, hoping the smile wasn't too tense. Brunner and Dyne were Grandma's lawyers, but even Brunner and Dyne had spies. Anya wondered how to tell if Laura was one of these. "I'm Anastasia Cartier," she said, "and I usually wash up at home, but this morning . . ." What could she, should she, tell a stranger about her home life?

"Too busy?" Laura supplied.

"My mother and father were having a fight." Anya turned off her water and shook the excess from her hands.

"Ouch. I know how that goes." The woman switched to her other eye.

Somehow Anya doubted it. But she could hardly tell a stranger how afraid she was of her father. She barely admitted the fear to herself. She took a deep breath. "Did you say you work for Brunner and Dyne?"

"Sure."

"Do you know Jamal Pantiri?"

"Of course, honey. He's the one who brought me into the firm. Introduced me to Roger."

"Roger?"

"My husband."

"Oh." She should have been able to figure that out. Roger Wilcox. She'd heard that name before. It took her a second to remember—but then she had it. Roger Wilcox was Ryan's commanding officer. Reasonably high in ship's crew. He might not be under her father's thumb yet, but most of the majors owed her father something. This Laura looked nice, and Anya hated not being able to trust anyone, but she couldn't risk grandma's fate with someone who might not be able to afford to cross Father. Still, a lawyer for Brunner and Dyne might be useful—if she could figure out how to get grandma what she needed without letting Laura realize that was what she was doing.

"He's a great guy, Mr. Pantiri. I've seen him up at Sunnydale a couple of times when I've visited my grandma. I half expected to see him this week, what with old Mr. Singh being so sick, and everybody talking about their arrangements."

"Mr. Singh is always sick."

"Oh, sure. I just thought maybe it was serious this time, since one of the aides told me he wasn't complaining. And he'd asked about getting a lawyer."

Laura Wilcox set down her torture stick and turned toward Anya. "Are you serious, honey?"

Anya shrugged. "The aide was a new one, so she might not know what she's talking about. But all the other residents were talking about stuff in their wills and other paperwork they wanted to tinker with—and I thought maybe this was the real thing—or close enough to the real thing that Mr. Singh might sign a will. I know if he dies intestate . . ."

"His family will tear *Hope* apart fighting over the money."

Anya shrugged again.

"Maybe we should send a notary up with a full set of blank documents, just to make sure. She can do some business with the rest of the jittery lot even if the old man still refuses to settle his affairs. And if he does sign—"

"Life will be a lot better for all of us. Look, I should go. It was nice to meet you, Ms. Wilcox."

"You too, Anastasia."

"Anya, actually." Now why couldn't she say that to Ryan or her father?

"Anya, then." The woman held out her hand, and Anya shook it, smiling.

Grandma would get the forms she needed to foil Father's plans in the course of the morning. Now all she needed was a clue about what was coming, so when she got the help, she could use it effectively.

The library was just opening when Anya got there.

"Morning, Anya," Mrs. Dominguez, the librarian, said. "You're here early."

Yeah, and Mrs. Dominguez would probably know that her paper wasn't due for another month. But there was always extra reading grandma wanted her to do—and Mrs. Dominguez wasn't one to talk. If she wrote a review properly, she might be able to make it a warning her grandma would understand, but her father wouldn't—even if he bothered to look at it. "I've got a detention this afternoon, but I promised my grandma I'd look at some history book she borrowed recently. Something about the Great Famine?"

"Doesn't sound familiar. Maybe you could glance through her recent borrowings." Mrs. Dominguez led the way in, turning on lights and starting up data stations.

"Thanks." Anya grabbed a spot at the first data station and ran a search on what books had been checked out by the over-eighty crowd. No sense in alerting her father's data trolls that someone was paying special attention to Grandma. It was far better if her queries looked like some college student researching the intellectual life of old folks.

She scanned several lists before getting to Grandma's. Hers was by far the longest and most eclectic, but Anya soon found what she wanted—a play, short enough for her to skim quickly, and old enough that her father had almost certainly never read it. As soon as she'd given it enough of a look to get the gist, she whipped off a message to Grandma: "Read *The Purple Haze* as you requested." Since Grandma had done no such thing, she would know immediately that this was meant as a message. "It's no *King Lear*, but I thought the characters were well-drawn, especially Ditton, who reminded me of Peglar in *Turinne*." Father had probably read some bits of Shakespeare—in translation—but if he knew the bard had written *King Lear*, that was probably the extent of his knowledge about the classic. And he wouldn't have read *Turinne* any more than he'd have read The *Purple Haze*, so he shouldn't know that Ditton and Peglar were nothing alike, nor that Peglar had betrayed his mother. "I also think it's great that Sarina surprises everybody." Sarina was Ditton's mother in law.

Anya tapped her finger against the desk. Would it be enough? She wished she could be more explicit, but if she spent too much time making the warning, Grandma wouldn't get it in time to profit by it. She added a couple of innocuous sentences to the review to make it more of the length and style of her usual ones, and then sent the thing off. Grandma would read it immediately. She always did with anything from her grandkids. Then Anya scanned another half a dozen old people's borrowing lists. If she'd really wanted to do a paper on the recreational reading of octogenarians, she could have made a credible start.

Once that was done, Anya still had an hour-and-a-half before school started, plenty of time to look around a bit for who had really bought Skreetches and write Ryan a note about the colony. She hoped that would work better than talking. And there was still the concert that might change his mind.

The news service took its time coming up, which wasn't surprising given the library's slow links, so she flipped through her personal messages. Homework reminders, an invite to Jamelah Park's birthday party, a notice from the bank, an ad for an old cooking show the archive folks had just updated to the latest data protocols . . . Wait. A note from her bank? It wasn't the end of a quarter or even the end of a month. She opened it. It seems they wanted her to log in to confirm a transaction. A transaction on the special account Father didn't know was hers? Well, no wonder flags had gone up. She never touched that thing. She deleted the notice, the way Grandpa had taught her, started a couple of security protocols to ward against hackers, and logged into her account.

At first, she couldn't quite believe what she saw.

She'd bought out Father's part of Skreetches? There was no way. She'd remember. Wouldn't she?

The stupid financial program wouldn't let her log out without either confirming or denying she'd made the purchase.

What was she supposed to do? If she confirmed, it was only a matter of time before her father's minions found the money trail—they were already halfway there. If she denied, an investigation would get started. Her father would learn of her fund, and its whole value—as a means to quietly escape his influence if she ever needed to—would be gone. Plus, if the person who'd made the transaction was good enough, an investigation wouldn't turn up anything. It would look like she'd made the purchase and then chickened out when her father found out about it. She was dead either way. The longer she sat here deciding what to do, the more likely one of her father's people would find her through this data stream. She quickly confirmed and logged out. That might have bought her a bit of time.

She leaned her head in her hands, willing herself to think. Who had done this to her?

The answer was so obvious, she almost hit herself. Borsk, of course. Who else had the motive and the skill? And here she'd thought he liked her art, maybe even wanted to be friends. She should have known better.

Well, that was one way to get out of this. She could just tell her father what she suspected Borsk of, and he'd take care of it. The confirmation she'd just made might get a little tricky, but with her father's lawyers, it probably wasn't insurmountable.

Father would put Skreetches out of business. Borsk would probably get thrown in the brig, and the concert would be off.

Anya breathed in sharply. Right now, she hated Borsk, but did she want to destroy his whole family that way? Plus, the concert might be her best chance of convincing Ryan to go with her to Golden Terrace.

What could she do now? She supposed she could try and divert suspicion from herself by throwing it on someone else. *Arnold Bates, William Newton, Oliver Forrest, and Diane Rutherford*, she reminded herself. They were the only other suspects. Besides Grandma, who had nothing to do with this mess.

Father was sure to find out.

She was doomed.

∞　∞

Borsk thought he'd be tired after his night of hacking. His eyes did look a bit bloodshot, staring back at him from the screen he'd set up with a camera so he could shave. But he found he was too tense to be truly sleepy. Though why he should be tense, he didn't know. He'd hacked cleanly. No one could trace him.

Whistling a bit to himself, he finished shaving, slipped out to the kitchen, and piled restaurant leftovers in a bowl for breakfast.

"You know Mama wants us eating at least two vegetables at every meal," Sarka said from behind him.

He glanced back. Her own plate was piled with green stuff. He set his food on the counter and stuck out his tongue at her. "There are onions and cilantro in the noodles."

"Not a whole serving's worth."

"So, go wake up Mama and tell her."

"You know she was up late last night."

"Then get off my case."

Sarka set her plate down on the counter so hard that his bowl and cup rattled. He smiled sweetly at her and slurped his noodles. He could do the whole bowl without stopping if he worked at it, and this morning he did, partly to get his mind off his tension, partly because he knew Sarka hated it when he ate this way.

"That's disgusting."

Borsk smiled around the noodles he was slurping. As soon as he finished, he took a deep breath, then downed his cup of water. "Later, sis," he said, dropping his dishes into the cleaner.

"Get back early tonight," she said. "Cousin Ketzia is still sick."

"Can't. Greenhouse detention again." He walked out of the kitchen, smiling at her muttered curses. He wondered if her mood would improve when she learned the restaurant was safe, or if she'd just find something new to grouse about.

At school, several people sought him out to commiserate about the soundstage problem, so word that the restaurant was fine hadn't gotten out yet. When Anya got to their homeroom, though, she met his eyes, then looked quickly away, standing where she'd stopped in the doorway for several seconds until someone behind her said something. Then, without looking at him, she walked to the desk next to his and dropped into it.

The tension he'd been feeling all morning crescendoed. She knew something. But she'd sat next to him. What did that mean? He decided to proceed as if everything was the way they'd left it last night. "Hi, Anya," he said.

She nodded.

"Work on any more sculptures last night?" he said, remembering how their best rapport had been over her art. The portrait she'd been working on last night was every bit as good as the flower, if a sight creepier. "Maybe of a boyfriend?"

"Are you threatening me?" she whispered.

"What?" He'd been teasing about the boyfriend thing. Any fool could see from a glance at the picture that she didn't care for the guy.

Her face went totally blank, as if she'd erased it. "You mean you didn't see how bad I was at math?"

He had no idea what they were talking about here, but math was one thing he was sure it wasn't. Before he could gather his thoughts, a shadow fell across the doorway. He glanced that way and saw Thomas Cartier. He stood in the doorway, tall, pale, and broad, with high cheekbones and thick brows, scarier than any ghost.

Their homeroom teacher, a tiny wisp of a woman, squeaked, "Mr. Cartier, can I help you?"

"May I borrow my daughter for a moment, Miss Franklin?" The man paused for a bit before the name, as if he'd had to look it up. "And perhaps young Mr. King as well?"

Someone behind him snickered, but Borsk didn't bother to look. He was too busy trying to control the thundering of his heart. What was wrong with him? The man couldn't prove anything, and he couldn't do anything to them in the school hallway.

Borsk stood as his teacher said, "Of course."

"Walk with me," Mr. Cartier said when Borsk got to the door. They headed toward the gym exit. The man's armband made an odd sizzling sound, and Borsk shot over a sniffer program to see what was causing it.

A crippled line of code limped back, just enough to tell Borsk what he was hearing: a signal blocker, powerful enough to knock out every recording device within twenty meters. The cameras would adjust, of course, but not fast enough to catch up with them if they were walking. He started to tap out a fix.

Mr. Cartier laughed. "Do you really want a file detailing our conversation about what you were doing last night, lad?"

Borsk's fingers fumbled, and he cursed and started over. "What, you think I'm worried about a couple more detentions? That's the maximum for co-opting a public record feed, right?"

"Don't toy with me, boy. I never run public record feeds in my house, but I know you were in my system."

That wasn't good. Borsk thought he'd wiped all trace of himself out of the Cartier electronics.

"Ryan set one up when we were in the bunk last night," Anya said. She was pacing so silently on Borsk's right he'd forgotten she was there.

"Ryan?" Anya's father scowled.

"Yes, Ryan. Borsk has been asking about him."

The man's scowl deepened. Borsk wondered what was so bad about asking about Ryan.

"But he understands, now, that Ryan was just tutoring me in math and science. Actually, Borsk has offered to tutor me himself instead, over in one of Skreetches' private rooms. That way there won't be any further misunderstandings."

Borsk tried not to let it show that this was news to him.

"Did he, now?" Anya's father growled. "And how much, exactly, is this tutoring costing me?"

"Actually, I paid for it myself," Anya said softly, "seeing how I had the cash."

"You?!" Thomas Cartier's face turned red.

Borsk was just as surprised (though not as mad) that Anya had all but admitted to the transaction he'd made last night. He wished he knew why she did it, but he didn't think now was the best time to ask.

Mr. Cartier's face went from red to purple, and he clenched a fist.

Borsk backed up a step, and would have gone farther, but at that moment, he gained control of the man's armband and shut down the illegal blocking program. The hissing stopped.

Mr. Cartier glanced down at his armband and took two deep shuddering breaths. Then he favored them with a ghastly smile.

"Well, that's one round to you, lad. Tell your mother I'm glad she found a buyer on such short notice. You two had better get back to class now." He turned on one heel and strode back the way they'd come as if he owned the place, which, come to think of it, he probably did.

Borsk looked over at Anya, who didn't say anything, just watched her father. Her hands trembled.

"What the hell just happened?" he whispered.

"You're smart, you figure it out," Anya whispered back before turning and walking slowly after her father.

Chapter Five

Anya still felt quivery inside hours later when she reported for her detention in the greenhouses. At least she had a detention to report for. David Ryerson, the engineer from last night, had stuck with the original punishment even though Father had pressured him to change it. David must have been one brave man. Nothing like Anya, who felt sick with fear about having crossed her father.

Her queasiness must have shown, because as soon as she got to him, Mr. Greeley asked, "Are you OK, Anya?"

"I'm fine."

Mr. Greeley rubbed the bald spot between his tufts of silver hair. "Are you sure? You seem a bit pale, girl. I was going to have you up on the trellises, but pollinating will wait a day or two if you're not feeling well. I can find something easier, or even write a note for you to go back home—I can use my judgment on detentions, you know."

Home was the one thing guaranteed to make her problems worse. "I'm OK. Really, Mr. Greeley."

He pinned her with an intense look for a long minute, then shrugged. "If you're sure. Here, pick a partner, someone you trust." He handed her his tablet which listed the detention kids working for him today. Fortunately, there were pictures, not just names. She tapped on the boy with the tattoo who'd asked her out last night. The name next to his picture said VJ Brown.

"How come Anya gets to pick who she works with?" DeShawn said.

Surprised, since she hadn't heard him arrive, Anya swung toward his voice, nearly whacking him with the tablet.

Mr. Greeley took it from her. "When you're down here volunteering every day for months, doing excellent work, you'll get to pick your partners, too."

He glanced down at the tablet. "Sorry, Anya. VJ is too heavy for the harnesses. You'll need somebody under seventy kilos."

"Who are my choices?"

Mr. Greeley tapped a couple of times and turned the tablet back towards her. Only two pictures remained—Borsk and DeShawn.

Just then, she was mad enough at Borsk, she almost picked DeShawn. Her good sense won out in time, though. Borsk might hate her as much as DeShawn did, but at least he didn't show it when he was with her. Plus, he had enough sense to maybe stay safe, which nobody could say of DeShawn.

She tapped Borsk's picture and headed for the trellis wall to get into her harness. It creaked as she adjusted the straps, and she wondered if it had been tested for material soundness in the last decade. Somehow, she doubted it.

Twenty minutes later, she hung next to Borsk just under the ceiling supports next to the trellis wall. Anya wiggled a bit to get comfortable and tested her mobility interface. Left, right, up—she about bumped her head, but managed to stop her ascent in time—and then down. Her stomach lurched as she fell a meter below where Borsk hung. The stupid things always went down too fast. She cranked herself back up using the manual reel, just to make sure it worked, then tried going down, more slowly this time. Better.

Borsk hadn't moved at all.

"Is your harness working OK?" she asked.

"You're really loving this, aren't you, you little snob? And for a second yesterday I almost liked you, almost felt guilty."

Anya could hardly make sense of the words, let alone the angry, bitter tone Borsk said them in. After what he'd pulled last night, and the way she'd covered for him this morning, what right did he have to be mad at her? "Sorry?"

"You ought to be sorry, dragging me up to the highest spot on *Hope* out of spite."

Anya looked down between her toes, at the green wall with the nubby white bits that counted as flowers for grapes. It stretched below her until the green and white softened into mottled abstraction and then ended sharply at turquoise floor some twenty meters below. Maybe it was the highest spot on *Hope*. Heights didn't bother her that much, but as she looked over at Borsk, she could see a funny green tinge under his normal golden brown. He was covering real fear with all that anger. She was still mad at him, but she couldn't stand to see anyone suffer. She sighed. "You're afraid of heights. I didn't realize. Did you tell Mr. Greeley?"

"It's in my file."

"He doesn't pay any attention to the files."

"What?"

Anya shrugged, making her whole body shake in the harness. Borsk winced.

"Sorry. I'll try not to move too much. Look, we can go back down. If I explain to Mr. Greeley how you looked up here, he'll find you something else to do. He's good about real problems."

"As opposed to what?"

"Have you seen the stuff parents put in the files? *Bobby can't lift more than three kilos this week since he strained his back playing mashball.* Or this was a good one—*Joe has shown adverse reactions to all ferto products and must not be exposed to them even when wearing gloves.*"

Borsk laughed, which made him look a touch less ill. "You've got to be kidding me. Come to think of it you *do* have to be kidding me. There are no Joes or Bobbys down here."

"I changed some names to protect the guilty. And Mr. Greeley, of course. He's not supposed to show me the files. But that *adverse reactions to ferto* one infuriated him so much one day, he showed me a whole set. Even before then he wouldn't look at the files until after he'd assigned chores for the day."

"And he assumes my fear of heights is like the ferto thing?"

"He probably assumes your whole file is fictional, designed for your own devious purposes. He's not stupid, you know." She sent her harness farther left, just in case Borsk decided to lash out at her, but he didn't even seem to notice that she'd criticized him. Her heart beat unreasonably quickly. She didn't usually get away with the most oblique dissent, let alone direct criticism or confrontation. Maybe Borsk wasn't feeling up to defending himself. He still looked kind of green. "We should get you off this wall," Anya sighed again and kicked softly at the vine in front of her feet. "It probably won't kill me to work with DeShawn."

"DeShawn? He said you got to pick your partner up here."

"Yeah, but Mr. Greeley says he doesn't trust the harnesses with anybody over seventy kilos, and you and DeShawn are the only ones besides me who are under. I guess there are no seventh or eighth form kids today."

"What's wrong with the harnesses?"

"Nothing. It's just fifty-year-old tech made of umpteen-times recycled materials."

"Knew I shouldn't have believed DeShawn. You wouldn't pick me to be your partner up here just because I'm afraid of heights, even if you are mad."

"I am pretty mad."

"And you're stuck with me, up here, halfway to the void. And here I thought you were Old Greeley's favorite."

"He trusts me not to get myself killed. Last cycle he had me up here with some kid—I forget his name—but the idiot was doing somersaults in the harness."

"Damn."

"Scared me to death before I could get him back down to the greenhouse floor."

"I can imagine. And I could just see DeShawn doing the same thing."

"Maybe if Mr. Greeley puts a scare into him, he'd behave himself."

"Up here? Nah—I'll stick with you. I figure I owe you one, and I can survive about anything. After all, this morning, I survived a conversation with your dad, even if, for a minute there, it got so intense I thought he was going to hit one of us. How crazy is that?"

"Not that crazy." Since Borsk was staying, and no longer mad at her, Anya pulled a brush out of a harness pocket and swabbed the topmost flowers she could reach, trying to get all of them in a smooth pattern from left to right.

"You think he'd really hit me? In a public hallway? Seconds after our whole class had seen us leave with him? Even with all the cameras off, touching either of us would have been a violence citation for sure."

"Maybe," Anya said, swabbing her second row of flowers. "Are you going to help with this? If I have to do it all myself, we're going to be up here a very long time."

"What are we doing, exactly?"

"Pollinating. You brush the flowers to move pollen onto those green capsule-looking things."

"These are flowers?"

"Not much to look at, are they? But they'll turn into grapes, eventually, if we get the pollen to the right parts."

"Makes you wonder how grapes survived before humans with brushes, doesn't it?"

"Insects."

"Like recycling grubs?"

"Sort of. But flying ones—they'd go from plant to plant spreading pollen around."

"Nasty."

Anya had forgotten he didn't like recycling grubs. "No, they were really pretty, some of them. And a few, called bees, would make honey."

"Actual honey?"

"I think the stuff we call honey was originally designed as a synthetic replacement for what the bees made."

Borsk stopped brushing for a second and stared at her. "I bet you're one hell of a poker player."

"Excuse me?"

"You tell the wildest stories like they're God's own truth."

"Bees are truth—I read about them in the founding diaries."

"Yeah, and that pile of shit you told your dad this morning?"

"Do you really want to talk about that here?" Anya glanced at her armband.

"Relax. You're not recording. Neither am I. And there aren't any other feed-optimized devices up here. I've checked."

"Still."

"Point taken. So how about whichever of us believes the biggest whopper buys dinner tonight?"

"How is that fair? Your family owns a restaurant."

"So, do you, stupid. Same one."

She'd forgotten for a second, but now that she remembered, the quivery feelings in her gut came back in full force. She couldn't believe she'd come right out and told her father that she'd bought his share of Skreetches. He seemed to have accepted her implied fiction that Borsk was blackmailing them about the betrothal. For now. Would the story hold up over time? Would it protect her when she went home tonight? Eating somewhere else suddenly sounded like a very good idea. She wished she could figure out a way to avoid ever going home. "You know, you're a very bad influence on me," she said to Borsk.

"*I'm* the bad influence? Before I tried being friends with you, I never hung from the ceiling supports, and I certainly never hacked strangers' armbands in public hallways."

What, you were too busy ripping off your friends? Anya wanted to ask but didn't. She never said stuff like that. Nice girls didn't, as her mother had taught her. Not that she was a nice girl, but she knew she didn't want the kind of trouble that came from speaking her mind, even to Borsk, who didn't seem to get out of control when he was mad, and who didn't seem to stay mad long.

She watched him for a minute as he brushed grape flowers, moving carefully and never looking down. He didn't let his fears master him, and he certainly didn't censor his speech.

How she envied him.

80   CealB

Borsk snuck Anya into Skreetches through the storeroom, hoping to get her alone in one of the signal-free private areas for long enough to get their stories straight, but as soon as they got within smell of the curry, they saw Sarka, restocking the spice shelves.

Sarka set down her jars, and yelled over her shoulder, "Mama, Borsk is home."

Mama came out of the kitchen, wiping her hands on her apron. "Borsk DeFranklin Menendez King," she said. "What have you done?"

Somehow, he'd imagined this moment going a little differently.

"I'm sorry, Mrs. King," Anya said. "Borsk said you wouldn't care if he brought me over for dinner."

Mama looked over at her. "Borsk's *friends* are always welcome." Borsk didn't miss the subtle emphasis on "friends," and he bet Anya didn't either. "You're Anastasia Cartier?"

"Yes, ma'am."

"Why don't the two of you go on back to the purple booth, and I'll join you in a minute, when I've got things in order here." Mama stepped back into the kitchen.

That was exactly what Borsk was hoping for, except that as he led the way out, Sarka grabbed a couple of napkin rolls out of the bin and followed right behind Anya. Sarka was Skreetches' most efficient waitress, but she could also make simple chores last hours when she was snooping. She'd still be fussing with the table when Mama got back to them, Borsk was sure of it. He had to think of something to get rid of her, but his mind blanked out.

"What made you buy out your dad's share of Skreetches?" Sarka whispered to Anya. Didn't she realize he was just two paces away, able to hear everything she said, even if she whispered?

"My illicit love affair with your brother," Anya whispered back.

Borsk tripped over his own feet, sprawling to the floor. At least down there he didn't have to worry about keeping a straight face.

"Are you serious?" Sarka gasped.

Borsk glanced back in time to see the look of horror Sarka gave Anya. Priceless.

"What do you think?" Anya asked. Borsk couldn't read her face, but apparently Sarka could read his.

"I think you're just as much of a pompous ass as your father," she said, shoving the napkin rolls at Anya and flouncing off.

Borsk picked himself up off the floor. "I think I love you."

"Even though I'm a pompous ass?" Anya's voice wavered. Whatever confidence had prompted her saucy answer to Sarka had apparently evaporated. Borsk didn't see why. Who cared what Sarka thought of her? "You're not a . . . Look, Sarka just said that because she was annoyed you teased her."

Anya closed her eyes and twisted the napkin rolls.

Borsk wasn't sure what to say to her, so he fumbled, "Here give me those—if you hold them that way all the tableware will fall out. Come on, let's get to the booth before Sarka remembers she hasn't found out what she wanted to know."

Anya nodded and followed him.

Of the private areas, the purple booth sat closest to the restroom and always smelled faintly of cleaning solution filtered through an aggressive air freshener. Mama tried to put guests elsewhere when possible, which was why it was often available for family business. Borsk ducked through the entrance and slid a good way around the bench that ran along the circular walls, half under the round table that filled the space. Once Anya slid in behind him, he tapped a button under the table, and the entrance panel slid shut, enclosing them in the booth.

Anya reached up and traced the quilted diamond pattern of the ceiling.

"I wouldn't recommend that. Some of the button shanks are wearing through, and they're a bit sharp."

Anya dropped her hand back to the table. "This is nice."

Borsk looked around at the brownish-purple foam that served as bench and walls, and at the white plastic table. "It's grungy and there's no signal. What's to like?"

Anya smiled. "It's cozy. And I like having no signal."

How could she like having no signal? Borsk already itched to connect after being offline for less than a minute. It was like he'd lost a limb—his arm-band arm. He shook his head. "You're a little bit crazy, you know it?"

"Maybe a little bit. Will your mother be long?"

"A couple more minutes, probably. Why?"

"I just wondered what you were going to tell her."

"The truth—or most of it. She'll eventually figure it out anyway, so it'll save time and trouble to get it over with at the beginning."

"But won't you get in trouble?"

"Hell, yes." Borsk laughed.

Anya didn't. She looked even paler than usual, and her eyes were huge.

"Anya, come on. Don't look like that. I don't know anything about your house, not really, but I have a feeling that trouble here isn't anything like trouble there. I'll get grounded or have to do extra chores or lose all but my educational net privileges." He grimaced. "But it won't be anything I don't deserve."

He shut up then, not because Anya looked any better, but because the light over the door shone red to indicate someone was coming in. Mama—with heaping trays of food that she set out even more beautifully and quickly than Sarka could. Then she shut the panel behind them, said grace, and stared coldly at Anya. "Well, young lady. I suppose you think I ought to be grateful to you."

Anya shrank back into the cushions and squeaked something that might have been, "I'm sorry."

"Sorry?" Borsk said. "Are you nuts? You haven't done anything wrong. Look, Mama. It was me. All me."

Mama turned her piercing gaze on him. His throat felt suddenly dry. He grabbed his water mug. Drinking gave him a second to collect his thoughts, but it wasn't long enough to come up with any good excuses for his actions. He had to spill the whole story from the beginning.

"Look, we all wanted to save the restaurant, right? So, we needed a buyer. An untraceable buyer. So, I figured out who on the ship had enough untraceable credits to buy out Thomas Cartier. The list is pretty short—Arnold—"

"Bates, William Newton, Oliver Forrest, Diane Rutherford, and me," Anya said.

"How do you know? That list was impossible to get."

Anya shrugged. "My father rattled off that list to my mom this morning when he found out about the sale. Except he didn't know about me. He thought my grandma—Grandma Anderson—had the money."

Mama half laughed and started in on Uncle Hirsch's roast eggplant.

Borsk felt a little shaken. Apparently, the secret accounts weren't nearly so secret as he'd thought. "Well, Anya—you're—in my class at school, and I figured if I spent a little time with you, I could get enough personal information to work the transfer. After a couple of days, school wasn't working out so well, and I was in a hurry, so I got myself in a little trouble, and made sure the detentions were in the greenhouse."

Anya gripped a fork so hard her knuckles went white. Borsk wondered if she was going to stab him with it. Maybe he should have told Sarka to give them the kid flatware rolls—the blunt tools would be less lethal if Anya decided to attack. Too late now.

Mama caught the direction of his gaze, and said softly, "Eat, Anya."

Eat. Mama's cure-all. It was a wonder the whole family wasn't pushing the ship's weight limits.

Anya looked down at her fork, as if seeing it for the first time. Then she nodded and poked tentatively at her own eggplant.

Borsk looked back at Mama. "Anyway, I got what I needed and last night hacked into Anya's system, and transferred her dad's ownership in the restaurant to her. I backed out cleanly, too. I don't know what made Thomas Cartier come looking for us this morning."

Mama looked up, her eyes large. "He knows."

Anya met his mama's eyes for the first time. "No. It's OK, Mrs. King. My father thinks I made the purchase—and I guess, in a way, I did. The bank sent me a notification of the transaction first thing this morning, and I confirmed it."

Borsk hadn't even thought about a confirmation notice. Damn. He thought he'd covered everything.

Mama lifted her head. "How much trouble are you in?"

"I don't know—maybe none. Father thinks Borsk blackmailed me to get me to make the purchase."

"Blackmailed you? About what?"

Anya hung her head. "I'd rather not say."

"Borsk? What is this about?"

He wished he knew. He'd been trying to figure it out all day. "All I know is we were talking about the video feed I used to hack into their house system, and then Anya said I'd been asking about her math tutor, and that I understood he was helping her with school, and now I'd do it instead. Then Mr. Cartier asked how much that would cost him. And Anya said she'd already paid for it, which I suppose means she'd bought out the restaurant in exchange for me tutoring her in math. All I can figure is this Lancet guy is doing more than tutoring—he's taking the tests for her or something—and they want to cover it up." Even as he said it, he knew that was the wrong answer. No way was keeping quiet about a little high school grading fraud worth fifty-thousand credits—or letting the concert go through without a hiccup.

"Don't be an idiot, boy. You say you'd been asking about her math tutor?"

"I only teased Anya a little about him—said he was her boyfriend—because he obviously isn't."

"He isn't?"

"Nah, I only said that because they had the bunk screens down when he was tutoring her. He's some thirty-year-old lieutenant that the Cartiers are probably paying to get Anya through school without embarrassing the whole family."

"Ryan's twenty-five," Anya said softly. "And the Lancets are friends of the family. He helps me because he wants to."

Mama looked over at Anya. "And the two of you spend time alone in your bunk with the screens down. I think I'm beginning to understand."

Borsk had thought maybe something was up too, until he saw them. "Mama, I'm telling you, they weren't doing anything but math."

"It's not what they were doing, but what they will do, isn't it?" Mama said.

What they will do? Could basic algebra be used as a cover for some kind of criminal code he hadn't yet learned about? He needed to look into it.

Anya kept her head down. "The Lancets are friends. That's all that's going on now, and maybe all that will ever be."

That didn't sound criminal. He was on the wrong track again. He had to think. Somehow Mama had figured out what was going on—he should be able to too.

Mama frowned. "We can't be part of this. I won't allow my restaurant or my family to be used to force you—"

"Nobody's forcing me to do anything."

Anya's denial didn't sound very convincing, and the flatness of her voice made Borsk feel guilty. "Anya, if I've gotten you into a mess. I can confess, and we can walk it all back."

"No! Don't you see that if you confess now, Father will know I was covering for you this morning?"

Duh. He couldn't do anything right, could he?

"Besides, what I said is true—no one is forcing me to do anything. Or at least, they aren't making me do anything that wasn't already happening. The restaurant and the concert—they've got nothing to do with the other. It would happen whether you used my money or not."

"That's another thing I don't like," Mama said. "My son, without consideration for either your feelings or your safety, pretended to be your friend so he could steal from you. I can't take pleasure in profiting from such actions."

Mama wasn't looking at him; she didn't even use his name. Borsk supposed he should consider himself lucky that she still recognized that they were related. And this after weeks of moaning about the imminent doom of the restaurant, and how they wished someone would do something to save it. Well, he'd done something, hadn't he? He'd saved their stupid restaurant, saved their damn concert. True, he'd picked a lousy way to do it, but what choice did he have? He couldn't get close enough to anyone else with enough credits. See if he concerned himself in their troubles again.

"I don't think he was pretending," Anya broke into his thoughts.

"What?" Borsk and his mother said at the same time.

"Borsk. I don't think he was just pretending to be my friend. Maybe I'm wrong, but today, up on the trellis wall, he stayed with me even though he's afraid of heights. You don't do that kind of thing if you're only pretending to be a friend."

Mama's mouth dropped open a little.

"And about the restaurant—you can't ever tell my father, but I'm glad it's going to be safe. Father shouldn't get to run everything all the time, and the concert—the concert should happen. I kind of wish I'd had the guts to buy it on my own." She nodded, and her eyes glistened.

Mama stared at her for a long moment, then nodded back. "OK. Then we'll keep quiet. But what about you? What will you do if you decide you don't want to go through with it?"

Go through with what? Borsk was going crazy trying to keep up with this conversation.

"Why wouldn't I want to go through with it?" Anya looked his mama in the eye and smiled the saddest smile Borsk had ever seen. He was afraid she was going to cry, but she didn't. She just rose from her seat as much as the table would allow and said she needed to be going.

Mama put out a hand and opened her mouth as if she were going to say something, but in the end, she just patted Anya's hand and opened the panel out of the booth. "You're welcome here anytime, Anya. Anytime at all." Then Anya left the booth, and Mama shut the panel behind her.

For a minute, Mama sat quietly, without moving. Her eyes glinted. Borsk wondered if she was going to cry. About what? Something Anya's parents were forcing her to do, that Borsk's family now agreed to keep quiet. Borsk ought to be able to figure it out. Maybe Mama would give him a hint when she remembered him again and said something.

He hadn't figured it out when Mama finally looked up and said, "Tell me everything you know about Ryan Lancet."

"Ryan Lancet?" The response was inane, he knew, but he still hadn't figured out what Ryan and Anya were doing that made his silence so valuable.

"Yes. Ryan Lancet. The pure-Euro scumbag they're breeding her with like some kind of plant, so their sickly line doesn't die out. What did you think you were agreeing to shut up about? Haven't you been paying any attention at all?" She pushed back from the table, slid the panel back open and left the booth.

Great. So, Anya was welcome back anytime, but he was so disgusting, Mama couldn't stay in a room with him.

It was nice to finally know what was going on, though.

Betrothal. That was the dragon he'd been holding by the tail—the secret Thomas Cartier hid behind his walls of security. He felt ridiculously stupid. If he'd had his head on straight, and remembered that Anya was pure-Euro, he wouldn't have had any trouble figuring out what was going on. He should have realized when Anya got worried about him teasing that Ryan was her boyfriend—no, even before that. He should have known yesterday in the shuttle. Nobody green but Anya? It had been right in front of him, and he hadn't even seen it. Maybe he was as dense as his family thought he was.

Still, he didn't see how he could have done any better for them, even if he had figured it out sooner. He might have done much worse. Mama might have preferred him to expose the whole mess and take the consequences, but he honestly didn't see how that would have helped anyone, least of all Anya.

On the other hand, when he thought of the creepy portrait Anya had made of her intended, he understood why his mom was so disgusted with him.

He was more than a little disgusted with himself.

Chapter Six

Anya had never thought much before about whether she wanted to marry Ryan since she knew her opinion in the case didn't matter.

Except it seemed to matter to Mrs. King.

And it must have mattered to Grandma, or she and Grandpa wouldn't have given Anya enough untraceable money to be independent at her age.

When Mrs. King had asked her what she'd do if she didn't want to marry Ryan, she'd had her glib answer ready, not realizing how dangerous it would be to let her own simple question echo in her mind.

Why wouldn't she want to marry Ryan?

Well, why wouldn't she? Ryan was good looking, smart and ambitious. He was scrupulously honest and always followed the rules, unless you counted the betrothal, of course. Anya wasn't quite sure how he squared that with his overzealous conscience, but she knew why he did it. Without her father's support, he'd never advance on ship's crew, and without going along with the betrothal, he'd never have Father's support.

True, Ryan didn't listen to her, and she wasn't sure he even liked her, but that might change. She was still a kid compared to him.

So why did the question of whether she wanted to marry him still bother her? Shaking her head, she tapped the combination for their quarter's screen into her armband.

As Anya entered the quarters, her mom turned away from the cooker. "Stacey! What are you doing here? Didn't you get your father's message to meet him in his office?"

Anya turned her left hand palm up. Sure enough, the message light at her wrist blinked. "Sorry. I was offline for more than an hour and forgot to check my messages when I came back on."

"Stacey, Stacey. What are we going to do with you? You'd better run. I think he scheduled the meeting for five minutes from now."

"Got it. I'm going." Anya stepped back into the hallway and jogged toward the lift, fiddling with her messaging as she went. Having as much information as possible was always a good idea when facing her father.

If the trellises weren't the highest spot on *Hope*, General Mercantile's main offices would probably win the title. Even Anya felt a bit queasy riding the lift all the way out to the observation deck on the outermost layer of *Hope*. On the other hand, this queasiness probably had as much to do with seeing her father as it did with the height, fast ride, and mere ten centimeters of manmade magic that separated one from the void up here.

She touched her hand to the miracle glass. Cold, so cold. She hadn't had time to grab her sweater.

"Stacey. You're late."

At the voice, Anya swung away from the viewing wall and saw her father's silhouette framed in his office doorway. Her heart pounded against her ribs and a babble of "I'm sorry, so sorry," ran an endless loop in her head, but she forced both responses down. She couldn't afford to be frightened, and apologies only made her father more brutal. "Am I?" she said instead, doing her best to sound like she neither knew nor cared.

"I don't suppose you've learned how to shorten an unpleasant business meal yet. I at least hope you've made good use of it. What have you learned?"

Anya couldn't see his face at all, backlit the way it was, but he could probably see hers. She was tempted to drop her head, but that wouldn't fully hide her from the light, and would likely make her look guilty. Keeping a tight rein on her fear, she raised her chin a bit so that she'd be staring right into his eyes if she could make out his features. This was a test, and she had to think fast to pass. "Well, I learned that Mrs. King wasn't very happy with the way Borsk handled things."

"The way *Borsk* handled things?"

Ferto. Father must have realized that Borsk couldn't have discovered the betrothal on his own: he wasn't that kind of smart. Or maybe Borsk's cluelessness that morning had been too obvious. "It was Borsk's idea to . . . um . . . persuade me to buy the restaurant. I don't think his mom had decided what to do with his information, and he was impatient."

"He told her what he learned?" Father sounded skeptical.

"Borsk tells her everything, near as I can tell." Anya let her surprise at Borsk's confession creep into her voice, hoping the real emotions would help convince her father.

"Come inside." Her father stepped back, leaving the doorway clear.

So far, so good.

Anya followed him in, blinking as she stepped into the brightly lit chamber. Father's office dwarfed every other private space on *Hope*. Twice as big as their quarters, it seemed even larger given its relative scarcity of furniture. A massive black table stood straight ahead, with her father's high-backed chair behind it. A few circles on the floor in front of it hid pop-up stools, but none of these were activated. Instead, the other occupant of the room leaned against the front right corner of the giant table.

Ryan.

As soon as Anya saw him, her heart slowed down. Well that was something to add to the positive side of the list. She was less afraid of her father when Ryan was in the room.

As her father stalked to his chair, Anya smiled at Ryan. Ryan nodded curtly. Not in a good mood, then.

Her father lowered himself into his chair and swung it to face the back wall with its priceless mural of *Hope* life in the mid J500s. Anya wondered if he even saw the piece. She suspected he only "contemplated" it so often to remind people of how important he was. And to raise tension, of course. It was a pity, since the piece truly was well done.

"Stacey, would you like to explain to Ryan what happened?"

Anya dragged her eyes away from the mural and perched on the table corner opposite Ryan's. She didn't want to explain anything, of course, but though her father's request sounded like something she could turn down, she knew it was really an order, dressed up politely for Ryan's benefit. "I bought out Father's portion of Skreetches," she said, staring at one of the circles on the floor.

"And why exactly did you do that, Stacey?" her father growled.

"Borsk threatened to expose our . . . arrangement." Anya carefully avoided making eye contact with Ryan. He had an uncanny knack for knowing when she was lying.

"How did he know anything about it?" Ryan demanded.

"That *is* the question, isn't it?" her father said.

Trembling, Anya grabbed the edge of the desk to hold herself still. She could do this. She just had to deflect attention from her own involvement. She shrugged with calculated nonchalance and said, "I think he got suspicious yesterday in the shuttle. Out of the twenty-five of us, I was the only green."

"What were you doing parading your color around?" her father asked.

"I wasn't parading it. Someone asked me out."

"Someone asked you out?" Ryan snickered.

"I don't see what's so funny. Just because you don't think I'm attractive—"

Her father swung his chair around and stared at her. "I'm sure Ryan would find you plenty attractive if you paid more attention to your personal appearance."

"Sir, Stace looks fine. I didn't mean to laugh."

Her father swung back around, and Anya blew out a long, soft breath.

"So, who wanted to ask you out?" Ryan broke into the silence.

Did he not realize what her father would do with that information? Or did he not care that he was about to ruin somebody's life over nothing? She smiled. "What does it matter? He wasn't green. None of them were."

"None of who were?" her father asked.

"The guys on the shuttle. You know, the greenhouse detention crew. They were all guys yesterday."

"Hardly the type of young man I'd expect my daughter to be interested in anyway. Stupid, uncouth—"

"They aren't all that way, you know. Borsk is actually brilliant." And so was DeShawn, though he had other issues. And some of the guys who weren't quite as smart—like VJ—were loyal and generous, quick to get a friend out of trouble, or help out with a hard job.

"Are you saying you like those—" her father started

"I'm saying that they're not worthless, and Borsk in particular is a force to be reckoned with. After the mess on the shuttle, I'm sure that when he saw the video feed Ryan set up . . ."

"We didn't do anything!" Ryan said. "That was the whole point of the feed—having documentation in case it came up in a court case."

"Video feeds are notoriously hard to use as court evidence," Father said, "and the fact that you thought you needed one is in itself enough to raise suspicion,"

"You think it was my video feed that made people wonder about the relationship? What about Stace drawing portraits of me instead of doing homework?"

"Anybody who knows me realizes I'd rather be drawing than doing homework. And I draw everybody. I doubt a portrait would have meant anything to Borsk if he hadn't already been suspicious. Neither would Ryan's video feed, for that matter. But once Borsk realized something was up, it's hard to say what all clues he found."

"Borsk does seem to have a few useful skills," her father said. "You were wise to deal with him directly. His mother is too stubborn to even see her own interest."

"There's nothing wrong with someone being too principled to take a bribe, sir," Ryan said.

Anya glanced over at him. She couldn't read his expression. Was he troubled?

"As you say," her father said, steepling his fingers. "Nothing wrong at all. It just makes for more protracted business negotiations, which would not be in anyone's best interest at this point."

"No, I quite see that, sir. I'm glad Stace solved the problem. Perhaps it would also be best to cut back on some of the behaviors that led to the problem."

"Stacey has already arranged to have her math tutoring with young Mr. King instead of you."

"You think our tutoring sessions might give someone ideas?" Ryan said. "I was talking about manipulating detention schedules and who knows what all else so that Stace doesn't run into other green guys. Is that even legal?"

"I assure you that in this matter, I was careful to be above reproach in every way."

Ryan's face stayed impassive, but at his side, below the level of the table, his hand tightened into a fist. His voice sounded perfectly calm, though, when he said, "Good to know. Still, it couldn't hurt to back off for a while. Surely you don't imagine I'm so horrible that the only way Stace will like me is if I've got no competition."

Father laughed a hearty, thoroughly fake, laugh." Of course not, lad. Of course not."

Ryan unclenched his hand. "Glad to know it. Was there anything else, sir?"

"No, no. I just wanted you to be aware of the situation."

"In that case, we'd better get out of your hair. I know you've got work to do." He stood up straight and put out a hand. Her father grasped it briefly, then Ryan strode toward the door. "Coming, Stace? I know you've got homework."

Anya scooted off the table and toward the door before her father could realize Ryan didn't really need her but was just giving her an excuse to escape.

"Do you really think our tutoring sessions are an issue, or were you just trying to get away from me?" Ryan asked when they got outside of the office.

So, he actually wanted to talk, and wasn't just giving her an excuse to escape. She stifled a sigh. How could he not know that her father recorded the conversations outside his office, and watched them even more religiously than he watched the ones inside? Or maybe he did know, and they'd set this up together as a trap. Good cop, bad cop. Now that she thought about it, she'd gotten out of her dad's office much too easily. And now she'd been thinking about Ryan's question much longer than she should. She forced a smile.

"Why would I want to get away from you? I might not like the math or science much, but I still have to deal with them. In fact, now I get to display my ineptitude to someone my own age who doesn't care about me at all."

"You really think it's a problem?" He looked directly into her eyes.

She fought the urge to look away. "I don't know exactly what gave the game away, but I'd rather not take any chances." She broke eye contact and walked toward the lift.

He followed her. "Fair enough. Perhaps we should be a little less familiar in public as well."

Less familiar? How much cooler could their public relationship get? "What did you have in mind?"

"I think you should call me by my title when we're not at home." He stepped past her, into the lift.

He had to be kidding her. "Lieutenant Lancet?"

"Exactly."

She forced another smile and got into the lift as well. "All right. Whatever you want." She wondered if he'd still want her to call him by his title when they were married. "Yes, major." Or even better, "Of course, captain." Just what she'd always hoped for. And she wasn't at all sure that this change would reduce suspicion instead of raise it, but what did she know? She was just Anya, the stupid, fifteen-year-old who couldn't even pass ninth-form math without intensive tutoring.

They rode down to Level One in silence. When the doors opened, she nodded at Ryan. "Lieutenant Lancet."

He nodded back.

Spectacular. Now he figured he didn't even need to speak to her.

Why wouldn't she want to marry Ryan, the smug, self-righteous hypocrite?

∞ ☙

Too wound up to work on homework when she got back to their quarters, Anya opened up her current art project. Ryan's portrait. Of course. Well, that wasn't going to help her mood, but she didn't have the processing capacity to work more than one project at a time. Even this would be better than the math and science she had to do for school. She closed her eyes for a long moment, remembering the way Ryan looked in the lift. Then she immersed herself in the work.

What seemed moments later, a violent banging on her bunk screen made her jump.

"What are you doing in there?" her father shouted.

"Homework." Anya stabbed the button on her armband to save changes and shut down the portrait.

"Like hell you are. You haven't even turned on your school tablet and you've been home for hours."

Oops.

Her bunk screen rattled upward.

Too soon. The portrait hadn't fully shut down yet. For a moment, the two scariest men in her life stared across the bunk at each other, more contempt in both sets of eyes than either ever let the other see. Then Ryan's image flickered and disappeared.

"Interesting," her father said. "Especially since I've told you specifically not to mess around when you've got homework to do."

Inside Anya cringed, but she knew better than to let it show. She took a steadying breath and nodded. "I was too frustrated with Ryan to work. He seems to think the best way to handle our conundrum is to stop speaking to me."

"Stop speaking to you? What did you do?"

"You mean you weren't watching the whole ride in the lift?"

Her father's eyes narrowed.

"You were watching. So, you saw him tell me I should use his formal title in public. And you saw him nod instead of say goodbye."

"That's got you upset, child? Grow a backbone. And do your homework. You know I won't stand for any of this nonsense. I'm deleting that monstrous portrait and cutting off all access to light-working programs for a month." He slammed her bunk screen down.

With shaking hands, Anya messaged a copy of her portrait to Borsk. Seconds later it disappeared from her storage file. Father wasn't wasting any time. She hoped her copy had sent cleanly, or the work was gone.

She wanted to cry but didn't dare. With her bunk screen unlocked, Father would hear. She had to get away from here before he destroyed everything worthwhile in her life. But there was nowhere to go on *Hope*. Her only chance was to earn a place on the Golden Terrace Colony. And for that she needed Ryan—who had just decided to take a step back from their relationship.

For the first time, Anya seriously tried to come up with another option. But she couldn't think of another single green guy between the ages of fifteen and thirty-five, and she didn't see how she could find someone, get to know them, and convince them to partner with her—potentially for life—by the start of colony try-outs a week from Saturday.

Which left Ryan.

Anya started up a masking program on her homework tablet, so that her father's snooping programs would register her doing exactly what she was supposed to be doing. Then, instead of even looking at her math, she crafted the most persuasive letter to Ryan she could think of. She focused on how the colony could be good for him—appealing to his desire to be important in history. And she threw in a hint about getting out from under her father's thumb. Ryan didn't experience Father's tyranny the way she did, but clearly, he was a bit uncomfortable with some of the things her father pressured him to do.

It wasn't half bad, she decided, reading it over when she was finished. Now all she had to do was get it to him without her father finding out. For that, she needed Borsk. Good thing she appeared to be having so much trouble with algebra—her homework tablet had gotten stuck on a problem even she could figure out with ease. Yes, she definitely needed tutoring in the morning.

Chapter Seven

An unholy buzzing invaded Borsk's dreams, and he woke to find himself fruitlessly slapping his head next to his ears in some bizarre, embedded response to a stimulus now long extinct.

Not that the buzzing was gone. It persisted annoyingly, leaking from his armband. His messaging system? Borsk stabbed at it, and Sarka's voice joined him in the bunk.

"About time, lazybones. Your girlfriend is here for some kind of tutoring appointment."

"What the—"

But the message had already shut off.

On reflection, it was probably better if Sarka didn't know how much that whining buzz annoyed him. He threw on clothes. As usual, he had no idea what was going on, but clearly, he wasn't going to be allowed to go back to sleep.

When he staggered into the kitchen two minutes later, there was no sign of Sarka, but Anya sat—slumped, really—on one of the stools by the biggest island workstation. So that's what Sarka meant by "your girlfriend." He wondered what Anya wanted at this horrible hour. He knew he'd never made any appointment for half past first bell.

"Anya?" he growled.

She startled upward, revealing reddened eyes. "Borsk—I'm so sorry. I thought you were up. Your armband registered active."

"My armband?" Borsk flipped his hand palm up and stared blankly at the regular flicker of bluish light under his thumb until he remembered the stupid project his mama had assigned him in lieu of more obvious punishment. "Oh, right. I'm running a simulation for my mom. Something to do with restaurant traffic, security, and that dumb concert." He yawned. "Are you OK?"

"I'm so sorry." Anya whispered. "I didn't mean to wake you. It's not important." She slipped off the stool and headed for the door.

"Hey, no. Don't go. It's fine. I'm up now." Borsk crossed the space between them in two steps and set a light hand on her arm. "What's wrong?"

Her face crumpled. "It's nothing, really."

"It's OK." Borsk helped her back up on the stool. "I'll get you some breakfast." It felt stupid and inadequate, but that's what you did when you were raised in a restaurant and somebody was having an emotional crisis—you fed them.

And maybe it wasn't such a bad plan. He had a little time to think as he got leftovers into the warmer. He glanced back at Anya. She wiped one eye with the back of her hand, but otherwise seemed under control. Good. He wasn't good with tears.

"You want to talk about it?" He put a plate in front of her, and settled himself, with another one, across from her.

Anya shook her head and reached for a pair of chopsticks.

"Someone's paying for that, I hope," Sarka said from the restaurant doorway.

Anya's chopsticks dropped with a clatter to the table.

"Go mind your own business, Sarka."

"Keeping track of where the food goes is my business."

"I can pay," Anya said softly.

"Don't be ridiculous," Borsk said. "You own part of the restaurant. Plus, Mama said you were welcome here anytime. She said anytime, Sarka. You know what that means."

"Children, is there a problem?" Mama stood, in her robe, in the archway from the stockroom and living quarters. "Oh, Anya! I didn't see you there." She floated over and gave Anya a light hug. "Is everything OK, honey?"

"I'm fine, Mrs. King. I just . . ."

"She came to see me about some homework trouble." Borsk put in.

"Not really. I just got in a bit of a fight with my father last night, and he blocked me from all my art programs."

And she figured Borsk could get her back into them. Great. He probably could, and he owed her, but he didn't see how that counted as a roust-everyone-from-their-beds emergency.

"Because of the restaurant?" Mama asked.

"Because I was working on a piece instead of doing my homework."

"Well, honey, if I were your father, I might take away your art programs in that case, too."

"No, you wouldn't," Borsk said. "You believe in kids using their talents. You might make her fix up those promotional materials for the concert, but you'd never take away her art."

"There's nothing wrong with the concert promos!" Sarka said, joining them at the island.

"Bet you two work details on garbage day that Anya can do them better," Borsk said.

"You're on. Come on, Anya. There's a workstation in the office that has some old art programs." She dragged Anya off the stool, and toward the storeroom.

Anya glanced back at Borsk.

"Don't worry. You can take the food with you." Sarka swept up Anya's plate and chopsticks with one hand and tugged on her sleeve with the other.

"OK. Just—" She shook herself loose from Sarka, and reached out a hand toward Borsk, resting it, awkwardly, on the table near his plate as if she weren't sure what to do with it. "Thank you."

Sarka rolled her eyes and marched Anya out of the room.

Mama looked after the two girls, worry wrinkles between her eyes. "Do you think the art programs are all that's bothering her?"

"How should I know? You and Sarka barged in here before she told me anything."

"It's our kitchen, Borsk."

"I'd have taken her back to my bunk, but you don't let us eat in there."

"True enough. Well, maybe you'll have a chance to talk to her later. So, tell me, how are you coming with my research project?"

"Which one?"

"Tell me about the boy first."

"You know he's ten years older than I am, right?"

"Still a boy."

Borsk shook his head and pulled up the notes he'd made on Ryan Lancet. "Lieutenant first class, likely to jump up to major any day now, glowing work reviews for efficiency, and believe it or not, even-handedness. If we've got to get security for the concerts next week, we should put the request into his office when he's on duty. He'll get the thing staffed if he has to show up himself to police."

"Even though he's in Thomas Cartier's pocket?"

"All I know is he fills every request within twenty-four hours, going strictly by the order they come in. So far, attempts to bribe or bully him have landed the other parties in the brig."

"Well, do we need security?"

Borsk tapped into his simulation.

"We definitely need a second night. Going without security might be OK, except—no, I'm getting some chatter from those goons who caused all the trouble at Steve's last concert."

"Kenneth Llourdes, and that crowd? Forget your simulations. If you really think this Lancet won't drag his feet on it, we'll get the security."

"I'll message you his schedule, so you can put in the request when he's on duty."

"Hard to believe the guy you're describing would agree to Cartier's nonsense."

"I know, right? And it's not just his work that's so upstanding—his personal life, apart from the obvious, is squeaky clean. No vices. No serious girlfriends—though he's flirting a bit with Leslie Wang."

"The girl who's played lead in every community play for three seasons?"

"That's the one."

"He's flirting with her?"

Borsk shrugged. "Not more than half the single guys on the ship do. Half the married guys, too. If it's more than flirting, they're hiding it well."

"OK, what else?"

"I don't know. He had stellar grades in school, played some hoops and cage-ball, and has a few records in stunt flying, but I wouldn't say there's anything exceptional about him—unless it's his music collection."

"His music collection?"

"Bigger than the restaurant's. And he listens to it all the time. All the time he's not working or actually in a conversation with someone, anyway."

Mama shook her head. "He sounds OK."

"Maybe he is."

"You don't believe that. Why? Has Anya told you something?"

Borsk thought of the portrait, even scarier in the version Anya had messaged him in the middle of the night. "Not directly."

"What do you mean?"

Reluctantly, Borsk projected the image out over the table.

"That's him?"

Borsk nodded. "It's what Anya was working on last night."

Mama whistled, soft and low. Then she walked over to him and tousled his hair. "Don't worry, kiddo. We'll think of something."

He'd heard that before—after his dad died, and they thought they were going to lose the restaurant because of all the hospital bills. That time, "something" had turned out to be a loan from Thomas Cartier. And hadn't that turned out well? He stabbed his chopsticks into his noodles, but then decided he wasn't hungry after all.

"I'm going back to bed." He cleared away the food.

Underneath where his plate had been, a small white cube sat. Borsk blinked, shifted his plate to his left hand, and picked up the cube.

"What is that?" Mama asked.

"Old style memory cube," Borsk said, softly. Anya must have left it.

"The same kind we use for the proprietary recipes?"

Damn. It was.

"You could just pop it into the reader over there."

"Yeah. Just a sec." He pocketed the cube, cleared away his food, and washed his hands. He wished Mama would leave, so he could look at this thing on his own, but she didn't look like she was going anywhere. He inserted the cube into the reader and scanned the brief message to him and slightly longer one to Ryan. The girl wanted to go to the colony with that guy? Was she out of her mind?

Mama came closer. "It's from Anya, right? What does she want that she can't trust to the net?"

"She wants me to get a message to Ryan without her dad finding out," Borsk said.

"Well, you can do that, can't you?"

Borsk nodded. "Probably. But she needs it fast. For that I need to send the guy something that this can ride in on."

"What about our request for security?"

"No. I need something going to him personally—or if it's official, it has to go to something he's in charge of."

"What's he in charge of?"

"He's a lieutenant, Mama."

"A lieutenant with ties to Thomas Cartier. He's got to be in charge of something."

Borsk shook his head and scanned through his notes on Ryan Lancet again. Mama was right, as usual. There was something.

"What is it?"

How he wished his mama couldn't read his face. "He's in charge of Camp Flight."

"Perfect. You can apply and send Anya's message at the same time."

Borsk made a face. "I don't want to be in Camp Flight. Even the simulations they do are boring."

"Anya didn't really want to buy ten percent of our family restaurant, either. You owe her."

"Maybe I can figure out another way."

"Then do it. But get that message sent by noon."

"I'll get it sent." He'd probably have to do it Mama's way and apply for Camp Flight to make her deadline, though.

Damn.

Maybe he was too much of a troublemaker to get accepted.

He could hope.

∞   ∝

Anya had never seen anything quite so gaudy as the promotional materials Sarka showed her.

"Not so bad, if I do say so myself," Sarka said.

The girl was proud of that junk? Ferto. Now Anya had to figure out something nice to say about it. She smiled to give herself time to think. "It's certainly colorful. But a mite text heavy, don't you think?"

"Can't afford better artwork than that," Sarka said. "And trust me, it's a good thing that bell rack is so small."

Anya zoomed in on the lone picture, a sad little piece from a commercial art set. It grew fuzzy at close range.

"What's constraining the size—projection density?" Anya asked.

"We're limited there, sure," Sarka said. "Can't go more than 5 X 5 X 8 on our weekly ad or it costs extra. But the main problem is commercial use royalties—we can only afford to pull from the art set we own." Sarka brushed her fingers against the wall-mounted screen in front of Anya, and an art catalog came up. The pieces were adequate, and nearly all food related.

Anya nodded. "I see the problem. But can't you use your own artwork however you want?"

"Kid, we're not putting up some school art project for a Steve Jackson concert. The guy is classy."

Anya glanced again at Sarka's concert advertisement. Classy it was not. "No, I see what you mean. What's he doing for his cover art—you know, for the recording?"

"He said he wanted to use Zhou's *Hope Rising*, but he couldn't get permission. So, he's just going with this." Sarka's fingers danced over the wall-mounted screen, and moments later a square of deep blue appeared. Across it in bold gold script were the words "Stepping Out." Steve Jackson's name ran across the bottom in smaller, plainer text.

"Nice," Anya said.

"It's boring. Doesn't suit Skreetches at all."

"That's a fair point. You wouldn't happen to have a picture of him playing in here, would you?"

"In here? Hardly. He's always been more of a classical, main stage performer. He's only in here because—"

"—the council won't let him play in either the main audience hall or the school performance center. I know. But surely he's done at least one practice in here to check out the acoustics."

"Yeah, he came in one night—Tuesday maybe—and messed around a little. But we didn't have a photographer here."

"But you've got security feed, right?"

"You can't put security feed on an ad. Do you have any idea how many rules that breaks?"

"I just want to look at it," Anya said.

Sarka grunted and pointed Anya to the relevant files. Anya flipped through the different camera angles until she found one that caught the stage and a bit of the restaurant. Then she triple-timed through the feed. There. She froze it. The young man in the center of the stage bent over his keyboard, a look on his face that spoke to Anya of deep joy. She thought that if she could feel that way, even for a moment, she would have lived a full life. "What have you got for light sculpting programs on here?"

"Light sculpting? Please. This is a thirty-year-old ad publisher. There's a basic drawing module, but not much more." Sarka pulled it up.

Anya nodded. "Better than nothing." She changed the background color to the saturated blue of Steve's *Stepping Out* cover, then sketched the scene from the security feed in bold gold strokes.

It took a while, but once she was satisfied, she added the concert information and Skreetches' logo.

"That looks OK, I guess," Sarka said from behind her.

Anya jerked. "I forgot you were back there."

"Yeah, still here, watching. That looks fine. Maybe even better than mine. But we'll have to run it by Steve. He doesn't like having his picture on his promotional materials."

"You couldn't have mentioned this sooner?"

"You didn't ask. But hey, there's still twenty minutes before school starts. You could sketch something else."

"In twenty minutes? How long did it take me to do this?"

"About an hour."

"Exactly."

"So, use something you've already done."

Anya thought of her trumpet flower. "I do have something that might work, but no one can ever know I made it. Actually, no one can ever know I had anything to do with any of this."

Sarka shrugged. "There's probably a way to arrange that. I'll have Mama check with Laura."

"Laura?"

"Restaurant lawyer. She's consulting on the concert stuff pro bono."

"OK, then." Anya copied her ad into a new workspace and in the copy replaced the sketch of Steve playing with a low-resolution, 2-D version of the trumpet flower. The colors didn't work perfectly, so she toned down the blue and added gold overtones to the thorns surrounding the flower. Striking, but not as hopeful as she wanted. She adjusted things a bit, so that the flower appeared to be emerging from a cage of gilded thorns. Perfect.

"I don't get it," Sarka said.

Of course, she didn't. Anya forced a smile. "Well, it's the best I can do right now."

"No doubt. You haven't had as much practice as I have. Come on, let's show what we've got to Mama."

"Isn't it time to leave for school?"

"Borsk left five minutes ago. It's too late to get there on time unless we run the whole way."

"Why didn't you say anything?"

"Didn't seem important. I figured you'd keep track if you cared about being late."

As if Anya could keep track of anything when she was creating. That's why she set alarms—so she wouldn't forget the world and miss things that were important to her father. Like school. She should have set an alarm before getting going on this project. But how was she supposed to know that Sarka didn't care about getting to school on time?

Anya snatched up her school tablet and ran. She couldn't believe she'd let herself get so caught up in making an ad.

Her only consolation was that Borsk was probably working just as hard on getting her message to Ryan.

At least she hoped he was.

If he didn't get it delivered, she'd never forgive herself for the time she'd wasted coming down here this morning.

⋆ ⋆ ⋆

Borsk tried a couple different paths for getting Anya's message into Lancet's personal software, but none got him close enough. So, half an hour before he usually got up, he found himself filling out the obnoxiously nosy questionnaire that served as an application for Camp Flight.

"Why do they need to know my favorite sport or most often used gaming software?" he grumbled to himself.

He wanted to answer with utterly ridiculous lies, but any half-decent fact checking software could verify those. Of course, he could reroute the fact checkers to his answers. He smiled. Maybe he'd get to have a little fun this morning.

Figuring out which fact-checking programs Camp Flight used was child's play. Hijacking the programs so they confirmed whatever answer an applicant wrote wasn't much harder. The trick was getting it to look like the hacked programs were still functioning normally. Then, of course, he had to erase all traces of himself from the system. It was just standard commercial security software, nothing fancy, but he took extra care. After getting caught in Thomas Cartier's systems so recently, he didn't trust his normal routines. Paranoid? Maybe.

He was so caught up in his new project, he almost forgot the reason he applied to the stupid Camp Flight program in the first place. He remembered in time, though, and piggybacked a Trojan horse on the application. His virus was a simple one, giving him access to Lancet's files for just long enough to drop Anya's message into his secure storage, along with a little program that made the message pop to the top of Lancet's workspace. Would that work? When unwanted files popped up in front of Borsk, he deleted them without even a glance. Lancet probably did the same. Borsk added a program that prevented Anya's message from being deleted until the machine registered Lancet's eyes scanning every word. When their work was done, both his Trojan horse and the trickier eye-scan reading program would erase themselves. No one would be able to track him through those.

He shook his hair out of his eyes and smiled. Not a bad morning's work. And he still had time for a second breakfast.

In the kitchen, Mama was cleaning one of the smaller refrigerators. "What are you having for vegetables?" she asked as he grabbed his normal plate of noodles.

"Cilantro and onions," he said.

"Nice try. You know they're flavors, not full servings in noodles."

Borsk sighed and grabbed a roasted sweet potato. "Better?"

"Not bad. Are you going to be able to get Anya's message out today?"

Oh, so now it was today, not noon? If he'd known that, he could have delivered it without the Camp Flight application. He scowled. "Already sent it."

"Do I want to know how you did it?"

Borsk shrugged and put his food in the warmer. "I applied for Camp

Flight."

"Well done. I'm sure the extra discipline will be good for you. Give you productive ways to channel your energies."

"They haven't accepted me yet." And likely wouldn't, given the bilge he'd told them about himself.

"But they will." Mama beamed at him. "They'd be fools not to."

Nobody but his mama would think that. Borsk shook his head, retrieved his second breakfast, and dug in. Poor Mama. She'd probably be outraged when Camp Flight rejected him. Hopefully, she wouldn't look into the process too closely.

Chapter Eight

Anya slid into her seat scant seconds before class started, leaving her no time to complain to Borsk about the job he'd saddled her with that morning—or to check how he was coming on the one she'd given him. On reflection that was just as well. The last thing she needed right now was whispers getting out about her relationship with Ryan—or her extracurricular artistic endeavors. *Hope*'s gossip mill worked fast, and the high school was one of the more efficient parts of it.

Telling herself all that only made her more impatient to get somewhere where they could talk alone. The longer the day went on without her even catching Borsk's eye, the more her pent-up frustration leaked out into her work. The legal documents related to her art that somebody in Skreetches sent her mid-morning didn't help her concentration any either. Just reading them took so much focused attention that she messed up on a science quiz that should have been simple. Then she had trouble (in front of everyone) on a math problem she would ordinarily find easy. She even got so distracted in history that Mrs. Patterson had to repeat one of the discussion questions.

If this kept up, one of her teachers would send a worried note to her parents, and Father would use that as an excuse to get her permanently removed from greenhouse work details. She had to get it together. She hastily signed the legal stuff on the pictures she'd done that morning and promised herself she'd corner Borsk at lunch and get the news out of him. Until then, though, she would pay strict attention to her classes.

Her plan worked fine until she couldn't find Borsk at lunch. She grabbed a salad without dressing and the last whole-wheat cracker (slightly burnt), and retired to her usual corner, away from the popular kids. Getting there, she went out of her way to avoid DeShawn's centrally placed boisterousness. She didn't want company, so she thumbed through her messages.

Ryan hadn't written her back, but that could be because he hadn't received her message yet—or if he had received it, he was still thinking it over.

What she did have was a notice from Kenneth Llourdes that effective immediately, she was no longer welcome in or near his house. If she had further contact with either her sister Kristi or her niece Tiny, he would see to it that they all regretted it.

He would, too. Anya worried her lip. She didn't get to see Kristi or Tiny as often as she liked, but she usually met up with them once or twice a week. Not at Kenneth's house. She wasn't crazy. But if Kenneth was rampaging, she should probably back off for a while. Maybe she could get Grandma Anderson's advice about how to stay in touch without putting Kristi and Tiny in danger.

She looked for one of Grandma's messages to reply to but found there weren't any new ones. Odd. Grandma usually sent three or four quick notes a day, often with articles or pictures attached, but there was nothing. There hadn't been anything yesterday, either—not since before Mother and Father had their fight. Anya hoped her parents hadn't done anything crazy—and that Grandma wasn't sick.

Suddenly worried, she dumped the remains of her lunch, mostly uneaten, into a recycling bin and logged herself out of the lunchroom. She still had half an hour before her next class. If she moved fast, she could get up to the assisted care unit, check on Grandma, and still make it back in time.

She hated running, but with the way today had been going, she would get enough in to make her physical fitness goals for the week. She guessed this was what the old saying meant about there being no trash without some reclamation value.

She had a stitch in her side and a blister on her right heel when she got up to Grandma's assisted living center, and she was looking forward to the comfy chairs in the common lounge area when the nurse guarding the reception desk stopped her.

"Where do you think you're going?"

Anya frowned. Though she couldn't recall the nurse's name, she recognized the woman. So, the nurse ought to recognize her too. But maybe she didn't. Anya shot the woman her ID codes. "I'm here to see my grandma. I'm on her 'visit anytime' list."

"Sure, but your parents sent over a court order yesterday. You aren't allowed to visit Mrs. Anderson—or have any contact—without supervision. Apparently, she got you in some trouble lately."

"No way. Mom would never . . ." Anya's message light blinked. She opened it, and a copy of the court order displayed against the desk wall.

"I'm sorry," the nurse said. "You're welcome to return with one of your parents."

With one of her parents. That was a good one. Father never came up here, and he only allowed Mom to visit once every couple of weeks. Joining those rare visits, even if she was allowed, wouldn't be enough.

First her art, then her access to Grandma. What else did her father think he could take from her? She smiled at the woman behind the desk and wandered away from the assisted living center, no longer in a hurry. She had plenty of time now to make it back to school, for all the good it would do her. Her father seemed determined to squeeze every drop of pleasure from her life.

Maybe Borsk could get her into her Grandma's place as well as into her art programs. If she could find him. She didn't share any afternoon classes with him, and he didn't show up for his greenhouse detention. When Anya asked about him, Mr. Greeley said he'd been reassigned somewhere—no idea where.

She could always find him later, at the restaurant, if necessary, but his absence seemed ominous to her. Was her father blocking her access to Borsk as well? Or was she just paranoid?

Either way, she wasn't having much fun. Funny how she missed Borsk, even though she'd hardly known him a week ago. She shouldn't depend on him so much. But she would find him. She wasn't going to let fate—or her father—keep her from her new friend, or her art, or Kristy and Tiny, or her grandma. And she certainly wouldn't let anything keep her from pursuing her dreams.

Maybe some of that seemed gone right now, but she'd get it all back.

All she had to do was figure out how.

ᛒᚱ   ᚲᛒ

Borsk could see that Anya wanted to talk to him from the way she kept looking his way, but he didn't want to discuss hacking in a place with as many monitoring devices as their school. He was almost relieved when he got the message to come home for lunch to run a few errands. If he cleared out as soon as the bell rang, he wouldn't see Anya until the greenhouses, where the recorders were far apart—if not broken or missing. That was worth the annoyance of a few restaurant errands.

Actually, the errands weren't all that annoying, he realized, as Uncle Hirsch shouted detailed instructions at him over the sizzle of a dozen lunches frying. Running down to Steve Jackson's and getting the guy to approve an ad before it hit the net might even be fun, especially if Steve approved Anya's design, and he got out of garbage duty for a few weeks.

He had to ring the bell at Steve's quarters three times before the man slid up the screen to reveal a standard one-by-two-by-two loft, packed to the corners with musical instruments and electronic gear nearly as complex as Borsk's own. Steve himself had a pair of giant earphones draped round his neck, and wires connecting his armband to a sixteen string minlay.

"Hey, Steve," Borsk said. "You should install a light or something, so you know when someone's at the door."

"Ah, but then I'd have to answer it, when I'd rather keep playing. This way I only have to respond to truly important things."

Borsk grinned. "Or truly persistent people. Mama says she can't reach you, but she needs your approval on an ad."

Steve shrugged. "I told her whatever she did would be fine."

"Ah, but that was before our art department came up with this." In the space between them, Borsk projected the ad that featured Steve playing.

Steve nodded. "I thought when you said your art department, you were kidding, but this is amazing. Who did it?"

"It's an anonymous gift," Borsk said.

"Don't be ridiculous. You have to know who it is. Work like this shouldn't be given away."

"We can only use the work if the artist remains anonymous," Borsk said, shooting Steve the legal file Uncle Hirsch had made him bring. "Sorry if you don't like it, but the alternative is this." He projected Sarka's advertisement up next to Anya's. Steve winced, then grabbed a reading tablet and frowned over it for a moment.

"What's this about two pieces? Surely that . . . second piece isn't done by the same hand."

Borsk skimmed his own copy of the legal document, and Mama's notes to him about it. "I guess Sarka told An—the artist—that you didn't like to have your image featured in your promotional materials, and she made a second ad—one my Uncle Hirsch didn't like as well as this one. Here, let me see if I can find it." Borsk hunted around for Anya's second advertisement and projected it next to the first two. When it came up, he gasped. The trumpet flower in the ad was even more striking than the one Anya had been working on in the greenhouse, and its pro-colony implications even more obvious.

Steve whistled. "Even more incredible than the other one. An artist like this simply can't stay anonymous."

"But she's got to," Borsk said. "It's too dangerous for her otherwise."

"You should have her come talk to me. I know it's hard to buck the system, but if we artists don't do it, who will?"

"I'm pretty sure she's not allowed anywhere near you," Borsk said. "She probably wouldn't be allowed near me either if we didn't have classes together."

"This artist is a kid?"

"Hey, watch it. I'm fifteen, not some baby."

"And her parents are opposed to the colony?"

"And quite possibly to art and music, at least when she's the one making it or enjoying it. But I think she'd like it if you used her work. Anonymously. It's her way of bucking the system, you know?"

Steve nodded. "I'd be a fool not to. But I still feel bad about not giving her credit."

"It's much better for her if we don't. At least not now," Borsk said. "I probably shouldn't have told you as much about her as I have."

"I won't say anything. Tell your uncle to go ahead with the image he likes—and maybe ask your friend if she'd be willing to let me use the other on my cover art."

"I'll check."

"And tell her that if there's ever anything I can help her with . . ."

Borsk nodded. "I'll tell her. Thanks." He switched off the projections. "I'll let you get back to your work."

Steve smiled and slipped the monster earphones back on, completely covering his ears. Before the screen snapped back down, Borsk saw him settle on a low stool in the center of the loft, and pluck at his instrument.

Borsk shook his head. He wished he had a job where he could hang out all day, focused on work he enjoyed. Maybe someday he would. But not today. His second errand wasn't so fun. He had to swing back by the restaurant, pick up a set of hot lunches for a trio of old folks down in Sigmore Landing, deliver them, and then somehow get back to school early enough that he didn't earn himself any more detentions.

He probably shouldn't have chatted as long as he had with Steve, but he'd been enjoying himself and lost track of time. He wouldn't have that problem with Great Uncle Elton, Old Doc Norman, or Ma Sweets. Down where they lived on the Landing, the air itself, with its slightly unclean haze and backed-up-sewer smells, screamed at him to get out. Ma Sweets and Great Uncle Elton liked to chat, but her recitations of her family's former glories and his political diatribes were no inducement to stick around.

At least the lunches were ready when he got to the restaurant, and no one, not even the ever-present Sarka, was around to ask why he was so late. Borsk grabbed the food, and it sloshed, threatening to spill. Well, that was spectacular. He balanced the buckets as well as he could and gingerly made his way down the ever smaller and grungier hallways to the Landing.

Usually the noise level grew with the dirt, but today Sigmore Landing was eerily quiet. No music blared. No arguments disturbed the peace. Not even a cooker or cleaner rattled its ancient protest at still being in use.

When he rounded the last corner to the common space he'd been aiming for, Borsk saw the reason for the silence. A uniform, complete with decorative cap, shone blue against the browns, grays and mustards of the Landing. What was a *Hope* security officer doing down here? Not much short of murder brought *Hope's* peacekeepers to this forgotten corner of the ship. Borsk hadn't heard about anybody dying lately, but down here, you never knew. He stopped, considering whether he should return to the restaurant without finishing his errand.

He hadn't made up his mind, when the uniform turned, and the subject of Anya's night-time artwork sized him up. That explained the hat, at least. Even in the meager light Sigmore Landing residents could afford on the dole, this guy's white-blond hair would shine. Ryan Lancet looked conspicuous enough, just wearing a uniform.

"Borsk King," Lancet said at last. It wasn't a question.

Borsk smiled weakly. He could tell his life had been simpler before this guy learned his name.

From beyond Lancet, Great Uncle Elton's querulous voice asked, "Is this purebred asshole a friend of yours, Borsk?"

Borsk panicked. Even if he were friends with Lancet, he wouldn't want to admit it in front of Great Uncle Elton. He jiggled a bit to his left, so he could see around Lancet. Or Ma Sweets or Old Doc Norman, either. He chewed on his lower lip.

Lancet glanced over at him and his mouth twitched. "Purebred asshole, huh? Somehow, I expected better. I'm sure someone told me that folks used colorful invective down here."

Borsk smiled, just enough to show he'd heard, not enough to make the old folks imagine he thought Lancet was funny, and turned a bit to squeeze past.

Lancet put out an arm to block him. "You can deliver their lunch after they've answered my questions."

"Y'all messed up in something serious?" Borsk asked the trio. He had no interest in impeding a murder investigation.

A torrent of words gushed out of Ma Sweets and Great Uncle Elton. They mixed old Mandarin and Spanish with bits of their Landing-accented Standard, and Borsk barely understood half.

If he got that half right, Lancet was down here asking questions about some new resident's overreaction to normal Landing life. Borsk looked over at Lancet. "You came down to the Landing on a *threat* of violence complaint?"

"I fully investigate every complaint that crosses my desk," Lancet said.

Borsk had just told his mom that this morning. He grinned. "I suppose you do, worse luck for you. You can't exactly force people to cooperate, can you?"

"I have the authority to . . ."

"Fine us," Ma Sweets said, "unless it would take our cash reserves below the bare survival line—oh, wait. None of us has any cash reserves."

"He could lock us up," Great Uncle Elton said. "What do you say to a vacation, Sweets?"

Ma Sweets giggled so hard, she threw herself into a coughing fit. Great Uncle Elton pushed himself off his stool, hobbled over to her side of the table, and whacked her on the back a few times.

When the fit had subsided, Lancet said, "I can stop this boy from delivering your lunch."

Ma Sweets lips trembled. If she got upset, and Mama heard about it, Borsk would be getting his snacks from the burnt and bruised bin for a while. He shifted the buckets a bit to make them more comfortable, and said, "Actually, you can't. They didn't order it; it's a gift from my mother. Even if you've got them down in the brig, they can receive gifts."

"I can search it."

"If you've got a warrant. Otherwise you'd better move your arm, or I'll issue a complaint of my own, and you don't want that on your spotless record, do you?"

Lancet dropped his arm and pulled backward just enough for Borsk to squeeze by.

"You're surprisingly uncooperative for a Camp Flight applicant."

Borsk set his buckets on the tiny common room table, then shrugged.

"You signed up for an officer-preparation course, Borsk? What were you thinking?" Great Uncle Elton asked as Borsk helped him back to his stool.

"Mama's idea, not mine. She thinks the extra discipline would be good for me."

Great Uncle Elton snorted and pulled the closest bucket toward him.

"She means well," Ma Sweets said, patting Borsk's hand.

"What exactly is wrong with an officer-preparation course?" Lancet asked.

"Nothing, if you want to slog away at a boring headache of a job for twenty-five years until your brains fry out and they take you to the recycler," Borsk said since nobody else looked like they were going to answer Lancet.

"You planning on dying at forty, Borsk?" Lancet asked.

"Forty-five," Old Doc Norman said from the back corner, where he'd been sitting so quietly Borsk had forgotten him. "B. has a decent chance of living to forty-five, even with the delta-zed gene he inherited from his father."

Borsk froze. He'd known his life expectancy for a while, almost since his father had died. It usually didn't bother him much—certainly not as much as knowing he was blocked from reproducing. Not that he wanted kids, exactly—but he had the feeling girls weren't as interested in guys who were banned. And he really didn't like the idea of having to explain a pregnancy termination to his mother. Or her God, not that he really believed in all that nonsense. But he didn't totally not believe in it either. So, he tried not to think about his future at all. Usually. With Old Doc Norman bringing it up, what could he do? Forty-five sounded so final. A long way off yet, of course, but not nearly so far off as the eighty-odd most people expected to live.

Silence stretched awkwardly, and Borsk couldn't think of anything to say.

Ma Sweets broke it with another of her giggles. "Norman, dear, we're talking about Borsk, here, not Big B." She turned to Lancet. "You'll have to excuse Norman. He gets a little confused sometimes."

"I'm not confused, woman. Big B. died three years ago, rest his soul. I'm talking about the boy here. He brought me his test results two days after the funeral, and I hope I'm still scientist enough to know what they mean."

Great Uncle Elton shoved a tin of noodles at the old man. "Of course, you're still a great scientist, Doc. We just don't get how you could have seen the boy's gene reports when Simone had both the kids' records sealed when they found out what was wrong with Big B. Didn't want anyone deciding their future before they had a chance to live it. Fierce, she was." He tapped the tin as if to remind Old Doc Norman what he stood to lose by crossing Mama.

Old Doc Norman stared blankly at the noodles. After a moment, he mumbled, "Maybe I was mistaken."

He wasn't, of course. Getting copies of his and Sarka's genetic files had been Borsk's first big hack. He'd been so frustrated when he realized he could make no sense of the medical jargon and lines of gene sequences. Old Doc Norman had been the only person he could think of who'd explain it all without reporting his misdeeds to Mama. That was back when the old man was clear-headed more often than not, and even in his best moments, disinclined for talking. Who knew that three years later, his silent helper would have a rare, lucid, talkative moment and spill the whole story? In front of Lancet. Damn.

Borsk couldn't do anything to change things now, though. Maybe Lancet wouldn't think too much of the incident. The old man was often unreliable these days. Borsk smiled at the trio. "I'll be back later for the tins, OK? Gotta get back to school."

"I'll walk with you," Lancet said. "It looks like I've got all the info I'm going to get here."

That sounded ominous. Borsk walked fast, hoping to make the talk with Lancet short, but the officer said, "No need to rush. I can write you an excuse for class."

"Thanks, but I'd hate to be late."

"To Calculus? Damion Huxton says you're late three times out of five, but still far enough ahead of your classmates that it doesn't matter whether you even attend."

Shit. Was the man stalking him?

"I checked because we've run into a bit of trouble with some of our software today, and my best IT guy says you might be able to put it right."

"Me?"

"That's what Martin Kim says."

Martin Kim. Of course. The guy was good—in an institutional, unimaginative way. He must have recognized Borsk's work and ratted him out. But Lancet had only solicited his help, not threatened to expose his hacking, so they must not think they could prove he did it. Borsk shrugged. "Well, maybe I could help you out, but why would I want to?"

Lancet smiled down at him. "I imagine you'll do it so I'm not forced to have a chat with your mother about your lack of interest in your own future and the possible reasons that might be so."

Borsk stopped stock still. "Bastard. You can't prove I did anything wrong."

Lancet's mouth twitched. "Oh, I realize the old man's word would never hold up in court. But I think we both know his story is generally reliable. You might be even better than Kim says if you were hacking into sealed gene records when you were twelve. We need to make sure that kind of talent stays on the side of the angels."

"Don't kid yourself. I know whose side you're on, and Thomas Cartier is no angel."

Lancet's smile tightened and his eyes flashed with a bit of the scary gleam Anya had caught in her portrait. "Your data mining skills may be impressive, boy, but your analysis could use some work. Go grab some lunch, and then meet me in the Level Three, west-side headquarters in half an hour. Without the attitude—or that awful mess on your head." Lancet started down the hallway at a pace that told Borsk his own earlier attempt at speed hadn't even inconvenienced the man.

"You talking about my dreads? You know they're a protected form of expression under Article Five of the Charter, and I could have you written up for an ethnic slur, right?" Borsk shouted after him.

Lancet turned on his heel and raised an eyebrow. "One point to you, kid. Keep the mop, then. But be on time."

"Fine," Borsk said.

"Fine, sir."

"Don't push it. I'm not *that* afraid of you talking to my mama."

Lancet clenched his left hand then released it. "Half an hour." He headed back down the corridor.

Borsk scowled but waited until Lancet was out of earshot to whisper, "Aye, aye, Sir Psychopath."

& &

By volunteering to help with packing up produce for the big Friday deliveries, Anya hoped to find a way to send a message to Grandma. As a bonus, she got to work with VJ Brown, the boy with the tattoo. DeShawn, together with a seventh-form kid, took over her job pollinating, now that the upper half of the vines were done.

She and VJ didn't say much at first, just loaded the baskets and schlepped them to the loading dock—by hand, since the mag-cart was broken, as usual. Anya's arms ached before they'd even finished the first truckload of pristine silver baskets with the General Mercantile logo.

The next set of baskets looked more used but held together all right. They were blue for the hospital, purple and orange and yellow with logos for various restaurants and green for the assisted-living centers. Anya kept her eye on the Sunnydale one, speeding her packing, so that she'd get to it before VJ could.

"Careful with that one," VJ said. "The old man gets mighty cranky if it's not perfect. I can handle it if you want."

Anya supposed Greeley had friends in Sunnydale. She smiled at VJ, to make sure he knew she appreciated the offer. "Thanks, but I can manage."

He smiled back at her. "I guess you can. I've never seen fingers fly so fast. And you don't complain either. It's a pity."

"That I don't complain?"

"That you're green. I'm kind of looking for someone to try out with me. You know, for the Golden Terrace Colony team—I figure it would be good fun, and it's my only chance of ever making an A salary. Might be nice to have the chance to have more than two kids, too. But I haven't found anyone to go with me."

"Oh, wow." Anya wished she could think of something better, but her mind blanked. VJ's wish was so close to her own secret desires. No wonder her father orchestrated her opportunities to meet eligible young men. Right now, if VJ were green . . .

"It was a stupid idea." VJ turned back to his basket, scowling.

"No, no. Not at all. I was just surprised. I don't think anyone's ever taken me seriously . . . that way . . . before. It's sweet." Anya pulled the Sunnydale basket toward her.

VJ gripped his basket hard enough that the tattoo on his bicep rippled. "You don't have to sugar coat it. I know I'm big and stupid." He swung the basket over Anya's head and strode with it toward the loading dock.

Anya half wanted to run after him and contradict him, but she couldn't ignore this chance to be alone with the produce going to Grandma's assisted living center. She grabbed a silverfruit from the bin and a paring knife off the tool shelf, but then couldn't think of anything to say. VJ'd be back in a minute, wondering why she hadn't gotten anything done. "Come on, girl," she whispered to herself.

In the end, she scratched the thick rind with, "G'ma ♥ you. C U when I can." It looked stupid, but wouldn't hurt the silverfruit, and whichever resident had unloading duty this week would guess she sent it and make sure Grandma saw it. Anya smiled to herself and loaded the fruit along with the rest of the basket.

She'd nearly finished when VJ got back and pulled a basket toward himself.

"You're not stupid, you know," she said, not looking at him.

"You haven't seen my mod scores."

Anya shrugged. "I've seen you explain the recycling system to the seventh-formers."

"But that's not hard."

"DeShawn didn't find it so easy last week."

VJ grunted. "I just have more experience messing with it than he does."

"So, you're better at understanding things when you can deal with them hands-on than when you learn about them in a classroom. That doesn't make you dumb."

"You sound like Old Greeley."

"You're just full of compliments today." Anya smiled, grasped the handles of her basket, and crouched, almost to a sitting position, so she could lift with her legs.

VJ bumped into her side and reached across her, covering her hands with his. "Let me get this. It'll go faster if you pack and I carry."

Anya's heart sped up. She wasn't afraid, was she? Slipping her hands out from under VJ's, she whispered, "Thank you."

He nodded, then leaned in so close, she almost thought he was going to kiss her, but at the last minute, he turned, then swung the basket up and away from her.

She found herself breathing as heavily as if she were running. That wouldn't have been a problem, except as she turned to watch VJ take the Sunnydale basket to the truck, she noticed a glint off the monitoring camera by the door. Did that mean it was recording? She made a mental note to ask Borsk how to tell when the cameras were on and turned back to the empty baskets. By concentrating on filling them as quickly as possible, she forced thoughts of cameras and impossible dreams out of her mind.

Soon she finished the job, and they'd loaded even the most ragged, lowest priority crates. VJ checked the manifest one last time, and then they sent the cart along the rails to make its way through *Hope*, delivering food everywhere food needed to go—from the posh General Mercantile processing centers to the soup kitchens and food pantries in Sigmore Landing.

Chapter Nine

Her father brought the cameras back to her attention the moment she got to their quarters that night. He sat at the far side of the table, playing and replaying her conversation with VJ on the family's wall-screen.

Anya stopped when she saw it, glad the table was up and between her father and her.

"I'm canceling your greenhouse hours. You'll have to find another work detail," Father said without turning around.

Anya's heart pounded. This time she knew she was afraid. But she couldn't let him take away the greenhouses. Perhaps she could make the alternatives seem so awful, he'd change his mind. She took a deep breath, straightened up, and forced herself to smile. "Well, I still have a few days of detention to finish, and I'd have to stop back in fairly often until my experiment ends, but perhaps it's time to pick up some new skills. I noticed they're a bit short-handed at Skreetches, and I might enjoy restaurant cooking. I certainly like—"

"No!" Her father swung to face her. "You spend more than enough time with that delinquent classmate as it is."

"You mean Borsk? I don't think he spends that much time in the kitchens, truthfully. And the rest of his family is very law-abiding." Anya didn't know this for sure, but she figured they had to be, or Father would have shut their place down long before now.

"I don't want you down there. Too many undesirables in and out."

By which he meant too many chances to meet an eligible boy who wasn't Ryan, Anya realized. The thought excited her almost as much as it probably scared him. Maybe she should consider trying something other than the greenhouses for a bit. Surely the restaurant wasn't the only place where she could meet young men. She searched her memory. Where could she go? Then she had it. "I guess it wouldn't have to be Skreetches. I've been invited to work down at the library or up at Mom's hospital."

Her father glared. His face turned red.

Maybe she ought to try a different approach before he got too angry to think straight. She thought a moment. "Or—I think they need an assistant up at Sunnydale. It'd be supervised, so I wouldn't be alone with Grandma, but I could—"

Her father snatched his cup off the table and threw it on the floor in front of her. Its contents splashed on her lower pants, and wet spots clung to her legs, uncomfortably hot. Anya wasn't sure if he'd meant to hit her and missed or meant the coffee to land exactly where it had. Either way he'd blame her for the mess in a moment.

Silently, she picked up the cup, found a rag, and cleaned up. Her father watched, the red slowly draining from his face. When she'd finished, her father turned halfway toward the screen, which was paused on a somewhat unflattering picture of her and VJ's backs.

"You can stay in the greenhouses until I've worked out something more suitable," he growled, "but this nonsense has to stop."

Had he figured out what she'd been doing with the knife then? It wasn't obvious from what Anya could see. "Working in shipment?" she asked tentatively.

"No. This flirting and encouraging young men to try out for the ridiculous colony team."

"Flirting? Father, V . . ." She thought better of using his name. Father could find it out, but why make it easy? "He's not even green. And if I'd realized you might think he was a valuable asset to *Hope*, I'd have encouraged him to apply for the mercantile exec program instead." That was a flat out lie, of course. She wouldn't recommend her father's exec training program to anyone she liked.

"I never said he was a valuable asset to *Hope*!"

"So, what does it matter if he tries out for the Golden Terrace Colony?"

Her father's face flushed bright red again. "Get out of my sight, girl! And don't return until you've learned some manners!"

Anya nodded and fled the living space, glad she'd put the cup in the cleaner and not back in front of him. This way, no hard projectiles followed her out into the corridor.

Chapter Ten

Anya didn't realize she was headed for Skreetches until she found herself, breathing heavily, under the lit sign that arched over the restaurant's main doorway. Behind the arch, Sarka stood, in a white uniform, rolling flatware into napkins.

Before Anya could decide whether to approach, the other girl looked up and grimaced. "Come to gloat about Steve picking your ad over mine, have you? Well, Mama's in back, and I don't have to seat anybody as grungy as you look right now. Where'd you pick up that foul smell, and what have you spilled on yourself?"

Anya felt her face get hot. She'd forgotten she hadn't made it to the shower after her afternoon in the greenhouse. Tears pricked at her eyes, and she ducked her head so Sarka wouldn't see. "Sorry. I don't mean to be a burden. I just wasn't sure where to go after Father threw his coffee at me and sent me out of the house."

Anya turned and walked quickly away. She thought she heard Sarka call her name as she reached the turn in the corridor, but she ignored it. Sarka was right. After an afternoon in the greenhouses, she wasn't fit to be seen in public. Besides, anyone who helped her now would incur her father's wrath. Skreetches didn't need any more of that.

What she needed was a wash-and-wear place. She'd never used one, but half her classmates didn't have showers or laundry facilities at home, so she'd heard a few stories. She was sure she'd heard Marya Dominguez, the librarian's daughter, say she avoided the one by the school because it was always crammed to bursting with athletes and ship-crew wannabes.

Now if Anya could only remember where Marya did go, she'd be in good shape. Someplace on Level Five, if she remembered right. She could tap a search into her armband and let her map program direct her, but then Father could track her movements, and she'd as soon make a meal of recycling worms as let Father watch her right now.

She slipped into the nearest level-stair alcove, climbed down to Five, and found herself in a residential and office district—all numbered entrances with understated screens. The colors got gaudier off to her left, so she walked that way, hoping the brighter patterns indicated a more commercial zone. She kept her pace brisk in hopes that anyone who saw her would assume she had a destination in mind.

After about five minutes, the plain numbered doors alternated with ones that had small light signs above them—a gaming lounge, a private gym, a small General Mercantile storefront, a hairdresser. Then she passed another hairdresser, and another. A fourth. A massage parlor.

Outside yet another hairdresser, a girl just a bit older than Anya lounged in little more than her underwear. Anya had seen her at school but couldn't remember her name. Something about the way the girl stared at her through listless hooded eyes made Anya uncomfortable. This couldn't be the part of Level Five Marya and her mother frequented, could it? If she didn't find the wash-and-wear place soon, she'd run a search after all.

Almost as soon as she'd made up her mind, she found one. Not, perhaps, the one the Dominguez's used, but a wash-and-wear place all the same. Anya brushed past the hanging beads in the doorway, making them crackle. Once inside, she couldn't help staring at the place—a claustrophobia-inducing corridor with narrow door screens every meter down both sides, except for the area immediately to her left. Instead of the corridor wall and a door, there was a chest-high desk topped by a full-service bank console. Nearly hidden behind that, a slim dark girl perched on a tall stool, tapping away at what looked like a school tablet. Anya didn't know the girl exactly, but she knew who she was. Georgia Lewis topped every class in the eleventh form and half the twelfth-form offerings as well. What was a genius like that doing manning the counter at a wash-and-wear? Not that it was any of Anya's business. "Excuse me," she whispered.

"Number seven is open," Georgia said, without looking up or stopping her tapping.

Number seven. Anya glanced to her right and saw a flashing numeral one on what looked like a payment pad next to the first door. OK. So, payment probably allowed you to unlock the things. That wouldn't be so hard, would it? She eyed the narrow hall that led straight back, and half wished that two or three had been available. But then it would be easier for Georgia to see her fumbling cluelessly with the payment pad, not that Georgia appeared to be paying any attention at all.

Anya took a couple deep breaths and walked down the tiny hall. Number seven was the second-to-last doorway on the left. Her armband couldn't connect to the payment pad, so she tried touching the thing. As soon as she stroked a finger over it, the flashing seven disappeared, giving way to a menu of payment options. Neither General Mercantile's GenM credit nor the Shippay system Anya used in the school cafeteria made the list. No wonder there was a banking console by the front counter. Anya made her way back to it.

"Don't tell me the unit's broken," Georgia said.

"No—I just don't have the right kind of money."

"Not even cash? Our deluxe packages top out at fifteen credits."

"My father says if it doesn't take GenM or Shippay, I don't need it, so I don't usually carry cash. It's easier than trying to explain. But I should be able to convert something." Anya got her armband talking to the banking console and logged into her Shippay account, figuring that would be harder for Father to keep tabs on than the GenM one. When she tried to withdraw cash, though, she discovered her account was a restricted one for minors that allowed only recognized school-related transactions. Ferto. She tried her GenM account and found it was also restricted—this time to places connected to the GenM system.

"That's not fair," she muttered. "All the money in there is from my work detail. I should be able to use it however I want."

"You're putting your paychecks in an account with parental access?" Georgia said. "I thought rich kids were supposed to be smart about money."

Anya hadn't realized her complaint was loud enough to be overheard. She peeked around the banking console and saw that Georgia had slightly lowered her tablet. "I'm only fifteen. I can't open an account on my own."

"Who told you that? The same asshole who's keeping you from your own money?"

"My father's not—"

"Believe whatever you want, kid. Financial advice for minors is the ninth item on the help menu."

"How do you know—"

"What? You think you're the only kid whose parents ever hijacked her work detail money? Just do me a favor. If you wind up using the social services forms, don't let on I pointed you toward them." Georgia raised her tablet back up, completely hiding her face.

Since her special trust couldn't be easily used for everyday transactions, Anya shifted back to the banking console and looked up the menu item Georgia recommended.

As soon as she glanced through it, she felt like a fool. There were a dozen different kinds of accounts that would be harder for her father to tinker with than the types she owned. She read through the options carefully, looking for one that would keep her father from messing with her finances, but still allow regular access to her money.

After laboriously sifting through the fine print, only two account options satisfied her. The first, a social services account, required a galaxy of forms. Scanning through them, Anya realized that to get one of these accounts, she'd have to prove that her parents were either abusive or financially irresponsible. She sighed. Father had a temper, but he'd never actually touched her. And he was anything but financially irresponsible.

The other option was a Golden Terrace account, designed to connect with the colony's slightly different financial system. Anyone eligible to try out could get one.

That would work for her. Of course, if she created one, she might enrage her father enough to give her sufficient evidence for the social services account. Her hands shook, so she held them together. She could not afford to give way to fear. She wanted to sign up for the colony next week anyway, and she'd need one of these accounts to pay the application fee. Sure, her father might hit her, but she could survive that, couldn't she? Mom always did. And if the cameras caught it, she'd be free of him for good. She smiled to herself at that thought.

Then she steadied herself with a couple of deep breaths and pulled her hands apart. Fingers still trembling, she pulled up the forms that would give her access to the colony and freedom . . .

Unless her father's temper destroyed her first.

∞ ᘓ

By the time Borsk dragged himself back to the restaurant that night, he was so tired he'd stopped fantasizing about strangling Ryan Lancet—even the daydream took too much energy. The jerk had made him undo all his work of the morning, and then recode all four major fact-checking programs so they were harder to hack. Borsk had imagined he'd get out of there after that, but Lancet had insisted on him reapplying for Camp Flight then and there. Then they did an interview.

Now all Borsk wanted was food and his bunk.

He snuck in the back way, grabbed a wrap from the leftovers bin in the smaller cooler, and bit in without bothering to warm the thing.

Before he could finish swallowing, Sarka flew into the kitchen, grabbed him by the elbow, and pulled him toward the public side of the restaurant. "Am I glad to see you," she said.

"What the hell?"

"I'll explain on the way. I've got to get back to the hostess desk."

Sarka had left the hostess station? The surprise of it flummoxed Borsk enough that before he could protest further, she'd propelled him through the swinging doors of the kitchen and out into the restaurant proper. There the dim light and raucous noise of a bigger-than-usual Friday-night crowd disoriented him. He almost thanked Sarka when she increased her grip on his elbow and guided him through the press of the crowd. He only tripped over people's legs twice. Before he got the thanks out, though, he remembered that he wouldn't even be here if she hadn't dragged him away from the kitchen. "Sarka—"

"Just a minute." She sped up, so that they reached the hostess station seconds ahead of a group of ship-system interns who looked restless and a touch effervescent. Borsk thought they looked a trifle young to be using, but who was he to judge? He wasn't hosting tonight—or any night he could reasonably get away with doing something else.

"Can I help you?" Sarka asked, beaming the group the kind of high lumen smile she never wasted on Borsk. "Six, is it? We're a bit packed tonight, but there's a table opening up in the underage section that might work for you all."

The smallest guy in the group started to protest, but his date, a willowy girl with purple streaks in her hair, calmed him down with a touch on his arm. "When do you think something on the adult side will free up?"

"The waiting list is running about forty minutes," Sarka said. "If you'd like to be on it, you can all flash me your IDs."

"No, no," the small guy muttered. "Underage is fine."

Sarka brightened her smile a notch. "Great. Follow me." Then hissing in Borsk's ear without breaking her smile, she said, "Don't move," and shoved him toward the hostess desk.

He sat on the stool behind it and inhaled the rest of his wrap. Sarka returned as he was finishing.

"Did you eat that whole thing? Disgusting!"

Borsk rose from the stool. "I don't have to put up with this."

Sarka stood in front of him. "Sorry. I shouldn't have said anything."

Sarka was apologizing? This was serious. "What's up?"

"Your g—, I mean Anya Cartier. She stopped by earlier, looking even grubbier than usual, and . . . look, I'm not proud of it, but I was kind of rude."

Borsk hadn't noticed Sarka being polite to Anya at any earlier point. "Yeah, so?"

"Well, when she left, she said something about her father throwing coffee at her and kicking her out of the house, and I got a little worried. But maybe it's another joke—you know, like what she said about you two being illicit lovers. I mean, who would actually throw something at their kid?"

Borsk remembered his one encounter with Thomas Cartier. "*Her* dad might."

"If you really think it's not a joke, we've got to find her! She needs help. And I can't leave. Unless you want to man—"

"No way. The only thing I hate more than cooking is working out here. I'll go see what's up with Anya."

"Good. She'll do better with you anyway. But tell her I'm sorry, will you? I had no idea."

Borsk nodded.

"Well, what are you waiting for? She went toward the third corridor lifts about twenty minutes ago."

"I'm going already!" Borsk sighed and stepped around Sarka. He didn't really want to do anything but sleep, but Sarka was right. Anya probably needed help. And she could be just about anywhere by now. Borsk shuffled down the hallway, half wishing that he'd left Anya Cartier—her money and her problems—strictly alone.

But if he had, who would help her now? His better half made him speed up. He needed to find her before her father did.

Chapter Eleven

Once she got her money straightened out, **Anya splurged** on a deluxe package, which turned out to be five minutes of steamy, scented luxury, and a further five minutes of gentle blow drying, by which point the cleaner had finished with her uniform. She buried her face in its fluffy warmth, breathing in the sweet, clean scent of the Wash & Wear detergent. She wished they used this stuff at home, but they couldn't. Father claimed to be allergic to anything with fragrance, and he wouldn't have it in the house. He'd probably throw a fit just smelling the perfume this place left on her.

Or he would if he didn't have other, more important things to be mad about.

Anya smiled grimly to herself, pulled her uniform back on, and studied her reflection in the mirrored surfaces around her. Not too bad. She smoothed her hair a bit. She might not look spectacular, but she should be able to get seated in a restaurant now.

A timer pinged, letting her know her turn in the stall was nearly up. She didn't feel ready to face the world yet, but buying more time wasn't likely to make her any more ready. So, when the door slid open, she stepped out into the narrow corridor between stalls.

"There you are," someone said. She stopped mid-stride. She had to remind herself that it didn't sound like her father before she could force herself to keep moving toward the entrance.

Halfway there, she realized the speaker was Borsk, and she stopped dragging her feet. She smiled at him. "Am I glad to see you."

"Funny. That's just what Sarka said. I guess I'm one popular guy tonight."

"Lucky you. Can you go be popular somewhere else? You're blocking the hallway," Georgia said without looking up from her tablet.

Borsk laughed. "Come on, Anya. Let's get out of here." He ducked back through the beads of the doorway.

Anya stopped a minute to smile shyly at Georgia. "Thank you. I feel much better."

Georgia lowered her tablet a smidgeon and looked over it. "Don't mention it. *Really.*"

Anya caught the older girl's glance and saw a warning there. Georgia was right. The whole Wash-and-Wear place could get in trouble if it got around that she had offered refuge and advice. Anya nodded to show she understood and followed Borsk out the door.

"You OK?" he asked, so low she wasn't sure she'd heard right.

She nodded again. "Want to find some supper?"

"I alr . . . Sure. I could eat."

Anya smiled at him. "At your place?"

"Let's get takeout. The restaurant is so packed you can't move in there."

"OK."

As if by some unspoken agreement, they didn't talk again as they walked back to the restaurant and raided the coolers. Only after Borsk handed her a bucket crammed with edible goodies did Anya ask, "Where to?"

"Not sure. The school cafeteria is usually quiet this time of night unless there's a game or performance."

"It's Friday."

"Good point. How about Central Park? I know a couple of hidden corners. They don't get very good signal, though."

Anya smiled. "Perfect."

Anya hadn't been to the park in months. Usually it depressed her to see the uniform lines of oxy-trees pruned into identical cones, as close to interchangeable parts of a machine as living things could be. Anya suspected that they only existed because *Hope's* engineers had never managed to come up with a mechanical air filtration system that worked half as efficiently.

She trailed the tips of her fingers along the trees on her right, enjoying the soft fur of the wide leaves.

Borsk led her through the air-recycling grove, ducking under branches now and then, so they could check the little caves formed wherever a water pump replaced one of the oxy-trees.

The first two were occupied by amorous couples, and a third held a noisy group of tenth-form kids playing a drinking game. A boy with unnaturally yellow hair asked Borsk to join them, saying something about a poker game later.

"Maybe another time," Borsk said.

"Can't you see he's with a girl, Sing?" asked a guy with dreadlocks almost as long as Borsk's.

"Since when has Borsk liked girls more than poker?" yellow-hair responded.

Borsk laughed and pulled Anya away. Leaning close to her ear, he muttered, "Let's get well away from that lot. They're bound to be kicked out within the hour."

Anya nodded, and they skipped the next couple of water pump clearings, finally settling on one so far from the park entrance that the park walls bordered it on two sides. That left just enough room for Borsk and Anya to sit, one on each side of the water pump, supper on their laps. Light filtering through the tree-leaves gave a sickly-green cast to the food, but the air smelled fresh.

Anya ignored the green color and ate. She'd barely eaten lunch.

"You know, I had to ask actual people to figure out where you'd gone," Borsk said.

Anya glanced up from a protein wrap. "Good. Then maybe Father doesn't know where I am."

"So, when you told Sarka your dad had kicked you out, that wasn't a joke?"

"Kicked me out temporarily. Why would I joke about that?"

Borsk shrugged. "Sarka wondered—"

"Sarka hardly knows me. And, sorry, Borsk, I know she's your sister, but sometimes she's a bit dense."

"You don't need to tell me. But in her defense, she did eventually figure out you might be in trouble. She sent me after you. She'll let you bunk with her tonight if you need to."

"Thanks, but it wouldn't be a good idea. Father will get over his mad soon, and if I don't go back home, he'll be filing kidnapping charges by morning."

"What happened?"

"He said not to come back until I'd learned some manners."

"You were rude?"

Anya shrugged. "Not particularly. He just needs some time to cool off. The trick with Father is to give him enough time to get over what got him upset, but not so much time that he's mad about me staying away."

"So, he's kicked you out—temporarily—before."

"Usually I go to Grandma's. But Father filed some papers yesterday that restrict my access to her."

"What about your other family?"

"Father restricted my access to the Shorehams years ago."

"You've got a sister who doesn't live at home, though, don't you?"

"Borsk, she's married to Kenneth Llourdes. Have you heard of him?"

Borsk remembered his report to his mother about restaurant security and troublemakers. "Yeah, I've heard of him. I take it that's not a good option."

Anya shook her head.

Borsk sopped up the sauce on his plate with a bit of bread. "So, when do you think you should go back?"

Anya turned her arm, so she could see her clock. "Another hour, maybe?"

"What do you want to do until then? Do you know how to play poker?"

Anya smiled. "Don't you think you've scammed me enough for this week? How about you show me how you know when cameras are running? How to turn them on and off would be even better."

Borsk lifted an eyebrow. "Wanting to hack now, are you?"

"Just show me, Borsk."

Borsk stuffed the bread he'd been playing with into his mouth and wiped his hand on his pant leg. Then he reached awkwardly around the water pump to touch her armband. "Your own system will show a light here when it's re-cording—unless someone has hacked it, which would be pretty damn impressive. But even if they have, you can check your camera's status with a simple command—push the check, then the camera, then input your personal icon. Two taps and a trace. Try it."

Anya set her plate of food to one side and found a napkin to wipe her fingers. Then she tapped her armband's screen—first on the check mark, then on a tiny black box with a circle in the center that for some unfathomable reason had come to mean "camera." Then she traced the silverfruit blossom pattern she'd come to use as her personal icon.

Her screen blacked out. Then words appeared. "Personal camera offline."

Anya giggled. "It works!"

"Why is it offline?" Borsk asked. "It should be connected to the system whether it's active or inactive." Borsk's fingers flew over his own armband. "Holy hell. Your whole surveillance system is a tangled mess."

And she'd signed up for a Colony bank account, just begging her Father to get violent. Anya's hand shook. "Can you fix it?"

"Maybe. If I work all night."

Panic made her voice rise. "I need the cameras to work when I go back home. If something happens, but there's no proof—" Anya stopped herself and took a deep breath. This was not Borsk's fault.

"Calm down. Your surveillance system has something crazy-wrong with it right now, but we'll figure it out. In the meantime, you can use the manual controls for the surveillance system on your home."

"What manual controls?" Anya didn't think anything about her house was manual.

"The panel under every nameplate has two ancient switches—one for the cameras, and the other for the entry screen. You push the switches up for on, down for off. When the newfangled stuff breaks, the old system still works. There are places down in Sigmore where the only way to lock up is with the manual."

"I think I saw that panel once when our lock had to be fixed, but I assumed only repair people could access it."

"No, it's not like a service hatch. Anybody registered as living in a space can open the thing. And if no residents are present, you have to have a warrant—level one warrant—to get in. Whoever was fixing your lock couldn't have accessed the panel unless you—or someone else in your family—was there."

The tension in Anya's chest eased a bit. "Oh. So, I open the panel and push the switch up to turn on the house video feeds?"

"That's right. Should be foolproof. But I'll show you how to make sure it's on. And I'll work on cleaning up the mess with your personal surveillance—that way you'll have a back-up."

Anya breathed out, slowly. "Thanks, Borsk. I don't know how I'll ever repay you."

"If you remember, I'm the one who owes you."

Anya smiled.

"Though if you wanted to do something, you could let Steve use that art piece you did with the trumpet flower. He wants it for his album cover."

"Really?" Anya almost squealed. Hadn't Sarka said Steve had wanted to get *Hope Rising* for his cover? And now he wanted her work?

"He wishes he could credit you. Pay you something too, I think."

"But Father will find out!" Anya's elation fell so hard she almost heard a thump. Then she remembered that she'd decided to go ahead and provoke her father—as a way to get free of him. "You know what? Father will find out eventually anyway. I may as well profit from my work, right?"

Borsk's mouth gaped open. "What will he do?"

"What can he do? Take my art programs away? He's done that already. Block me from seeing my grandma? He did that too. Make me quit working in the greenhouses? He's working on an alternative right now. Stop me seeing you? Oh, wait. He can't really do that, can he? Not with you and your mom knowing our business."

"Do you think he'll get violent?"

"If he does, and we've got it in the feed, I'm free of him."

Borsk closed his mouth and swallowed so hard Anya could see his Ad-am's apple bob. "I guess we'd better make sure you know how to work the cameras."

Something woke Borsk from a light snooze. His body rested against a hard, lumpy pole, and odd greenish light flickered on his face. He knew he was tired, but tired enough to fall asleep sitting up? And, where was he?

"What is this?"

Borsk turned toward the voice. On the other side of one of Central Park's water pumps, Anya Cartier bent over a school tablet—*his* school tablet. "What the—" He stood up, hitting his head on a branch of one of the damn oxytrees.

"Are you OK?" Anya shifted, so that they now faced each other.

Borsk crouched back down, rubbing his head. "Fine. What are you doing with my tablet?"

"You gave it to me. Fifteen minutes ago—to practice controlling cameras. Remember?"

That's right. He had. He hadn't thought she would mess around with anything else. "So, you decided you could do whatever you wanted?"

"When I shut down the query file, it dumped me back at your main menu. I noticed a folder marked *For Anya*."

"Oh, that." Relief washed over him. "That's just math stuff. Since I'm supposed to be tutoring you."

"This is math?" Anya turned the tablet so he could see the screen. A fractal crawled across it, painting a wild landscape in purples, reds, and blues.

Borsk smiled. "I figured you'd like that. You probably aren't ready for the math involved yet, but I thought you'd enjoy seeing the possibilities."

"But what is it?"

"A fractal—a graphical representation of a mathematical set, just like the curves you've been doing are graphical representations of mathematical equations."

Anya snorted. "Those curves aren't art."

"Maybe not. Or at least not yet. You could make them into art, though. I've seen what you can do with lines and curves." Borsk flashed her portrait of Steve into the space between them.

"I did that with a drawing program. I can't do that with my graphing calculator."

"I bet you could if you figure out what kind of equations make what kind of lines."

"Show me."

"OK." Borsk stifled a yawn. He'd need to find some caffeine soon if he had to stay awake long enough to beat algebra into Anya's head.

She surprised him, though. Instead of needing hours of explanations, as she had when Lancet helped her with her homework, she caught on quickly. After a brief review of what she'd learned already, and a slightly longer dip into inequalities, she entered a series of equations into the calculator, pushed enter, and out popped an oxy-tree.

"Amazing," Borsk said. "I can't believe—"

"I'm not stupid, you know. I just couldn't see what this was all about before."

Borsk thought about telling Anya that math wasn't only for making pictures. But maybe, for Anya, it was. He smiled. "I've never thought you were stupid."

"Just slow at math. And science. And tech."

"I don't know. You picked up the surveillance tracking skills in minutes. And you weren't slow learning your math either. Maybe you've never been properly motivated before."

Anya laughed in a way that made Borsk wonder if she was quite sane. "That must be it. All I need to do to learn the engineering core is have my father take away my art programs and threaten me with grievous bodily harm."

"Did he threaten you?"

"Not with words. Nothing I could take to the social services people. Most of the time he's very careful. He doesn't like anything, even his temper, to be out of control for long. Which reminds me I've been gone long enough. He's probably calmed down as much as he's going to."

"Are you sure?"

"There's no being sure when Father is in a rage." Anya gave Borsk a half smile, handed him his tablet, and ducked under the trees out onto the path.

"Do you want me to come with you?"

She crouched down at the opening of the clearing and looked back at him. "Thanks, but Father's taken a dislike to you. It's probably better if you stay away. But if you can track me—make sure I'm doing it right with the cameras and all—that would be a great help."

Borsk nodded. Tracking her wouldn't be easy, not with the mess her personal surveillance system was in, but he'd figure out a way to do it. He'd work all night if he had to. He'd make Sarka help him stay awake—tell her that Anya's life depended on them getting it done.

After all, it might.

Chapter Twelve

With the way her hands shook, it took Anya five full minutes to pry up the nameplate next to their door, and even longer to tap in the armband code sequence Borsk had taught her. The camera was off, so she flipped the switch. Then she tested the camera, just to make sure. On. She took a deep breath, carefully replaced the nameplate, and entered the family quarters.

The quarter's main overhead light flickered on as she entered, and mother's disembodied voice floated out from the sound system. "The Chang-Smythe baby is coming, so don't wait up for me. Anya—no more than four-hundred calories for dinner, dear. You were a bit over yesterday. And do your homework."

Anya scowled at the sound system, but kept her voice polite as she said, "Yes, Mom." The stupid manners program would be on her if she sounded too disrespectful.

Where was her father?

A quick search proved he wasn't in the house. Perhaps he'd gone out for dinner when he discovered Mom wouldn't be home in time to make him anything.

It made Anya nervous, not knowing where he was, or when he'd come home. Anya chewed her lower lip. The silence of the house grew heavy.

Perhaps she'd better take her mom's advice. Homework might not be much fun, but it would occupy her mind.

She ducked into her bunk, pulled the screens down, and debated locking up. The locks would separate her from her father if he came home in a towering rage, but they would also make it impossible to reach an exit without getting past him.

No good choices. The story of her life. When her lip started to bleed, she forced herself to stop chewing on it. When all choices were equally bad, what did it matter? She left the screen unlocked and settled back into her bunk.

Homework. What fun.

Anya had finished all her science and math for the week and was working on drawing a silverfruit blossom with her equations when her screen rattled upward.

"What do you think you're doing?" her father growled.

Anya tapped her school tablet so only the equations showed. "Getting a little extra practice with my math homework."

Father grabbed the tablet. "Let me see that."

He tapped a couple of times. "I know that little bastard is a hacker. What has he hidden in here?"

Anya held her breath, waiting for the explosion when Father saw the pictures she'd been drawing.

It never came. Instead, Father shoved her school tablet back at her. "You may think you're getting away with something, but you're not. I'll find out your secrets. I'll have Ryan lean on young Mr. King if I need to."

"Ryan?" The word slipped out before Anya could catch it.

"Didn't your little friend tell you he's joined Camp Flight? He didn't, did he?"

Anya tried to wipe her face of all emotion, but the effort must not have worked because her father laughed.

"You really shouldn't rely too heavily on that boy, Stacey. Remember, whatever you're paying him to hide your shenanigans, I can pay him more." Her father stepped back and slammed the bunk screen down.

Borsk would never betray her to her father, would he? He hated her father, and he didn't care about money.

Still, Anya worried. Borsk knew so many of her secrets—her lies to hide his hacking, her desire to join the colony, her art for Steve Jackson; her message to Ryan; her new method for creating pictures that looked like math . . .

Why hadn't he told her about joining Camp Flight?

☿   ☽

Despite his exhaustion, Borsk was enjoying himself. He'd never seen such intricate hacking as the web of code he'd found in Anya's armband surveillance system. It took hours to map out what was there before he could even begin to try and figure out what it all did.

Somewhere around one, Sarka slapped a coffee cup in front of him so hard a bit slopped over onto his hand.

"Hey!"

"Hey, yourself. I'm going to bed. You're obviously fine staying up without me."

"But—" What if he fell asleep, and Anya's dad beat her up? Sarka had promised she'd keep him awake.

Sarka slapped a tall thermos next to the cup. "You'll be fine." She stomped off for bed.

Borsk didn't miss her until the coffee ran out hours later. By then, he'd spent so long trailing elegant lines of code that the glowing paths of logic seemed more real than the kitchen he sat in. He saw it all clearly now. The programs in Anya's armband high-jacked the ship security protocols, not only controlling what the feeds caught, but also diverting all surveillance feeds to a private account, and only releasing a few back out to ship security. It did all this without alerting the security systems to any problems.

By four in the morning, Borsk had proof that the private account belonged to Thomas Cartier. The asshole was getting away with felony corruption of ship systems.

If Borsk had known this a week ago, he could have turned the bastard in instead of messing around with Anya's money. Except who would believe him over Thomas Cartier, especially when Borsk had acquired his knowledge illegally?

Borsk took a washroom break and refilled his coffee thermos. That's all the time it took to decide it would be unutterably stupid to turn over the evidence to *Hope* Security. Even if the people he talked to weren't on Thomas Cartier's payroll, they'd have to open a formal investigation, and Cartier's lawyers would find a way to get their man off while landing Borsk in the brig for his pains.

He couldn't leave the code there, though. Beautiful as it was, it endangered Anya. Besides, its elegance tempted Borsk. It was so good, he couldn't resist proving he was better.

Carefully, knowing his freedom depended on not leaving any trace of himself, he began weaving code around Cartier's hacker's code, subverting the subversion, so that the security surveillance programs reverted to their original functions.

Thomas Cartier was going down.

Chapter Thirteen

Borsk had only half finished his work when it was time to leave for school. He debated ditching but decided now was not the time to draw attention to himself.

Leaving himself an easy path back into his work, he pulled out, then cleaned and triple-cleaned his machines until he was sure they showed no evidence of his hacking. That took time. Some things couldn't be hurried.

Dressing and eating could be, though. He tossed on some clothes, raced through the unusually quiet kitchen, and made his way down to the high school.

Only after he got there did he remember that it was Saturday.

No school.

Brilliant.

Now that he was here, though, he might as well make use of the computer lab. The equipment in there was state-of-the-art.

People were supposed to sign in and pay up to use the school machines, but nobody with any skill did that.

Borsk slipped into the lab using a purloined access code, hoping one of the better machines would be available.

Luck was with him. Nobody sat at the Wellspeed 5000 station. In fact, nobody sat at any of the stations. Borsk smiled softly and took control of the third-best public machine on the ship. With this much power behind him, he might be able to finish his work before the payment systems kicked in and started sending auto-alerts to actual authorities.

Forty-five minutes in, he realized he'd been overly optimistic. For the second time that morning, he cleaned up after himself. This time, in addition to dealing with his code, he took time to literally wipe down the equipment, removing fingerprints and other physical traces of himself.

The principal had caught him that way once. His fingerprint on a lab machine the day the school grades had been hacked had won him detention for a month.

Ironically, he hadn't done that particular hack.

But he knew the guy who had. Hiram had a pad down in the Landing, so close to a utility hub, you could tap into almost any system on *Hope* right from his bunk. The "sweet spot," Hiram called it. After Borsk got nailed, Hiram had offered him use of the place whenever he wanted.

Trouble was, the place smelled like a latrine after a party. Borsk grimaced at the thought of it, but decided the smell might be worth the access, at least for this project. He swung by the restaurant to pick up his trash-and-toilet nose clip, then ran down to Hiram's place.

Rousting Hiram proved about as difficult as getting Steve Jackson to open his door. Borsk finally resorted to the horrible whining buzz Sarka had used on him a couple of days ago.

Hiram threw up the screen on his double-high bunk and poked out his wild mop of white-splattered black hair. "What the fuck?"

"I did bring up the lights and try my whole repertoire of chimes first."

"Borsk."

"You said I could use your place any time."

"What the hell are you doing up this time on a Saturday, kid? Don't you know decent hackers work at night?"

"I did. Project's not finished yet."

"Do I want to know what it is?"

"Probably not."

"Then if anybody asks, I never saw you, and don't know how you got yourself into my place." The man lifted himself out of the bunk with arms so scrawny Borsk thought they might break from the strain. Then the guy shuffled off down the hall.

Borsk shook his head. Was that what he'd be in thirty years—a scrawny guy living alone in a stinky hole—all he could afford on a C salary? But he wasn't going to live that long. He grimaced, put on the nose clips, and climbed into the bunk.

Five hours of intense work later, he emerged from the hole. Finished.

He stumbled home and had nearly reached the shower when he bumped into Sarka.

"Where have you been? You smell like—"

"I slept in a toilet. I know. Do you need my nose clip?" Borsk pulled it off.

"Disgusting. Get scrubbed up and get down to the kitchen. You're supposed to be working tonight."

"Sarka, I haven't slept since the night before last, and that was only a couple of hours."

Sarka pursed her lips. "Did you finish?"

Borsk nodded.

"Then get cleaned up and get to bed. I'll switch shifts with you. This time."

"Thanks, Sarka."

She smiled in a way he didn't quite like, but he was too tired to figure it out. Instead, he did as she said—washed the stink off and collapsed in his bunk.

He didn't know anything else until a ravening hunger woke him. He dragged himself from his bunk down to the kitchen.

A glance at the restaurant clock-schedule showed that he'd slept through the rest of Saturday all the way to Sunday morning. No wonder he was starving. He didn't think he could wait for the family breakfast Mama always held before church. He grabbed a slightly burnt turnover out of the leftovers drawer and munched on it while he took a closer look at the schedule.

It listed him as the host for the Sunday noon-to-eight shift. That had to be a mistake. He hacked in, and a message popped up on his armband screen: "You switched with me, remember? I already explained to Mama, so it won't do you any good to mess with the board."

Damn. Mama paid more attention to verbal reports than the clock-schedule. They all knew him too well to trust anything electronic. But hosting during a rush? What made Sarka imagine he could even do that?

He stuffed half the remaining turnover into his mouth and chewed disgruntledly.

Sarka came in then. "Good. You're up. You can help me get breakfast ready."

"Excuse me?"

"Anya dropped by while you were sleeping. Explained how much you'd exaggerated the danger."

"And you believed her? Shit, Sarka. The other day he almost hit her—in a school hallway in front of a witness."

"What witness? You? Who'd believe you?"

"Fair point. I guess it's a good thing I got the cameras working again before he could do anything."

"If she's in real danger, why would she lie to me about it?"

"Yeah. That's a puzzler. You've been such a sweet, considerate friend to Anya. She's bound to trust you with her deepest secrets."

"Right. And she trusts you because you're so loyal and supportive. Puh-leeze. Tell it to someone who doesn't know you." Sarka grabbed a large pot from its hook above the stove and shoved it at Borsk.

"What am I supposed to do with this?"

"Start some water for the noodles. Really, Borsk. For a guy who grew up in a restaurant, you are clueless in the kitchen. Hence the hosting. You've got to learn something if you want to inherit."

"Why would I want to inherit?"

"Borsk," Mama's quiet voice came from behind him, "you're too young to know—"

"What? What I'm good at? What I like?" Borsk swung to face her. "What kind of training I need? When do you suppose I'll be old enough, Mama? After all the college spots for my year have been taken? Or once we've learned I have the disease, and it sinks in, and I can barely move? You think I'll be old enough to make decisions for myself then?"

Mama's eyes welled with tears. She pressed her lips together, barely opening them, as she said, "This is exactly why you aren't allowed to see your gene records."

"Because you can't handle the truth? Yeah, I've known that for a long time." Borsk shoved the pot at her, and she clutched it, anguish in her eyes.

Almost immediately, guilt washed over him. "I'm not hungry anymore." Borsk stumbled out of the kitchen, ignoring Mama's "Borsk!"

So, she couldn't handle the truth. Why'd he need to go throwing that in her face now, when she had so many other worries?

⋈ ⋊

By the time church finished, Borsk felt so guilty about the way he'd yelled at Mama, he headed straight for Skreetches without arguing at all. He'd just thrown the host apron over his restaurant uniform when Ryan Lancet and Martin Kim walked through the business entrance.

"We're not open yet, gentlemen," he said.

"We're here about an application for concert security," Lancet said. "But since you're here, you may as well help Crewman Kim with a security problem that has come to our attention. Show him, Kim."

Martin Kim shoved a display screen under Borsk's nose. "Have you ever seen anything like this?"

Borsk stared at the code he'd written yesterday—wrapped around the code Cartier's hacker had wound about the programs that controlled security footage. Damn. He thought he'd covered his tracks this time. "Can't say that I have," he said. He hoped his voice didn't reveal too much. "What is it?"

"A program that compromises ship security. Thomas Cartier alerted us to it," Kim said.

"Didn't know Thomas Cartier was on ship crew," Borsk said.

"He's not," Lancet said. "But civic-minded private individuals do help us out from time to time. Much as you did Friday. Perhaps you can help us again today."

If they were asking for his help, they probably couldn't prove he'd done it, right? How much did they know? And how long could he stall? Anya needed those cameras working. "I'm sorry I can't help you. We've had some illnesses in the family, and business is brisk these days. I'm needed here."

Lancet nodded. "Tomorrow afternoon, then."

Tomorrow afternoon? Anya needed at least the week—her conflict with her dad was bound to come to a head before Colony try-outs on Saturday. "I don't think that will work. This week, in case you haven't noticed, the restaurant is getting ready for Steve Jackson's concerts. I could probably spare you some time when that's over—if Crewman Kim hasn't solved the whole problem by then."

Lancet's eyes narrowed. "You do know that interfering with ship surveillance is a felony, don't you?"

"You think I've been interfering with ship surveillance?"

"This code interferes with ship surveillance." Lancet jabbed a finger at the tablet Martin Kim held. "And you know perfectly well it's your code. It's only a matter of time until we prove it."

"I'm sure you can prove all manner of things that aren't true," Borsk said.

"I don't falsify—"

"Yeah, yeah. Save the righteous act for someone who might believe it. And do me a favor. Let me know which of these viruses you think I'm responsible for, so I can let our lawyer know what kind of crap we've got to deal with."

"Kim, what is he talking about?"

Martin Kim turned the tablet back toward himself and flicked his finger across it. "He's right, sir. There are at least three styles of programming here. Look."

Borsk leaned in so he could see what Kim was doing. So did Lancet. They nearly knocked heads.

Kim highlighted some of the code in blue. "Original program." He traced other lines in yellow. "Hacker A." He marked a few other lines in green. "Hacker B."

"Are you sure?" Lancet asked.

"Positive. Different styles, different programmers."

"So, if you're accusing me of writing this code, which do you think I wrote?" Borsk said.

"What does it matter? It all interferes with the proper functioning of ship surveillance," Lancet said.

"Does it? I have to admit that after looking at it for just ten minutes, I couldn't have told what any of these programs, even the original did. Undoubtedly you two have had more time for a detailed analysis, though."

Kim and Lancet exchanged a look.

"Maybe it's better if he doesn't work on this until we've had a chance to verify . . ." Kim said.

Lancet nodded. "We'll discuss it back at the station. Mr. King, you want to think very seriously about your role in this. A felony conviction for hacking could lose you your net access. Permanently. If you insist on working against ship systems instead of for them, you could find yourself in a world of hurt."

Borsk wanted to punch the guy. Instead he smiled just enough that his teeth showed. "That's why I make a point of working *for* ship systems. And for the restaurant. Which reminds me I'm due out front. If you were looking for my mama, she's probably in her office."

As he left the kitchen, he could feel Lancet's eyes on him. Not a friendly feeling. Not friendly at all.

Chapter Fourteen

Anya spent the weekend avoiding her father and hunting down the other men in her life. The first task was easier to accomplish than she feared—her father worked all weekend. All she had to do was to pretend to sleep in the mornings until after he left and come up with legitimate occupations away from home for the evenings.

Locating Borsk and Ryan proved more troublesome. Borsk disappeared completely on Saturday, and Sarka claimed not to know where he'd gone or when he'd be back. Anya might have waited for him at Skreetches to see when he'd show up—Sarka certainly invited her to. The older girl fired off nosy questions as quickly as she wrapped dumplings, though, and Anya decided to postpone her own questions for Borsk until later. She wanted to ask about cameras, math, and the note she'd wanted him to deliver to Ryan, but that could wait until a Sarka-free moment.

The note worried her. Had Ryan received it? Why hadn't she asked Borsk about it last night, when she had the chance?

Borsk would have told her if it hadn't been delivered, wouldn't he? She was nearly sure. Ryan must have seen it by now. But if so, why hadn't he written back? Anya could only guess that he didn't want to commit himself to any recorded medium. He must intend to answer face-to-face. Time stretched on, though. She'd have to seek Ryan out to learn what he thought of her proposal.

He wasn't hard to find—he was pulling a weekend shift at work, so anybody on *Hope* could locate him just by looking at the duty roster. There'd be no point trying to talk to him there, though. Even if there weren't other crew members around, he'd be recorded, and if there was one thing she'd rather not have on record, it was the talk she hoped to have with Ryan.

With him pulling long shifts and crashing in the crew bunkhouse when he was off duty, she didn't see how it could be arranged. Finally, she resorted to bumping into him accidentally on purpose. She timed her walk home from the library so that she got to the Level 3, West crew station exactly as he was due to get off work on Sunday. By watching closely as soon as the station came in view and modulating her speed, she managed to draw even with it just as he stepped out of the door with a scrawny coworker.

She hadn't counted on an audience. Her mouth felt dry, but she still managed to say, "Lieutenant Lancet." That was all she could come up with? She could kick herself.

It was enough, though. Ryan glanced up. "Miss Cartier. Is something wrong?"

"No, I'm heading home from the library." Now why couldn't she have figured out something that would get them alone?

"Ah. Well, as long as you're here, perhaps you could let your parents know I can't make it for dinner on Wednesday. My unit's been asked to provide security for the Skreetches concerts on Thursday and Friday, and we'll be setting up on Wednesday."

"You're providing security for the Steve Jackson concerts?" A seed of hope sprung up in Anya. If Ryan listened to the concerts, the music might convince him of the worth of the colony. Music spoke to Ryan so much better than she could. She smiled.

"My unit and I, yes. It's nothing personal. The request came in while I was on duty, so I had to respond to it. Your father should understand. All the same, I'm glad I have an excuse not to see him this week. I'm not crazy, like some people who live with him."

"Excuse me?"

"What did you think he'd say when he saw who made the album cover Steve is using?"

Anya's heart sank. So, the album was out. No wonder Ryan didn't want to be at her house right now. He was no fool.

"*You're* Anastasia Cartier?" The skinny guy next to Ryan interrupted her thoughts. "No way. I thought the Skreetches buy-out cost something like fifty thousand credits. And that light sculpture . . ."

"So?"

"I just thought you'd be older, that's all. You must be incredibly brave."

Not brave. Never brave. But the way the guy looked at her made her feel like maybe she could be. She took a deep breath and smiled a challenge at Ryan, even while she kept her eyes on his companion. "I'm old enough to make up my own mind about the Golden Terrace Colony. Old enough to try out, too. You don't happen to be green, do you?"

Ryan's eyes flashed and he clenched his right fist. So, he was angry. Why? Could it be jealousy? She'd directed her comment mainly at the other guy. She wished Ryan would say something, so she had a clue what he was thinking.

He didn't, though. The scrawny guy was the only one who spoke. "Sorry, yellow. Not sure it would be worth risking your father's displeasure anyway. They say the computers planetside will be rudimentary, and the network non-existent."

Ryan chuckled softly.

Anya glared at him. "Fair point. I guess I'll have to look for someone a bit more adventurous and less computer dependent. Evening, gentlemen." She walked off quickly, wondering how she'd managed to mess up a chance to talk with Ryan quite so spectacularly.

"Miss Cartier?" Ryan called after her.

She turned.

"How much money, exactly, is this venture making you?"

She shrugged and turned back around. What an odd question. What was he trying to tell her?

∞ ℝ

Anya's father was waiting for her when she got home.

"You shouldn't joke about joining the colony team," he said, his voice surprisingly non-threatening.

Anya's hands clammed up anyway, and she rubbed them on her pant legs. How had he found out about her conversation so fast? Was he watching her full time now?

At least she'd checked her bank accounts on the way home. In trying to figure out Ryan's comment, she may have found an excuse for her behavior that her father found acceptable—Skreetches had doubled its daily profit since she'd bought her dad's portion. She still wasn't sure why Ryan wanted her to know that—unless he was trying to camouflage her interest in the Golden Terrace Colony as a good business decision. Certainly, that was the only smart way to present it to Father. "I don't see why not. It's remarkably good for business. Have you seen Skreetches' sales numbers since I bought you out? And the projected numbers on the concert? Do you think we could have a really public fight about the colony Thursday afternoon? We could guarantee everybody in the ship cycles through Skreetches while the concert is going."

Father chuffed half a laugh. "I'm glad to see you're developing some business sense. If I'd any idea you had a flair for investment and marketing, I'd have had you in my management training program years ago. I think I can squeeze you in when the next cycle starts a week from tomorrow—at least I can if you pass your math test Thursday."

Anya blanked her face to keep her dismay from showing. Management training for the General Mercantile was the last thing she wanted. She'd flunk her test on purpose—but that would keep her from getting picked for the colony team as well. She sighed. "I'll schedule an extra tutoring session Wednesday night."

"That's the night—"

"The Lancets come over, I know. But I bumped into Ryan on the way home, and he said he's got a work obligation to deal with, and to send you his apologies. I would have thought you knew that if you knew about my comments to his friend."

"Ryan didn't mention it when he called me to discuss his concerns."

Ryan had ratted her out? Her stomach clenched. But he hadn't told Father she wanted to join the colony—even though he knew it. And he seemed to have handled things so that any move she took to support the colony would seem motivated by a desire for better profits on her first investment. Did that mean he wanted to go too, and was handling her father for her?

Father broke into her thoughts. "It would be better for you to be here on Wednesday."

But her best chance of seeing Ryan and figuring all this out before Golden Terrace try-outs was Wednesday—at Skreetches. "I'll do better on my test if I study as close to the time as possible. Besides, I thought maybe you and Mom would like a chance to hang out with just George and Janet." They wouldn't, of course. Her father hated the Lancets, especially George—and only pretended friendship to facilitate the betrothal. But what could he say?

"I don't like it, but you need to pass that test. Make sure you do."

Anya nodded.

"And be more careful how you talk about the colony. Some things are more important than making money."

Her father said that? No way.

"Don't get me wrong. Making money is important—it leads to opportunities and influence. But you've got to think a little about how your influence will be taken. The more people who see that concert, the more will be trying out for spots on the colony team. Do you want to be responsible for blighting the future of an entire generation, just to make a bit of money today?"

Was there a good answer to that? Whatever she said would need to be bold—and to maintain his illusion that she was joking about wanting to join the colony team. Otherwise, his anger would flare. Anya fought to keep her voice steady. "I don't think the colony is taking more than thirty couples. Even if you're right about what Golden Terrace means for people's future, that's hardly a generation. Or were you planning on being vindictive toward anyone who tries out and fails?"

Father's eyes narrowed. "I'm never vindictive. And the fate of this generation depends a great deal on which thirty couples DeLang and his sycophants take. If they convince our best minds to abandon ship for that stupid little hunk of mud, it may as well be an entire generation."

DeLang and his sycophants? Anya hadn't realized before that her father's objection to the colony was personal. She wished she could remind him that his supposed "stupid little hunk of mud" was *Hope*'s destination from the outset. And never vindictive? She wished. Anya smiled as sweetly as she could. "I guess I don't agree about the danger. Whoever goes to the planet, there will be plenty of people—talented people—left here."

"You can't know that, and you ought not gamble with people's lives. One shouldn't tempt brilliant young engineers to try out for jobs that stupid oafs with broad backs can do."

Anya was pretty sure the colony needed more than oafs with broad backs but arguing wouldn't convince her father. "So, I guess that's a 'no' on the big public fight."

"I refuse to be involved with anything that might help that scumbag DeLang or his pet project."

Scumbag? Anya wondered what DeLang had done to her father. She wiped the sweat off her palms again and tried to keep up her smile. "I'm sure no one expects you to help him. The whole ship knows how you feel about the colony."

Father glared at her.

She pressed her hands tighter to her thighs. "Sorry. Didn't mean to annoy you. Mind if I head to my bunk now? If I'm going to pass that algebra test, I'd better start studying now."

"Fine, but no funny business. I'm watching you."

As always. Which was one of the many reasons Anya wasn't joking when she talked about trying out for the colony.

Thank goodness her father thought she was, though. She apparently had Ryan to thank for that.

She really needed to talk to that man.

Chapter Fifteen

he week of Steve Jackson's concerts, Borsk worked so hard in the restaurant that even Sarka paid him a half-hearted compliment. She paused as she passed the table he was bussing. "You've been almost responsible the last few days. What's happened to you?"

Borsk glanced toward the stage where the lights glinted off the gold accents of Lancet's cap. He was definitely close enough to hear. "I decided you were right about Mama needing special consideration this week."

"Yeah, right." Sarka put the back of her hand on his forehead.

Borsk shrugged it off. "I'm fine."

"You haven't slipped away from the restaurant all week."

"I'm getting away from chores tonight for a couple of hours."

Lancet stepped off the stage and approached them. "Did I hear you say you'd be free this evening, Mr. King?"

"He's tutoring his girlfriend," Sarka said. "I'm sure he could put it off a bit if you really need him to."

Borsk scowled at Sarka. Hadn't she figured out yet that he didn't want to help Lancet? "She's not my girlfriend, and she has a test tomorrow. Her messages are starting to sound desperate."

"Only because I've never had a high pass on a math test without extensive studying."

Borsk swung toward the voice. Anya leaned against the next booth. It was way too easy to sneak up on people in this place. "Hi, Anya. I'll be with you in a sec."

"You look busy. If your mom needs you, maybe Lieutenant Lancet could help me. He seems to have finished whatever he was doing by the stage."

Lancet's eyes flashed. "Does your father know you're here?"

Anya broke into a phony-looking smile. "Yes. Actually, he's the one who wants me to do well on the test tomorrow—seems to think it's all I need to get into GenM's management training course."

"Your dad wants you in GenM's management training?" Borsk asked. What was up with that? Even though he'd only been hanging out with Anya a week, he was sure she didn't want to be a GenM manager.

"Someone," Anya directed a pointed look at Lancet, "seems to have convinced him I have a flair for investment and marketing."

"You did an OK job with our ad," Sarka said.

Borsk glared at her.

"See, noticeable skill," Lancet said.

Anya shrugged. "Anyway, Father wants me to pass the test. I'm sure he'd rather you tutor me than Borsk if—"

"I wish I could, but there's a lot more to see to than just the stage." Lancet jerked away from the table.

"At some point we should talk," Anya called after him. "Among other things, I need to know exactly what you've told my father."

Lancet paused. "I'm afraid I'll be busy until after the second concert Friday night, but you can look me up any time after that." He touched his cap and strode off.

"He's checked those pass-throughs to the kitchen twice already," Sarka said.

Anya dropped her smile. "He's very thorough."

And obviously avoiding Anya. Borsk grinned. "Let me get this mess cleared up and I'll be right with you." He hummed, happier than he'd been in days, as he whisked his tray into the kitchen and dropped the dishes into the cleaner. It looked like all he needed to do to avoid Lancet was stick close to Anya. If he'd known that, he would never have spent the last few days slaving away in the kitchens.

☯ ☯

Ryan didn't want to talk until after Friday's concert? Even if she located him the second it ended, she'd have less than a day to persuade him before Colony try-outs began. Maybe it was time to think about somebody else. Past time.

So why was she watching Borsk deal with dirty dishes instead of checking out the personal ads that came with her new Colony-connected bank account?

"You all right?" Borsk asked.

Anya smiled. She must look terrible if Borsk noticed something was off.

She needed to do a better job hiding her feelings.

"Don't want to talk about it here, huh? Come on."

Anya wasn't sure she wanted to talk about it anywhere, but she followed him back to the comfy purple booth-room where they'd talked with his mom. Today a small tower of strawberry plants bloomed on the table. "Beautiful."

"Yeah, Mama thought you'd like that."

"She put it here for me?"

"And because we pulled the screens back on all the first-row private rooms so we could increase main restaurant seating for the concert. Mama didn't want it getting trampled in the chaos. As long as we were moving it anyway, Mama said we should put it in here where you could see it."

Anya's eyes misted. "Tell her thank you for me."

Borsk reddened. "It's nothing."

Great. Last time her gratefulness embarrassed him, he'd been planning to invade her bank accounts. What was he up to now? Or was he still embarrassed about that? Should she ask him? She decided against it. If he was planning something devious, he wouldn't tell her. She scooted into the booth and fingered a smooth strawberry leaf.

Borsk slid in across from her and shut the door behind them. "Lancet's got you upset, hasn't he? Why's the asshole avoiding you?"

"He's not an asshole, and I don't know why he's avoiding me. Maybe he doesn't want to talk about colony try-outs. I know he has other plans for his life—but he's not totally comfortable with my father, and I thought I made a pretty good case for going to Shindashir—or at least making an attempt."

"You did. If he still doesn't want to, maybe you should find somebody else."

She'd been thinking almost the same thing herself, but now that Borsk said it, she realized what a stupid idea it would be. "Who? I don't know anybody green. Even if I did, why would they want to try out with me? I'm not good at math, science, or tech, and I'm on the young, controversial edge of the eligible age spectrum. Chances are, anybody who tried out with me wouldn't make the team, but be stuck here, dealing with my father's wrath."

"Oh, come on, if you didn't make it, what would your dad have to be mad about?"

He thought her father needed a reason? She stared at him, slack jawed.

"Right. Stupid question. Still, you could look around, see if there's someone willing—"

"Sure. Do you know anybody green who's decent enough I might want to hook up with him for life—but enough of a jerk that I can avoid feeling guilty if we don't make the colony team?"

Borsk leaned back in the booth and rubbed his head. "You think *Lancet* is that guy?"

"My father needs Ryan to marry me, so he can't afford to get mad at him if we fail."

"But he's such a—"

"Ryan's decent."

"If you say so."

"Really. He's smart and fair and he has great taste in music, and . . ." She couldn't think of anything else. Spectacular.

"I guess you'll just have to persuade him, then. He'll be here until eleven on Friday. You can catch him as the concert lets out. That gives you three days to perfect your proposal."

Three days. Anya stroked the silky edge of a strawberry blossom and tried not to panic. Three days gave her plenty of time to think of how to persuade Ryan. She'd come up with something. She had to.

Chapter Sixteen

Anya muttered her proposal to Ryan under her breath as she picked her way from one surveillance-free spot to another, following the map Borsk had loaded onto her armband at lunchtime. Her father thought she was at the library.

She hoped.

As she approached Skreetches, the concert was letting out, spilling into the corridors.

Anya hated crowds. Her stomach churned, and she had trouble catching her breath. If it weren't so important to see Ryan—and soon—she'd turn around and go home.

But Ryan was in there, and she needed him. She closed her eyes, took a steadying breath, and squeezed against the flow of people.

Inside, the restaurant was more packed than outside. This kind of crowd had to be against code. But it couldn't be. Ryan would never stand for a code violation, and he had eyes all over this place. Literal eyes—Anya counted three uniforms within paces of her, not a one of them Ryan. Where was he?

Anya stood on tiptoe, holding onto one of the poles that supported the ceiling, so she wouldn't get knocked over by the people surging toward the exit. At first, she couldn't see any sign of Ryan. Then she caught a glimpse of light flashing against white-gold hair. That had to be him. She wove her way under and between bodies until she was close enough to call out, "Ryan!"

He looked around, scowling. She'd forgotten he didn't want her to call him by his first name in public.

Before she could worry too much, the woman next to him turned, too.

"Anastasia Cartier. I thought I recognized that voice."

Anya smiled and held out a hand, frantically trying to remember where she'd met this woman before. Fortunately, before they finished a warm hand-shake, she remembered. The woman from the bathroom last week. The law-yer. What was her name? Leila? No. Laura. "Hi, Laura," she said.

The woman smiled. "Sweetheart, when I saw Steve's album cover, I was amazed. An artist of that caliber on *Hope* in our lifetime? And then I realized I'd met you and how young you are. Incredible."

Borsk elbowed his way to her side. "Nothing compared to what she's been working on this week."

"No," Anya said, but Ryan's image sprang from Borsk's armband before she'd half said the word.

At least it wasn't the ferocious version she'd done last week. As soon as Borsk returned it to her and hacked her back into her art software, she'd started tinkering with it. Every time she got stuck in her colony-proposal for Ryan, she worked on the portrait, creating a vision for herself of what Ryan could be if he went to the planet with her. Now her portrait had him building a library. Still full of icy fire, he now focused his unyielding will on creating a civilization.

Laura whistled, and several people near them turned to look.

"Borsk!" Anya said.

"If she didn't give you permission to show that, turn it off now," Laura said in a voice that could stop the ship turning.

The image flicked off, and at a glare from Laura, the strangers who had stopped to look cleared away. "I guess I don't need to ask if you two are con-sidering trying out for the Golden Terrace team," Laura said.

Ryan smiled, but his eyes stayed grim.

"I haven't quite convinced Ryan," Anya said.

"Then why not ask someone closer to your age?"

"Borsk isn't my color, and I don't much like any of the other boys my age." Anya thought of DeShawn and grimaced. Of course, he wasn't her color either.

Laura laughed.

So did Ryan. "Let's talk about it at lunch tomorrow. Here would be better than your place, don't you think?"

Any place would be better than her house. But lunch? "Tryouts start to-morrow evening. What about breakfast?"

He smiled at her. "I've got something I need to take care of in the morn-ing, but the discussion shouldn't take that long."

He sounded almost like he'd decided to go with her, and she wished she could see his eyes better, so she knew how serious he was. "But part of the test is what you pack—they look at what you'd take for the trip."

"You haven't packed already?"

Ryan sounded surprised. Did he imagine Anya would pack without some reason to believe he'd go with her?

Maybe he'd already given her reason to believe, and she'd just missed it. "I'll go do it now," she said.

Ryan nodded and smiled at her. The smile felt a bit condescending, but who cared? He thought she should pack for colony tryouts.

She couldn't quite believe this was happening. She hadn't even used her spiel.

— —

Borsk blocked two foreign queries on Skreetches' in-house video logs before Anya made it to the door. Damn, her father was paranoid.

"What did I tell you about messing with ship systems, Mr. King?" Lancet said.

Borsk wished the lieutenant had left when Anya and Laura Wilcox had. "What makes you think I am?"

Lancet served Borsk's armband with an official request for Borsk's activity log for the last five minutes. Borsk let it go without alteration. He hadn't been doing anything illegal—or even suspect—not in the last five minutes anyway. Besides, if Lancet dug deeply enough, he might find proof of Thomas Cartier shoving his nose where it didn't belong.

Lancet grunted. "You're walking a very fine line here."

"Shove it. I'm protecting my family restaurant from outside threats. You think you're the only security they count on—or even the best?"

"And that picture you stole—did Miss Cartier even know you had it?"

Borsk rolled his eyes. "Are you mad because people saw what you could be and aren't?"

"Stealing valuable artwork is a felony."

"Anya gave me permission to copy her work." Borsk played back a holo of Anya saying "I don't mind you having a copy of this—or any of my art."

"And what did you do to get that?"

"Admired the piece she was working on. Surely you've noticed how well she responds when people genuinely like her work."

"I wouldn't know."

Hadn't the asshole ever praised even one of her pieces? "You should try it sometime. No telling what you might get." Borsk turned away to clear the table next to them.

"The concert's over." Lancet sounded like he expected something from

Borsk.

"And now we clean up. Are you helping?"

"I have other work to do—and so do you, as soon as you're done here."

Anya couldn't afford for the cameras to go back to her father's control yet. "I'm not sure when—"

"Tomorrow at lunch time with Miss Cartier will be soon enough. I'm sure you can get things put back together by then."

"But don't you want . . ."

Ryan walked off before Borsk could finish ". . . your meeting with her to be private?"

🙳 🙵

The morning of Golden Terrace Colony tryouts, Anya brought her backpack to the greenhouses when she went in for a morning shift. Her father wouldn't have access to her pack if it sat in Mr. Greeley's locker all day, and she could easily retrieve it if—when—she and Ryan tried out. The Golden Terrace leadership team had reclaimed a large area in this sector for their testing center, bringing enough new materials back from their exploration of the surface to stabilize it.

Mr. Greeley kept her busy, perhaps recognizing that if she had time to slow down or work on art, she might cry. If she and Ryan made the Colony team, she wouldn't be back here much, and she'd miss it. In fact, the greenhouses might be the only place she'd miss.

Superwheat supports—tomato harvesting—Anya didn't have a moment to slow down until it was time to check on her experimentals.

Nothing in the sterile lab environment encouraged her to linger, but the B-9s were ready to harvest. She stripped the ugly little plants of their pods and did a full nutritional analysis. Mr. Greeley came in as she finished.

"What have we got here?"

"I just put in my report—you should have a copy of the results."

Mr. Greeley tapped on his armband a couple of times, then grunted. "A glowing success. Low-light, quick-grow, calorie-dense, complete protein. So how do they taste?"

Anya wrinkled her nose. "I'm afraid to try. They smell awful."

Mr. Greeley chuckled. "You never know. They might surprise us. Better to have a complete report anyway." He scooped up a handful of the beans, dropped them in a bowl, and speed cooked them for four minutes. While they waited, he showed Anya how to preserve sample seeds for storage. "One for the lab, one for the greenhouses, and one for you."

"But I don't think . . ." Anya stared down at the shiny, seed-filled envelope Mr. Greeley had pressed into her hand. "I mean—"

"You never know when one of these things might come in handy—and rights that aren't exercised disappear."

"Sorry?"

"Did you know that *Hope*'s charter grants every person aboard the right to a garden?"

"I've seen that, but—"

"A couple hundred years of non-use and gardens disappeared with hardly a murmur. Now all we've got is the right for a new strain-developer to keep a little seed-stock without it counting against their organic allowance. You'll keep this, child."

"Yes, Mr. Greeley." Anya stowed it in her colony pack, which had more space than her pockets.

"What's that, girl?"

"Maybe nothing. But I'm talking with a guy about trying out for Golden Terrace."

"Let me see that."

Anya handed the pack over and closed her eyes as the old man rummaged through it, grunting occasionally. She hoped that meant he approved of her choices.

"What's on the memory chips?" he asked.

"Grandma's art collection, my library, a couple of ancient Earth books on cooking with primitive equipment—and on something they called camping."

Mr. Greeley grunted again. "Not bad. I think you could live without the doll, but perhaps by the time you're old enough to figure that out, you'll have a little one of your own to give it to."

A little one of her own? Anya was so not ready for that.

Mr. Greeley chuckled. "Never mind. Why didn't you pack your sampler?"

Anya glanced at the chemical analysis tool she'd left on the counter by the cooker, which was flashing. "The B-9s are finished."

"Don't change the subject, girl. Why didn't you pack your sampler? It would come in handy sorting edible from inedible indigenous organisms."

"You need it in the lab."

"You'll need it more at Golden Terrace, and Charles DeLang's budget is even leaner than mine."

"Mr. Greeley, I'm not even sure I have a try-out partner, and I'm not very good at school—the important parts anyway. They probably won't take me."

"You have a green thumb, a kind heart, and an inquiring mind. Unless I'm very much mistaken, DeLang and his team know how to recognize and properly appreciate all three. Pack the sampler."

"Yes, sir."

"Then we can celebrate your coming of age by trying those beans."

Anya didn't know how much influence Mr. Greeley had with the colony team, but his insistence encouraged her. She smiled as she stowed the sampler in her pack and the pack in the locker.

When she returned, Mr. Greeley handed her a bowl full of dusty brown B9s. They smelled as foul as the plant had looked, and Anya limited her first spoonful to a single bean. Once it was in her mouth, she regretted even that much. She wished she could spit the thing back out.

Mr. Greeley spewed his bite onto the floor and made a face. "Bleurgh. I've tasted ferto I'd rather have in my mouth. Those things might sustain a person for a month, but who'd want to live that way? I hope you're getting a decent lunch."

Anya laughed. "Skreetches. Which reminds me, I'd better get going. Are you OK?"

"Go—go. I'll get rid of this mess."

"Are you sure?"

Mr. Greeley shooed her out the door so fast, she didn't have time to worry about meeting Ryan.

Chapter Seventeen

When Anya arrived at Skreetches, freshly scrubbed and in a clean uniform, she found the place almost as packed as it had been after the concert. A harried-looking middle-aged woman with the name "Ketzia" embroidered over her shirt pocket stood at the hostess desk.

Anya smiled tentatively at the woman. "Hi, I'm—"

"Anya!" Sarka bustled over. "Right on time! I've got this one, Ketzia."

"Sarka, you know we don't have room for your parade of free-loaders today."

"Anastasia Cartier is not a freeloader," Sarka said, shaking her glossy black curls. It was the first time Anya had seen them without a hairnet. Wasn't Sarka working today, then?

"Come on, Anya." Sarka tugged on her arm. "You can sit over by the kitchen window with me and Borsk."

"But—" Anya didn't particularly want Borsk, let alone Sarka, hearing her conversation with Ryan.

"Best I can do for you today. Besides, your security man wants to talk to Borsk too."

Ryan wanted to meet with Borsk? What for? And wouldn't he want to do that privately? Or at least talk to her privately? The twirling worries caused a headache just behind her eyes. She wanted to close them but couldn't. Not with Sarka half-dragging her through a maze of round tables and wide posts.

They wound their way around the stage and under the left wing of the adult balcony to a booth near the pass-through window to the kitchen. An overpowering smell of sweet-potatoes deep-frying made Anya instantly hungry, while the clatter of dishes and rattle of cooking machines blocked out most other noise. Anya felt sorry for anyone who might have been sitting here during the concert, but she thought it would do nicely for her talk with Ryan. They probably wouldn't be overheard—she might have trouble hearing Ryan herself. And there was good artwork on the wall at the back of the booth—an unsigned hall-style painting in vivid colors.

"I like the energy," Anya shouted, nodding towards it.

"I guess." Sarka let go of her arm and shoved Borsk over so that she could fit next to him, leaving the other bench for Anya.

"Sarka, don't you have somewhere to be?" Borsk asked.

Anya smiled. She didn't really want either of them there, but if she had to choose one, she'd pick Borsk.

"You know Mama gave all my weekend hours to Ketzia. Medical bills and whatnot."

Borsk rolled his eyes. "OK, but—"

"But nothing. There is nowhere else for me to go."

As if to confirm this, Ketzia stumped over to them and whisked plates of food onto the table. "Try to be quick today, would you? We've got a zillion people in here wanting to talk about the colony thing."

"*We're* talking about the colony thing," Borsk said.

"No way can your mama spare either of you."

"Anya's going to try out for Golden Terrace," Borsk said.

"Please. Anya and who else?"

"Ryan Lancet," Borsk said.

"Actually, he should be here any minute now, and he doesn't like mushroom wraps. Could we possibly get him a pinehurst and tumbler? I can p—"

"You don't pay here," Sarka said. "Mama made that very clear."

"Right," Ketzia said. "When you lot stop fooling around, clear out of here, would you? I've got work to do." She swung back toward the hostess desk.

When she was out of earshot, Sarka leaned forward. "Are you serious about testing, Anya?"

"Absolutely. I'm dying to go."

"Bad enough you'll put up with Lancet?" Borsk asked.

"There's nothing wrong with Ryan." Anya picked up one of the mushroom wraps.

"Nothing. Except he's an uptight pure-Euro asshole. Last week he tried to make me get rid of my dreads. I had to invoke the code."

"New experiences are broadening for the mind," Ryan said as he slid into the booth next to Anya. She choked on her bite of mushroom and coughed into a napkin.

"Lancet," Borsk said.

"So, you're going to try out for the colony team?" Sarka asked.

Ryan glared at Sarka. "No. I came to tell Stace that we're not trying out for Golden Terrace."

"What?" Anya could barely think, let alone get words out. "But you said—"

"That we'd talk about it today. Last night was not the time."

And he thought this was talking? Where was that little speech she had prepared? She couldn't remember a single word. The only thing to come out of her mouth was, "You said I should pack."

"I said I figured you'd packed already. Hadn't you? You've been way more focused on this crazy scheme than is good for you."

"But—"

"Look, Stace," Ryan lowered his voice, so Anya had to lean toward him to hear what he said. "It's bad enough I'm stuck with a kid whose chief interests are mud and doll babies."

And art—Anya thought, but she couldn't make a sound.

"I'm not ruining my career as well."

"We could at least try."

"Forget it. I'm aiming for Captain Bates's job when he retires, and I'm on track if Roger Wilcox grants this next promotion."

"Laura Wilcox's husband?" Anya asked.

"Yes. And that reminds me. Do *not* call me Ryan when I'm on duty."

Anya stared at him, stunned. He said he'd talk to her, and instead did this?

"Glad we got that cleared up. I have places to be, and so do you, Mr. King. If you continue to show so little interest in your Camp Flight duties, I'm afraid I'll need to have that talk with your mother." Ryan stood up, barely avoiding Ketzia, who was shepherding a foursome to a table.

"I'll have that pinehurst and tumbler out in a jiff," she said.

"Don't bother, I'm not staying," Ryan said. "Coming Mr. King?"

"When I've finished my lunch and restaurant chores," Borsk said.

"You want to be very, very careful, Mr. King."

Anya didn't know what was going on, but she didn't much like the sound of it.

"If you're not eating, you should leave, Lieutenant Lancet," Sarka said, her voice hard. She rose and looked Ryan directly in the eye.

"Miss King, your brother—"

"Told you he'd come by when he was finished here. Do you need help finding the exit?"

Anya almost smiled. She'd never liked Sarka quite as much as she did at that moment.

"Of course not." Ryan clenched his fist. "I'll see you this afternoon, Mr. King. No later than fifteen hundred hours." He turned on his heel and strode out of the restaurant, as straight as could be managed around the closely packed tables.

Sarka sat back down. "Pure-Euro asshole doesn't begin to describe that jerk's issues. You're better off without him, Anya."

Anya felt herself smiling the humorless smile her mother always wore when Father had been particularly brutal. "It's nothing. I misunderstood."

She picked up a crisp and ate it mechanically. She didn't taste it, though. If those dark spots on the edges meant it was burnt, that might be just as well.

She kept smiling until Sarka found an excuse to leave.

Borsk leaned over the table toward her. "Are you OK?"

Anya nodded. It was a lie, of course. She could see her life stretching forward bleak and uninterrupted. She'd be trapped forever on this ship with a man who hated her greenhouse work and who couldn't bother to remember she was an artist.

She'd be trapped forever in her mother's smile.

ɉ Ƀ

Anya wasn't sure how long she'd been sitting in the booth, numbly munching her crisps and mushroom wrap unaware of the world around her. She was surprised Borsk had bothered to stay with her, but when an angry buzz of conversation brought the world back to her attention, there he was, across from her, sitting still, not even tapping on his armband.

Anya caught his eye and tried to make her smile a bit happier.

From the booth next to theirs, Shilana Young's voice rose above the general discontent. "That's the worst idea I've heard in my whole life." Shilana appeared suddenly in the aisle. "Forget it." She stomped toward the entrance.

DeShawn popped out of the booth behind her. "Shilana, wait!"

"What's the worst idea she's ever heard?" Anya asked Borsk.

"He wants to try out for Golden Terrace. She doesn't."

"Sure it's Golden Terrace and not DeShawn she wants to keep away from?"

"Pretty sure. They've been going out, so she must think DeShawn is OK."

Anya made a face.

Borsk laughed.

At a table across the aisle from them, Gabrielle Martin stood up, the better to shout at Robert Dahl. He stood up and shouted back. Even if Anya had known the language they were speaking, she might not have understood them, they yelled the staccato words so rapidly.

Anya leaned toward Borsk. "It's getting really intense in here."

"Yeah, Lancet's jab at you is sounding more and more refined and private all the time."

For three seconds, Anya had forgotten Ryan. Now tears swam to her eyes, and she fought them back.

"Sorry."

Anya shook her head. "It won't help to pretend it didn't happen. Give me a second to pull myself together, and we can go."

Borsk nodded.

Across from them, Gabrielle flounced out, and Robert sat back down.

In the lull that followed, a high-pitched voice rose. "You thought *I'd* go live somewhere that doesn't even have private quarters?"

Anya looked up. She knew that voice but couldn't quite see the right wing of the adult balcony, where it was coming from.

Before she could recall who sounded like that, another voice responded, "You promised you'd at least try."

Anya knew that voice too—it had shouted at her from darkness, half frightening her out of her wits. The guy who'd given her a detention—and had the guts to go through with it. David Ryerson. Too bad he was having a fight with his girlfriend. And from the silence around her, she guessed she wasn't the only one listening in.

"That was before I saw the specs," the woman said in carrying tones, almost as if she wanted people listening. What did she think this was—a performance?

"You knew—" David said.

"I had no *idea* it would be so primitive," the woman said, projecting as though she were on Skreetches' stage instead of at one of the tables. That thought helped Anya remember who owned the voice. Leslie Wang, star of the last five *Hope* Theater productions. Well, perhaps she was so used to an audience that she couldn't help herself.

"We talked about—" David said.

"We talked about a house of our own. Not a lodge with the whole colony. I can't believe there's even one woman willing to put up with the conditions, let alone twenty or more."

"Really? Would you like to test that?"

"Excuse me?"

David raised his voice. "Is there any eligible woman from the green reproductive group who'd be willing to try out for Golden Terrace with me?"

Green? He'd said green. If Anya spoke up, maybe she could still go—if

Leslie still refused, and she and this David could make the team. But it seemed like David was just trying to persuade Leslie to go.

"Anyone?" David repeated. He sounded as desperate as Anya felt.

"I'm green," she said. Her voice sounded loud in the silent restaurant, and way too many pairs of eyes turned her way. Cameras too, probably. Well, she was in it now.

She stood up, wound her way around the tables and support poles until she got near the stage, and looked up into the adult balcony, where a handsome, medium brown man with black curls leaned over the railing. A quick ID check confirmed he was David Ryerson. If Anya had realized he was so good looking, she might have been even more afraid to say anything. No way was Mr. Gorgeous giving up Leslie Wang for her.

"Are you the one who said you're green?" he asked.

Anya held up her left hand, palm out, so the green light showed.

"And you're old enough to try out?"

Anya's mouth felt dry, but she managed to say, "Fifteen last January."

"Then I guess we should talk." David vaulted over the railing and landed lightly on his toes in a bare space between the tables nearest her. He was even better looking up close, with black velvet eyes that twinkled as if the two of them were sharing some private joke.

Anya tried to smile.

"David, don't be ridiculous," Leslie called, as she stalked to the balcony stairs. "You can't honestly imagine pairing up with that child."

"No?" David said. He leaned toward Anya. She stepped backward, only to find her way blocked by one of the balcony supports.

David took a step forward and rested his hands on the post on either side of her head.

Her heart sped up with a mixture of fear and attraction. She wanted more space. "I'm—"

He interrupted her with a kiss.

Her first ever.

She forgot what she was going to say.

His lips were gentle, and he carried with him a clean, fresh scent that reminded her of sitting beneath the oxy-trees. Someone who smelled like that couldn't be all bad, could he? She closed her eyes, so she could concentrate on the feeling of his mouth against hers, his warmth surrounding her, making her feel safe.

Not that she was, she realized when Leslie's voice broke in. "Oh very, very cute. Even you can't pretend you're enjoying that."

Anya opened her eyes and tried to pull back, but David kissed her for a long moment more before pulling away. Anya gasped for breath.

"It wasn't bad," he said with a wink at Anya, "and I suspect it would get better with time."

"Please. She's pure-Euro. Those girls don't even get undressed for bed. Besides, she's betrothed to Ryan Lancet."

How on *Hope* could Leslie know that? Anya's hands shook, but she still managed to sound calm as she said, "Betrothal is illegal."

"So's underage drinking. Doesn't mean it doesn't happen."

David stepped farther from Anya and raised his eyebrows.

She supposed he wanted to know if the accusation was true. He probably wasn't the only one wondering, either. She had to get people thinking about something else, but she couldn't get her own mind off the question of how Leslie knew. In her head, Anya zipped through the people who knew about the betrothal—Borsk and his mom wouldn't have said anything—they could lose the restaurant. Her parents and Ryan's mom could lose so much more. Which only left her—and Ryan.

Ryan had told Leslie about the betrothal?

Why would he do that?

Then it hit her. Knowledge that seemed to come with her mother's smile—a part of her that hadn't existed this morning. Ryan would only have told Leslie about the betrothal if he and she were . . . .. Anya couldn't even finish the thought in her mind. In a strange voice that didn't sound like her at all, she said, "Ryan Lancet told you he was betrothed to me?" She forced out a giggle. "What was he trying to do—get you to sleep with him without the bother of a relationship?"

"You little bitch!" Leslie's hand whipped out, and hot pain seared across Anya's left cheek.

David forced his way between the two of them, and half a dozen people at nearby tables jumped to their feet.

Anya held up her hand. "It's OK. Nothing. I'm not hurt. No offense taken." She leaned around David to lock eyes with Leslie. "We'll stay out of each other's way."

Leslie glared, but gave them space as Anya reached down, grabbed David's hand, and led him from the restaurant.

Chapter Eighteen

Anya wasn't sure where to go, so she led David toward Central Park. Halfway there, he stopped and dropped her hand. She figured he'd leave at that point, but instead, he opened a service hatch and ushered her into a small alcove filled with a tangle of brightly colored wires. Then he squeezed in after her, tapped something on his armband that made the lights come up, and pulled the panel shut on them.

His presence filled the space, making Anya realize for the first time how big he was. Her mind flitted back to the sensation of his lips on hers, and her heart sped up. She ordered herself to calm down. David had only kissed her to make Leslie jealous. He didn't show any signs of wanting her now. In fact, he slumped against the opposite wall of the conduit, eyes closed, looking deeply weary. Definitely not amorous. Anya took two deep, steadying breaths.

"You know," David said before she worked up the nerve to speak, "We'd been going out for a year and a half."

Anya closed her eyes against the pain in his voice. "Sorry."

"Better to find out now than after we're married, right?"

"Maybe she—"

"Wasn't sleeping with other guys? Then why'd she slap you? Besides, she'd already reneged on her promise to go to the colony."

Anya tried another deep breath. It didn't steady her much, but she managed to open her eyes so she could see David when she asked him, "Then you'll consider trying out with—"

"Kid, I want to go to the colony, but I can't afford to be anybody's declaration of independence. If I don't make the Golden Terrace Team, I've still got to work in this place."

Anya nodded. Her eyes filled with tears, but she fought them back. "I have to go to the planet. I've dreamt of living among flowers . . . and trees. But R—my first choice of partner won't go with me. I shouldn't have involved you, but you sounded so . . . Anyway, I had no idea Leslie would . . ."

"You're telling me the betrothal is real?" David laughed hollowly. "Of course, it is. Lancet thinks too much of himself to lie to a woman just to get her into bed. I'm so screwed." David rubbed his temples.

"If we make the Golden Terrace team—"

"We'll be OK, but my family—"

"I can pay for start-up supplies—yours and mine. So, your full compensation package can go to your family. You'll make an A salary, right? So that should keep them current enough on their bills that Father can't—"

"Kid, colony start-up supply lists start at twenty-thousand credits."

"Even after the Skreetches buyout, I should be able to swing two. Barely."

"We need three. I've got a dependent."

"You have a kid?" Anya whispered. "Why isn't the mom—"

"Not a kid. My gran. She'll never see the planet if she doesn't go now. She was going to sell her place in Sigmore to pay for this, but if we're blacklisted—"

"No one will buy." Anya thought for a minute. "OK. So, her set-up comes out of your comp, and we send mine back to your family. The specs suggested we wouldn't need much to live on."

"That's very generous. What about the extra kid benefits? My sister Joyce would really like at least one extra, but if we need to take the pressure off . . ."

Anya envisioned Kenneth forcing extra kids on Kristi and shuddered. "Joyce can have both. Really. It's better that way."

David stared at her. His forehead crinkled for a long moment. Then his forehead smoothed. "You're Kristi Llourdes's sister. Yeah, Joyce gets both kids."

Not many people made that connection. Kristi was so much older, and Kenneth kept her pretty isolated. But David would have gone to school with her. Anya hoped they hadn't had a fling. She loved Kristi, and was happy to have her leftover clothes, but a leftover boyfriend?

A buzzer on David's armband sounded. He glanced down. "Shit. Leak in the blue layer on Level Three. That has to be fixed, and I'm on call until six. Here."

He tapped on his left forearm, and an address showed up on Anya's armband screen.

"That's my gran's place. You'll need to tell her we're trying out together. I don't know if I'll have time after this job. We can all meet up at the testing center at seven. And tell your parents. I think there's some clause in the contract about minor applicants having to inform guardians. I don't want to get this and then lose it on some technicality." He maneuvered them out of the maintenance alcove, refastened the panel, and brushed a sweet-smelling kiss across her lips. "We're going to make it."

They had to. The alternatives were too awful to contemplate.

Anya couldn't keep them out of her mind, though. She watched David stride toward the level stairs, wishing she could be so confident.

℘   ℭ

When Leslie slapped Anya, Borsk watched the net traffic in Skreetches go wild, and there wasn't a thing he could do to stop it—not without losing his net privileges. Permanently.

Unless his interference didn't directly affect the security feeds. He typed furiously on his armband.

Sarka appeared at his elbow. "Borsk, what should we do?"

He turned, so she couldn't see what he was up to and typed in the last bit of code.

Seconds later a fryer in the kitchen buzzed. Perfect. That meant a new cycle would be starting, and with the way he'd rerouted the power supply—

Something crackled and all the lights and mechanical sounds in the place shut down.

Silence.

Then backup generators kicked in, and a roar of shouts rose simultaneously with the house lights.

Borsk could only hear Sarka's "Borsk, what did you do?" because she shouted it in his ear.

"Not here," he shouted back.

She grabbed him by the upper arm and dragged him toward the stage, but Uncle Hirsch got there before they did. He stood tall, letting a full ladle drip something greasy onto the floor, as he gave a deep-voiced, soothing recitation of the restaurant's safety features and back-up systems.

The crowd quieted.

Borsk leaned toward Sarka. "He doesn't need us."

Sarka stared for a moment at Uncle Hirsch, then nodded and pulled Borsk toward the kitchen.

They found Mama in her alcove office, filling out forms on the main screen and two smaller ones.

"Mama, Borsk just—"

"Not now, Sarka. Something just short-circuited the system and even working fast, it'll take me half an hour to get all the reports down to operations.

And the video logs wouldn't go to security until operations was through with them. Well, at least he had bought Anya a bit of time. Borsk smiled. "Yeah, sorry about that."

Mama pulled away from the wall screen and turned around. "Borsk, what have you done?"

"I was tinkering with the wires, trying to find a more optimal configuration, and it just—"

"Borsk!" Sarka glared at him.

"Yeah, I know I should wait to do experiments like that until the restaurant isn't busy, but—"

Mama sighed. "All right, you two. Thank you for telling me. Now is there anything else?"

"Actually, yes. Lancet's been a pain. He's pressuring me to fix some code that I'm pretty sure helps Anya's dad illegally spy on her. Lancet's expecting me to report at three, but I'm going to turn in my resignation to Camp Flight instead."

"That's what Lancet's been on you all week about?" Sarka said. "I should hope you're turning in your resignation. I don't know why you even bothered to sign up in the first place."

Borsk winked at Mama. "Stupid, I know. But here's the thing. If I resign, Lancet's planning on coming down here and telling Mama about that hack when I was twelve."

"What? No. How does he know about that anyway?"

Mama rubbed her temples. "What are you two talking about?"

"I ran into Old Doc Norman about a week ago. When you had me run those deliveries at lunch. Remember, Mama? When I got there, Lancet was already down there investigating a complaint, and while we were both there, Old Doc Norman suggested that he'd helped interpret my gene records for me."

"He couldn't have," Mama said. "I had your records sealed. Yours and Sarka's both. Even I don't know what's in them."

Borsk caught Mama's eyes and held them until her eyebrows rose and her mouth made a little "o" of understanding. Borsk dropped his eyes.

Mama turned to Sarka. "You knew about this and didn't tell me?"

"She didn't have anything to do with it, Mama. She only knows about it because one time when she was stressing about the delta-zed gene, I showed her she didn't have it." Yelled at her to stop whining, she had nothing to worry about was more like the truth, but Sarka was kind enough not to correct him.

He took a deep breath. "Anyway, it's not Sarka's fault. It's all mine. You should probably ground me or something, but not until I find Anya, OK? I think she's going to need some help."

Mama glared. "Borsk—"

Sarka broke in, "Anya probably does need help, Mama. Did you see the security feed before the power went out?"

Mama pinched her lips together and shook her head.

"Leslie Wang slapped Anya. Slapped her face. Then Anya left with Leslie's boyfriend."

"Leslie's boyfriend?"

"David Ryerson," Borsk said. "They were talking about trying out for Golden Terrace."

Mama stared at him, blinking, for a long moment. Then she shoved him toward the trade entrance of the restaurant. "Go. I'll deal with you later. Sarka, come help me with these reports."

"But, Mama, I've never done them before. I'll slow you down."

"You have to learn sometime. It won't hurt operations to get these filed a few minutes later than usual."

"A few minutes? I'll be lucky to finish in an hour."

Borsk smiled to himself as he made his way to the back door. An hour or more of delay was better than he'd been hoping for.

All the same, he wondered if it would be enough.

℠ ℞

Anya stared at the address David had given her without seeing it.

A woman passed by, staring, and Anya realized she had to move. The longer she held still, the easier it would be for her father to find her. No doubt someone had told him about the restaurant by now. Unless Skreetches had been so packed with Golden Terrace supporters, none of them would report her actions to her father.

Yeah, who was she fooling? He was sure to know.

She breathed in deep and moved toward the level stairs, so focused on making forward progress that she bumped into Borsk.

"Anya! I've been looking everywhere. Hey, are you OK? Where's David?"

Anya dragged out her worn smile. "I'm fine. And David is . . ." She'd forgotten exactly what David said he was going to do. ". . . fixing something."

"Figures. The genius can fix anything. Does that mean you two are trying out together?"

"Would you mind not shouting? I'm sure my father—"

"Sorry." Borsk lowered his voice. "But are you?"

Anya nodded.

"Excellent. So, what now? Hide until the start time?"

Wouldn't that be nice? Borsk could find somewhere her father wouldn't know about if anybody could. But first she had to find David's grandma and inform her parents she was testing. She wasn't sure how she'd manage the notification without messing everything up, but first things first. "Do you know where Sigmore Landing is?"

"Sure, but you can't think hiding there is a good idea. They might not have many working screens, but—"

"David wants his grandma to come along, so I have to tell her to get ready."

"You ever been to Sigmore Landing?"

"No."

"I'll go with you. It's a little scary the first time."

Scary? Anya knew it was a bad neighborhood, but how awful could it be? Not that it would hurt to have Borsk along. "Thanks." She straightened her uniform and took a deep breath. "There. I'm ready."

But she wasn't. Not for Sigmore Landing. Not for the grime on the walls. Not for the dimness of the light. Not for the stench of close-packed human bodies. And especially not for the miniscule cubby holes that counted as quarters. Most of them were no larger than her bunk.

She was glad Borsk had come with her even if the halls were now so narrow that they had to walk single file. She wished she'd taken him up on his offer to go first.

From pocket-sized communal kitchens and filthy lounges, conversation drifted out. The words were from a dialect Anya didn't know, or perhaps several dialects she didn't know. Every time she got close to a doorway, the voices hushed, and didn't pick up again until she was well past.

Anya tried to control the panic rising in her throat. Labeling it irrational silliness didn't help. Fear—her fear, anyway—couldn't be reasoned with.

Mrs. Ryerson wasn't in her quarters, which wasn't surprising, given that no normal-sized adult could have sat upright in them.

"Where do you suppose she is?" Anya asked.

Borsk shrugged. "Let's try this section's lounge." He led the way to a tiny open space where a broken wall screen loomed over six women, all of them ancient. Four sat at a rickety table playing mahjong. Another sat on a bench against the side wall, knitting a sweater, and the sixth leaned in a corner. All fell silent when Borsk and Anya approached.

"You gringos lost?" one of the women asked.

Anya's words stuck in her throat.

"Nah," Borsk said. "*Jiao ren*. Abuela Ryerson."

"Who's asking?" the woman on the far side of the table said. She was a tall woman, yellow-brown, with flesh that hung loose on sharply angled bones. Her eyes were deep-set, and she fixed them on Anya with an unfriendliness that bordered on hostility.

Anya gulped and then found her voice. "I'm Anya Cartier—that is, Anastasia." The woman's stare unnerved her. She started again. "David had to go repair . . ." What was it he'd said?

Borsk tapped on his armband. "The blue layer on Level Three. So, he asked Anya here to come tell his grandma that they're testing tonight. Isn't that right, Anya?"

Anya nodded. "We're supposed to meet at the testing center at seven."

"Why couldn't he send his girlfriend to do it? She afraid to get her pretty hands dirty?" the woman in the corner asked.

"I'm testing with him," Anya said. She wished she could make herself sound less whimpery.

"You putting me on, girl?" asked the woman with the knitting—a short dark woman with closely-cropped white hair. "We know the boy has a fetish for light skin, but this is ridiculous."

"And he'd never touch any chick that wasn't pretty—could you imagine it?" The mahjong player to their left laughed.

"The pretty girls won't go to the planet." Anya's fight to keep tears out of her voice made her sound angrier than she wanted to. "So, he's stuck with me. I'm sure he could do better with more time, but he hasn't got it."

"Lucky for him," Borsk said. "Leslie Wang hardly passed high school, let alone tests like the A-16. But Anya's grades are respectable. Great in some subjects."

Not the ones that counted. Anya hung her head.

"What did you get last mods?" the tall woman demanded.

Anya jerked her head upward. Mod scores were supposed to be private. No one, not even her parents, had asked her before (not that her parents needed to ask).

Everyone else around the table looked at her like they expected an answer, though. Her cheeks got hot. "93 technical, 92 math, 99 arts," she muttered.

The tall woman grunted. "That'll do, I guess. I'll be there tonight. See that you're on time."

Anya gulped, nodded, and backed up, nearly hitting the corridor wall behind her.

Borsk steadied her. "Thanks so much, Abuela Ryerson."

"I'm not your grandma," the woman said. "Nor hers neither if she don't perform up to scratch."

"Got it," Borsk said. "We'll get out of your hair."

The tall woman's glare followed them down the corridor. Anya had to force herself not to run.

Chapter Nineteen

By the time she and Borsk made it back to familiar corridors, Anya's hands were trembling and slippery. She wasn't sure whether she was reacting to the encounter with David's grandma or her worry about telling her parents her decision. Maybe it was both. She wiped her hands on her pant legs.

"Where to now?" Borsk asked.

"David said something about informing my parents. I can send a legal document, but since it's Saturday, they could pretend they hadn't read it."

"I could track when they read it."

"Legally?"

"Well . . ."

"Borsk, this has to stick. I should probably send a document to each of them and inform them in person as well. On record, if I can manage it. Where are my parents now?"

"Give me a second."

While Borsk tapped away at his armband, Anya found the documents she'd need for official notification of her intent to try out for the Golden Terrace colony team. Filling it out only took a few moments. Figuring out when and how to send it might be tougher. She needed to give her parents enough notice so that her try-out would be legal, but not so much that they could stop her. Of course, they might already suspect something after that debacle in Skreetches, in which case, they were already plotting how to stop her, and sooner might be better.

"Looks like your dad's at a small GenM store on Level Eight, and your mom's at home."

"Makes sense. Mom had a late shift last night and Father often tours stores on Saturday afternoons." Anya thought for a minute. "I'll head home and tell Mom first. Even if she messages the news to Father, he won't look at it until he's done with his tour. He never interrupts business for personal stuff."

"When will you tell him?"

"When he gets to the GenM flagship on One in about an hour. There should be plenty of video feeds in there, but if you could show up with your recorder on, it would make me feel a lot more secure."

"No problem. Do you want me to come with you when you tell your mom, too?"

Anya considered it. "No. The house surveillance and the form should be enough to make it legal if Father tries to dispute it, and if I talk to her alone, she might even see my point of view."

"You sure?"

Anya wasn't sure of anything right now. She smiled at Borsk. "Don't worry. It's just my mom. She might not be willing to help me, but she won't hurt me." Not physically anyway. Anya tried not to think about how it would feel if—no, when—her mom reported her doings to her father instead of helping her. She wasn't sure why part of her kept hoping Mom would come through for her. The larger part of her knew it would never happen.

No matter how hard she tried to force herself to be realistic, something inside her kept hoping. That something whispered encouragement to her as she walked home, as she flipped the camera switch, as she keyed in the screen code.

The screen parted.

All hope switched off.

Father, not Mom, leaned on the kitchen counter.

∞ ❧

Anya knew she should run, but her feet refused to cooperate. They stood, as rooted to the entry as a silverfruit bush was to the greenhouse.

Father tapped on his armband, and the entrance beads snapped into place behind her. "We need to talk. Ryan says you embarrassed him in public today."

"*I* embarrassed *him*?" Shock got Anya's legs moving again, but anger propelled her forward, not back. "Do you have any idea what he did to me?"

"I'm not interested in adolescent whining. Ryan Lancet is a man I value and respect, and you will treat him accordingly whenever you deal with him."

Ryan cheated on her, but he was the one Father valued and respected. Of course. "I guess it's a good thing I won't be dealing with him much, then. I'm trying out for Golden Terrace, and once I make it, I'll never have to see him again." Anya reached for her armband to send her notification to Father.

Before she could reach it, he grabbed her arm, twisted it behind her back, shoved her against the wall next to her bunk screen, and leaned against her so hard she could barely breathe. "What did you just say?"

Anya's anger deserted her. She wiggled, trying to get away.

Father twisted her armband arm behind her back too.

She screamed and squirmed but couldn't escape. She couldn't even protect herself when he pulled her slowly away from the wall, then slammed her back into it, twice.

"I asked you a question!"

Black swam in front of her eyes, and she realized her head had hit the wall. "You can't do this. Someone will come."

Father laughed. "No one watches this house when I'm in it unless I want them to. No one's going to see. No one's going to come. So, tell me again, what did you just say?"

Anya feared the threat in his voice, and she wondered if he was right about no one seeing or coming. Had he fixed the cameras so they wouldn't run, even when she had turned them on manually? Fear rose in her, but she refused to let it rule her. "I said I'm trying out for Golden Terrace."

Father pulled her backward and held her against him as he whispered in her ear, "No, you said you're sorry about Golden Terrace and will never embarrass Ryan or me again. Isn't that right?"

Anya trembled, but she still said, "No."

Father slammed her into the wall again. By jerking her head backward, she managed to keep her head from hitting this time, but air whooshed out of her chest. She couldn't suck any back in, hard as she tried. She couldn't breathe.

Dark spots danced at the edge of her vision, and the room seemed to fade.

She gulped at the air around her, but none made it down to her lungs. Panicked, she tried harder.

Father said something, but she couldn't hear him properly.

She gasped again, but no air came. Was this what dying felt like?

Father slammed her into the wall again. A sharp pain assaulted her nose, but she didn't care—at that same moment, air rushed to her lungs.

"Answer me!"

Anya couldn't remember what the question was. Her breath still came in gasps, and her whole torso ached, but what really bothered her was not being able to wipe at the blood that dripped down her face. She struggled to free her arms from Father's grasp.

He tightened his grip. "Say you're sorry and won't embarrass me again."

He was going to kill her if she kept disagreeing with him.

But if she agreed, she'd never get to Golden Terrace. She'd be stuck with Ryan. Her head throbbed. "No. I'm trying out for the colony."

Slam. "You're sorry, right?"

Pain and fear engulfed Anya, but some deep instinct wouldn't let her give in. "No. I'm trying—"

Slam. "Say you're sorry."

"Never."

Slam. "Say you're sorry."

Tears clouded her vision, and her whole body cringed against what she knew was coming. She sobbed.

"That's better. Now say you're sorry."

"No." She couldn't manage more than a whisper, but it was a fierce whisper.

Slam. "Say—"

"Step away from the girl, Mr. Cartier."

Anya fell when Father released her arms. Her head whirled, and blood dripped from her nose. She reached a hand up to stop it.

"Are you all right, sweetheart?" Father had never used such a sweet tone toward her before. Anya staggered upright, trying to catch her bearings.

"I hope you gentlemen have a good reason for bursting into a private residence, making a man drop his daughter when she's having a nosebleed and dizzy spell." He sounded so protective, so angry on her behalf, that Anya couldn't quite believe it was her father who spoke.

She lifted her head, so she could see. Three ship's crew crowded just inside the quarter entrance, pointing stunners at Father. Three? Crew didn't usually work in more than pairs. Was her head spinning that badly?

"Mr. Cartier, we have a warrant for your arrest for assault and child endangerment," the short one in the middle said. He licked his lips and nodded toward Father.

The guys on either side of him stepped forward. So there really were three. That was good, she guessed. She rubbed her head as the two men took her father into custody.

"Get her a seat," Father barked at the short man who had spoken. "Can't you see she's having trouble standing up?"

The short guy found the dining chairs, unfolded one, and helped Anya into it.

"Better. Now sweetheart, don't worry. Your mom will be with you in a minute, and so will I as soon as I get this little misunderstanding cleared up."

Little misunderstanding? His audacity stunned her but helped her find her voice. "It's not a misunderstanding. You did assault me."

"It's OK," the short man said. "We saw. Just relax now, and in a bit, when your mother and social worker are here, you can give a statement. Do you want a glass of water?"

Anya started to nod, but the movement set off a wave of dizziness. "Yes, please. And a washcloth, if you don't mind. They're in the bathroom cupboard."

She'd washed her face and nearly finished the water when her mom rushed through the door. "Oh, my poor baby! What happened? Where is your father?"

"They arrested him for assault. He kept slamming me into the wall after I told him I was trying out for the Golden Terrace Colony."

"Sweetheart, I can see you're mad at him right now, but don't lie that way. Your father would never—"

"Ma'am, we saw the full attack on the security feeds."

Mom looked at the short man as if he were a bacteria culture. "That's impossible. Thomas said he wanted a private conversation with Stacey."

"So, you *let* him trade electronic signatures with you and wait for me in here with all the feeds turned off?"

"Stacey, your father would never—"

"Excuse me, ma'am," the short man said, "Did you exchange electronic signatures with your husband?"

"Don't answer that, Sylvia," said a voice from the door. A blond-haired, green-eyed woman stood in the entryway. Julie Randall. She'd been here that time Father broke Mom's arm. Anya sat up straighter. Bruises all along her front caught at her breathing. She gripped her water glass tighter. "I want a different social worker."

"Stacey, Mrs. Randall is the best—"

"Somebody not pure Euro."

Julie Randall flushed. "Ethnic background can't be taken into account when choosing a person for a particular job."

"Unless reason can be shown why it matters. In this case—"

"Stacey, have you lost your senses?" Mom's hands trembled.

Anya watched her mom's shaking hands. That's where she got it from—the shaky hands when she was afraid.

Mom was afraid? Of what Father would do if Anya spilled the beans about the betrothal? But if Mom would explain how he bullied her, the only person who'd get in trouble for that was Father. Mom would never explain though. Mom always covered for Father.

Anya closed her eyes. Pain rolled over her, and she wasn't sure if it was bruises or her heart. She should have known her mother would cover for her father. "I. Want a. Different. Social worker," she repeated.

"But . . ." Mother said.

"And I want Officer. . . . Sorry, I didn't ask your name," she said to the short man.

"Gupta," he said.

"I want Officer Gupta to stay. And I want a lawyer in here."

"Of course. I should have thought of that myself. I'll call Oliver Forrest right—"

"Not Father's lawyer. My own lawyer," Anya said. Not that she had a lawyer. But Grandma had one. He'd help her, wouldn't he? "Jamal Pantiri."

"Stacey, think about what you're doing." Mother's voice sounded panicky.

"It's all right, Sylvia." Julie Randall put a hand on Mother's shoulder. "If the girl feels uncomfortable with me, it will be better to have someone else. I'll just run down to the office and see who's available. It's a busy afternoon, so we might not be able to get someone here for a few hours, but I'm sure we can find an alternate."

A few hours? Anya didn't have that kind of time. She was about to protest, when Mr. Gupta said, "No problem. I've contacted the girl's lawyer. He can get here within ten minutes and serve as her advocate until a new social worker arrives. If you would hurry along the medical professionals before getting your replacement, that would be very helpful."

Julie Randall's eyes narrowed to slits, but she said, "Of course," before leaving the room.

Mother watched her go, "Oh, Stacey, are you sure you want—"

"My name is Anya, Mother. You know that."

"My poor baby. You're hurt, and you don't know what you're saying," Mother reached a hand toward her shoulder.

Anya shrugged away. "Don't touch me. Don't ever touch me again."

Chapter Twenty

Borsk didn't consider how awkward it would be to wait around in the GenM flagship on One until Anya had disappeared from sight. It had sounded like a reasonable plan when she suggested it, and he knew she didn't think it would be a big deal for him. But then, her armband probably didn't even trigger the huge "No Loitering" signs at the store's entrance. How was she supposed to know that such signs were designed with kids like Borsk in mind?

The last time he'd been up to the store on One, a perfectly coiffed employee had latched onto him the moment he stepped through the arch. She'd trailed him through the electronics section, and made clucking noises as he tested the processor he was interested in. As soon as he'd declared himself satisfied and completed his purchase, she'd hurried him out the door.

He'd thought about complaining, but what could he say? That the service had been too efficient? The woman hadn't made any rude or disparaging comments. She'd made him feel like something she wanted to wipe off her shoe without saying a single impolite word.

He knew that any time he walked into that store again, she or one of her fashionably-clad clones would be there, right at his elbow, to make sure he didn't stay long enough to lower the tone of their high-class establishment.

If they wouldn't let him stay long, he'd have to time his trip just right. And he needed to do it without any iffy electronic activity, so that Anya could use his armband camera feed in a court if need be.

Borsk scratched his head. As Anya had reminded him, tracking Thomas Cartier's movements wasn't strictly legal. Neither was periodically pinging the man's armband. But he was within his rights to set his proximity detector at the widest possible range. Then all he needed was a reason for being in Anya's dad's general vicinity.

Borsk brought up a ship map and smiled. Cartier's marketing team had done Borsk the favor of highlighting every GenM store on it, so he could easily locate parks or open spaces within fifty meters of each store.

Borsk was checking out his third open space when he picked up Thomas Cartier's armband signature at the edge of his proximity sensor. The man didn't appear to be moving, so even though he wasn't much good, Borsk agreed to substitute for one of Uncle Hirsch's boys in a game of wallball.

Within minutes, Kirsch demanded his spot back, and Borsk leaned against the open space entrance, panting. It was exasperating to be shown up by eleven-year-olds, even in a sport he didn't like. He had to practice more.

Cartier's signal moved toward the elevators.

"I'm off," Borsk said. "Going to find a game I *can* play."

Kirsch jerked his head but kept his eye on the ball. Definitely a better player than Borsk.

Borsk shook his head. Maybe he could just avoid wallball from here on out. He trotted toward Thomas Cartier's signal, and got to the level-exit alcove as the signal entered the elevator.

Before the doors closed, he noticed that the person broadcasting the signal had way nicer legs, and way less scary eyes than Anya's dad. He shot a deep level query at the woman's armband, forgetting he was supposed to be avoiding iffy net activity.

As the elevator cranked upward, his results returned. The woman's armband specs matched those of Sylvia Cartier.

If Anya's mom was here, using her dad's armband signature, then the person in Anya's house using her mom's signature had to be her dad.

Borsk raced towards Anya's house, but halfway there, he changed direction. If he broke in or hacked the cameras, that would be no help to Anya at all. It would do plenty of harm to himself and his family, though. Sometimes official channels were best.

He didn't stop running until he reached the biggest security station on Three, where Ryan Lancet stood outside the door. "Lancet, we've got to—"

"Mr. King. I'm glad to see you've heard the voice of reason, but there's no need to run. There are ten minutes until fifteen-hundred hours yet."

Fifteen hundred hours? Oh, right. The deadline for showing up and getting to work. Borsk shook his head. "You think I'd run for that? I'm here to put in an official complaint—a threat of imminent violence complaint."

Lancet stepped backward into the station. "A threat of *imminent* violence complaint? That's serious, Mr. King. Are you aware that making such a complaint maliciously can result in a felony conviction?"

Would result in a felony conviction given who he was complaining about. Borsk gulped. "I'm sure. I believe Anastasia Cartier is in immediate danger from her father Thomas, who is currently using Sylvia Cartier's armband signature."

Lancet's face paled, but he took two steps toward the back of the station, where Martin Kim sat at a console against the back wall. "Did you hear the young man, Mr. Kim?"

"Sir, if this is a bogus complaint, Borsk won't be the only one in hot water."

"Mr. Kim, we're sworn to uphold the security of this ship. You know that requires taking every threat of violence complaint seriously."

"Yes, sir." Kim waved the work he'd been doing to one side and muttered into his headset. The screen at the workstation to his right flickered to life. It gave a good view of the largest quarters Borsk had ever seen. At the back right of the front room, Thomas Cartier slammed a girl against the wall.

"Get someone in there," Lancet barked. "Who's closest?"

"A group on One is already going in. They've been watching for a couple of minutes."

On the screen, ship's crew burst into the room. Anya's dad moved away from her. She crumpled to the floor, as if she couldn't stand up on her own.

"I should have got here sooner," Borsk said.

Martin Kim shrugged. "Don't beat yourself up. The team from One got there about as soon as anybody could. They've been monitoring those quarters since the girl turned on the house camera a few minutes ago. See the . . . Hey, what's happening to the feed? I'm losing it!"

The video in front of Borsk broke up into lines of code that scrolled so fast they blurred.

"Mr. King, help him!" Lancet said.

Borsk slid into the seat next to Martin's, rested his hands on an old-style control board, and lost himself in the streaming lines of code.

Thomas Cartier's hacker. Borsk would recognize this guy's style anywhere. Especially since this was nothing new, just a version of the program he'd fought with a week ago.

Just like the code in Anya's armband, this new code high jacked a whole set of videos and hauled it off to Cartier's private storage. Borsk located the source, cut it off, and rerouted the data to the console in front of him. Once it arrived, he made three copies on permanent storage cubes, and disconnected them from the console, to keep them safe from any further attacks from the net.

Finally, he straightened up. How long had that taken? A little while, if he went by the tension in his shoulders. He stretched from side to side to loosen up. "I think I've got it, but we'd probably better look at it to make sure. I didn't notice any resistance from Cartier's hacker, but the man is good enough, he might have pulled off something amazing without my knowing."

"What do you mean, 'Cartier's hacker?'" Lancet asked.

"Look at what I've done." While he was thinking about it, Borsk saved off a permanent copy of all his work since the video had broken up in front of them. Twenty minutes worth. Was that all? "Here. See this? This is where the guy latched onto any video feed from the last four hours that contains Anastasia Cartier."

Martin Kim nodded. "That's true. And these lines here route all those videos to a private account. It's the same account as in the other code I'm detangling, sir. So far, I've only been able to trace it back to Prime Security, a company that died more than a century ago."

"I take it you've done better, Mr. King?"

"Sure. It's Thomas Cartier's account. Not that my word will be any good to you, if you have to prove anything. My family has a well-known grudge against the man."

Lancet nodded. "Then we'll stop referring to our hacker as Cartier's."

"But . . ."

"At least until Mr. Kim independently verifies your conclusions. In the meantime, we'll watch these videos together, all keeping an eye out for tampering." Lancet ordered the console in front of Borsk to play the captured videos in chronological order.

The code on the screen in front of Borsk disappeared, but what took its place wasn't Anya's home. It was Skreetches, and David Ryerson was swinging over the balcony rail to meet Anya.

"What does she think she's doing?" Lancet asked.

Covering for your sorry butt, Borsk thought, but didn't say. He'd promised to keep quiet about Anya's betrothal, after all. Besides, they'd all see what it was about if the video hadn't been altered.

It hadn't been. When Leslie Wang accused Anya of being betrothed to him, Lancet sank onto a stool next to Borsk with a look in his eyes that almost made Borsk feel sorry for him. Almost. Then he remembered how Lancet had treated Anya at lunch and figured the man deserved whatever misery was coming to him.

A couple minutes later, he hoped Lancet would rot in Hell. The scene in Skreetches had run all the way to Leslie Wang slapping Anya's face. They'd fast forwarded through the next video capture—a mostly inaudible feed that showed David Ryerson and Anya Cartier in a maintenance hatch. Then the video had jumped again, this time to Anya's quarters. Thomas Cartier paced from side to side. Anya entered.

"We need to talk. Ryan says you embarrassed him in public today," Cartier said.

"*She* embarrassed *you?*" Martin Kim said as Anya said almost the same thing.

Borsk would have said it more profanely.

Lancet pressed his lips into a thin line. Borsk thought he looked mad. But when Anya's dad started slamming her into the wall, Lancet covered his eyes. "I can't believe . . . He's never done anything like this before."

"What are you talking about?" Borsk said. "He was about to hit her last week—in a school hallway, in front of me. At least I think he was going to hit her. Maybe he was going to hit me. He pulled back when I got surveillance unblocked."

Lancet shook his head, like he still couldn't believe it.

"Sir, this looks bad," Kim said. "First the betrothal rumor, and then you set the kid up for a beating? If this gets out, your career is over."

Lancet straightened up. His eyes blazed. "*If* this gets out? Are you a security officer, or aren't you?" Lancet stood all the way up, clenching his fists at his side. "A horrible act of violence has been committed, the kind of thing we haven't tolerated in centuries. We will do whatever it takes to bring the perpetrator to justice and protect our fellow officers. They risked their careers to stop him, and you think we should lose the video because it might bring me a spot of trouble? If you ever hint at something like that again, you are done on ship's crew. I'll see to it."

Borsk had thought Anya's portrait of Lancet on the Golden Terrace team was wishful thinking, but the Lancet of her artwork stood before him in the flesh now. Except instead of building a civilization with his bare hands, he was taking apart his own dreams of being captain.

Borsk wasn't sure he knew anybody else who would do that.

Maybe he'd hold off a bit on turning in his resignation to Camp Flight.

Chapter Twenty-One

Having her own lawyer didn't speed things up as much as Anya had hoped it would. Jamal Pantiri showed up within minutes, but he insisted that Anya be checked out by three different doctors (not including her mother). Then he and Oliver Forrest—apparently Father thought his lawyer could do more good at their house than the brig—squabbled every time the ship's crew asked her a question.

When it was 5:30, and the interrogation showed no signs of stopping, Anya got panicky. "Please, Mr. Pantiri. I have to be at the Golden Terrace try-outs before seven. Is there any way to hurry this up?"

Mr. Pantiri tilted his head to one side and smiled, causing the laugh lines at the corners of his eyes to deepen. "Is there anything else Security needs to know?"

Crewman Watson scrolled through his notes. "I have four more questions and then the appointment of a temporary guardian."

"Temporary guardian?" Mother's voice hit a crazy-high pitch. "I'm her mother!"

"In cases of alleged child endangerment, minors are always placed else-where until such time as the home environment is certified as safe, Mrs. Cart-ier," Oliver Forrest said. "Though as the girl's true guardian, and one not charged with any wrongdoing, you will naturally have a good deal of say in who is chosen."

Anya felt like arguing, but that would waste time. And if Mother was helping with the choosing, Grandma Anderson wouldn't be an option. "I don't care who my guardian is, so long as it's not Kristi or Kenneth." Kenneth was far more out-of-control than Father, and he'd be particularly obnoxious if she'd been trying out for Golden Terrace with David. "Also, whoever it is, we've got to meet the legal notification requirements for me to try out."

Mr. Pantiri nodded. "That can be arranged. Crewman Watson, your questions?"

With Mother and Oliver Forrest slowing things down, it took a good half hour to get through them, and there was still that guardian issue to solve.

"I have to go," Anya said. "Can't you all choose without me?"

"If she names a representative to speak for her, that should meet your requirements, Crewman Watson," Mr. Pantiri said.

Oliver Forrest's tablet beeped. The man frowned over it. "It does appear that is true."

"Then Mr. Pantiri is my representative," Anya said. "Can you make sure that whoever it is gets notified soon enough that my try-out is legal, sir?"

"Certainly," Mr. Pantiri said.

Anya smiled. "Now, may I leave?"

Crewman Watson nodded.

"Thank you," Anya flew out of the room. If she ran—as fast as sore lungs and legs allowed—all the way to the shuttle, she could still make her appointment with David on time.

She would have met David on time, too, if the shuttle hadn't broken down three quarters of the way to the greenhouse station. Had Father figured out how to hack the shuttle's systems, like Borsk had? It didn't seem likely, given his limited hacking skills. Perhaps he'd hired someone. Or perhaps, she was letting herself imagine her father was way more powerful than he was. Shuttles broke down all the time.

Besides, what did it matter how it happened? She was stuck in the middle of nowhere, waiting on a repair that could take hours. Most of the other passengers sat—they were guys who now have a good excuse to be late for a shift tending the recyclers, or couples heading for try-outs who figured the repair was minor. But Anya had seen too many shuttle breakdowns to trust this would be fixed in a reasonable time. She sighed, rubbed her aching head, and took to the pedestrian bridges.

Unfortunately, she'd forgotten to ask David for contact information, so she couldn't tell him what had happened. Plus, she had trouble moving, as sore as she was. Even going at her top speed at the moment, and messaging Mr. Greeley to meet her at the greenhouse door with her pack, she was running more than five minutes late.

As she approached the last corner of the hall before the registration point, she could hear David's grandma. "Where is the little bitch? Think she got scared?"

"Now, Grandma, I know you didn't take to her right away, but there's no reason to talk like that. I heard the girl talk about the colony, and she might be as passionate about seeing Shindashir as you are. She promised she'd come."

Anya sped up, even though it made every breath feel like a knife against her ribs.

"Easy to give a promise and not mean it. Especially when it's you doing the listening. I hate to say it, boy, but—"

"I'm here," Anya gasped. She wondered when she'd be able to breathe normally again.

"Shit, child. What happened to you?"

Anya closed her eyes. She hadn't looked in a mirror yet and wondered if she looked as bad as she felt. Shame swept over her, and she had to remind herself that she wasn't the one who had done anything wrong. "My father . . ." Why couldn't she say it? "He wasn't happy when I said I was trying out. He slammed me into a wall. There was an official inquiry."

David whistled, and he stroked her right cheek with a cool finger. "I should have come with you."

"What, so you could look like her? Don't be ridiculous. Let's get checked in. We're late enough as it is." David's grandma led the way toward a long table. Two men stood behind it, one tall and gaunt, the other medium height and jolly. They fell silent as Anya, David, and his grandma approached.

"Names?" the jolly man said.

David's grandma jerked her head in Anya's direction.

Had the old woman forgotten her name? She took a deep breath. "Anastasia Cartier and David Ryerson," she said.

The tall gaunt man threw an unfriendly glance her way. "Thomas Cartier's daughter?"

"Yes." She didn't like the look in the man's eyes. Had Father done something to him?

"Do your parents know you're here?"

Anya sighed. "I told them in person, and also sent them both legal notifications." And Mr. Pantiri was taking care of notifying whoever would be appointed as her temporary guardian. Did this man need to know that?

Hopefully not, because he didn't give her time to say anything about it. "Fine. Stanley, you process this pair. I'll send Lisa out to help." The tall man stalked through a door off to their left.

The shorter man—Stanley—watched him go, his eyes wide, and no longer looking jolly.

David put an arm around Anya's shoulders and gently drew her closer to him. "Captain DeLang take off like that often?"

The tall man was Captain DeLang? How odd that she'd never seen his likeness. Captain Bates, who ran *Hope*, had his picture everywhere.

"Not to worry," the man behind the table said. "Best man in the universe, Captain DeLang. If he needs to take off, he's got a good reason for it. Let's get you all checked in. I'm Stanley Kuhler, Golden Terrace Chief of Medicine, and . . ."

Anya had trouble listening. Why had Captain DeLang needed to leave? Did it have anything to do with the personal grudge she suspected her father had against the man? Why hadn't she researched that more closely, so she knew what was going on? Would the history she didn't know about hurt her chances of making the colony team?

For weeks Anya had worked so hard at getting to stand in this spot, that she'd forgotten this was only a try-out.

If she wanted to stand on Shindashir's surface—to see real mountains with her own eyes, and feel what it meant to have sunshine on her face and wind in her hair—she still had to earn a spot on the Golden Terrace team.

She smiled at Dr. Kuhler as she tapped her armband's note-taker so she could review what he'd been saying, and make sure she hadn't missed anything.

She only had one shot at this.

She meant to make it a good one.

୫୦ ୦୪

Since Lancet wanted him to help recode camera controls, Borsk stayed at the security office for hours. He only got away at eleven by promising Lancet he'd return to work more on the problem as soon as church was over the next day.

They'd already finished clean-up when he got home. He tiptoed through the strangely eerie dining area. In the dim light, long shadows and the exposed legs of upended chairs made him feel like an interloper in a surreal landscape.

He jumped when Mama rose from the booth nearest the kitchen door.

"Mama."

"You've been gone for hours."

"Yes, well—"

"You can't have been with Anya the whole time. I saw her father's arrest on the news—and it made no mention of a second minor."

"No, I—"

"When I said I'd deal with you later, I meant as soon as you'd finished your necessary business—business you appear to have failed at quite spectacularly, by the way."

"That's totally unfair. Anya wanted to talk to her mom alone. How was either of us supposed to know that her mom and dad had switched armband signatures?"

"Switched armband signatures? But that's a—"

"Class two felony. I know. Soon as I found out, I reported the breach to Lancet."

"Lancet? But he . . ." Mama clamped her lips and eyes shut.

Borsk waited. No good ever came of interrupting Mama when she looked like that.

At last Mama opened her eyes. "And what did Ryan Lancet do when you told him?"

"He secured the evidence—for the signature switch and for the assault on Anya. Since then, he's had me working on security camera programming, so it's harder to hack."

Mama raised her eyebrows. "Does he imagine he's immune from Cartier's wrath?"

Borsk thought back to Lancet's set face after he'd seen all the camera feeds. "No, I think he knows exactly what this will cost him."

"So, you stayed to help." Mama nodded her approval.

Borsk felt both pleased and embarrassed. "Didn't seem like the time to turn in my resignation."

"No. But it would have been a great time to let me know you'd be late."

Borsk knew that. Why hadn't he remembered at the time? "Sorry."

"Don't let it happen again. Now, how are we going to schedule both your new appointments and your new work hours?"

"New appointments?"

"I've arranged for you to meet with Dr. Young twice a week."

"The shrink? No way, Mama."

She glared at him until he straightened up and tried again. "What I mean is, I'd rather not see a therapist, Mama."

"Yet you clearly aren't willing to talk to your uncle or to me. You need help. I'm your mother, and I'm going to see that you get it."

"But—"

"There are no buts. You're going. Now get yourself to bed. We've got one of our quarterly Sunday dinners tomorrow."

Borsk sighed. He hated those things. "Yes, Mama."

He didn't see how it would help to see a shrink. All they did was encourage him to talk. No amount of talk would stop him from getting disabled and then dying. Just like none of the therapy sessions after the funeral had been able to bring his father back.

He didn't want to talk about living.
He wanted to live.

- 154 -

Chapter Twenty-Two

After Anya and David turned in their initial application, **Dr.** Kuhler ushered them into the strangest test Anya had ever seen. Instead of testing pods, or even desks with computers, there was a large open room with small groups of people clustered near piles of crates in each of the four corners. Dr. Kuhler pointed them toward the group at the back right and said, "That's your try-out team. Get to know them, and in a few minutes, we'll give everyone more instructions."

"When does the testing start?" David asked.

The doctor smiled. "Right now."

David's brow crinkled. He looked as confused as Anya felt.

Mrs. Ryerson reached up and shoved him in the shoulder blades. "They want to see how you function in a team, stupid. So, they're putting you in one. Let's go. We're wasting time."

"Gran," David said.

But Dr. Kuhler's smile told Anya the old woman was right about what the leadership was testing for. She reached for David's hand. "I think your grandma is right. Not about you being stupid, of course. You're not stupid. Who could expect this?"

Mrs. Ryerson sniffed, as if to say Anya was no genius herself.

Well, Anya was used to people thinking she was stupid. What she wasn't used to was the way she seemed to warm up when David beamed a wide smile at her.

"Shall we?" he said.

Anya nodded. She didn't trust herself to talk.

He led the way toward the back corner, Anya and his grandma trailing in his wake. Anya wasn't sure why Mrs. Ryerson stayed back, but she herself couldn't overcome her shyness.

Shyness didn't seem to be David's problem. Long before they'd reached their corner, people drifted away from the group to say hello. David seemed to know everybody—a tall beautiful woman who worked with him in Materials Science—well, of course he'd know her. And the mechanical engineer with electric blue hair—he probably worked with her too. He almost certainly worked with the leggy, glossy-haired structural engineer. But how had he become such good friends with Bria Huxton, a tiny dark woman whose work with textiles probably didn't bring her anywhere near him? Should Anya be worried about the way David flirted his way through the group?

None of the husbands or boyfriends seemed to care—except Bria's. Mr. Huxton glared at David with such practiced threat, that Anya remembered he was a high-school teacher. Not one of hers. She'd probably never learn enough math to wind up in one of his classes. But Borsk had him. In fact, hadn't Mr. Huxton given Borsk some of the fractals he'd shown to Anya?

Anya lifted her head, stepped out of David's shadow and found her smile. "Mr. Huxton, it's nice to meet you. I really liked the fractals you let Borsk show me."

A voice from behind Mr. Huxton rang out. "Anastasia Cartier? Is that you? What happened to your face?"

DeShawn Philips. Anya knew cameras were on her, judging how she reacted to this, and she still froze. Why on *Hope* had she wound up in a group with DeShawn Philips?

"Seriously. Did you fall down a stairwell or something?"

David drew her closer to him, and Anya took courage from his warmth. "My father took exception to my trying out for the colony."

"What do you mean? He beat you up?"

"Slammed me into a wall a few times, yeah."

Several nearby conversations came to an abrupt stop. Eyes turned her way. Anya wished there was a cubby nearby she could crawl into.

"Oh, honey. I'm so sorry." Anya barely had time to recognize Laura Wilcox—the lawyer married to Ryan's boss—before the woman enveloped her in a giant hug.

Anya wasn't sure what to make of having a near stranger hug her, but before she could decide, Laura whispered in her ear, "Have you seen a doctor?"

"Three," Anya said softly.

Laura pulled back a bit and looked her in the eye. "They said you're well enough to try out?"

Anya nodded.

"Oh, good. Come on, then." Laura drew them after her into the heart of the group and introduced her to so many people in such a short space of time that Anya's head reeled. She hoped her notetaker was catching all this, so she could study it later. It would take some serious concentration.

Though most of the group (including David and his grandma) seemed to know each other, she'd met hardly any of them.

She knew DeShawn, of course. As it happened, he had teamed up with Georgia Lewis, so Anya knew her, too—if you counted exchanging a few words in a Wash and Wear as knowing.

Anya didn't recognize any of the others—except for Steve Jackson. After having drawn his picture for Skreetches, she'd never forget his face. Since he'd so publicly recognized her art, she was excited to meet him in person. But Laura hadn't quite reached him when the colony leadership team interrupted, sent them all a flurry of files on the testing process and schedules, and told each group to use what it found in its crates to set up a camp in its corner.

"What's a camp?" DeShawn asked.

This Anya knew. She'd seen references to camps in some of her ancient literary works. "It's a kind of primitive living quarters, I think," she said.

"Ah—a dormitory. That shouldn't be hard." Laura's husband took charge. He assigned them all tasks—first carrying and unloading crates, then constructing eating and sleeping areas, and finally organizing schedules for cooking and cleaning.

Anya had thought herself pretty handy with tools, but when she saw the way David's beautiful coworker and some of the others held hammers and wrenches, she felt awkward. Plus, today she tired easily. She was glad when at last everything seemed organized enough for them to go to sleep.

It was strange sharing a screened area with Mrs. Ryerson and David. She rather wished they'd split the tent by gender rather than family, but that was silly. Most of the couples were already married and would presumably be more comfortable together.

She rolled out one of the bed mats, shoved it next to the screen, and sank onto it.

David dropped down next to her and stroked her cheek with the back of a finger. "Holding up OK?"

Her breath hitched, so she couldn't speak. She smiled a weary smile at him.

"Can't you see the child is too tired for your nonsense tonight? Shoo, so she can get changed." Mrs. Ryerson chased David out beyond the screen.

Anya stared after him.

Mrs. Ryerson popped back in. "Don't look so heartbroken. He'll be back." She slapped a sleeping mat down next to Anya's. 'Tomorrow's plenty soon for hanky-panky. You're in no shape for it tonight."

Anya supposed she wasn't. Her head throbbed, her arms ached, and her ribs groaned every time she breathed.

All the same, as she pulled her nightshirt over her head, she wished David, not his grandma, had claimed the middle spot.

ဢ ◌ ဧ

Anya ached. From her tender, throbbing forehead to her stiff and scraped knees, a thousand separate nerve-endings screamed discordantly at her. No wonder she'd woken up. She was surprised she'd slept at all, though a quick glance at the clock on her armband told her she must have.

She shifted, trying in vain to find a comfortable position. She'd do better on tomorrow's tests if she was well rested, but she might as well wish for an automatic spot on the colony team—or a new father. Sleep was not in her near future.

Noises around her grew loud. Mats squeaked and whispered as people turned. Half a dozen different snores filled the air, with Mrs. Ryerson's irregular honk the loudest. A sprinkler system hissed as it geared up. An air purifier pinged.

Wait. A sprinkler system hissed? She knew they were close to the greenhouses, but close enough to hear the sprinklers? Surely not.

But why would this section have its own sprinklers? They couldn't grow anything in the week allotted to try-outs. Even her new B-9s didn't mature that fast. Anya flipped on her armband projector and flashed the light at the ceiling to reassure herself that nothing was up there.

The narrow beam fell on a giant sprinkler head, bigger even than the misters used for mangoes. Sweeping her arm in a wide arc, Anya counted four-no-five more sprinklers in the area above her head. Judging by the sound the system was making, they'd all let loose within the next five minutes.

Anya dragged herself to her feet and stumbled around Mrs. Ryerson. She'd nearly reached the screen when someone gripped her left ankle. Anya suppressed a scream.

"Where do you think you're going?" David whispered.

"Supplies. We need a roof."

Anya flashed her armband projector back at the ceiling, so that it illuminated one of the sprinkler heads. "They're going to go off."

David released her ankle. "OK. Right behind you."

At least he didn't argue. Anya slipped past the screen and ran to the pile of still-unused supplies. By the time she got there, David had caught up with her.

"How much time do we have?" he asked.

"Not sure. Maybe five minutes."

"Quick and dirty, then." David's armband projector lit up the pile of supplies. "Here." He yanked out a thin sheet of fabric and a shiny pole. He shook the latter, and it telescoped out to five times its original length. Then he threaded it through a casing in one side of the fabric. "Now all we have to do is get it raised above the camp."

"Will something on the wall help us?" Anya flashed her light toward the corner of the great room they were testing in. "What about that set of pipes halfway up?"

"That'll do, if we can get a line over them. I don't know if I can throw that accurately."

Anya was sure she couldn't. But the wall wasn't solid—it looked like lattice. "I could probably climb up."

"The hell you say."

"Do you have a better idea?"

"Fine." David handed her the ends of two coils of rope. Pull them out as you go. I'll deal with this end.

Two? Why two? Better not to ask, there wasn't time, and he was the engineer. She ran to the corner, wishing with each shaky breath that she were in her normal condition. She never liked running, but it didn't usually hurt this much.

At least her hands didn't hurt. She tied the ropes together, slipped her right arm between them, and started up. Climbing was definitely better than running.

The lattice seemed sturdy, but the area beyond was black and felt hollow. Anya wondered how much of it was structurally sound. If she fell through, would she keep falling all the way to *Hope's* axis?

The hiss of the sprinkler system rose in pitch. They were running out of time. Anya shook her head, to clear it of thoughts of falling. She needed to concentrate on climbing. Grip, grip, step, step, repeat.

The pipes she'd seen were higher than she'd realized. When she finally reached them, she didn't want to let go with even one hand to deal with the ropes. She should have carried them in her teeth or something. Too late now. She hung on tight to the lattice with her right hand and her toes while yanking the rope up and over the pipes with her left hand. Then she gripped the rope in her teeth, brought her left hand back over the pipe and pulled at the rope.

She had pulled the rope one, maybe two, meters down when she realized it would take too long to reel it in while she clung to the lattice. Instead, she looped the ropes around her left hand a couple of times and slithered back down the wall as quickly as she could. She didn't quite let herself fall, but she didn't climb carefully either.

She heard a whoosh behind her. The hiss stopped, and with a loud click, the sprinklers turned on. Water streamed down. People shouted.

They were too late, then. But Anya couldn't worry about that. The now slick trellis gave her no place to hold and her controlled descent became a free fall. She scrabbled at the wall, but only managed to scrape up her toes and knuckles, not slow herself down.

Just when she was sure she was going to crash, David caught her, enfolding her in water-slicked arms.

He steadied them both, then gave her a hard squeeze. "Don't you ever take that kind of risk again. People can get wet."

"Aren't people getting wet?"

David laughed. "Only in the other corners. And us." He unwound the ropes from her wrist, slipped them through the lower part of the terrace, and tied them to a crate he must have brought over from the supply pile. "Come on, let's get out of this shower."

As David took her hand, she realized she was soaking. Her nightshirt clung to her body, and water dripped from her hair. She probably looked awful, but was that a good reason for David to shove her behind him when an armband beam caught them and a voice called out, "Everything OK out here?"

"We're just a little wet, Roger." David said. "We'll get back in and dry off."

Anya wondered how David knew who it was in the dark. But the other voice didn't correct him, only said, "Are you two responsible for our canopy? Good work. Should have realized we'd need that extra tarp for something. It's not like DeLang to dole out useless supplies."

"Sounds like we weren't the only ones fooled," David said.

"True. How did you all catch it in time?"

"No clue. Anya somehow knew the sprinklers were going to go off."

"That's the trouble with testing for the colony while we're still on *Hope*. Too many ways to hack the system."

Did he want to get wet? And what did he mean hack the system? Did he think someone had told her about the sprinklers somehow? "Actually, I heard them."

"What's that?" Roger asked.

"The sprinklers. I heard them. The greenhouse ones make a sound just like that when they're about to go off. I think it's the pump."

"You work in the greenhouses? I thought you were Thomas Cartier's daughter."

"Just an accident of birth," David said. "Roger, could we save the rest of the interrogation for morning? Some of us are freezing out here."

"Sorry. I was just surprised." Roger moved his light off their faces. "You kids get dried off."

David steered Anya toward their section of the camp, keeping himself between her and Roger. Why did he think they needed to be separated? She'd ask, but her teeth were chattering too much. David pressed her to him and kept her close as they moved under the canopy, and then slipped behind their screen.

"Come on, let's get out of these wet clothes." David stripped off his shirt, and then his shorts.

Even in the darkness, Anya could see he wasn't wearing anything underneath. She glanced away.

David wrapped himself in a blanket, then seemed to notice that she hadn't moved. "Do you need help?"

"I'm fine." Anya pulled away from him, trembling, and not just from the wet and cold.

"Can you two keep it down? I'm trying to sleep," Mrs. Ryerson said.

"Yes, ma'am." Anya reached in her pack for her spare nightshirt. "Could you . . . turn?" she whispered.

"If it will make you more comfortable." David turned away, laughing softly.

"What's so funny?"

"He's already seen everything there is to see, child. That wet shirt don't cover nothing, even in this light."

Anya wished she could hide, but there was nowhere to go. She quickly swapped nightshirts and hung the wet one over the edge of the screen.

Her teeth still chattered.

"Let's get you warm." David wrapped her in her own blanket, lowered them both down to his mat, and snuggled up next to her. Then he kissed her cheek and leaned close to her ear. "In case you're wondering, I liked what I saw. You're a beautiful woman, Anya Cartier."

Anya gasped.

David kissed her again, this time on the mouth

She wondered how far he would go, but he didn't push. After the kiss, he held her, keeping her warm and comfortable—or as comfortable as she could be with her bruises and the pounding of her heart.

David's breathing evened out, and his embrace relaxed.

Anya didn't think she'd ever sleep.

If Borsk hadn't been hanging out with Lancet recently, he might have granted the request. Zig, Boss, DD and Con were all long-time players, and Borsk had dug deep enough into their financials when he was setting up their accounts to know that they could all afford a more expensive game.

Letting players risk real credits instead of lunch money would take his poker franchise from shady right over the line to illegal, though. Normally Borsk wouldn't have cared about that, but the day after he'd been helping Lancet with ship security, he was sensitive about breaking rules. He was sure his inconvenient attack of conscience would fade away with time, but for the moment, he sent the players a polite but firm rejection.

Con threatened to cancel his account.

Borsk let him. Then he logged out of his admin account. Mrs. J had started addressing every question to Borsk personally, as if she knew he was paying less than half a mind to the Sunday school lesson.

Sunday school and therapy—two things he'd never do again once he left home.

Not that Mama was ever going to let him leave home. Not now that she knew he'd inherited his father's illness.

"There's no need to scowl like that, Borsk," Mrs. J said.

She thought this was scowling? Borsk sunk lower in his chair. Would this class never end?

It did, but only after Mrs. J had asked him a dozen more questions, and then kept him afterward to lecture him on his attitude. He escaped as soon as he could and made up a school errand so he could take a back-route home instead of getting a repeat of the lecture from Mama.

He was a couple of corridors from the restaurant when Thomas Cartier stepped out of an alcove in front of him.

Borsk yelped and dropped the school tablet VJ Brown had asked him to fix.

"Sorry. Didn't mean to startle you. Naturally, I'll pay for any damages to your machine."

Borsk snatched the tablet from the floor. What did Anya's dad want with him? Was that bit about the tablet supposed to make him like the man? After yesterday? Why was the jerk even out of the brig? Borsk made to move around him. "I'm sure it will be fine."

Mr. Cartier put a hand on his arm. "Not so fast. We should at least check to see if it's broken."

"If it's broken, I'll—"

Mr. Cartier laughed. "Hit me up for four times the actual damages and broadcast what a miser I am when I get my lawyers on it. I insist on seeing what's wrong now.

Maybe on an ordinary day. Today Borsk wanted out of Mr. Cartier's vicinity. "The tablet was broken before I dropped it. I officially waive all rights to compensation."

"You must have come into money. That's the second lucrative opportunity you've passed up today."

"Second?"

"The poker game?"

How did Mr. Cartier know about that?

Anya's dad laughed. "You should see your face right now. I'm not a mind reader, boy. I'm Boss. Thought you knew that."

Thomas Cartier was Boss? Obviously Borsk's poker background checks didn't go nearly far enough.

"I guess I was misinformed about your computer skills."

"Excuse me?"

"I was told that you're the best programmer currently living on *Hope*. But if you can't even lift an ID from a payment record . . ."

"Chose not to is different from can't. I can trace anything anywhere."

"That's what Mr. Singh said."

Mr. Singh? Oh, right. Hiram. Hiram had called him the best hacker on *Hope*? Nice.

"If you're as good as you think you are, I might have work for you. You'd start with GenM's regular B compensation package—B salary, plus company housing if you want it, and school tuition. As with all our B-level positions, there'd be opportunities for advancement. Oh—and in this case, I'd be willing to throw in a special signing bonus—a 50,000 credit contribution to the King Syndrome fund. I know how much that means to your family—especially to you." Mr. Cartier winked, as if he knew all about Borsk having the disease. But, how could he?

Borsk's brain crunched to a halt. His smart response reflex completely failed him. Thomas Cartier was offering him a B salary package with benefits while he was still in school?

"Not ready to answer just yet, hey? No worries. The offer's good for a little while. Take your time. Think it over. We can talk again after your appointment with Dr. Young tomorrow." Mr. Cartier clapped Borsk on the back and strode down the hall.

Borsk watched him go, unease boiling like oil in his gut.

He wasn't fool enough to want a job from Anya's dad—even a job as highly compensated as this one.

But he wasn't fool enough to want to directly cross the man either.

Why couldn't Thomas Cartier have gone on thinking he was a stupid, delinquent schoolboy?

Chapter Twenty-Three

As an early riser, Anya had signed up for the first chore of the morning—carrying water—but when her armband alarm beeped in her ear Sunday morning, she wished she hadn't. Making it to the colony depended on her getting her aching, weary body off this mat. With a soft groan, she disentangled herself from David's arms, threw on a fresh uniform, and staggered out into the common area of their corner.

Laura Wilcox was already there, frowning over her armband. As Anya approached, she looked up and smiled. "I don't suppose you know why they've got us walking halfway back to the inhabited side of *Hope* for water when there are pipes running into the latrine and those crazy sprinklers?"

Anya shook her head. "Unless the plumbed water isn't potable. Some of the water we use in the greenhouses isn't."

"I didn't know that."

Anya shrugged. "Cheaper that way, and it doesn't seem to hurt the plants."

"So, you think that's what's wrong with the water from the sinks?"

"I don't know, but I could check." Anya ducked back into the sleeping area, crept around David to her pack, pulled out the sampler Mr. Greeley had made her bring, and returned with it.

"What's that?"

"Chemical sampler."

"Nice. Where'd you get it?"

"Bought it a year ago when my experiments got complex, and the greenhouse ones weren't reliable. Let's see what we've got." She led Laura to the latrine and sampled some of the water from the sink.

"Well?"

"I wouldn't recommend it. There are more trace minerals than I'd like, and the biological contaminants are outside the acceptable range. We could drink it, but a lot of us would spend a fair amount of the day in here."

"So, we walk."

Anya nodded, then returned the sampler to her pack. By the time she made it back to the common area, Laura had found four collapsible water bottles and a couple of poles they could use to help carry them. "Are you sure you're up for this? If your father hurt you yesterday . . ."

The last thing Anya wanted was people thinking she needed to be coddled. "I'm just a little sore. I'll be fine."

"Let me know if you need to slow down."

"Absolutely." She smiled, wondering if Laura could tell what she really meant was "not a chance."

Maybe not, because Laura smiled widely at her, said "OK," and started off with two of the water bottles attached to one of the poles. Anya hurried to gather the remaining gear and catch up with her.

The trip out wasn't bad. Laura talked about her son, Jimmy, and encouraged Anya to talk about her grandma and her niece, Tiny. It was all very pleasant until halfway through filling the third water jug, when Laura said, "I was surprised to see you show up with David Ryerson yesterday—I was sure you and young Lancet would come in together."

Awkward. Laura—and half of the people at Steve Jackson's second concert—had seen that picture she'd made of Ryan. Anya might as well get used to the question. She smiled. "We did consider it, but Ryan felt he'd be happier on *Hope*. Since I've found somebody else, I'm glad to let him do what he wants. David is even smarter, and he wants to be here as much as I do."

"You do seem to know how to pick them, honey."

Anya smiled. She hoped Laura never figured out how she'd come to pick Ryan.

They didn't talk as much on the way back, mostly because Anya had to focus all her attention on keeping up. By the time they'd made it back to the big testing room, she was fighting for every step, but she kept to the pace Laura set. She walked behind the other woman, so Laura couldn't see how much she was struggling.

They'd passed the two camps closest to the door and nearly made it to their own when Anya heard DeShawn.

"David, good to see you—and without Miss Moneybags. Where is she? Trying to get some beauty sleep? She needs it."

Anya stopped moving.

A woman laughed. "I suppose she deserves to sleep in after getting a roof over the rest of our heads last night. Though if she knew the deluge was coming, why couldn't she warn us when we were all still awake?"

"I don't think she did know, Bria." David said. "She said she heard the sprinklers warming up, and that's what warned her. You've got to admit, the things *were* making an unholy racket."

"I guess she'd have to come up with some cover story, wouldn't she? Even if her family is paying off the top brass to give her an edge, the rest of us won't put up with the kind of favoritism she's used to. The colony is supposed to be a new start. A fair start. They shouldn't even allow purebred Euro trash."

"Amen, sister," DeShawn said.

Anya's head dropped, and her face got hot, but why should she feel ashamed? So, she was pure Euro. She couldn't help that. And even if her family had helped her out plenty, they weren't helping with this. Quite the opposite. She'd laugh if her ribs didn't still hurt too much.

Laura was now far enough ahead that Anya could see around her. Anya raised her head and caught the eye of the petite bronze-haired woman next to David. So that was Bria. At least there was now one fewer name she'd need to remember. She straightened and held her head high as she carried her water jugs the remaining distance into the camp, setting them down right at Bria's feet.

"What, you can't carry it the rest of the way into the kitchen?"

David glared at her. "You know that's not why she put them there, Bria. Never could admit when you were wrong, could you?" He picked up the jugs. "Come on, Anya, let's see what's cooking."

Anya followed him around the sleeping area to a table strewn with bags of flour, crates of vegetables and fruits, and a mess of hardware. Laura had already found her way there with her own water jugs, and stood, kissing her husband. Next to them, tinkering with the hardware, stood a short, very thin, dark brown man with wiry black hair and a goatee.

"How's it going, Forrest?" David asked.

The man with the goatee looked up and scowled at them. "I'll have a hot plate going in about two minutes. It would be done already if some people hadn't gotten distracted. Now all we need is someone who knows what to do with all this—he pointed at the food. There aren't menus or instructions or anything."

"I think I've got one of my cookbooks loaded into my armband storage," Anya said.

"Of course, you do," Forrest said. "Wouldn't want to live off cooker-boxed food like normal people."

Great. Somebody else who thought she didn't belong. Anya closed her eyes and tried to think of something to say, but David beat her to it.

"Come on, Forrest. Plenty of people like real cooking. You're just cranky because you haven't had your morning coffee yet. They did give us coffee, didn't they?"

Roger pulled away from Laura. "Not a bean or a packet. I think the leadership team might be trying to kill us. Here, young lady. Did you say you've got recipes loaded on your armband? Find some directions for griddlecakes. That will be fast, and we've got A-16 comprehensive tests at nine. David, can you put together that cleaner?" He pointed at a crate behind him that prickled with wires.

Anya wasn't scheduled to cook breakfast, but she wanted to eat, and didn't want a reputation for being uncooperative. She already had enough trouble with people thinking she was a spoiled rich kid. Besides, she reminded herself, cooking was fun, and griddlecakes smelled heavenly.

Laura helped expand her recipe to feed thirty, then organized the supplies while Anya flipped little cakes and slipped stacks off onto a seemingly endless stream of plates.

Arms circled her from behind. Anya tensed up until she realized it was David nuzzling her neck. Her heart still pounded, but she wasn't afraid when he said, "I hope you got to eat some of those because they're delicious."

"Really? I haven't."

"Then this stack is for you." David slid a clean plate under the griddlecakes she was lifting and gently pushed her away from the hot plate. "Go on, eat. I can finish here."

Anya nodded, carried her cakes to the circle where everyone was eating, and squeezed in next to Mrs. Ryerson. Several people got up as she sat down. She felt they were trying to get away from her even though she knew that was paranoid. They'd had plenty of time to eat already, and she'd just started. They were probably finished. Leaving as she arrived was a coincidence.

She didn't convince herself.

At least the griddlecakes were good—golden and flaky, melting in her mouth. They almost made up for the disappearing circle and the way Mrs. Ryerson looked at her—as if she were month-old fruit that needed to be scraped off the floor.

No sooner had they finished than they were off to the first test. A slim dark woman with an elaborate braid who identified herself as Commander Lisa Tehled led them out of the main testing center into a smaller room packed with silvery oval pods. Anya's stomach flip-flopped at the sight of them. She'd never had to use a testing pod before—all her school exams took place at basic computer stations.

She wished she hadn't eaten so many griddlecakes.

David stretched an arm around her. "First time in a pod?"

"How could you tell?"

He chuckled. "You've got the newbie look. But don't worry. If you can talk sensibly in a maintenance hatch, you can perform well in a testing pod." He brushed a kiss across her lips.

"I've never taken an A-16," she whispered.

"You'll do fine. I believe in you."

They'd reached the front of the line, and Commander Tehled waved them toward the next two silver ovoids. David released her with a bright smile. Anya's returning smile felt wobbly, but she walked firmly toward her pod and ducked through the opening. As soon as she settled in the black squashy seat, Commander Tehled shut her in.

Anya closed her eyes and took two deep breaths. An overloud burst of "Triumph" caused her to open them again. A rotating image of *Hope* came up on the screen.

"Welcome to the A-16 Academic and Commercial Skills Placement Test," a female machine voice said over the racket.

"Is there a volume button on this thing?" Anya asked, "And do I have to listen to Kracken? Almost anyone else would be better: Bach, Sven Wang, even Sousa."

"There is a volume control on the left side of the console," the machine voice said in the same calm tone. That was the way with artificial intelligence. It was so maddeningly unemotional. "Background music is a fixed part of the system but may be turned off if desired."

"I desire it," Anya said.

"Triumph" ended mid-note.

"The A-16 Academic and Commercial Skills Placement Test is designed to comprehensively survey your talents and abilities, allowing for ideal job placement and career implementation."

"That so?" Anya said as she fiddled with the buttons on the left side of the console, trying to find one that reduced Madame Tester to a reasonable level. "Does it have any questions on botany?"

Silence fell. The pod hummed.

At last Madame Tester's voice returned. "No. Botany is an imprecise and unnecessary study."

"It's pretty useful when it comes to feeding people," Anya said.

The pod hummed again. Finally, Madame Tester said, "Botany is not a useful branch of knowledge for careers on *Hope*. Now on to your test. There are five main sections: Mathematics, Physical Sciences, Other Sciences, Engineering, and Humanities. Each section will last one hour. Questions posed to you must be answered either verbally, on the console, or with the keyboard before a new question will be given. Press the red button to the right of your console to declare your answer complete. Once the red button has been pushed, no changes may be made to your answer on a particular question. Do you understand the directions?"

"Yes," Anya said.

"The red button must be pushed to declare your answer complete."

"Do you know, I really don't think I like you," Anya said as she pushed the red button.

The first math questions were easy, but by the time half-an-hour had passed, Anya's head hurt. She hadn't had this stuff about cosines yet, though she thought she might be able to guess it from something they'd done in geometry last year. She drew some lines on the screen with the stylus Madame Tester prompted her to find in a crevice above the console and used them to derive a formula from the ones she knew. Twenty minutes later, she'd come up with an answer. Odds were, she was wrong. She pushed the red button anyway. Moments later, a story problem came up—something about a man on a frictionless surface throwing a ball.

"Seems a rather stupid thing to do," Anya said. "He'd fall and break his neck."

"Please answer the question."

"Fine." The problem didn't give nearly enough information for Anya to form a basis for answering. From what she could see, it wanted a distance and a time. "Thirty-seven meters. Twelve seconds." She hit the red button.

The next question had symbols Anya had only seen before in Ryan's textbooks. That was years ago. She'd been at his house, with her doll, and he'd given her a cookie.

"I can't have cookies."

"Nonsense," he said.

"Mommy says they'll make me fat, and then you won't love me." She handed it back to him.

A long silence fell. Then Ryan gave the cookie back. "Don't be silly. One cookie now and then isn't going to make you fat. Come on, you can help me with my homework." He boosted her onto the stool next to his at the counter and brought up his Math text. He held his arm around her shoulders while he worked the problems. Funny how she could still remember those strange squiggles.

"This is the end of the Mathematics Section of the A-16 Academic and Commercial Skills Placement Test. The next section will be Physical Sciences."

What, no break?

Apparently not. Madame Tester launched directly into the next section. Anya sighed, rubbed the sore spots on her wrists from where her father had gripped her yesterday, and got on with it.

The science tests went about the same as the Math test—OK until halfway through, and then painful. She did hit a reprieve in the Other Science section when a series of questions on genetics came up. Every Euro child on *Hope* knew about genetics, and her greenhouse experiments helped some, too. Those questions passed quickly, though, and soon she got bogged down in some questions about polymers that were over her head.

Engineering was even worse. For one thing, by that time she was sore and cramped, yesterday's bruises paining her with every breath. There was no comfortable way to sit, and her head hurt. She asked for a bathroom break, and Madame Tester brightly pointed out a drawer with a deep space tube and disinfectant. She didn't have to go that bad. She shut the drawer and let the machine get on with it.

It only took fifteen minutes to get beyond her depth. How would she design a bridge to span this chasm? She took a good look at it and its specifications. There was no way she could do that problem. "I wouldn't," she said at last. "It's supposed to be crossing a river, right? Well, I'd go upstream until I found a more crossable point—somewhere with a narrower opening and build my bridge there. Then all you'd need is a material that could stand your three-ton load. Even basic steel would do." She hit the red button.

Shockingly, the machine took that as an answer. It wouldn't take "I don't know." She'd tried that already.

As for how she'd design a machine to lift a three hundred kilo weight ten meters, she was similarly clueless. She thought back to a picture she'd seen in a library book once of an ancient musical instrument called a grand piano being lifted into the ballroom of a fourth-story apartment. What had they used in that picture? Some kind of platform, and a system of cables and pulleys—Anya sketched quickly, then considered her work. Of course, a three-hundred-kilo weight needn't be that big, but it could be.

She'd done no calculations. It probably wouldn't work. She'd for sure test a contraption like that with something other than a priceless antique. But she didn't want to look at the problem any longer. She hit the red button.

The next problem was even worse. Would this never end?

After Engineering, Humanities felt like a vacation. Anya breezed through the questions, waiting for them to get hard. She talked about philosophy, political science, Earth religions, ancient culture, modern culture, and authors new and old. It was like talking to Mrs. Dominguez, the librarian, except Anya got to debate both sides.

Madame Tester interrupted in the middle of a question about how eighteenth and nineteenth century Earth Romanticism affected the Barler period of *Hope* literature and art. "This is the end of the Humanities section of the A-16 Academic and Commercial Skills Placement Test."

"That's it?" Anya said.

"Scores for this test will be accessible on your armband starting 7th month, 12th day."

"Thanks." Anya brought up her calendar to mark the date, and realized it was the same day the pass lists for the colony would be out. At that point, who cared what the individual scores were?

The pod door slid open, and she staggered out.

"Bit more than you bargained for, hey?" DeShawn sneered. He was leaning on the pod next to hers. "You should go home now."

"And waste my spectacular performance on this thing?" David said, from the doorway of the pod on the other side of Anya. "When they average us out, I bet we beat you by thirty points."

DeShawn laughed. "Whatever, man. You shoulda stuck with Leslie. Equally brainless, but at least there were compensations."

David extricated himself from his pod, and hugged Anya to him, painfully close. She supposed he'd forgotten about her injuries. He certainly sounded nonchalant, almost jovial as he said, "I doubt Leslie could fix an insta-noodle packet, let alone a griddlecake. Speaking of griddlecake, I want some lunch and a restroom before my next incarceration. Come on, Anya." He steered her past DeShawn and down the hall to their camp. "How are you feeling?" he asked when they got out of earshot.

"Sore. If you could ease up just a bit . . ."

"Sorry." He loosened his grip before she could finish her sentence. "I'd forgotten."

"Wish I could."

"It will go away. Didn't the docs yesterday say there was no permanent damage?"

Anya nodded.

"At least no physical damage."

Tears welled up in her eyes. She shook them back. "Did you really do that well on the test?"

"Better. Except on that Humanities crap. That always gets me. I've been studying, but still—"

"Really? I thought that was the easiest part. I'm sure I did well there. The rest of it—"

"Was good enough, I'm sure. Come on, let's go see if Grandma has scared those kids out of their wits yet."

∞ ∞

"What took you so long? We've all been waiting." Sarka shoved a stack of plates at Borsk and directed him toward the dining area.

"They don't have plates yet, but they're waiting on me?"

"You know what I mean."

"Hardly ever." Borsk ducked through the arch to the dining room.

"Ah, Borsk! The plates. Excellent," Uncle Hirsch said as he relieved Borsk of them. "We're just about to start. I believe there's a spot left in the kid corner."

"Is that the only seat available?" Borsk asked, not because he minded, but because Sarka was two steps back, and would notice if he sounded too enthusiastic. True, it was a drag to chaperone the toddler and elementary school cousins, but none of that crowd would ask him about where he'd gone after church. They probably wouldn't pay any attention to him at all. As long as he kept the chaos to an acceptable level, he could think in peace.

He'd hardly settled in with his dinner platter and his thoughts when all the kids around him sat up straight and dropped their voices to whispers. Borsk straightened instinctively as well, even before he saw Mama drop her hand on Kirsch's shoulder.

Borsk didn't hear what she said to Kirsch, but his cousin brightened, took his platter, and without a backward glance, left for the seat next to Sarka at the head table. Mama slid into his vacated place.

"It shouldn't have taken half an hour to get a broken tablet from VJ Brown. What happened?"

Borsk choked on his chickpea salad. All the kids who hadn't yet tuned into his mama's question now looked his way. Wonderful. He coughed a few times to clear his throat and said, "I don't know. I guess I'm just slow." She wouldn't accept that answer, but maybe it would stall her for a moment.

"Don't be ridiculous! You're efficient when you want to be. Are you avoiding me?"

"Of course not, Mama. I just ran into a little complication on the way home."

"What kind of complication?"

"Mama, I'm not sure this is the best place to talk about it."

Mama's eyes narrowed. "You'd better not have been doing anything you can't talk about around your younger cousins. After the report I got today from Therese Jenkins about your performance in Sunday school—"

"Oh, so Sunday school is a performance now, is it?"

One of his younger cousins snickered. Mama turned toward the girl, and she shut up instantly. Mama turned back to Borsk. "Don't get smart with me. What happened on your way home?"

"Thomas Cartier offered me a job."

It was Mama's turn to choke on her salad. Borsk hoped he'd said enough to shut her up.

He hadn't.

Mama coughed twice into her napkin, then glared at Borsk. "Did you just say Thomas Cartier offered you a job?"

"Yes, ma'am."

"What kind of job?" Uncle Hirsch's younger boy, Shan, wanted to know.

Borsk shrugged. "A well paid one, B-salary now, and more when I've got my degree, which he'd pay for."

"You're not working for Thomas Cartier as long as you live in my house," Mama said.

"That's probably why he also offered me company housing." Now why had he said that? He wasn't seriously considering Cartier's proposal, was he?

"You're only fifteen!"

"Which you obviously think is way too young to decide anything on my own."

Mama stood up abruptly. "If you think anything that man can give you is worth what he'll take, you *are* too young to decide on your own."

Borsk's guilt kicked in as he watched Mama retreat to the kitchen. All around him, his cousins stared with wide eyes. He'd tell them to shut up, but they weren't making any noise.

At least none of them made a sound until Shan spoke up. "What does Mr. Cartier want you to do for a B-salary, tuition and housing?"

"He didn't say," Borsk said.

But he knew.

What could Cartier want from him—from any hacker—other than to make a certain video disappear?

Mama was right. No amount of compensation was worth Anya's safety.

Too bad. It would have been nice to get out on his own.

Chapter Twenty-Four

As they returned to their camp, Anya was surprised to find Mrs. Ryerson getting along remarkably well with the kids other families had brought as their dependents. Little Jim Wilcox sat on her knee, telling her a story.

"We'll finish after lunch, Jimmy." She shoved him off her lap. "Go see your mom and dad."

Anya would have been offended, but the little boy skipped off toward his parents.

"So, how'd you do?" Mrs. Ryerson asked.

"Better than last time, I'm pretty sure," David said.

"Not you, her."

Anya shifted uncomfortably. This must be another of those things—like the mod scores—that other families discussed, even if hers didn't. "I don't know. I'll get the lunch."

That didn't stop Mrs. Ryerson. As Anya poured juice and made sandwiches, the old woman followed her and peppered her with questions. David didn't say anything, but he seemed to be listening intently.

"Well?" Mrs. Ryerson demanded at last. "What do you think, David?"

"It sounds good." David took a plate of sandwiches from Anya. "Really good." He laughed. "I bet she pulled a sixty, and all the extras will count in our favor."

A sixty? Sixty was respectable. Not genius, like David, but not bad, either. "Extras?"

"How you handled problems beyond your reach, how you dealt with the computer, your age."

Mrs. Ryerson sniffed. "You've always been an optimist."

"It's stood me well so far." He gave her a hug.

Anya settled down on the floor with her lunch. So, David Ryerson thought she might have scored a sixty? Maybe they had a chance at this thing after all. And then she'd be married to David—a near stranger. Anya glanced over at him. He laughed when his grandma pushed him away and told him to eat. His smile dimpled, and his eyes shone. Anya loved the warm brown of his skin, the shiny gloss of his hair. She wondered what it would be like to touch—

David caught her looking, and the mischief in his eyes suggested he knew exactly what she was thinking. Her face burned, and she dropped her eyes. David laughed again.

Whatever else it was, marriage to David wouldn't be boring.

Anya never knew how she managed to finish that sandwich.

She recovered enough to join him when he carried his dishes to the cleaner. Bria Huxton reached the machine at about the same time they did.

"Go ahead." Anya stepped back.

"Oh, no. You were here first. Please."

David dropped his dishes in and took off. Then Anya did hers. "There's room for yours, too." She held out a hand. Bria gave her a couple of plates and watched, critically, as Anya placed them in the machine, set the dial for low energy, low water, and started it.

"Very economical." Bria made it sound like a complaint.

"They weren't that dirty." Working in the greenhouses, Anya had developed the habit of using energy and water as sparingly as possible.

"Ah."

The cleaner finished, and Anya stacked the clean dishes in a crate next to it. "Good luck this afternoon," she said to Bria before heading back toward David and Mrs. Ryerson.

"Thank you, but not being insane, I doubt I'll need it."

Anya felt her face heat. She'd forgotten that this afternoon's test was the psych evaluation.

A weird test it was, too. Full of questions about her family and her aspirations interspersed with profoundly strange and personal questions like "Who on *Hope* do you trust, and why?" and "When did you last tell a lie and why did you tell it?" and "How do you feel about what happened between you and your father yesterday?"

Anya blinked. Of course, it *would* ask that. In a suave recorded male voice, just as annoying as the feminine computer voice this morning. Anya looked directly into the console. Her heart raced, and she knew the testing pod had access to her vitals through her armband. She hoped this wouldn't blow her score. "I don't know, and I don't want to talk about it with a computer."

The machine hummed as it processed, taking even longer than Madame Tester had needed for the botany questions that morning. At last it said, still suave and calm, "Who would you talk to about it?"

Anya closed her eyes. "My grandma."

The machine hummed, though not for as long this time. "Anyone you're allowed to speak to?"

Anya closed her eyes tighter. *Anyone not purebred*, she wanted to say, but that answer would be disastrous. Thank goodness, these machines couldn't read minds.

Besides, it wasn't true. She didn't want to talk to just anybody. "I'd talk to Borsk King. Or Mr. Greeley. Or Lucretia Dominguez. Maybe even Kristi."

"That's Mr. Samuel Greeley and Kristi Llourdes?"

"Yes, on Kristi. I'm not sure what Mr. Greeley's first name is. Mr. Greeley in the greenhouses."

"Mr. Samuel Greeley."

"OK, then."

"None of the people you've mentioned are trying out to go to the Golden Terrace Colony. Is there anyone you're trying out with that you'd be willing to discuss yesterday with?"

Anya thought for a moment. "Laura Wilcox, I think."

The machine processed again for a while. Anya sat, growing more and more tense.

"Please describe your relationship with David Ryerson," the machine said at last.

Anya laughed. The sound, even to her own ears, was high-pitched and nervous. They probably thought she was crazy for sure, now. She took a deep breath, then another. Then she chose her words carefully, trying to pick around the stress fractures in this subject—the brief time she'd known him, Leslie and Ryan, the way he made her feel when he looked at her with sparkles in his eye, how it felt when he kissed her, and whether either of them would ever speak to the other again if this thing fell through.

She tried not to lie. She had an uncomfortable feeling that the machine could tell when she lied.

Psych scores could be accessed immediately. Anya was relieved, if a little surprised, to find she'd scored well over the minimum requirements for the colony.

In fact, their whole testing group qualified to continue trying out. However, everyone looked as exhausted as Anya felt. They ate quietly and turned to their mats.

When Anya awoke on day two to find that they'd be doing another standardized test, she couldn't help groaning. "I don't see what use all this traditional math and science is going to be on the planet. Why not do something more practical?"

"You mean more subjective, so your family can buy you in," DeShawn said.

"No, I mean tests that will measure what we'll actually be doing."

"Haven't you kids heard about the simulations Group A did yesterday?" Roger Wilcox said. "DeLang is nothing if not practical. But he's fair, too. If he's offering A salaries, he's going to make sure he's got A-qualified people earning them."

And that meant another day of incarceration in an egg-shaped pod. Lovely. At least there was a simulation to look forward to. She'd never done a full sim before. Her parents believed life should be lived in one's own skin as much as possible.

Today's test, however, was nothing to look forward to. The B-32 was like the A-16, but longer and harder, with a section entitled "leadership" that set problems like "You are working on a team of five. Persons A and D don't get along because of an old family grievance. You're the team leader. How will you proceed?"

Nobody in their right mind would make Anya a team leader. She was the youngest person trying out, and her family had made so many enemies that being in a room with her made some people jumpy. Besides, she was good at art and taking care of plants, not dealing with people. But she had to answer the question somehow. She hardly knew how to start, but then she remembered that Ryan seemed to be able to make people work together, even when they all hated him, so she tried to picture what he'd do, and went with that.

The computer took her answers with the same impassive deliberation that it took everything else. Anya wished it would show a reaction to something. She wanted to dance when the thing finally released her. She really did skip her first few steps back to their camp.

After an early dinner, a few of the group started up a pick-up game of netball. Though terrible at all sports, Anya went along with it since so many of the other candidates seemed interested. She did her best, too, but her best tended to be balls knocked clear off the court and services that didn't make it over the net. Her team lost three games to nothing.

When the last game point went through, and everybody else agreed it was time to quit, DeShawn said, "Yeah, but maybe Anya needs a little more practice. What do you say Anya?"

Anya had been walking off the makeshift court, glad to be finished, but she turned, shoulders slumping. "What?"

"Just give this a good return." DeShawn sent one of his famous serves straight for her face.

"DeShawn!" somebody said.

Anya was too stunned to duck, and the ball hit her on the nose and upper left cheek before bouncing back toward DeShawn. She laughed; she wasn't sure why. When she brought her hand to her face, it came away covered in blood.

David materialized at her side, hugged her to him, and half carried her back toward the latrine.

"It's OK," she said. "Just a nosebleed. I should have ducked."

"Nonsense." Laura Wilcox appeared on her left and pressed a soft wet cloth into her hand. "He shouldn't have served a ball like that to you."

Anya mopped her face with the cloth. "He was just trying to help."

"He was venting anger at losing, which wasn't entirely your fault," David said.

"But mostly," Mrs. Ryerson said. She'd watched the whole game.

"Grandma," David said in a tone that meant "Shut up."

"I know I'm no good at sports," Anya said. Through the cloth and nose-bleed, she sounded even more pathetic than she felt.

"Or much of anything else," Mrs. Ryerson said.

David's eyes blazed, but he was gentle as he drew away from Anya, leaning her toward Laura. "Can you deal with this?"

"Course. Love to," Laura said.

"In that case, if you'll excuse us, please." David grabbed his grandma's arm and marched her toward their screened sleeping area growling something that Anya couldn't distinguish.

Before they got out of earshot, Anya heard Mrs. Ryerson say, "All I was saying . . ." She wondered how the sentence ended. It couldn't be good. Mrs. Ryerson obviously hated her almost as much as DeShawn did.

"How is that feeling now?" Laura asked.

Anya took the cloth away from her face and touched the bruised area. The blood flow had at least slowed down. "I think I'm fine. I'll go clean up, and then come help with supper."

"Honey, you've cooked every meal. It's time you got a break. In fact, I think young Mr. Phillips should take a turn in the kitchen."

"But I like to cook and have the recipes we've been using, I don't mind cooking, but it won't be as much fun if DeShawn has to help." Then Anya remembered she was supposed to be trying to get along. Teamwork. "Whatever you think is best, though."

Laura nodded. "I'll meet you back in the kitchen area, then."

Anya got herself the rest of the way to the latrine and finished cleaning her face in the washbasin. Then she set her armband to mirror mode and checked out her face. She wasn't sure which of her bruises were new and which were yesterday's, but she looked a fright, and probably would keep looking a fright for at least a week. And David was so good looking, she didn't measure up when she had her normal face. She sighed.

Back in the kitchen area, she found Laura and David's beautiful co-worker Denise Jackson looking, with some consternation, at a large clump of red stuff.

"What is that?" Laura asked.

"I think it's meat," Denise said.

It did rather look like the pictures of meat Anya had seen in some library books.

Laura made a face. "They expect us to eat meat?"

"People back on Earth did," Anya said. "Or, at least, that's what I've read. Some really liked it, too. The founding diaries are full of complaints about the meat running out, and the meat substitutes not tasting like the real thing."

"You've read the founding diaries?" Denise said.

"Well, yes. It was one of the enrichment options in lit last year, when we did the charter."

Denise laughed. "And here I thought Steve was the only person on *Hope* who ever did a humanities enrichment. Well, did the founding diaries say how to cook the stuff?"

Anya thought back. She thought she remembered a stir fry description that had made her mouth water when she read it. Maybe there'd been enough details to replicate the dish. "Just a sec. Let me get my school tablet. I think there might be something."

When she came back, they pored over the diary entry together.

"It's like gossip," Laura said.

"Only they've all been dead so long, nobody can be hurt by it," Denise said. "And this recipe does look good. Even if we all gag on the meat, the vegetables will be tasty."

"Let's give it a try," Laura said.

Anya nodded, found a knife, and approached the red stuff. It felt cold and a bit slimy to the touch, and wobbled when she tried to cut it, much more than tofu ever did. It was easier when she got to a section that was still partially frozen—the meat stayed in place as she cut.

"You look like you've been doing that your whole life," Denise said.

"Do you cook at home?" Laura asked.

"Some. When my mother lets me."

"Tell you what, kid," Denise said. "You teach us how to cook, and we'll teach you how to play netball."

"Really?"

"Of course," Laura said. "There's nothing wrong with your game that a little instruction and some practice couldn't fix."

"OK, then," Anya said, and they arranged for a practice session after dinner.

Anya found herself looking forward to it, which might be the strangest thing that had happened to her so far.

&&&&&& &&&

Borsk had promised his mama he'd show up for his appointment with the shrink on time and with a cooperative attitude. It was the only way she'd let him go on his own.

So here he was, staring at a set of moss green entrance beads. Before he could make up his mind to go in, the beads parted.

Dr. Young had spiky hair, the exact same color as his beads. It made him look far younger than thirty-two, the age listed on his public profile. "Ah, Borsk. You'll have to excuse me—I need to wash my hands. But go on in, go on in. I'll join you in a minute." The man brushed past him, leaving the beads swinging.

Borsk watched him saunter down the corridor toward the nearest lavatory. Once the shrink disappeared from sight, Borsk turned back to the beads and watched them until they stopped swinging. Then he sighed. He'd better go in. He'd feel pretty stupid if he was still standing here when Dr. Young returned.

Borsk pushed through the entrance with such decision that he nearly propelled himself into the back wall of the office. He hadn't expected the place to be so small. He knew private office spaces cost a fortune, but this was ridiculous. When they'd pulled the two fold-down chairs into position, he and the shrink would knock knees. He shook his head. He'd be more comfortable in one of the private booths at home, if it weren't for the claustrophobic feeling of being cut off from the net.

Borsk brushed his armband to reassure himself, and discovered, to his horror, that he had no signal. This office was shielded? He bolted back through the beads, directly into Dr Young.

"Steady there, Borsk. You look like you've seen a ghost. Is my artwork that scary?"

"Um . . ." Borsk hadn't noticed any artwork.

"Not the problem, eh? Well I did try for innocuous geo prints. What did you think of them?" Dr. Young held the beads aside, so Borsk could see the muted green squares mottling the walls. No wonder he hadn't noticed them

- 181 -

on his first foray into the room. He shrugged.

"I agree wholeheartedly. I'd get something better if I could afford it. Your mother didn't tell me you were an art connoisseur."

"I'm not."

"You could have fooled me. The only other person who's shown such studied disdain for my walls is Renfro Singh—back when he was still in charge of the art collection in the *Hope* archives."

"If you don't like it, why don't you use blank walls?"

"Oh, the art has its uses. Helps me get reluctant patients inside, for one thing." Dr. Young sketched a motion with his forefinger, and the entrance beads clicked shut behind them.

Borsk hadn't even realized he'd stepped back into the room, but now that he knew he was cut off from the net, his heart sped up, and his breath got shallow.

"Strange. You look like you're experiencing claustrophobia, but you don't have any of the markers for it."

"Markers? You mean gene markers? How would you know? My file is sealed."

"I thought you knew—this is gene counseling. Naturally, the court made an exception."

Borsk blew his breath out in a long slow stream. "So that's how he knew."

"Sorry?"

"Thomas Cartier. He knew about me having King's Syndrome, and I couldn't figure out how he'd learned the information. But if you've got it in your files, he could have lifted it from there."

"That's impossible. My files have A-level encryption, and my office is shielded, so—"

"I noticed. Believe me, I noticed." Borsk stroked his armband. "The thing is, your typical A-level encryption isn't that good. You may be stopping yourself and your clients from accessing the net, but you're probably not stopping anybody from getting in."

"This is state of the art—"

"Want to bet?"

"Excuse me?"

"We'll step outside. If I can hack back in within ten minutes, I can skip the session, and you won't say a thing to Mama."

"If you can hack back in within ten minutes, we'll do half-sessions for as long as your mama wants you coming, and I'll hire you for the remaining time as a security consultant."

His second job offer in as many days. Borsk smiled. At least he didn't feel bad about accepting this one.

As soon as they got outside and his armband came back online, Borsk relaxed. This was more like it.

He wished he had one of his more powerful processors, but he'd work with what he had.

It turned out he didn't need the power. Breaking through Dr. Young's shielding was disappointingly easy. He found dozens of weak spots, not just one.

Within minutes, he had the interior of the office projecting on the corridor wall, and a stream of patient information scrolling across his armband screen.

"Fascinating," said a smooth voice behind him.

Borsk jumped and closed down the screen before turning to see who had snuck up on them.

Thomas Cartier.

"You look surprised to see me, lad. You shouldn't be. I told you I'd meet you here, and I must say, the demonstration of your skill is most impressive, though I wonder at the wisdom of bringing confidential files out into the open. But then, you've never been one to play by the rules, have you?"

"I don't know what you're talking about." Borsk tried to sound nonchalant, but he wasn't sure he pulled it off.

"Nor I," Dr. Young said. "Mr. King is doing exactly what a security consultant should—showing me where the holes in my system are. And now, if you'll excuse us, we need to see about fixing them."

Before Borsk could register his surprise, Dr. Young propelled him back inside the tiny office.

Borsk looked back and caught a glimpse of Thomas Cartier's eyes before the beads clicked closed.

They seemed to threaten, "We'll finish this later."

Chapter Twenty-Five

Anya stared at the tiny silver disks with trepidation. She'd already been painted with the equally silver substance that communicated sensory impressions from some computer directly to her skin and her armband. Now she had to put a foreign substance onto her eyes as well. She wondered if her parents' objection to simulations had more to do with this crazy suiting-up process than philosophical or moral questions.

"Are you all right?" asked the short woman in doctor's green who was in charge of this test.

"Fine. I don't think I've ever deliberately put something in my eyes before."

"Is this your first simulation?"

Anya nodded.

"Surprising. I assumed that with your family—"

"They think simulations encourage escapism and spoil one's taste for reality."

"Do you agree with them?"

Anya shrugged. "How would I know? I've never done one." She stabbed a silver finger at the left-hand disk and raised it to her left eye. It took three tries to get it in. Tears leaked out around it, but the disk stayed put. She felt the doctor's eyes on her and worked more quickly with the right-hand disk.

As soon as she got it securely placed, the world blacked out. Anya stifled a scream. She was fine. Everything was fine. People survived simulations every day. In fact, they paid thousands of credits for the privilege of painting themselves silver, so they could live in phantom worlds.

Ordinarily, the panic would make her sweat, but now all her pores felt blocked.

Then they weren't. A tickling sensation whispered across her right arm, as if she were standing too close to an air vent. She turned toward the feeling and heard something that sounded like a broom sweeping across a tile floor. She opened her eyes and found herself in a steel cubicle. She was back in her normal school uniform, with normal peachy-pink skin. Tools and gear hung from hooks all over the walls. On a table in the middle of the room sat her pack. She opened the flap and found all her things, exactly as they'd been the night they checked in. How had they simulated that?

Something behind Anya creaked. She turned in time to see the silhouette of a man enter through a slender door. All around him, bright white light glowed. The door swung shut, and Anya blinked a few times before she could see the man clearly. It was the tall, gaunt man from the night of registration—Captain Charles DeLang. This time, instead of scurrying away from her, he handed her a small round instrument that she thought might be an old-fashioned compass. Then he pointed to her armband.

She turned it screen up, and saw a map scrolling across it.

"That's a map of the area around the campsite. When you leave this shed, you'll find yourself somewhere on that map. Your task is to get yourself back to camp within five hours. You have the map and the compass, and you may also take your pack and any five additional items you find in the shed. Do you have any questions?"

At first, Anya's mind blanked. She should ask something, shouldn't she? What might be useful to know? She looked around the shed for inspiration. On a wall full of clothing, she saw hats—both thick, cloth ones and wide-brimmed ones that appeared to be made of something like thin cornhusks. "What season is it out there?" she asked.

"Summer," DeLang answered.

"What time of day?"

"Afternoon."

That helped some. She wished she had more experience with this kind of thing. Not that anybody did. Except Captain DeLang himself. "What five items would you take if you were doing this?"

"I can't answer that question." The man flashed a slightly crooked grin.

It was her grandfather's grin. Her grandfather's way of standing, her grandfather's terse way of talking.

"Is there a problem?"

Anya pulled herself together. She could figure out DeLang's relationship to her grandfather later. "No. You just reminded me of someone for a moment there."

The simulated DeLang didn't seem quite sure what to do with this information. "If you've no other questions, you'd better get started."

Anya nodded. "No other questions. Thanks."

The man grunted something inaudible and left the shack.

Five things. Anya looked around. Besides the clothing, she saw lights, knives, rope, spades, a light blanket, small jingle bells . . .

Jingle bells? Why on *Hope*?

She closed her eyes, trying to remember everything she'd ever read about surviving in the wild back on Earth. It took a bit, but she eventually remembered that making noise could keep a person from startling animals and causing them to attack. She picked up the jingle bells and attached them, to her uniform.

If it was summer, she'd want something to keep the sun out of her eyes. Perhaps the cornhusk hat would work. She pulled it down and plunked it on her head.

And she'd want water. She found a canteen.

That left two things. She located a sturdy mid-sized knife and a coil of bright yellow rope and stowed these in her pack.

She was ready. Or as ready as she'd ever be. She shouldered the pack and stepped out of the door of the cube.

A dazzling wash of light and heat made her wish she was back inside. She turned, only to find the steel cube had disappeared. If she wanted to get back inside somewhere, she'd have to find the camp, which was nowhere in sight.

Well, of course it wasn't. That would be much too easy.

She looked around, hoping for a sign that could tell her where she was.

She was on a knoll covered with springy, acid-green plant life. Below her, both ahead and to her right, wound a line of darker green. Overhead, a bit to her right, an unbelievably bright, glowing circle presided over an expanse so vividly blue that Anya reached out to touch it. It felt no more real than her light sculptures.

Anya turned, slowly, soaking in color and form and space.

This, she had to capture. Bringing up her sculpting software, she sat. But before she could start, she noticed a sweet cloying smell that came off the odd little plants beneath her. Fine white mist puffed from the ends of the flabby coiled tubes.

What was that? She dug in her pack for her sampler and tested the air above one of the plants.

Her sampler beeped and flashed red. Poison! Anya straightened up so fast that her head spun. Or was the chemical affecting her already? She tapped the display to bring up more information but couldn't decipher the long string of chemical symbols. What she did understand was the countdown ticker at the lower-right corner of the screen. Less than an hour until fatal exposure. She had to get out of here.

Could she get out of here? Or was the whole planet slightly poisonous?

Her heart sped up. Not helpful. She took a deep breath to calm herself. The breath was full of the sweet smell, and her heart beat even faster.

Think, Anya! Think!

There had to be places on the Shindashir that weren't poisonous to humans—she'd seen pictures of DeLang and the other explorers working on the planet without breathing apparatuses. In fact, there hadn't been any breathing apparatus in the shed.

Anya turned again, now deciding where to go. The land behind her was all the acid green of the plants beneath her feet. She started down the shortest route to the darker green line she'd seen. Part of her wanted to run. Her more sensible side argued that running would increase her chances of tripping. Plus, she'd have to breathe more deeply.

The dark-green line was farther away than she'd guessed. She jingled along, never seeming to get closer, a headache forming behind her eyes. Was that the poison? How long did she have before it caused real damage? At least the bruises from her father's beating had faded to a minor, though constant, irritation.

After what seemed like forever—though the sampler's ticker said it was only twenty minutes—the dark-green line became a line of soft mounds in at least two colors of green. Five minutes more, and Anya could make out leaves and branches, as if the green belonged to giant bushes, though why bushes should be so low to the ground, Anya couldn't figure out.

Then Anya reached the side of a ravine, and realized the foliage wasn't low to the ground, but the very tops of giant trees. If she hadn't had a splitting headache, and if the ticker on her sampler hadn't been counting the minutes down relentlessly, she'd have taken a break to sketch this as well.

As it was, she looked for a path down. She stood at a point every bit as tall as the grape arbor in the greenhouses, though not as steep. Still, she had no harness. There wasn't even anything on the top that looked sturdy enough to tie her rope to.

Anya spent precious minutes searching for the best route. Nothing looked safe, but she eventually found a narrow dirt track with odd little dimples in it. Could water have made the path? Or animals of some kind? She crouched down and rubbed one of the dimples. It felt rough and dry, like ferto in a bed that hadn't been irrigated for months. She shook her head. The marks remained a mystery, but one she couldn't waste time solving.

Anya made sure her pack was fastened securely and started down the track. By hugging the wall and not looking down, she made slow progress toward the valley floor. After five minutes, her sampler's ticker slowed, then stopped. The warning lights cleared. Within another five minutes, her head stopped pounding.

Around the next turn of the track, Anya saw a black beast nearly as tall as she was, with a narrow face and a single sharp horn in the center of its forehead. As Anya stared, it opened its mouth, and a sound unlike anything she'd ever heard before came out—half laugh, half trumpet.

Anya screamed and slipped, landing on her rear end, and sliding half a body length along the track. Her descent sent clumps of hard dirt tumbling toward the animal. The beast made its curious call again, and skittered away, right up the side of the ravine. Anya couldn't believe anything could climb like that. She supposed it helped that the creature climbed with four feet instead of trying to balance on two.

At least it had left the track. She didn't want to find another way to the bottom, but neither did she relish advancing on an animal with a weapon on its head. Picking grit from her palms, she rose to her feet. Her backside now ached almost as much as her front. Balance. Less beautiful when it came to pain than when it came to art.

She grinned wryly to herself and continued along the track. Afraid she'd meet another of the horned-animals, Anya sped up, slip-sliding down the next stretch of hill. The path narrowed, so that she could barely stay on. She turned sideways and tried to slow herself, but only seemed to rush faster. She'd have sat down again but wasn't sure the path was wide enough. She hugged the ravine wall.

Her descent ended when the track turned to avoid an outcropping, and Anya missed the turn, instead ramming into the stone wall shoulder first. At least she'd halted her descent before she fell off the hill. Her relief more than made up for her sore shoulder.

Carefully, she turned.

After the bend, the hill grew less steep and the track widened. Soon, Anya scrabbled over rocks in the shade of giant, silver-barked trees. Their branches began so high above her, that she couldn't even reach the lowest ones standing on tiptoe. The occasional red-barked trees interspersed among the silver were every bit as tall. Anya stopped and took a swig from her canteen.

All around her, the world buzzed and hummed and chirped. Anya didn't recognize a single one of the noises except—she was fairly sure—the splash and gurgle of running water.

Wasn't there a river on the map? She turned her arm palm up and swept a finger across her screen to bring it up. Yes, it showed a river running from the top left edge in a winding curve to the lower right. A feeder and two tributaries branched off from it, but the camp sat near the middle, on the eastern bank of a section where all the branches joined. If the water she'd heard was the river, then all she had to do was follow it, one way or the other, to the camp.

Rubbing her shoulder, Anya stumbled toward the sound.

After a few minutes of winding her way through the trees, Anya found the water. Off to her left, It flowed down a rocky slope, gushing as fast and strong as the pumps that filled the greenhouse rice paddy, but not so uniformly and far wider—a thousand times wider. It flowed past her, off to her right, white and foamy, moving swiftly over boulders and around a log until it disappeared in the trees. She'd seen video recordings of things that looked like this but had always thought they were the wild imaginings of drugged up film makers. How incredible that they were real.

Anya knelt to dip her fingers in the water. Stony ground pressed uncomfortably into her knees, but the cool liquid passing through her fingers felt invigorating.

She'd found the river. Should she follow the water flow—down to her right? Or go the way it came from, up to her left?

Anya checked the map on her forearm, then stared at the water in front of her. She couldn't see even the remotest similarity. The river wasn't straight, exactly. It had rough edges that reminded her more of plants than plumbing. Still, nothing here seemed to be the great sweeping curves that showed up on the map.

She supposed she couldn't see enough of it at once. This map covered an area twenty kilometers across, and she was looking at, what? Half a kilometer at most?

She needed perspective. Then she remembered that perhaps she had some. When she'd first stepped out of the shed, she'd seen a dark green line that turned out to be the tops of trees. If trees lived by the water here, surely, they hugged the river elsewhere as well, and that dark green curve marked the river.

Anya glanced at her map again, but still couldn't relate the landscape she'd walked through to the sharp lines on the map. But there was an easy way around that. Anya sat at the riverside, back against a tree, and opened her art software. (Thank you, Borsk, for getting access to that back.) As quickly as she could, Anya light-sculpted the vision she'd seen when she stepped out of the shed. Then she manipulated it until she was looking at the line of trees, from directly above, and plugged in the data from her fitness tracker to give her picture the same scale as the map.

It was now easy to see that the curve swept in a wide turn that matched a turn of the river on the map, south of the camp. But wait. Anya rotated the light sculpture over her map. It also matched one of the feeder rivers north of the camp.

That left her with two very different possibilities for where she might be now, but still, she knew more than she had known a few minutes ago, and figuring out the rest would be easy. If she was on the northern curve, the river should be north of her. If she stood on the southern curve, it should be to her east.

Anya whipped out the compass DeLang had given her and let the little needle wiggle to a resting point.

Was she reading that right? It said the river was south of her.

She must have done something wrong. She compared the map to her picture again but couldn't see how she'd made a mistake. She was sure she must be in one of two spots. She marked them on her map.

Maybe she had read the compass incorrectly. Anya dug in her backpack for her reader and asked it to search for information on compasses. An ancient book that called itself a field guide loaded. Anya scanned the highlighted section. According to the book, she'd read her compass correctly, but apparently there were things that could throw the mechanism off—certain rocks, for example. Fascinating.

If something was interfering with her compass, perhaps she could solve the problem by changing her location. Anya pushed to her feet and stepped away from the river, back into the woods. The compass swung wildly for a moment, and then settled, pointing off to her right. So, the river was east of her after all? She took a couple more steps, and the compass shifted to point directly away from the river again. In a few more steps, it pointed to her left. Then back to her right.

What on *Hope* was going on?

Anya stood still, let the compass settle, and then followed it in the direction it said was north until she ran into one of the silver-barked trees. As she circled it, she noticed that the compass-needle swung so that it stayed pointing at the tree all the way around.

The tree attracted the compass? Anya tried another one. The same thing happened. It happened again with a third silver tree. A red-barked tree did not attract the compass, but every silver tree she tried did.

Her compass was worthless near silver trees. Anya dropped the thing in her pocket.

How could she tell direction without it? She racked her brain but couldn't recall anything she'd read that could help, so she dug out her reader again. Once more, the field guide had an answer. The thing was becoming useful enough that Anya transferred it to her armband—using the manual clip since there was no net here.

The guide said the position of the sun could tell her where she was—if things worked here as they had on Earth. And they should, shouldn't they? She bit her lip. She knew she should have paid more attention in her science classes, but she was sure she'd heard teachers explaining how similar Shindashir and Earth were when it came to orbit and rotation and a dozen other things she couldn't remember now, but that she thought meant Shindashir and its sun would relate to each other in much the same way Earth and its sun did. She hoped so. It was all she had to go on.

She squinted up at the sun in the sky. It was above her, but not quite straight above, not even as high as it had been when she first got out on the poison-plant plain. According to the field guide, that direction was west, which meant the river was to her east. She tapped the spot on the map to mark it. If she was right, she had to go about six kilometers upstream, and somehow cross the river.

Upstream meant up, Anya realized after a few minutes of scrambling along the riverbank. She wasn't sure she could do it all in one stretch. She'd need to plan breaks. Maybe she could rest for fifteen minutes after each third of the course. The first third would take her to the point where the river split in three. She ought to be able to recognize that.

It took her longer than she expected. When she stayed close to the river, she had rough going through stands of thorny bushes and over rough boulders. When she moved farther away, the ground under the silver trees was smoother, but she had trouble following the path of the river.

It was a bit over an hour before Anya reached the curve she'd been aiming for. She was glad to finally be sure she was on the right track, but worried that she was taking too long. She would have kept going, skipping her break, but a stitch in her side forced her to stop. She set her armband alarm for fifteen minutes, found a comfortable spot beneath a tree, and sketched, making her fingers fly as fast as they would go, knowing she had only a few minutes. She drew the one-horned beast, then a silver tree, then her first glimpse of the river, and finally, with broad strokes, the point in front of her where the river split in three.

She'd barely started this last drawing when her alarm buzzed. She sketched a final few lines before dragging herself to her feet. If she ever wanted to do this on the planet, next to an actual river, she had to get moving.

The river turned west here, and the terrain smoothed out. Anya whistled as she walked. The river beside her splashed. The air smelled fresh, cleaner even than the air under the oxy trees, and ever-so-slightly perfumed with a floral scent. Ahead of her, the sun hung low in the sky. Her armband said she had about two hours remaining. She began looking for a likely spot for crossing the river.

A kilometer further on, she found a wide, shallow section of river that had stones poking above the water level all the way from this bank to the opposite one. It was as good a place as any to cross over. Anya stepped onto the first stone, adjusting her weight as it shifted beneath her. The second stone was wider and firmer. It stayed solid when she moved onto it. The third was far enough away that Anya had to stretch to reach it. She raised her arms out to her sides at shoulder height to steady herself. Once secure, she moved forward again, but as she was about to set her foot down on the fourth rock, it turned and looked at her with small beady eyes.

Anya screamed, lost her balance, and fell into the river, scraping her right leg from ankle to thigh, but managing to stop her fall before her torso and head fell underwater. Cold washed over her. As she struggled to her feet, fighting the pull of the river, the animal she'd thought was a rock, rose, lumbered to the edge of the larger stone it had been sitting on, and launched itself into the water.

It shot away with a speed and grace she wouldn't have believed possible from something that looked like a rock. She watched it speed out of sight. Only when she returned to crossing the river did she realize the water had pushed her a body length downstream from the line of rocks she'd been using to cross.

Rather than go back to them, she waded across, holding her pack above her head when the water got chest high in the center. She worried that not returning to the stones was a mistake, but soon after that, the water level dropped to her thighs, then to her knees. Then she scrambled up the opposite bank, a goodly way downstream from where she started.

She didn't think she'd gone far enough to take a break again, but she couldn't go on without paying attention to her leg. The scrape was bleeding, the uniform above it in tatters. Thank goodness Mr. Greeley had put that first-aid kit in her pack the day Father beat her up. She located it now, soaked the washcloth in the cleaning solution, and washed the cut, wincing at the sting. The scrape was long, but not deep, except for a short span above her knee, where she used one of the butterfly bandages.

Long before she finished tending the wound, she was shivering in her wet clothes. She stripped them off and changed into a dry uniform from her pack. She wasn't sure what to do with the wet uniform, and finally tied it to the outside of her pack, where it slapped wetly against the back of her legs as she walked, until she figured out a way to tie it up better.

Her break hadn't felt very restful, but she feared she'd run out of time if she didn't get moving. The worry twisted in her gut, pushing her onward, limping and fighting weariness and pain. She hurt in places she didn't know she had. Her legs alternated between screaming in protest about the indignities the rocks and dirt had subjected them to, and grumbling about the hard, uneven terrain. They felt weak and unsteady, and blisters on her heels punctuated every step, but Anya pushed on, ignoring the discomfort.

She told herself not to think about it, and when that failed, actively looked for something else to occupy her mind. Fortunately, there was plenty to see. She didn't think she'd ever tire of the silver trees, which were as plentiful on this side of the river as the other. The lacy-fronds of deep green that occasionally tucked themselves near the red-barked trees' roots were fascinating as well, and every plant, every tree, every rock and fallen branch and puddle was different from the last. Hardly a straight line could be seen, but there was still an order to it all, somehow. It reminded her of those fractals Borsk had shown her.

She sped up, hoping to get to a place where she could stop and sketch.

Forty minutes on, she came to a wide straight path, clearly made by humans. On her left, it crossed over the river on a sturdy bridge. She cursed. Had that been marked on her map? She brought it up, but nothing was there, not even a line to indicate that this path or the safe river crossing existed.

"Those idiotic—" Then Anya remembered that the same idiots who'd given her the map would be watching this, deciding if she got to join the Golden Terrace team. She bit her lip and stumbled onto the path, bearing right. She had to be close now.

She dragged her weary, protesting body steadily up the rise, which was nearly as steep and every bit as rocky as the ravine side she had climbed down on the other side of the river. She thought she'd nearly reached the top when an animal barred her way. It was tawny brown and bigger even than the horned beast she'd encountered on the other side. What looked like tree branches sprouted from its head.

Anya managed not to either scream or fall this time, even when the thing raised its branch-crowned head to stare at her.

"All right, you brute," she said. "I suppose you weren't expecting me on your path any more than I was expecting you on mine."

The beast blinked, then apparently decided Anya was no threat. It lowered its head and tore up some delicate sprays of purple flowers that grew out of a stony outcrop next to the path. It chewed in a side-to-side grinding motion, with bits of flower and leaf sticking out of the side of its mouth.

It ate plants. Well, that was promising. Probably it didn't eat people. But it didn't seem afraid of them either. Maybe it didn't move because Anya hadn't screamed.

She worked up her best high-pitched screech. The big animal merely raised its head, stared at her for a moment with liquid reproachful eyes, and returned to its snack.

Anya backed down the path until she got to a wider section. There were no paths that branched out, and no good way up the last rocky hillside. She checked her armband. She didn't think she had enough time remaining to scramble over rocks finding a new way to the campsite, but she didn't fancy squeezing past the beast, either.

Her eyes lit on a clump of the same purple flowers the animal had been chewing. It seemed to like those. She bet it would enjoy this bunch. If she could lure it down here, to enjoy these flowers, the path was wide enough, she could probably get around the thing. She picked several handfuls of the flowers and headed back up the hill.

When she was back near the top, she held the bunch out to the beast. "I brought you some of those flowers. There's a whole big patch of them back this way."

The animal, which had nearly finished its own patch of purple, lifted its head. Then it stepped closer. It took all Anya's strength of mind not to drop the flowers and run away, especially when the animal lowered its head and pulled the flowers right out of her hand.

She'd convinced it to move, but not far enough. "Come on, there's a whole patch this way."

The animal looked at her but stayed stubbornly put.

"I'll show you." Anya walked down the path, but the animal didn't follow. She supposed it wanted more flowers. Stumbling back down to the big patch, she picked another bunch and returned, holding them out to the animal again. This time, when it shuffled forward, she backed up, keeping the flowers out of its reach until they reached the place where she'd picked them. "There you are. See, isn't that better?" Anya fed her bunch to the animal, then scooted around it and headed up the path.

This time, she crested the hill to discover an unimpeded, winding descent. She rushed forward. Ten minutes of her time remained. She hoped it was enough.

She'd gone halfway to the next curve in the path when she heard something like a drumbeat behind her. She looked back.

The flower-loving beast was running her way.

Anya raced ahead, but it followed, catching up as she reached the turn. She pressed herself into the rocks, hoping the beast would pass her by, but it stopped, and nudged her with its nose.

Anya stifled a scream. "What do you want now?"

It nudged her again, knocking her off balance. She caught herself before she fell, but it was a near thing.

Perhaps it wanted more flowers. Anya spotted a few nearby, plucked them, and fed them to the animal.

While it chewed, she moved ahead, but it followed. She supposed she'd better keep feeding it, so it would stay happy.

Anya descended as fast as she could while stopping to pick flowers every few steps. After the next turn in the path, she could see a flag and a couple of wooden sheds. She smiled and ran the last bit, the animal thumping along behind her.

As she approached, DeLang stepped out of the shack to the right of the path. He smiled her grandfather's crooked grin at her.

"I see you've brought Bonnie with you."

Chapter Twenty-Six

Borsk stayed hypervigilant at school, worried that Thomas Cartier would come into one of the classes again, but the man didn't show—not there, and not on the route home. Borsk had changed into his restaurant whites and was halfway through an agonizing shift of waiting and bussing tables when Anya's father had the audacity to walk through the front door and demand a table in Borsk's section.

Overhearing him, Borsk jerked and dropped the tray of dirty plates he was carrying back to the kitchen. They clattered and crashed to the floor, splattering a group of nearby diners.

Sarka glared at him. He apologized to the table, ducked down, and started recovering the soiled dinnerware. Sarka turned away, beaming her brightest smile and slickest difficult-customer voice at Mr. Cartier. "As you can see, my brother still lacks finesse when it comes to serving. I'm sure you'll be much more comfortable in the stage-side area."

Borsk was surprised she'd admitted they were related. He kept his head down and his hands busy.

"Thank you, my dear, but I must insist on one of your brother's tables. We have a conversation to finish."

"You have a lot of nerve coming into my place of business and harassing my children." Mama's voice so startled Borsk that he dropped the few plates he'd managed to recover. He couldn't remember when Mama had last come out of the kitchen to speak with a customer.

Even Sarka must have been surprised. She forgot to glare at Borsk over his fresh bout of clumsiness.

"Mrs. King. What a pleasure. I deeply regret that there was no time to discuss the loan situation two weeks ago. I fear we misunderstood each other. I'd prefer there be no such misunderstanding as I begin working with your son."

"There will be no misunderstanding. Borsk won't be working with you."

"Under Section 12 of the Optimal Employment Code, that is for Borsk to decide, not you. And as I understand it, he has already begun freelancing as a security consultant. He can't refuse to offer me the same services he's offering others."

"Borsk isn't—"

"Mama, maybe we should take this to the purple room. It sounds like it could take a while." Sarka placed a hand on Mama's arm and led both her and Mr. Cartier back toward the purple booth.

Borsk stared after them. When had Mama ever followed Sarka's lead?

Sarka glanced back over her shoulder. "Are you coming?"

"Right." Borsk scooped the scattered dishes onto his tray, dumped the lot on the nearest empty table, and followed the others to the back of the restaurant.

The purple booth felt even more claustrophobic than usual when Borsk shared it with Mama and Mr. Cartier. He slumped down in his seat, fighting his panic over being cut off from the net, and trying not to meet anyone's eye.

For a while, no one said anything. Then the red light flashed, and the booth door slid open. Sarka passed around cups of water. "Can I help you with anything else?"

"The special will be fine, young lady," Mr. Cartier said, smiling at her.

"And . . ."

"We're fine," Mama said, with a look that sent Sarka scurrying.

When the booth had relocked, Mama turned her stare on Borsk. "Care to tell me what all this is about?"

"Mr. Cartier was passing by when I had my appointment with Dr. Young the other day. He noticed me giving the doc some advice on security and suggested I work for him as well."

"What were you doing . . ." Mama stopped. She closed her eyes, as if praying for patience.

Mr. Cartier spoke into the gap. "Your son seems to enjoy helping people, an admirable trait. I only wish to remind him, and you, that *Hope*'s charter requires that businesspeople offer their services to all who wish to receive them."

Borsk knew about those laws. His dad had said they were meant to keep pure Euro jerks like Mr. Cartier from discriminating against the rest of *Hope*. Trust Mr. Cartier to twist them to his own ends. But at least he could think of a way around them. "Under normal circumstances, maybe. But I'm a minor, and you've just been charged with assault and battery against another minor.

I don't have to deal with you."

Mama sat up straighter and gave Borsk a glance that made him feel proud of himself, if only for the second it took for Mr. Cartier to speak again.

"Those charges are completely unfounded. They'll get thrown out before trial."

"Well, if they get thrown out, Borsk can consider your request then. For now, enjoy your meal." Mama scooted toward Borsk, as if to chivvy him out of the booth.

"Not so fast, Mrs. King. I was hoping not to bring this up, but there is another item to discuss. When I passed by your son's security demonstration the other day, I quite accidentally picked up a number of files that perhaps I shouldn't have. The lad's intake form was one of them. While I only glanced at it, I saw enough to think that *Hope* Security might want to take a look as well. Remind me what the penalty for felony hacking is?" He looked at Mama, who stopped sliding toward Borsk.

Borsk thought she looked scared. He'd never seen his mama look scared before. What had she put in the stupid intake form? And could Mr. Cartier legally use it to prosecute him?

Mr. Cartier smiled at Mama. "You don't know the penalties? I'm sure your son does. Permanent armband removal, isn't it? Though in juvenile cases, especially ones like this, where the records hacked affect mainly the young person in question, the sentence is often reduced to a class three-shut down until the young person becomes fully of age. Still, six years without an arm-band? I could see why the young man might worry about that. All it would take is a whisper of what's in the files, and ship security could subpoena them from Dr. Young."

Borsk couldn't help grimacing, but he wasn't going to let Mr. Cartier have it all his own way. "Actually, in a several-year-old case, the penalty is likely to be only a warning."

"If there's no evidence of hacking in the intervening time. In your case, however—"

"I've had no criminal prosecutions for hacking, and there's no evidence that I've done anything I shouldn't lately." Borsk hoped.

"Boy, you've been in my house system within the last two weeks!"

"Are you sure? Both that I was there, and that I wasn't asked in?"

"What do you mean, asked in?"

"Your daughter is a lot smarter than you think she is, sir, and she hasn't trusted you in a long time."

Thomas Cartier pounded on the table. "Leave my daughter out of this, you little—" Thomas Cartier stopped. He took two deep breaths, sat up straight, and unclenched his fist. Then he took another two deep breaths. His face, which had been turning red, returned to a lighter color. "What I meant to say, lad, is that I doubt my daughter gave you permission to be in my house system, but even if we can't prove that, there are some things on your school record that suggest you haven't given up hacking at all. Even the old offense ought to get your armband shut down for a year. However, since I'm the only one who has the leaked file—" Mr. Cartier broke off again as the red light over the door flashed.

The door slid open, and Sarka slapped a plate in front of Anya's dad. "Everything OK in here?"

"Fine," Mama said in a strangled voice.

Sarka didn't even smile at them before shutting the door.

Anya's dad stared at the light for a moment. Then he returned his gaze to Borsk. "As I was saying, I'm the only one who has access to the file, and I'd see no reason to report the 3-year-old peccadilloes of someone working for me."

"But if I refuse to work for you . . ."

"I'd feel it was my duty to inform ship security of what I'd seen."

"What exactly would you want me to do for you, Mr. Cartier?"

"To hire you on a freelance basis for security work, much like the work you provide for Dr. Young. I've brought a sample contract." He pulled an old-fashioned memory chip from a pocket, ran it over his armband, and handed it to Borsk.

Borsk grit his teeth, took it, and ran it over his own armband, glancing at the file as it scrolled over the screen. Generous terms. Too generous. Borsk shook his head and worked to hold his voice steady as he said, "If I did decide to work for you, it would only be to do legitimate, legal work."

"Oh, I think you'll find that working for me will stand up to every bit as much scrutiny as your other activities." Mr. Cartier looked down at his untouched meal. "Do you know, I find I'm not hungry after all. So rude of me. But perhaps it's just as well to give you time to think this over. Take it to your lawyer. You can respond to me by tomorrow after school?"

Borsk nodded mutely.

Anya's dad smiled. "Then I'll take my leave. Mrs. King, Borsk." The door sprang open, and he gracefully uncoiled himself from the booth and exited.

From his smug look, it was obvious he thought Borsk would be signing the contract before morning.

Borsk let the door close, and the light fade. "Mama, what exactly did you put in my intake form for Dr. Young?"

"Borsk, he needed to know."

"Let me see it." He handed Mama the memory chip from Mr. Cartier, so she could use it to transfer the file to him.

"Borsk, you can't be thinking—"

"I need to know if it's enough to get me convicted of felony hacking."

Something in his voice must have gotten through to her because she answered in a businesslike tone, "Of course. We'll go to Laura—no, whoever's covering for Laura while she tries out for the colony—and see what the lawyers have to say."

Borsk nodded. They had to check it out. Mr. Cartier could be bluffing, of course. But somehow, he didn't think so. He was sure the lawyers would tell him Mr. Cartier could make good on his threats. Then he'd be left with deciding which he'd prefer: covering Thomas Cartier's tracks, so he could go on controlling and even beating Anya or condemning himself to years without access to the web.

He'd be cut off from any meaningful work for half his remaining healthy years, maybe more than that. What good would he be at twenty-one if he hadn't been able to hack since he was a teen?

But he couldn't betray Anya again and live with himself all that time either.

He turned to his mom. "Yeah, let's talk to the lawyers. Maybe they'll know how to reduce the time I'm without an armband."

Mama stared at him for a moment, and then smiled. "Oh, Borsk. I'm so proud of you. I'm sure our lawyers can minimize the penalty. You'll probably get a warning, or . . . ." She bit her lip, "at the most a year without your armband. That's not so bad, is it?"

"A year without any access to the net, stuck in this stinking restaurant unable to do anything I love?"

Mama gasped.

"What? You thought I loved this place like you and Sarka do? Sorry to disappoint you, Mama."

Borsk pounded on the release button for the door and stormed out the second the opening got wide enough for him to escape.

⁎ ⁎

When the Golden Terrace Colony dissolved into pure white light within a minute of Anya finding it, she cried. Actually cried.

Her mood wasn't improved by the uncomfortable sensor-peeling that followed or by the stinging shower required to remove the silver paint. She tried to comfort herself during her post-simulation check up by looking at the art she'd created on her journey, but when she tried to access it, the pictures were gone. She moaned.

"Are you OK?" Carolyn Kuhler, the short, green-clad doctor asked.

"My pictures are gone."

"What pictures?"

"The ones I created in—"

"The simulation was a test. Anything you created in there has been uploaded to the colony servers for analysis."

And wouldn't be available to her—they wouldn't want anybody cheating on the simulation if they had to run it again. "Of course. I should have realized." Perhaps she could recreate them. She'd recovered lost art before. Sometimes it was even better the second time.

As soon as Dr. Kuhler released her, Anya dragged herself back toward their camp.

"What took you so long?" DeShawn asked as soon as she approached their group, which was mostly gathered in a loose circle in the common area. "Don't tell me you survived the whole simulation."

"Survived? Did some people die?"

One of David's tall beautiful admirers—Anya thought she was called Savannah Leigh—laughed shortly. "Half of us died," she said. A number of heads around the circle nodded.

"Oh," Anya said. She glanced at the people seated on the floor. Everyone looked tired and glum, including David and Mrs. Ryerson. Anya walked across the circle and sank down next to David. Mrs. Ryerson leaned across him. "So how bad was it?" she muttered.

"I only made it back with a minute to spare," Anya said, keeping her voice as low as Mrs. Ryerson's.

On her other side, Steve Jackson laughed. "Hey, you all, we have another finisher," he said to the group. "That makes three of you," he said, more quietly, to Anya. "Roger and Laura both made it through too."

Anya glanced to the other side of Mrs. Ryerson where the Wilcoxes were sitting. "Why do they look so sad, then?"

"They each had a simulation of Jimmy along," David said. "The kid died in both their scenarios."

"Ouch," Anya said.

"Steve, did you just say that somebody else finished?" Bria Huxton asked. "Who? Surely not Anya."

Anya looked up and said, "Yes, I finished."

DeShawn grunted. "What did they do? Drop you within sight of camp?

"No, about eight kilometers southwest as near as I could tell."

"Ah, so your compass was working," Steve Jackson said. "I wasted the first two-and-a-half hours going around in circles."

"I hear you there," Bria Huxton said, slumping. Even her bronze spikes of hair seemed to droop. "Mine didn't work either. It didn't take me long to realize it was broken, but I never could figure out where I was, either."

"Yeah, those silver-barked trees sure mess with compasses," Anya said. "Mine was useless too."

"So, how'd you find the stinking place?" DeShawn asked.

"I used the sun to get my bearings and followed the river."

"Well, of course, if they dropped you by the river . . ."

"Actually, they dropped me in a field of springy plants, but once I realized they gave off poison gas, I made for other vegetation, and that brought me to the river."

"How'd you know the plants gave off poison?" Savannah asked.

"The smell was off, so I tested it with my sampler."

"Sampler? Who has their own sampler?" Bria asked.

Anya's cheeks got hot. She'd forgotten most people couldn't afford tools like that. "I got it when the greenhouses couldn't replace their broken one. I needed it to do research. Father wouldn't let me keep working there without the research."

"You wanted to work in the greenhouses that much?" Bria asked.

Anya nodded.

"Why?" Georgia asked.

"Well, it's beautiful. And Mr. Greeley let me sculpt after all my work was done."

"Can we see?" Steve asked.

"If you'll play. I've never heard you play."

"You've never heard Steve Jackson—" Bria said.

"Her father doesn't approve of my music. Would you listen to it if you thought you'd get beat up for doing so?"

"My father doesn't beat me up every time I do something he doesn't like," Anya muttered at her shoes. She couldn't say why she was defending him, but she couldn't stop herself either. "He only lost control when he heard I was trying out for the colony. He has some kind of issue with Captain DeLang."

DeShawn snorted. "Some kind of issue with DeLang? Are you sure his problem wasn't with the idea of you and David Ryerson?"

"He wasn't thrilled about me and David, but his problem with the colony definitely has to do with DeLang." That was true, of course—or at least she thought it was, but it also covered up the betrothal. Why was she acting like she cared if her parents got caught? She didn't understand herself. She decided to change the subject. "Anyway, did you say you would play, Steve?"

Steve pushed up from the ground. "Let me get my trillium."

"Hungry, Mama," Jimmy Wilcox said.

"Of course, you are, sweetheart. Just a moment, and I'll get up and fix something." Laura sounded and looked more exhausted than Anya felt.

Anya pushed herself to her feet. "I can do it. You look like you need a rest."

"But you just got here, and it's not your turn for dinner detail. Besides, you were going to show some pictures."

"They'll go better with dinner, don't you think? I'm hungry too, now that I come to think of it, and I doubt whatever's back there is instantly edible."

Georgia got to her feet, too. "No such luck. The leadership left us another load of unrecognizable stuff that probably has to cook for hours. I'm supposed to be over there, but I didn't want to face it. If you're going, though, I'll come."

The two of them headed toward the makeshift kitchen. "You said the food is unrecognizable?" Anya said.

"Never seen anything like most of it before."

"Give me a sec, then." Anya ducked into her sleeping area and grabbed her sampler. She didn't trust unrecognizable food from the leadership team. Not after the compasses and maps in the simulation. And sure enough, one of the foods, a dull orange fruit, turned out to be a strong diuretic.

"I can't believe it," Georgia said.

Anya shrugged and dumped all the orange fruits into the compost bucket. "At least the rest of it is edible."

Georgia and Anya had already whipped up a batch of biscuits and cleaned most of the vegetables when Bria Huxton turned up.

"I'm supposed to be on dinner detail, too," she said.

She didn't sound happy about it, but at least she was there. Three people working would be better than two. "Georgia is starting to serve people, so if you'll keep the biscuits going, I'll get after some of the rest of this," Anya said.

Bria scowled. Perhaps she didn't like being ordered around by a teenager. Anya smiled in what she hoped was a conciliating way and got busy chopping vegetables.

It took nearly an hour to get everything ready to eat. It wasn't so much the difficulty of preparing things, though there was a brownish root that hadn't noticeably softened despite boiling all that time. Rather, it was the amount of food that had to be made up. But at last everyone had a plate of something, and Anya settled back into the circle between David and Steve Jackson.

"Ready?" Steve asked.

"Um, sure," she said, trying not to look too longingly at the plate of food in front of her.

"Then go." Steve raised a set of pipes to his lips and blew out a long clear note. It reminded Anya of the pale lines of superwheat just before harvest, so she flashed up a sculpture of those.

She heard several people gasp, but she couldn't pay attention. Steve had moved on to a melody that triggered a different memory, a different sculpture, this time a ripple of light on the grape leaves. When she flashed this second sculpture up, the music hitched for a second, then continued almost the same, but not quite, and the new notes matched her sculpture even better, almost as though Steve was altering his song to accommodate her art. She gasped. He winked at her, and then changed up the music again. She laughed and closed her eyes to remember just the right piece. She wasn't sure she'd ever had so much fun in her life.

They might have gone on forever, but suddenly, Desiree Leigh, Savannah's two-year-old daughter, threw up into the middle of the circle.

Savannah pulled the child toward her. "Desiree, honey, what's—" She broke off, dropped the child onto her husband's lap, clutched her stomach, and dashed toward the lavatory.

"What's wrong?" Anya said. "Is it the food?" She pulled her untouched plate toward her and sniffed. It smelled wonderful. Her stomach growled, and she lifted a small portion toward her mouth.

"We tested all of it," Georgia said. "Besides, you don't see anyone else getting sick, do you?"

"Get a doctor," Jordan Leigh said.

"DeShawn ran toward the leadership table, but before he got even halfway there, Stanley and Caroline Kuhler both met him. Without listening to his explanation, the doctors strode toward the group, Stanley moving on toward the lavatory, and Caroline stopping at the circle. "Not to worry, not to worry," she said briskly. "Some people's systems can't take meat. That's almost certainly what's happened here. Come along, little one. We'll get you fixed up." She maneuvered Jordan and Desiree Leigh out of the circle.

The party broke up. Denise Jackson, the Wilcoxes, and to Anya's surprise, DeShawn cleaned up the sick and cleared the dinner dishes.

Anya rushed to finish her food before one of them took her plate.

"Oh, honey, take your time," Laura said. "After that show, you deserve it. I had no idea the greenhouses were so beautiful. Maybe Roger and I can plan some dates over there once this is finished."

"Once this is finished—but you and Roger both made it back to camp. Surely you'll make the colony team."

Laura dropped into the space Steve had recently vacated. "We're thinking of withdrawing our application. After what happened to Jimmy in our simulations—I mean, Vera and Charles DeLang have been our best friends for years, but I'm not sure I'm willing to risk my child, even for them.

"I never thought about the danger to kids," Anya said. "But this was a test situation. I shouldn't think we'll be running those kinds of risks very often."

"Maybe."

"Please don't give up, Laura. The Golden Terrace team needs you."

"Needs me and Roger? A lawyer and a ship's crewman? I doubt either of those professions are on DeLang's must-have list."

"I don't know. With the way my father has been opposing the colony, a lawyer might come in pretty handy. Besides, there's more to all of us than our professions. You and Roger are both so calm and wise and warm."

Laura laughed. "Well, we haven't made up our minds yet."

Roger came up behind her. "But all your pictures tonight have us appreciating the beauty of *Hope* in a new way."

Mrs. Ryerson, one of the few who hadn't yet left the circle, snorted. "Only an artist could make those greenhouses look good. Show us what you did with your simulation today, child."

"How did you know I made pictures?"

Mrs. Ryerson rolled her eyes.

"Anyway, I lost them—they got uploaded somewhere, and I can't access them."

"If you did it once, you can do it again," Mrs. Ryerson said.

Anya wasn't used to creating in front of people, but this was the first sign of real approval Mrs. Ryerson had shown her. Besides, she wanted to recapture the lost art anyway. "OK," she said.

She settled herself back into her seat, pulled up her drawing program and tried to block the sounds of the people around her, but their shifting and muttering intruded on her thoughts.

"Ignore them," she muttered to herself. "Remember what you saw." She closed her eyes for a moment to recall the scene she'd stepped out of the shed to. Then she opened them and sketched with all her might, first the whole valley, then the springy plants, then the ridge and the path she'd scrambled down.

Dimly she was aware of others joining Mrs. Ryerson and the Wilcoxes. DeShawn muttered something about how the hills weren't that green, but several voices, including Mrs. Ryerson's shushed him, and Anya was left in peace to sketch and sculpt and sketch again, putting down all she could remember of that glorious simulation, right down to Captain DeLang's welcoming grin at the edge of camp.

"She really did finish," DeShawn said.

Anya looked up. Her creations surrounded her, all of them hanging in the air, casting shadows over the people around her. "How is that possible?"

"How is what possible?" David asked.

"They usually disappear when I finish working on one. My armband can't project more than one at a time."

"Oh, I've been boosting your capacity a bit," David said. "Remember, I asked if I could help back when the early ones started to disappear?"

Anya couldn't remember anyone saying anything other than DeShawn complaining about her colors. She shook her head. "I wasn't paying attention, I guess. But thank you."

"No, thank you. This wasn't much of a day until I got to see Golden Terrace through your eyes."

"Plenty of time for mushy stuff later," Mrs. Ryerson said. "If that's all you've got, child, you'd best get to bed. You have an interview in the morning, and we'll have to clean up all this camp mess, too, no doubt."

Anya glanced over at the old woman, who gave her a half smile. Well, well. Was Mrs. Ryerson softening up towards her? "Yes, ma'am," she said before shutting down the projections one by one, making sure each was well saved in her long-term storage.

She didn't want to lose a single pixel.

Chapter Twenty-Seven

After consulting the lawyers, Borsk bought freedom from Thomas Cartier by turning himself in to Central Security in exchange for six months with severely limited net access and no armband function at all.

By mid-morning, he was already regretting the choice. Without his armband, he'd had trouble getting up, accessing his work schedule, and turning in his homework. His school tablet had so many security protocols running on it that it stalled out every third minute. He had no idea how he was going to survive six months of this.

The only bright spot of the morning was when Anya's father showed up at his school, in person, and cornered him in a short corridor between his history and physics classes.

"Mr. King, a word."

"Mr. Cartier? Should you be here?"

"Lad, have you lost your mind? What good are you to anyone if you can't use your armband?"

That was exactly how Borsk had been feeling, but it wouldn't do any good to let Thomas Cartier know how much he was hurting. "Actually, I'm lots of help in the restaurant, and it's only for six months."

"We can walk this back."

"Thanks for the offer, but our conversation yesterday made me realize I'm better off taking responsibility for my actions."

Cartier grimaced, and Borsk had to repress a smile.

"Son," Cartier put a hand on his arm.

"Please don't touch me," Borsk said, loudly enough to bring his history teacher out from her classroom.

"Sir, you can't be here. You've got a Class A restriction on dealing with minors—at least until after your trial. I don't know how the door let you through. Please come with me."

With more spunk than Borsk would have given her credit for, she escorted Anya's dad toward the door. The look on his reddened face almost made the misery worth it.

Almost.

Borsk just had to get through six more months of it.

Well, five months, thirty-and-a-half days.

Why had he made this deal again?

&ℬ   ℭ

Anya's last day of try-outs whizzed by in a whirl of cleaning and packing. Near the end of the morning, Anya and David were the last of their group to be called to a small white room with uncomfortable white stools around a rickety, once-white table. On the side opposite the door sat the two doctors and Lisa Tehled, the second in command of Golden Terrace Colony.

"I thought Captain DeLang was interviewing all candidates personally," David said.

"He had a conflict of interest in your case," Commander Tehled said.

David shot a questioning glance at Anya, but she couldn't explain it any more than he could. She ought to have looked into it before now, but the tests had kept her so busy, she hadn't had a chance. She hoped whatever it was her father had done to Captain DeLang wouldn't hurt their chances. She shrugged at David, and they sat.

Anya had never done a formal interview since the greenhouse took any willing (and quite a few unwilling) workers, so she had nothing to judge this one by, but she thought they did well. David sounded relaxed, confident, enthusiastic, and unbelievably smart, and even she managed to let her enthusiasm for the colony overcome her shyness. The leaders seemed particularly interested in her greenhouse work, and though they kept to the technical parts Ryan and her father found so important rather than the beautiful parts she loved, she thought she did well with that part of the interview.

She and David also seemed to do all right handling the awkwardness that came when talking about their fledgling relationship. But then, Commander Tehled asked how they thought Anya's being pure-Euro might affect how she fit into the team.

David bristled. "I didn't know you got to bypass articles seven through ten of *Hope's* charter when making up this team," he said. "Race is not supposed to be an issue when selecting people for a work detail."

"No, but it can be an issue for living together peaceably," Caroline Kuhler said. "We'd like to know how Anya plans to handle it."

Anya touched David's arm, trying to let him know she didn't mind answering the question. "There's a lot of history—personal as well as ship history—that interferes with peace. I guess I can understand why a lot of people don't like pure-Euros. They've dominated ship leadership and culture even as they've become an increasingly small minority on *Hope*. People like my father sometimes act like they're above the law—and get away with it.

"I can't change any of that. I try to be different. I don't expect special treatment or favors, but I know some come to me anyway." She thought of her personal library and the sampler that helped her get through the simulation. "I can't help the fact that I'm wealthy—privileged in many ways."

"You don't act like a wealthy, privileged kid," David said. "You serve others, clean up after them, do jobs usually relegated to those who couldn't make the tertiary education cut."

"Well, I don't mind, and somebody's got to do those jobs. Besides, if I didn't do them, there would be people who figured I think I'm too good for that kind of thing."

"So, what people think of you is important to you," Stanley Kuhler said with a warm smile.

"Well, sure. Who doesn't want to be liked?"

Commander Tehled stared at Anya until she felt her face get hot.

David squeezed her shoulder. "I'm sure that anybody who had a problem with Anya would mellow out once they got to know her."

Anya wasn't so sure. After all, she'd worked with DeShawn at least twice a week for years up in the greenhouses, and he'd never warmed up to her. But this wasn't the time to bring that up.

"On a different note, how would you feel about leadership?" Caroline Kuhler asked.

"I'm fine with it," David said. "I've been project lead on a number of significant repairs and—"

"Sorry," Commander Tehled said. "We meant that question particularly for Ms. Cartier."

"Me? But I have to be about the youngest person trying out—and anyway, isn't the leadership team set? Captain DeLang, you three and Matthew Smith?"

"We're still looking for someone to lead our food and textile team, and the scouting party has insisted that person be someone with experience in the greenhouses."

"Oh." The idea of leading anything made Anya feel squirmy inside, but if that's what it took to get on the colony team, she'd have to try to convince them she could do it. She pasted a smile on her face and tried to sound enthusiastic and intelligent about heading up a team. It was easier if she thought about it in terms of what it took to grow food for a group. That she could talk about with some authority.

After a couple of minutes, as she was talking about superwheat harvests, Caroline Kuhler and Commander Tehled exchanged a cryptic glance and moved the subject on to which of their try-out companions they felt made good teammates and why.

Anya wondered if David really got along with everyone as well as he seemed to or if that was an act he put on for the interview. She herself found it easy to talk about the Wilcoxes and Steve and Denise Jackson, but then stumbled trying to find others she thought she got along with well. Georgia had been wonderful when she'd been in trouble, and very helpful last night—if only she wasn't linked to DeShawn.

Mercifully that line of questioning didn't last long, and when it ended, Commander Tehled wound up the interview.

As soon as they were well away from the meeting room, David swung Anya up into his arms. "Unless I am very much mistaken, we're in," he whispered in her ear. Then he kissed her breathless.

When he finally released her, Anya felt dizzy, both in body and spirit. Jubilation spiked with doubt washed through her.

She wished she could be sure David was right.

❧　❧

Try-outs ended an hour after Anya and David emerged from their interview. There was one last form where they gauged their own excitement about the colony team and evaluated their try-out teammates' contributions to the group. Then, along with the rest of the candidates, they grabbed their bags and made their way to the greenhouse station to wait for an available shuttle. The Golden Terrace Colony team list would be posted tomorrow.

Anya wondered if the hollow feeling in her stomach would last until then. She chewed on her lower lip.

"Hey, don't worry," David said, drawing her close to him. "I think we're in great shape. We're going to make this team, I tell you."

"You and everybody else who still wants in," DeShawn said. "Haven't you heard? After the simulations, half the people trying out have withdrawn. There's chatter on the net that the captain might have to draft a couple or two."

"He should have sent Anya around to all the groups," Laura said. "She convinced Roger and me to stick with it."

"Thanks," Anya said. She wasn't sure what to do with all the attention that seemed focused on her and was glad when a shuttle pulled in.

Standing in the crowded car with David's arm firmly around her shoulder kept her well separated from DeShawn but gave her far too much time to think about what she was going back to. She wouldn't even be going home. She wondered who the lawyer and her mother had picked as her temporary guardian. Funny that she couldn't figure out how to bring the information up on her armband. It should be available now she was reconnected to the net.

"You OK?" David asked.

Anya nodded. They were almost to *Hope* Central Station, and she could see a crowd of people waiting to meet the shuttle. When their car shuddered to a stop, and the doors opened, spilling first the standing passengers and then the sitting ones out onto the platform, they were surrounded and embraced by loved ones who acted as if they'd been gone years rather than days.

All the passengers, that is, except Anya. At first, she saw no one she knew.

Mrs. Ryerson, after enduring a few hugs, stomped off through the crowd, leaving David to field his family's questions. There seemed no end to them—either the family or the questions, so Anya let her hand slip from David's and headed for the back corridor, not knowing exactly where she was going, but wanting out of the press of people.

"Anya, hang on," David said, catching up to her, "Where are you going?"

"I think I'll head for Skreetches," she said. She hadn't realized where she was going until she said it, but now it seemed the logical thing to do. Borsk and Mrs. King would help her figure out who her new guardian was. Too bad there wasn't much chance it was the Kings.

"I'll walk you," David said.

Several people behind him groaned. David turned, pulling Anya toward the group, stopping in front of a tall, astonishingly beautiful middle-aged woman. "Mama, this is Anastasia Cartier. She's the sweetheart who agreed to try out with me, and whose mad greenhouse skills are going to get me and grandma on the colony team."

"I wouldn't be too sure of that," said a voice behind them.

Anya twisted, so she could see who had spoken. Ryan Lancet. A weight like a number eight ball bearing dropped to the pit of her stomach. "What are you doing here, Ryan?"

"I came to collect you. My parents have been named your temporary guardians, but they couldn't get off work in time to meet you."

"Then I will walk you back there," David said.

"No need. She's perfectly safe with me, and I can see your family wants your attention. If you do, somehow, make the colony team, there won't be that many more opportunities for them to see you."

"That's true, David," his mother said. "Though perhaps Anastasia and her friend would like to join us all for dinner."

Before Anya could figure out whether she wanted to accept the invitation or not, Ryan said, "That's very generous, ma'am, but my parents are expecting us back at home quite soon."

"Of course, of course. Well, say goodbye, David."

David scowled as if he didn't much like his mother telling him what to do, but he drew Anya in close and kissed her soundly. Before releasing her, he murmured in her ear, "Don't let him convince you there's anything wrong with us. We might not have known each other long, but we were destined to be together on the Golden Terrace team." Slowly he released her.

When her heartbeat slowed, she followed Ryan through the remnants of the crowd, glancing back every few steps until she could no longer see David.

It felt like they were heading toward her home since the Lancet place was only a few corridors down from hers.

Ryan didn't speak to her until they were up ten levels and the corridors were nearly deserted. Then he said softly, "You shouldn't let Ryerson kiss you like that."

"Why not? We tried out together. If we make the team, we're going to get married. And I don't see why you care anyway. It's not like you want to kiss me. I'm the kid you're stuck with—the one whose hobbies are doll babies and grubbing in the dirt if I remember correctly."

"I shouldn't have said that."

Tears welled in Anya's eyes, and she shook them back. "No, you shouldn't have." Though if she hadn't heard, from his own lips, what he really thought of her, would she have found the courage to try out with someone else?

Maybe Ryan was thinking along the same lines. "But Stacey, just because I was a jerk doesn't mean you should throw yourself at the first dirtbag who shows an interest in you. David Ryerson—"

"Is brilliant and thoughtful and at least knows my name."

"What are you talking about, Stace? I've known your name since you were born."

"Everybody but you and my parents calls me Anya. Has for years. If you paid any attention to me at all, you'd know that."

"You're right. I'm sorry. I'll try to remember, but—"

"It doesn't matter." Anya wiped the tears away from her eyes with the back of her hand. "It really doesn't. We were never friends, and now we're not anything else either."

"S—Anya, you've got to understand. There's no way your father is going to let you go to the planet with that womanizing jerk."

"David is not a womanizing jerk," Anya said.

"Right. Because you know him so well after a couple of days in his company." They reached the Lancet door, a tasteful blue screen. When Ryan punched in the door code, the beads swung loose in waves that reminded Anya of images she'd seen of the sea.

Something calmed inside her. This had always been one of her safe places. Was that going to change now? Anya chewed her lip. "I know David likes me better than you do. And he wants to go planetside almost as much as I do. It sounds like a better recipe for happiness than hooking up with a womanizing jerk who doesn't like me and doesn't share my goals."

"Maybe, but your dad still won't allow it."

"There are some things even my father can't control," Anya said, hoping desperately that it was true.

Chapter Twenty-Eight

As it turned out, they could have joined David's family for dinner. Mrs. Lancet's rotation at the hospital lasted until two, and Mr. Lancet only came home long enough to say hello, get Anya settled in Ryan's bunk, which she'd be using until they could clear out his older sister's, and get called back to work.

"I guess it's just you and me," Ryan said.

Anya didn't want to be alone with him. "Why don't we go up and visit my grandma?"

"You know you aren't allowed to visit her without one of your parents. Last Friday didn't change that. But hey, I'm not such bad company. I'm not much of a cook, though. Are you any good at making noodles?"

Anya could make anything, but she didn't feel like playing nice for Ryan after the way he'd treated her on Saturday, the way he'd been treating her for years. Didn't he realize how mad she was at him right now? She opened her mouth to argue, and then realized she didn't want the fight. Ryan wasn't worth it. "I'm not hungry. I think I'll turn in early."

"Sta—Anya, you can't avoid me forever. You—"

Anya slipped into the bunk she'd been assigned and slammed down the screen. Ryan's voice clicked off like a music program when a teacher found her running it. Anya smiled. She was tired enough to drop into sleep and not wake until morning when the Golden Terrace team list would be posted. If David was right about them making the team, she might never have to deal with Ryan or her father again. She squirmed until she got comfortable in the cramped space, then shut down the bunk lights and let the darkness take her.

Anya woke abruptly to violent banging that shook the blackness around her. She jerked upright and hit her head on a low ceiling. Her heart pounded. Where was she?

Old instincts took over, and she fumbled at her armband, typing in codes by touch.

"Stace? Stacey? What the hell are you doing?"

Ryan? Oh, Ryan. She was staying at the Lancets. She remembered now.

She found the bunk lights and brought them up. Yes, here was a cubby full of neatly stacked music cubes and another with crisply folded uniforms. Anya took deep, slow breaths, forcing herself to calm down. It was only Ryan. He was a jerk, but he wouldn't hurt her—not physically anyway.

"Stacey? Are you all right? What's going on in there? Why can't I open this thing?"

Anya took another deep breath. "What do you want Ryan? And how did you override the soundproofing?"

"Priority message came in for you ten minutes ago, overriding all sound-proofing in the house. Why do you think I've been banging on the screen? And what have you done with my bunk?"

Anya stared at her armband. "Sorry. I changed the code before I realized it was you. Kristi taught me to do that if anything ever woke me up at night, back when . . . back when . . ."

Back when Kenneth was still around at all hours. Just thinking about it made Anya's heart speed up, and she found she couldn't even whisper the words. Fortunately, she didn't need to.

Ryan sighed. "Stace, Kenneth Llourdes hasn't been allowed in this house for twenty years. Not since he made a pass at my sister when she was barely ten."

Anya hung her head. She knew that. "Sorry."

"Don't be. I'm only telling you to help you feel safe. I'm not going to touch you, Stace. Not until you want me to."

Anya got hot. "You're not going to touch me ever, Ryan."

"You don't mean that, Sta—Anya. You're angry right now."

"Of course, I'm angry!" Anya started before deciding the issue wasn't worth pursuing. He'd find out soon enough what she meant and didn't mean. "What's the message about?"

"You've been summoned to a meeting up in your father's office. Some-thing about the Golden Terrace Team."

"In my father's office?" Anya shrieked.

"Yeah, Dad thought that was fishy too. He said I needed to go with you to make sure your interests are protected. He'd go himself, but he can't get away from the job he's on. It's a critical repair, but I doubt they'd insist on Dad doing it if your dad weren't pressuring them."

Anya massaged her head. "And he thought *you* should come along to protect my interests?"

"Not the best choice, I know." Ryan sounded tired. "But possibly better than going to the meeting alone."

"What about my lawyer?"

"Tried to reach him, but he's offline, and the junior associate fielding calls is in your dad's pocket."

It was Anya's turn to sigh. "All right, then." She performed a complicated swirl over her armband and unlocked the bunk screen. "Give me a sec to clean up."

"We'll barely be on time if we leave right now."

"Tough. If whoever it is needs to see me so badly that they've got to wake me from a sound sleep, they can wait until I've freshened up."

"It's Captain Bates."

"He can wait."

"And Captain DeLang."

That was different. "I'll just be a moment." She ducked into the lavatory, splashed water on her face, and ran her fingers through her hair. As she worked, Ryan asked what the new combination to his bunk screen was.

"Oh, I don't know. I think it'll only take my security swipe now."

"*Your* security swipe?"

Anya shrugged. "Get Borsk to help you put it right. He's good at that kind of thing."

"I can't. Borsk has been banned from the net."

"What? Why?"

"Officially or actually?"

Anya was too tired to deal with riddles. "Just tell me."

"Officially it's a punishment for a hack he did several years ago."

"That's crazy! Why bring it up now?"

"He turned himself in without consulting me, but I'm guessing it was to avoid working for your dad."

"What's my father got to do with it?"

"There are certain video logs from a few days ago that your dad would like to have disappear, and Borsk is one of the few—perhaps the only one—currently living on *Hope* who has the skills to make that happen."

Anya gasped. He was talking about the record of the beating. "They're not gone already?"

"Borsk helped us save them, and I made sure they were properly filed, with plenty of redundancy."

"*You* did? But . . ." Anya ducked back out of the lavatory and stared at Ryan. He'd destroyed any hope he ever had of being captain. And he knew it, Anya realized as she looked at his face. Wow. Maybe he didn't like her. Maybe he was cheating scum. But It might be good to have him with her to deal with Father. She smoothed out the wrinkles on her uniform and said, "I guess I'm ready."

Anya had never been out in the corridors during sleep cycle before. It was eerie, walking in a puddle of light that moved with them, illuminating their next few steps, but leaving empty blackness before and behind them. It felt as though the whole world had shrunk into a tiny bubble of light containing only her and Ryan. She knew houses and businesses existed beyond the circle, but they felt as unreal to her in that moment as a dream remembered days later.

She spoke as much to break the silence as to satisfy curiosity. "Is this—"

Ryan put a finger to his lips. Seconds later, the message light on Anya's armband flashed. She glanced at it. "No talking in the corridors after curfew," it said, and the relevant articles of ship code were linked. Anya glared at him but didn't try to say anything else.

They had to wait five minutes for the lift, and when it slid open, Borsk was in it, slumped against the back wall, his dreadlocks falling over his eyes.

"Borsk, are you OK?"

He raised his head, and a mix of emotions Anya couldn't read played across his face until he settled on a smile.

"Anya. How'd it go?"

"The try-outs? Good, I think. David says we got in." As she said the words, all her excitement and nervousness returned.

"Quiet," Ryan hissed, ushering Anya into the lift and getting them started on their upward climb. "Don't you two care at all about ship security?"

"Not much," Borsk said with a ghost of his former grin. "It's not like we're disturbing anyone. Everybody on this level has good soundproofing."

"You think it'll help to have a noise citation going into this meeting?"

"You're coming to the meeting?" Anya asked Borsk. "Why?"

"Message said there might be a way to adjust my sentence—did you hear about that?"

"Yes," Anya said.

"Figures." Borsk glared at Ryan. "Anyway, there were no details, but if there's even a chance I can get this undone, I have to hear about it." Borsk twisted his arm so that his left forearm faced up. His armband screen was oddly blank, even the color indicator near his wrist had gone black.

"I'm so sorry, Borsk," Anya whispered.

"Me too."

Chapter Twenty-Nine

Borsk couldn't believe how big Thomas Cartier's office was. The ceiling vaulted up three times a man's height, and the empty area in front of the enormous desk could hold a wall ball tournament, one with a live audience. The mural on the wall facing them had to be the largest piece of art on *Hope*. Borsk tried not to feel dwarfed by it as he, Anya, and Lancet approached the desk, but suppressing his reaction to the outsize space only gave him more time to notice the other intimidating features of this gathering.

Every face in the room but his own was white—Lancet, Anya, Cartier, the bland-looking woman beside him, Captain Bates, who sat on Cartier's other side, and a tall, rangy guy Borsk didn't recognize. This man sat, scowling, a bit apart from the others, but still behind the desk. As Borsk and the others neared, the man looked up, and Borsk realized who he was—and that he wasn't pure-Euro. Captain DeLang. So, this had something to do with the Golden Terrace Colony. That explained why Anya and her parents were involved.

But what was he doing here?

He must not have been the only person wondering that because Captain Bates leaned toward Cartier and whispered something in his ear. Cartier looked up. "Ah, yes. Borsk King. Glad you could make it, but we aren't quite ready for you yet. If you could wait in my foyer."

"You yank me out of my bed in the middle of the night to wait in your foyer?" Borsk managed not to yell it. Barely.

"Lieutenant Lancet, would you please keep our young guest company?" Captain Bates said.

"No," Anya said. She looked even paler than usual but spoke clearly and loudly enough they could all hear. "Lieutenant Lancet is here at my request, and at the request of his father, my temporary guardian. And if you called for Borsk, he should stay too."

"Stacey, my dear, your mother has never stopped being your guardian," Cartier said. So, the woman sitting next to him was Anya's mom. Borsk should have realized; he'd caught a glimpse of the woman the other day in the lift.

"My mother may not have stopped being my guardian, but she stopped looking out for me ages ago. If you're going to be in this room, Father, then I also want people I know and trust here as well."

Cartier scowled, looking for a moment so like DeLang that the two could be twins.

Then DeLang's mouth quirked upward in what might have been a fleeting smile, and the illusion was gone. "Let them both stay. You've room enough, and time is pressing."

Cartier jerked his head and moved his hand over his armband. In front of the desk sat a sturdy folding chair, intended for Anya, Borsk supposed. Next to it, two circles in the floor before the desk irised open. Poles shot upward out of them, and tops folded out. Within about thirty seconds, two stools sat there, looking like red-capped mushrooms.

Anya looked at them with distaste, but perched on one, glanced at Borsk, and patted the more comfortable-looking folding chair to her left.

"Yeah, OK," Borsk said, sitting down on it.

Lancet took the second stool.

"So, what's all this about?" Borsk asked.

Captain Bates glanced at Cartier, who nodded. "The Golden Terrace Colony Personnel List has triggered a couple of protests."

"Sure. Mr. Cartier objects to his daughter going. He beat her up trying to stop her," Borsk said.

Bates glared at him. "Young man, you'd best watch what you say. Thomas Cartier has not been convicted of any wrongdoing."

"Yet," Anya said, again in that unusually clear, loud voice. "He will be. He—"

"Slammed you into a wall multiple times, leaving well-documented injuries," Lancet said. "It will come to trial, but not today, and arguing about it here isn't likely to help anything. What protests did the Colony List trigger?"

Captain DeLang answered. "Cartier has accused me of violating Article 10 of the charter."

"Article 10?" Borsk frowned. "I thought that had to do with not discriminating against people based on their ethnic background."

"Precisely," Cartier said.

Borsk snorted.

"DeLang has knowingly, and with full intent, followed a course of action designed to destroy the continued existence of pure Euro-descended people," Cartier said.

"Just by giving Anya a place on the Golden Terrace team? You all must be pretty fragile."

Cartier pressed his lips together, and Bates choked, but Anya giggled. "We are, but I don't see how Captain DeLang could have known that. It's not like he has full access to any pure-Euro gene files. He's not family."

Lancet laughed, or maybe it was coughed. "You're kidding, right?"

"Excuse me?" Anya said.

Lancet glared at Cartier. "You never told her?"

"Told her what?" Borsk asked.

For a minute nobody answered. Then Lancet sighed. "Captain DeLang and Thomas Cartier are brothers. Only half, sure, but the captain would have access to his father's files."

Borsk half expected someone at the table to jump up and deny this, but no one did. He shifted in his seat. Next to him, Anya had turned even paler, which he wouldn't have believed possible, and her face seemed oddly blank, like a bad game character's. She didn't seem able to speak.

"OK, so the guy's related. How do you figure he set out to destroy you lot? He couldn't have planned on Anya being on the team—she didn't get a try-out partner until the day testing started."

"If Ms. Cartier hadn't tried out, we would have drafted her," DeLang said. "We need someone with her particular set of agrarian skills."

"And five years ago, you asked Sam Greeley to train someone with those skills," Cartier said.

"I did," DeLang said. "I did not, however, ask him to train your daughter." His lip curled. "In fact, if I had any idea that Ms. Cartier was his protégé—"

"You'd have asked him to train someone else," Anya said softly. Borsk wasn't sure how anyone besides him could hear her, but they must have because all eyes turned toward her.

"That's beside the point," Cartier snapped.

Lancet cleared his throat. "Not entirely beside the point, sir. You did say knowingly and with full intent."

Anya's dad glared at Lancet. "Well, he is knowingly and with full intent pursuing such a course of action now. Though we requested the team substitute someone else for Stacey, he refuses, even knowing what that refusal means."

"There is no one else with Ms. Cartier's skills," DeLang said. "We've checked. The survival of the colony may well depend on Ms. Cartier's involvement. Nothing less would induce me to include one of your children on my team, Thomas."

"You see," Cartier said to Bates, "clear prejudice against our kind. Once he knew he had to make do with one of us, he set out to see there were no more."

Borsk stifled a laugh. Prejudice against their kind? DeLang's issues with Anya sounded more like a completely reasonable prejudice against Thomas Cartier. "Don't be ridiculous," he said. "If Lancet there hadn't been such an asshole, Anya would have tried out with him, and they could fill a whole new world with pure-Euro babies. The colony lot can have as many kids as they want, right?"

DeLang smiled a crooked smile. "Once we're stable enough, yes."

"Obviously that's why DeLang has made sure Stacey is NOT partnered with pure-Euro lad, and why he's begun these persecutions against me—to separate my daughter from her family and friends, and cast dark enough aspersions on my character to nullify my influence with her."

"Persecutions? Father, you beat me up."

Anya's voice was so startling, Borsk's head jerked. On his right, Anya sat straight and bright-eyed, her chin up and her voice strong. He'd never seen her look so good.

"And you've never appreciated my strengths—my reading, my plants, and my art. You don't even know my name. Nobody but you is responsible for nullifying your influence in my life."

Cartier sat up straighter as well. "Your uncle may have taught you to say that—"

"My uncle! I didn't even know he was my uncle until I came into the room tonight! I've never spoken with him. Your normal searches of my armband will prove he hasn't been around enough to teach me anything."

"I'm sure your armband shows whatever you want it to show, given your young friend's proclivities," Cartier said. "He alters proximity logs for fun."

Borsk smiled. "You think I can hack an armband proximity log without leaving a trace?" It was nice to be appreciated, even if the appreciation came as an accusation, but he had no desire to earn more time without an armband, and for once someone had overestimated his skills. "Thanks, but I don't think anybody can do that. Besides, if Captain DeLang was trying to "end your kind" as you put it, don't you think he was running an awful risk, letting Anya ask Lancet here to join her on the team? I mean, Lancet turned her down, but for a second on Friday night, it looked like a near thing. Lancet's a jerk, sure, but if he'd publicly agreed to try out with Anya, in front of his boss, no less, he'd have gone through with it."

Borsk looked over at Lancet, who gave him a strained smile.

"Ms. Cartier asked you to try out for the colony with her?" Captain Bates asked Lancet.

"Yes, sir. Just after Steve Jackson's second concert wrapped up. Major Wilcox and his wife were both there."

"So were about thirty other people, who certainly saw Anya ask, and who probably heard you muttering positive non-committal noises," Borsk said. "Hell, the restaurant security tapes might even have caught the interaction. You set them up for complete coverage, seeing how we were expecting trouble."

"DeLang still—" Cartier started.

Captain Bates held out a hand. "Enough, Thomas. If she asked young Lancet here, and there seems to be irrefutable evidence that she did, then we can't move forward with the charter protest. Even a sympathetic judge would throw it out for lack of grounds." He sighed and passed a hand over his head. "Maybe we should take a break, let you children get a snack. Lieutenant, perhaps you could get coffee and pastries for the rest of us as well."

Wait. Was that it? What did it mean?

Lancet was already on his feet. "Come on, Borsk and Anya. The captains and Anya's parents seem to need a bit of time to regroup."

Borsk thought about resisting since the idea to leave had come from Bates but decided against it. It might help Cartier and his pal to have time to think, but that same time might help Anya and him figure out what to do next.

He got up and followed Lancet across the wide office space. As he thought about what Lancet had said about the adults needing to regroup, he couldn't help smiling.

If Cartier needed to regroup, they'd won the first round.

∽ ⟡

Anya stumbled after Ryan and Borsk, her head reeling. Mother hadn't spoken, hadn't even looked at her once, not even when Anya accused her of not looking out for her own daughter's interests. Anya wasn't surprised, exactly, but it still hurt, her mother's not being willing to even acknowledge her presence with a nod.

And then the news that Captain DeLang was her uncle. Her uncle! And they'd never said a thing. She turned her arm, so she could use her armband more easily, and started a record search. Now she knew what to look for, it took only moments to get access to the entire story. The sordid details stopped her in her tracks. The boys stopped, too, but Anya didn't have much attention to spare for them. She was reading how grandfather had raped an employee, and then grandmother had tried to bribe the young woman into having an abortion. When that hadn't worked, Anya's grandmother had sued to deny the child—Charles DeLang—any breeding rights. The suit had dragged through the courts until DeLang was almost ten, bankrupting the entire DeLang family. The settlement the DeLangs had received when they won hadn't even begun to make up for what they'd lost.

No wonder Captain DeLang didn't want her on his team. But apparently, he needed her. She was going to the planet—assuming she could make it through whatever devious plot her father came up with for his next protest.

Ryan put a gentle hand on her shoulder. "Are you all right?"

"I think so. The snack station is this way." Anya stepped around the boys and led them away from the elevators toward a small door opposite them. Beyond was a twisting hall with dozens of unmarked doors draped in gray beads. The last on the left opened into a small service hatch with a cooker, a cooler, a drink station, and a cupboard of edibles.

"How much is this, then?" Borsk asked.

Anya shrugged. "Free on this floor. GenM executive perk. Take what you like." She wasn't hungry, but water never hurt. She grabbed a cup and filled it.

"Are you sure you're OK?" Ryan asked.

"Of course, why?"

"You never drink straight water."

"What are you talking about?" Borsk grabbed a couple of rolls and filled a glass with fizz. "She drinks straight water at the greenhouses and Skreetches all the time."

Anya stared down at her cup. She supposed she did usually drink water around people who couldn't afford anything else. And it had seemed the best thing here. "I'm fine."

"You're also not eating. And you didn't have supper." Ryan looked concerned.

Borsk swallowed a big chunk of roll. "That *is* strange. Are you sure you're alright?"

Anya shook her head. They didn't have time for this. "Guys!"

"That was a lot to have thrown at you," Ryan said.

"Sure. I'll no doubt be thinking about it for years, but right now, the only thing I have time to worry about is whatever Father has up his sleeve. I wish I could guess what it was."

"I suspect he'll protest Ryerson being your partner," Ryan said, "or at least your mom will. She's still got parental rights, and you are underage."

"There's nothing wrong with David," Anya said.

"Of course, you wouldn't see it. Not with him laying the charm on thick like he was this afternoon," Ryan said.

"David Ryerson is an OK guy," Borsk said.

"If he were the right color, you'd have no problem with him dating your sister?" Ryan asked.

"Well . . ." Borsk started, then stopped. After a pause, he said, "Better him than you."

Ryan smiled wryly. "Touché. And almost certainly how you come into it. Much better match for Sta—Anya than either of us, right?"

"Borsk?" Anya looked over at him. He looked as shocked as she felt. "Borsk doesn't feel that way about me. Besides, he's not even green."

Borsk shoved his darkened armband with the odd black light under her nose. "I'm not any color anymore. I've got my dad's delta-zed gene sequence. King Syndrome. Can't have kids at all."

King Syndrome? Wasn't that fatal? "Oh, Borsk, I'm sorry. I didn't know."

Borsk shrugged. "Nobody was supposed to know. Mama thought it would be better that way."

"Then why are you telling us?"

"I couldn't live with not knowing, so I hacked in shortly after my dad died. Mama recently found out and used the information to find me a shrink. The doc's files weren't very secure, and that's how your dad got the info—or so he says. It's only a matter of time before everybody knows."

"Why does my father care about your health problems?"

"At a guess, he doesn't," Ryan said. "But when the Kings admitted Borsk had the intel., they were also admitting that he'd pulled off a felony hacking job at twelve."

That *was* the kind of thing her father would be interested in. "I can't believe he prosecuted instead of hiring you," Anya said.

"He definitely tried to hire me," Borsk said. "I'm pretty sure he wants me to make certain evidence disappear, not that he said as much in so many words."

Certain evidence. Borsk meant the proof that Father had beaten her up. "I'll bet he did."

"That's a serious accusation," Ryan said.

"A hundred-fifty credits an hour is serious money," Borsk said. "You think he meant to pay me that for entirely legal security services?"

Ryan pressed his lips together. His brow furrowed.

"Ryan, if Borsk goes to the planet with me, or if you do, what are the chances that *Hope* holds Father responsible for his actions?"

Ryan turned away.

"What are they?"

"Slim to none," Ryan finally admitted.

"And once he's restored to full power, what do you think he'll do to the Ryersons, and Borsk's family, and yours?" Not to mention the Golden Terrace Colony. Anya didn't see how her father could wreak havoc on *StarRacer* or the planet, but she'd be a fool to underestimate him.

"Stace—Anya, I mean, you don't really know David Ryerson."

"I know that he wants to be part of the colony as much as I do. So, does his grandma. But neither one of you do."

"I might want to go if I get the use of my armband back again," Borsk said. "Though I hate to think what might happen to Mama and Skreetches while I was gone."

"Why should anything happen to your mother or Skreetches in your absence?" Father's voice so frightened Anya that she jerked backward into Ryan, who steadied her as Father came into view from around the last curve in the corridor, still talking. "Particularly if you had left to oblige me? I look after those who do me favors." He glowered at Ryan.

A shudder snaked up Anya's spine. She wasn't particularly happy with Ryan herself at the moment, but he didn't deserve whatever Father's look threatened.

To Ryan's credit, he didn't even flinch. "Sir, the colony team will never accept Borsk. Even if he wants to go, he's banned from reproduction, and he has a degenerative illness that will affect his physical fitness within a few years. He might even be showing symptoms by the time *StarRacer* reaches the planet."

Father laughed. "I hope they do reject him. If they can't put together a working team, personnel selection reverts to *Hope* leadership, where it always should have been."

"No!" Anya said. "The colony is a separate entity, equal in power to *Hope*. Its leadership has the right to choose its own workers."

"Your uncle certainly did a good job on you," Father said. "What did he promise you? The chance to drop out of school and fritter away all your time on those childish drawings of yours?"

Anger rose in Anya. She lifted her chin and moved away from Ryan. "Captain DeLang has never promised me anything. And I didn't even know he was my uncle until this evening."

Father smiled. "You've developed quite the talent for lying, my dear. I hope your uncle appreciates it."

"What are you talking about?" Borsk said. "As Lancet said, the Colony leadership won't take me. If that lands team selection back in *Hope*'s hands, there's no way Anya gets on that team. You may want her gone, but others don't. You're not the only one who cares about the continuation of the pure-Euro line."

Anya slumped. Borsk was right. If Father somehow managed to tie her participation on the colony team to Borsk's—and it looked like he intended to do so, it would mess up DeLang's team and probably still not get her to the planet. Everything she'd worked for, hoped for, planned for, crumbled, at only a flick of her father's fingers.

Nothing had changed.

Nothing would ever change.

Chapter Thirty

No doubt Anya's father would figure out some way to wriggle out of the child abuse charge as well, and soon she'd be stuck back at home, banned from the greenhouses, kept from her art and her friends. Anya's hands shook so badly that the water she was holding spilled over her knuckles and dripped onto the floor.

Ryan handed her a handkerchief. Then he stepped between her and her father. "Sir, you need to back up. You're scaring your daughter."

"Of course, I'm not scaring my daughter. Her whole complaint is a fantasy, designed to discredit me."

"Her hands only shake like that when she's afraid," Borsk said. "Maybe you don't realize it because she's always afraid around you."

Father laughed and stepped sideways, as if to get around Ryan, but Ryan and Borsk both moved to block him.

"Sir, I've asked you nicely. I don't want to have to cite you. Back up."

Father laughed again, but this time he didn't sound quite so aggressive. "You're not even on duty, lad, but I'm backing up. In fact, I'm going back to my office. You three can join us there when you're done playing around." His footsteps faded into the distance.

Well.

Something had changed. She had friends willing to stand between her father and her, friends who believed her side of the story, friends who could make him back down, if only temporarily. That made her feel better, but also more scared than ever. What would Father do to Borsk and Ryan? To anyone else who dared to stand up to him for her sake?

Anya took a deep breath and mopped up the water she had spilled. "Thanks, guys."

"Just doing my job," Ryan said.

"I don't like bullies," Borsk said. "What now?"

Anya wasn't sure. She sipped her water and let her thoughts tumble in her mind, combining and recombining what she'd heard in the last few minutes, hoping that some new configuration would point to a way out.

Then something clicked. "Borsk, did you mean it when you said my father wants me gone?"

"Sure. He'll go down for child abuse if you stick around to testify. What will that get him, Lancet?"

Ryan tapped on his armband. "Sentences are variable, of course, but I don't see how he avoids time in the brig and the rest of his life under observation."

Father wouldn't like time in the brig, but he could probably make it work for him. The rest of his life under observation? That would cramp his style, for sure. "And if I'm not here?"

Ryan answered. "He might still be convicted, but he's got a much better chance. If you and Borsk both go, I can almost guarantee that the vid feed will disappear or get corrupted, and *Hope* will be hard pressed to prove anything at all."

That is, Ryan would be hard pressed to prove anything at all. Who else would even try? Anya nodded and gave her once-betrothed a smile. She'd always known Ryan was a decent guy.

So, she and her father had at least one goal in common now—her removal to the colony. And he'd always said that one goal in common was all you needed for successful negotiation. All she needed to do now was beat her Father at his own game.

She stifled a wry smile. It wouldn't do to let her father see any sign of hope in her at this stage.

Let's see. What was next? Deciding what she wanted, right? Well she knew that—the success of the colony team, and her on it with David and Abuela Ryerson. A future for Borsk and his family. And for the Lancets. And she wanted Father to face the consequences of his temper for once. She wouldn't get all that, she was sure, but she'd get as much of it as she could.

What did Father always say the next step was? Oh, right. Know the rules. That meant the agreement on colony selection that her father had referred to, and also the Golden Terrace Charter. She wished there was some way to ask the guys to help without letting her father know what she was up to. She wasn't sure she could read both documents in time to do any good.

She called them up on her armband anyway.

"Are you almost ready?" Ryan asked.

"Give me a sec," Anya said, skimming the colony selection document as fast as she could. From what she could tell, it tallied with her Father's account of it far too closely for her liking.

"I should get the coffee," Ryan said, "but I'm not sure how to work this thing." He pointed at the beverage dispenser.

"Move over," Borsk said. "I didn't grow up in a restaurant for nothing. What are the orders?"

"Black for Father, sweet as syrup for Mother, sugar and soy for Captain Bates, and . . ." She wasn't sure what Captain DeLang drank.

"Strong enough to chew with cardamom and nutmeg for Captain DeLang. Got it." Borsk set the machine whirring and humming.

Anya looked up. Captain DeLang took his coffee the same way her grandfather had? How bizarre. One more thing to put in the back of her mind to think about later when she had time for it.

She nodded to Borsk and looked back down at her armband screen. The colony selection agreement wasn't helping any. She switched over to the Golden Terrace Colony Charter.

Finally, she'd caught a break.

It read exactly like *Hope*'s original charter, which she knew as well as her own art collection. Maybe excelling at history wasn't so useless after all.

"All set," Borsk said. "Are you ready, Anya?"

She was, but she didn't want her father's ever-present cameras to pick up on that. Suppressing her mounting excitement, Anya kept her head down and her voice low as she answered, "As ready as I'll ever be, I guess."

❧ ☙

Having seen Borsk handle a tray, Anya insisted Ryan carry the drinks while she followed with an assortment of pastries.

The gray hall was just as long and dull on the return trip as it had been on the way out. When it dumped them back into the space-view lobby in front of Father's office, Anya took a moment to look out at the star-studded blackness. As usual, she felt humbled by its vastness. Her little affairs seemed so paltry in the face of the universe.

Then again, so did her father's. "Come on," she said to the boys, who had also stopped to stare out at the deep. She started to lead the way into her father's office, and then remembered that she didn't usually lead anyone anywhere. She let Ryan go first, and then Borsk.

By the time she'd set the pastries on the desk and settled onto her stool, Ryan had passed out the coffees.

As Ryan had predicted, Anya's mother had registered a protest against Anya being sent to the colony with David, a horrible philanderer who Anya barely knew.

Once Anya finished reading the protest, she looked up. "David does seem to enjoy flirting. But he wants to go to the colony, and none of the other green guys I know do."

"Always a flaw in the design of Charles's recruitment plan," Father said. "Insisting on couples. And fifteen-year-olds should never have been allowed to apply. No teenager's judgment about who to marry can be trusted."

"And yours can be?" Ryan said. "Didn't you encourage Kristi to marry Kenneth Llourdes?"

Mother pressed her lips together.

Father sighed. "Kristi's unhappiness is much of what makes us want to keep Stacey from making the same mistakes."

Anya blinked. Her father sounded so sincerely concerned that for a moment even she was fooled. Then she remembered the last time Kristi had visited and how Father had revised his will to make her sole owner of GenM after he died—provided she went back to Kenneth for long enough to have her second child.

"Did you have another option in mind?" Captain DeLang asked Father. "A young man acceptable to your daughter who isn't opposed to life on the colony?"

"That's why we asked young Mr. King to be here," Father said. "The two young people are good friends, and I believe they'd work well together. You wouldn't mind going to the planet, would you, lad? Obviously, we'd get your armband back online before you went—could do it this evening, in fact. I'm sure there's something in the colony charter, article seven, about forgiving offenses in a case such as this.

Article seven. But that section was meant to prevent the colony from being overrun with criminals. If Father was citing that section, he was offering Borsk use of his armband tonight whether he went to the colony or not. "You're all agreed about this?" Anya asked.

"Absolutely," Captain Bates said.

"I've looked at the lad's record," Captain DeLang said, "and nothing there concerns me. He isn't green, though, is he?"

"Black," Borsk said. "Genetic condition that bars me from breeding. I guess it could work if we had our kids with donor . . ." Borsk colored, and Anya wasn't about to help him. "Sperm" wasn't a word she had any intention of saying in front of her parents.

"I mean, you will be taking a full donor bank, right?" Borsk faltered on.

"Just in case something happens to *Hope*? So, the kid side of things could work."

"And you would like to be part of the colony team?" Captain DeLang asked, sounding way more interested than Anya thought reasonable.

He must not have fully understood Borsk's health problems. "But—"

Borsk cut her off. "I'd be happy to do just about anything honest that gets me my armband back."

Obviously, he didn't realize he had his armband back already. "Oh, Borsk—"

"I mean it. It's not such a bad idea, Anya. We work well together. You know we do."

They did. But his health could threaten the survival of the colony. And he didn't awaken those feelings that tingled through her every time David was in the room. Before she could say anything, though, her father spoke up.

"Seems like a perfect solution. I'll have my lawyer program draw up the papers."

Captain DeLang nodded. Anya had to say something—anything, fast. "But Borsk's whole family is Christian!"

"What's that got to do with anything?" Borsk said. At the same time, Captain DeLang and Ryan both leapt to their feet spouting the freedom of religion sections of both the *Hope* and Colony charters.

Anya gathered her courage, then rose to her own feet and shouted over them, "Yes, yes, I know all that." The noise lessened a bit. Anya turned to face Borsk. "But Borsk, honestly, do you mean to say that if we . . ." She fumbled for the right way to say what she had to say, "get to doing what married people do, and there was an accident, do you really think you wouldn't have any problem with me getting rid of it?"

A look of horror washed across Borsk's face. "I can't go. Sorry. Wasn't thinking. Sit down, Anya. We'll think of another way."

Anya sat. So did Ryan and Captain DeLang.

Anya smiled at them. "The best, simplest way would be for Mother and Father to drop their protest and let me go with David and Mrs. Ryerson."

"Absolutely not," Father said. "You're too young to make that choice."

What did Father hope to accomplish by continuing this line of argument after Borsk said he wouldn't go? Perhaps it was time for her bluff. She looked down so her father couldn't see her eyes. That shouldn't seem strange to him. She hardly ever met his gaze. "Then perhaps I'd better stay, so I can be where David is when I am old enough to make that choice on my own."

"Young lady," Captain DeLang said, "Didn't you hear me say the colony needs you?"

"I'm glad my skills impressed you, but you could probably make do with VJ Brown."

"VJ Brown?"

"He didn't try out because he didn't have a partner, but a leadership spot on the team would make him seem more eligible, wouldn't it? He knows almost as much about the greenhouses as I do, and he's good at teaching what he knows to others. Smart too, though I get the sense he doesn't usually do well on standardized tests.

Captain DeLang gave her an appraising look. "You wouldn't mind not going?"

"I'd mind not going horribly! But I don't want my involvement to put the colony at risk. Besides, I'm only fifteen. I'll be forty-five when *Hope* gets to Shindashir. Being in the second wave of colonists won't be as good as being in the first, but I can wait. David too, probably. But Mrs. Ryerson?" A tear welled up in Anya's eye. "She really wants to go," Anya whispered. Then she pulled herself together. "Of course, if she gets angry enough about not getting to go, the family won't care how much it costs them to get back at my parents. They might even be willing to support my marriage with David, just to inconvenience my father."

"Stacey, we're *blocking* your partnership with David," her father said.

"*Mother* is blocking my partnership with David, and she can only do it because I'm underage. But in three years, I won't be. I can marry whoever I like, then."

"But your babies wouldn't be white," Mother said, speaking for the first time all night.

On Anya's left, Borsk whispered, "I can't believe she just said that."

Anya stifled a laugh. She supposed, though, that she'd always known this was the sticking point—her parents couldn't live with any choice that didn't allow for pure-Euro children. But if that was the only obstacle between her and a life in the colony with David, there was hope.

"No, Mother. My babies won't be white. Not if I stay on *Hope* where I'm limited to two. But perhaps, seeing how it's so important to you, we could work something out. If you drop all your protests and let the Golden Terrace leadership put together their own colony team, David and I could have a few pure-Euro babies in addition to our own.

Mother sucked in breath. "I don't know," she whispered. "Thomas?"

"I'd like more than a perhaps."

"If you agree to drop all protests and not begin any new ones, the colony will grant your daughter the right to have ethnically Euro children as soon as it is deemed safe for new children to be part of our community, and she's not carrying any of David's." Captain DeLang said.

Father sighed. "I suppose that will have to do, but I don't like the idea of my grandchildren being raised in such an unsafe environment."

"You could improve the conditions," Anya said. "I understand the colony needs more samplers, has only been granted a partial library, and has medical equipment more than twenty years old."

Father shrugged. "I've always said I'd be happy to invest—"

"If GenM gets a half share in any resources we return to *Hope*!" Captain DeLang said, "We're not interested in your investment."

"What if he donated money or equipment without any conditions attached?" Anya asked.

Captain DeLang snorted. "Thomas Cartier never donates anything without strings. He's too insistent on getting good returns on his investments."

Anya smiled. "But there would be a return on this investment—just not a monetary one. Making the colony safer could directly affect the chances of the pure Euro-descended genetic line continuing. If I'm not mistaken, that's worth quite a lot to my father."

"It should be worth quite a lot to you," Father growled.

Anya's hands shook.

Ryan reached over and patted her knee.

Anya glanced at him, puzzled.

He pointed at her armband.

She turned it screen side up and saw a message from him scrolling across it: "He can't hurt you here."

She nodded and focused on her breathing until she thought she had herself under control. "I'm not sure what the continuation of an ethnically Euro line is worth to me, but I know the colony is worth more."

"Apparently. Well, Caroline, I don't see that we have much choice. Stacey seems intent on destroying her future, and we'll just need to salvage what we can. Drop your protest as soon as Stacey and DeLang sign the contract."

"The contract?" Anya asked.

Ryan pointed to her armband a second time. This time she looked at her screen, paragraphs of her father's worst legalese were scrolling across it, but despite the awful language, her spirits lifted. This was an agreement she could live with—or it would be as soon as she put DeLang's proviso about not having pure-Euro kids if she was already pregnant back in. She tapped in the change.

Her father grunted. "Sorry. Forgot that."

Sure, he did.

"I see you've specified the number of pure Euro children Anya will have, as well as required a surrogate to step in for her if she dies before the quota is reached," Ryan said.

Captain DeLang barked out a short laugh. "Of course, he has. But it's no skin off my nose—I'm not the one who will be having them. Or raising them."

His signature appeared on the document.

Four kids? Plus, however many of David's she had? Could women even have that many children? She'd heard myths about such things, but of course no one had given birth to any more than two—or in extraordinary circumstances, three—for hundreds and hundreds of years.

Mother's signature appeared on the contract right above Captain DeLang's. So, it was up to her now. She read through the contract carefully one more time, looking at every phrase. In a couple of places, she pulled up a lawyer program to clarify a word.

Borsk leaned close to her, and she adjusted her arm, so he could see the screen too. When they got to the end, he said, "It's not a bad contract." He sounded sad. Because she was going? Or because he thought he'd missed the chance to get his armband working again? She wasn't sure, but she thought he was right about the contract. She carefully traced her security swipe over the top of it, and her signature appeared on the line for her name.

"Well that's done," Father said as she was lifting her finger from her arm, "and I, for one, want to get to bed. Coming, Arnie?"

"He needs to get Borsk's armband working first," Anya said.

"Excuse me?" Captain Bates said.

"You agreed, about ten minutes ago, to put Borsk's armband back in service tonight. Remember?"

"But that was only if I went to the colony," Borsk said.

"No, it wasn't," Anya said. "It depended on Article Seven of the Charter, the article designed to prevent *Hope* from populating the colony entirely with criminals. Both Captain Bates and Captain DeLang agreed to clear your record and put your armband back in service whatever you decided."

"Thomas?" Captain Bates said.

He sounded worried. Father must not have told his poker buddy what he was agreeing to. Silly man. He'd known Father long enough not to take anything he said at face value.

Father didn't answer the captain, so Anya decided to push. "I could have my lawyers called in—or any lawyers, really."

Father nodded slightly.

"But . . ." Captain Bates spluttered. "I'm not sure how . . ."

"I can set it up, sir," Ryan said.

"Oh, very well then," Captain Bates said.

Ryan stood up. Anya scooted backward off her stool, so he could reach Borsk more easily. As he tinkered with Borsk's armband, Anya noticed Captain DeLang eying her appraisingly.

"Is something wrong, sir?"

"You negotiate surprisingly well."

"Well, sir, I did learn how it was done from my father."

An odd look—one Anya had never seen before—flitted across her father's face.

It looked almost like—

But it couldn't be.

Was her father proud of her?

Chapter Thirty-One

Borsk spent the entire walk back from the meeting plucking Cartier's annoying spyware out of his armband. He didn't notice Mama sitting in the dark kitchen until she rose from her stool and said, "Borsk what have you done?"

Borsk bristled. "Why do you always assume the worst about me, Mama?"

Mama sighed. "Because it's so often true. How did you get your armband function back? How much of your soul have you sold?"

A wave of anger rose in Borsk, but he clamped his mouth shut. This was too good a night to ruin with a fight with Mama. "Give me a sec," he said, closing down a sneaky string of code that had lodged itself in his health-management software. Only after he'd ensured his armband was clean down to the smallest bit, did he look back up. He thought he could talk calmly now. "Sorry. Had to make sure it was still my software and nothing else."

"Why is your armband functional?" Mama asked.

"They've dropped all charges and cleared my record," Borsk said.

"In exchange for what?"

Borsk grinned. "In exchange for nothing, as it turns out."

"That's ridiculous," Mama said. "I thought you were with Thomas Cartier."

"Among others, yes. Bizarrely enough, he proposed me as an alternative to David Ryerson as a companion for his daughter on the colony team. The colony needs Anya badly—something to do with her greenhouse work."

"I could see that, but why would the girl need an alternative to David Ryerson? And why would they want you?"

Borsk shrugged. "Mama, you know David's reputation with women. Would you let a guy like that near Sarka?"

Mama shrugged. "I'm not sure he's as bad as they say. But even if I believed the hype—why would you make sense as a replacement? You're a lovely young man when you want to be, but you've got—"

"King's Syndrome, which will totally cripple me within a few years. Where but the colony can I make a difference to anything in that time?"

"But—"

"But no leader in their right mind would take me this way. I get it. I think Anya's dad was hoping DeLang didn't have the whole story and would accept me, and that the resulting brouhaha would fracture the colony leadership team."

Mama sank back onto her stool. "Surely he saw through that. I'm sure Captain DeLang would never—"

"Captain DeLang approved me."

"No," Mama whispered. "If you go, I'll never see you again."

Borsk stepped closer. The dim light cast by the emergency exit lamps glistened off the tear tracks running down Mama's face.

The only other time he'd seen her cry was after his father's funeral. The lingering bits of his anger dissipated. He took another long step closer and enfolded her in his arms. "Don't cry, Mama. I'm not going anywhere. Anya reminded us all that even when they're careful, a married couple that's not supposed to reproduce could still . . .. Anyway, neither of us wanted to deal with that. Besides, now that I've had time to think about it, I'd rather stay here anyway."

"You said you hate Skreetches," Mama said, her voice back to brisk.

Borsk let her go. "I said I didn't love it the way you and Sarka do. But I'm fond of *Hope*. I love the net and the layers of code our people have been laying down for centuries. Nothing on the planet can compete with that. I mean to explore it as fully as I can with the time I've got left. And if I can get enough work doing that to move out where I never have to peel another potato, I'll do it. But Mama, that's a ways off yet, and might never happen. Cartier can't be happy with how things went down tonight, and I'm sure he's already plotting to make my life difficult."

"No son of mine is going to let a little thing like Cartier's plotting stand in the way of his dreams," Mama said.

"No, ma'am." Borsk smiled. "I'll be out of here before you know it. But it won't be to avoid you—or even Sarka. You know that, right?"

Mama reached over and gripped his hand. "Just like your father. You know, he always felt stifled by the restaurant, too."

"What? He loved Skreetches."

"No, sweetheart. Your father loved me and understood that Skreetches came with me. It was enough—usually."

"Then you understand."

Mama rose off her stool, pulled her hand out of Borsk's, and tousled his hair. "Get some rest. The colony list posts in a couple of hours, and I imagine the restaurant will be overrun with people celebrating."

"In a minute. I'm kind of hungry."

Mama shook her head. "I don't know where you put it all, child. You're lucky you were raised in a restaurant."

"I know it." Borsk hugged her to let her know he meant it, then let her go, so he could dig through one of the cleaners for a bowl."

"Remember at least two vegetables," Mama's voice floated back to him from the doorway.

Borsk shook his head. He might have lucked out with his family, but he still couldn't wait to get out on his own.

ᗺ   Ꮳ

Somehow Anya dragged herself out of bed and down to the public message board outside Skreetches where she'd promised to meet David and Mrs. Ryerson to wait for the Colony Team List announcement.

When she arrived, ten minutes before the list was scheduled to be posted, people filled the hallway, blocking the message board from her sight. She recognized a few of the people—the Wilcoxes, the Jacksons, the Huxtons and DeShawn—but many more were strangers to her. At first, she wondered if David had come, but then she heard Mrs. Ryerson's grating voice behind her. "What do you mean, 'She might not be here?' Do you mean the child has withdrawn and is too spineless to tell you herself?"

"No, Grandma. It's just she had a long night."

Anya turned toward the voices. She couldn't see Mrs. Ryerson, but David's glossy curls were visible above the crowd. Anya squeezed through, silently cursing the mass of people. Soon she could see her new family—a vast improvement on her old one, even taking Mrs. Ryerson's caustic manner and fuzzy house slippers into account. She smiled at them. "I'm here."

David's face lit up with a grin, and he pulled her close. "Anya, you're so amazing." He kissed her, and for a moment, the crowd disappeared along with Anya's worries, and there was nothing, no one, in this universe but the two of them absorbed in each other. Then someone wolf-whistled, and Mrs. Ryerson said, "Time enough for that later if we've made it in, you two nitwits. The list is posting, and I can't see."

Anya pulled away from David in time to see Mrs. Ryerson making her way through the crowd with the judicious use of a cane.

"Does she even need that?" Anya whispered to David.

He laughed. "Sometimes. Should we follow, or let her see on her own that they've added you to the colony leadership?"

"You know, then?"

"The captain came around very early to tell me what was going on and make sure I wasn't going to mess up his team with my notorious womanizing."

"There's enough truth in that for him to talk to you about it?"

"Not really. I've liked lots of girls. But the only girl I'm into now is you, Anya. Nobody but family has ever stood up for me the way you did last night." He brushed a kiss across her forehead.

"Did he tell you about the . . . the . . ."

"Kids? Yeah, and I'm fine with that. I've always wanted a house full of kids. But, Anya?"

"Yes?" She dreaded what might come next.

"We're going to love them all, you hear? We're not bringing kids into this world to ignore or dislike them. Every child we have, whether biologically mine or not, will be ours—yours and mine. They'll all, equally, be ours."

Anya didn't know what she'd been expecting, but it wasn't that. Passion blazed in David's eyes, and she wondered what made him care so much about this. She'd hardly thought about these children she'd agreed to have, but now that she did, she could see how David was right. Slowly she nodded her head. "You're a good man, David Ryerson." She stood up on tiptoes to plant a kiss on his lips.

Before the kiss could become more than a taste, DeShawn Phillips's voice rang out, "What is this crap? Anastasia Cartier on leadership? The little bitch is only fifteen!"

"I heard there was some kind of secret meeting in Thomas Cartier's office last night," Bria Huxton said. Her bronzed spikes of hair seemed to bristle, and Anya had to remind herself they always looked like that.

Anya pulled away from David, cleared her throat, and focused on projecting her voice over the angry muttering of the crowd. "There was a secret meeting in my father's office last night, but it wasn't about getting me into leadership."

The crowd, which had been pressing against the message board, shifted so that dozens of faces, both familiar and unfamiliar, pointed toward Anya. Silence fell. She swallowed hard and forced herself to go on. "Somehow, my father got a copy of this list before the rest of us, and he tried to block my presence on it. I dare say Captain DeLang would have been happy for the excuse to get rid of me, but apparently some of my greenhouse work has made me indispensable. So then, Father tried to stop David going with me."

"Likely story," DeShawn said. "Who would object to you going out with David?"

David wrapped an arm around her shoulder and squeezed. "Half the fathers on *Hope*. Bria, didn't your dad throw a fit when you and I started dating?"

"Sure, but he didn't call any secret meeting with any captains."

"Only because he's not friends with Bates," Mrs. Ryerson said, emphasizing her point with a stamp of her cane. "As I recall, he got some of his buddies to lock David in that unstable maintenance tunnel for a day."

Roger Wilcox laughed. "I heard about that. By the time Security was called in, the tunnel wasn't unstable any longer. Glad DeLang convinced Anya's father to let you come, David. You're exactly the kind of man I like to have around. And if the leadership put Anya in charge of a team, I'm sure they had their reasons."

"Yeah. Sucking up to her dad," DeShawn said.

Anya laughed, but before she could say anything, the grate over Skreetches' entrance rolled up and Borsk stepped out. "Hey, everybody. Mama says to come on in and have some coffee or tea if you're going to be chatting awhile. We have another message board inside, and we'll get cited if people keep blocking this hallway."

The crowd must have seen the logic to that. They filed into the restaurant and quietly waited their turn for Sarka, Borsk or Mrs. King to whisk them to a table and supply them with drinks. By the time Anya and David's turn came, the group had settled into gentle conversations that didn't sound nearly so hostile. Borsk winked at Anya as he came up to seat them. "They should be ready to listen to you now—unless you want me to take a go at it," he said as he led them to a table in front of the stage where the Wilcoxes, Jacksons, and Mrs. Ryerson were already sitting. "I saw most of your speech, and could probably take over, if you want. I think I know what to say."

Anya smiled at him. He probably did know what to say, and she trusted him. But if she was going to make this leadership thing work, she'd have to start standing up for herself. Borsk wasn't coming with her. "I'll handle it. But if you could get some things projecting when I ask for them?"

"Absolutely."

"You want some sound backup as well?" Steve asked.

"I . . . Yes, please." Tears filled her eyes. So maybe her parents would never see her as more than a baby-making machine. Other people appreciated her true worth, and some of them she'd be spending the rest of her life with. She blinked back the tears and climbed the steps to the stage.

Looking out, she saw many more hostile faces than encouraging ones, but some of the encouragers, like Mrs. Ryerson and Sarka, had been hostile just a few days ago. Somehow, she'd convinced them, and somehow, she'd convince all these others. She nodded at Steve and Borsk, and started in.

"I can't tell you why the leadership team put me in charge of a group because I don't know myself."

A couple of people laughed.

"But Captain DeLang said it had something to do with my work in the greenhouses, and that I can tell you about. You see, it all started with my first class detail up there as a sixth-former. I'm sure you all remember what those details were like. Dirty, manual labor. I probably would have thought the same as everybody else, but I happened to see this." Anya projected her first silver-fruit blossom picture from her armband, and Borsk captured it and set it rotating from the house projectors. "I knew I had to draw this beautiful flower, and I was willing to do anything—even extra greenhouse work—to have time in the greenhouses to do it."

Steve started up a sweet tune on simple pipes. The sound gave her courage. She turned her eyes to her flower instead of the still-angry looking crowd, and told about her deal with Mr. Greeley, the things she'd learned from him, the art she'd made, and how her love affair with the colony had started. As she talked, she illustrated her story periodically with her art. Slowly the faces around her lost their angry looks.

"Anyway," Anya said, flashing a display of the Golden Terrace colony picture she'd drawn after the simulation, "That's why I want to get to the planet and how I picked up the skills the leadership team seems to think will be useful down there. Anybody else want to tell their story?"

Borsk left the colony projection up as she stepped down, and it served as a fitting background to the stories that followed.

Roger and Laura spoke of friendship and the desire to help make a new, more just civilization. Bria talked about exciting new opportunities. DeShawn spoke of adventure. As the stories went on, Anya settled into her chair, leaned against David, sipped the cup of cocoa Sarka brought her, and listened to the dreams of her new tribe. She felt proud to be part of such a brave, creative, brilliant group of people. They were going to be OK. No, more than OK.

Together, they would create a better world than the one that had birthed them.

It was time to do more than *Hope*.

Acknowledgements

Thank you so much for reading this book. If you have left a review (or are about to), I thank you also for that, because reviews are an enormous help to authors, especially to those like me, who are just beginning their publishing journey.

This book has been long years in the making, and many people have helped bring it into the world. I thank my God for my health and ability to do the work.

My thanks also go to my critique group, the 93rd Street Irregulars, who help me stay on task, make sure people who don't live in my head have a chance of figuring out what I'm talking about, and laugh with me at the Freudian slips. Every time we get together, I learn something, and my writing is much better than it would be without their wisdom, keen observations, and brilliant examples.

Thanks also to my beta readers, Charity, Deborah, Kaitlyn, Katie, Phyllis, & Mom whose encouragement and good sense have also improved this work.

Thank you to my fellow members of Imago Dei, who help me focus on what's most important.

And most of all, thank you to my family. Your love, encouragement and support are priceless treasures.

R. L. S. Hoff

Want More?

Look for *StarRacer*, book 2 in the Golden Terrace Colony Series, due to come out in 2021.

Interested in YA fantasy, not just science fiction? Try out R.L.S. Hoff's *Songs of Healing,* available now on Kindle and in paperback.

Sign up on my website (URL below) for the R.L.S. Hoff newsletter to get the latest installment of *Hope Gardens* (A serial story about Sam Greeley and his friends when he was a teenager). There are also book reviews, news stories about upcoming releases, bits about R.L.S. Hoff's life, occasional giveaways, and other fun stuff.

http://pencilprincessworkshop.com